ONE OKTOBER

One Oktober

Joseph Donnelly

Beach Read Press

One Oktober
by
Joseph Donnelly

ISBN# 978-0-9821265-8-5
LCCN# 2008909150
SAN 857-3247

To order additional copies, please contact us
www.oneoktobernovel.com

Beach Read Press
2310 N. Hwy 77
Ste. 110 Box 343
Lynn Haven FL 32444

First printing: 2009

Cover art: Karen Siugdza
Interior: Ronald L. Donaghe

Printed in the United States of America

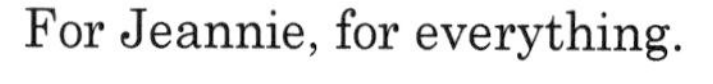

For Jeannie, for everything.

Acknowledgements

If you are of a certain age, then you are aware that during the cold war, the Soviet Union did, in fact, insert people into the United States for nefarious purposes. After 1991, as the movies and novels tapered off, I occasionally wondered—*what ever happened to those guys?* Russia in the mid-to-late 1990s would not have been a pleasant place to return to.

I would imagine the intelligence agencies know the answer to that one. I, on the other hand, get to make stuff up. Much cooler.

Still, I would bet a few of them stuck around.

For reading when it was mush and being polite about it: Steven Levy, Alison Levinson, Nancy Hemphill, and Jeannie Donnelly.

In the editing process, Nancy Hemphill was first and turned it into a proper manuscript.

Ron Donaghe and Katie Hillelson at Two Brothers Press turned a manuscript into a novel. I am fortunate and very grateful for their professionalism.

Karen Siugzda provided the cover, and as you can see, she is a true artist.

And, hey Kevin...thanks for that line.

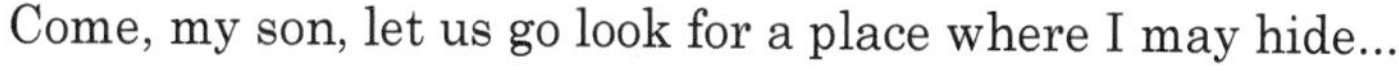

Come, my son, let us go look for a place where I may hide...

—Cervantes (Don Quixote, 1605:565)

Chapter 1

767s FROM THE NORTH and from the East. Beautiful, precision-built American aircraft, fully fueled for the long trip west.

The obscenity has begun.

Stuart Rafkin sags into his executive rolling chair on the seventy-eighth floor of the South Tower in lower Manhattan, listening vaguely as Devard Montrane relates the overnight undulations of the Nikkei. It seems the dollar is falling against the yen, and Montrane has bet heavily on the buck in his personal portfolio of clients.

"If you trend this out over the previous one-hundred-and-eighty-day cycle—excepting August of course—you'll see that we're due for a big-time uptick."

Rafkin nods or otherwise makes gestures of acknowledgment. He is thinking of Helen Pardue. An hour or two in one of the nearby luxury hotels would do it. He has studied her. He knows she is studying him. They have waited long enough.

Rafkin looks out through the checkered-glass partition. On cue, Helen appears. She stands at a desk in the cubicle farm, holding a sheaf of papers in one slender hand. Rafkin dips his head and nods, adding what he feels to be a dash of charm. A pale rose of crimson flushes high into those magnificent cheeks. She looks away to say something to some fat girl, who Rafkin thinks of only in mediocrity. He tilts his head back into the leather, allowing the thinnest of smiles.

Helen has no purpose with the woman at the desk. She is preening for him, and he is pleased.

Montrane is on a roll. His laptop is open as he illustrates something to Rafkin on PowerPoint. Something about loss ratios and spread dynamics—all the buzzwords of their industry—high-roller investments. Rafkin smiles, when appropriate—an unspoken pat on the head. Through the floor-length window, Helen turns in a peripherally sexy gesture peeking over at him, and then averting her eyes.

American Flight 11, closest now to infinity, banks slightly over Baychester in the Bronx, settling into a six-degree glide. The passengers whisper into their phones. Some pray. In the cockpit, Atta catches his first clear view of the skyline, and he begins to shiver with excitement, jerking the craft, overcorrecting and tumbling people into the aisle.

It begins as a hum in the distance. The sound a radio might make, rumbling low on the dial on a starless night. What was common background noise is now enough to get in the way of conversation. It grows and borders on a roar. Rafkin cocks his head, drawing a pen from the corner of his mouth. Helen turns to him, flashing a quizzical smile, as if asking someone to repeat a question.

Atta wipes his hands free of perspiration, glancing over at Abdulaziz, who has joined him in the cockpit. Abdulaziz stares hard at the skyline of Manhattan, and at their altitude. He is beginning to understand.

Atta ignores him, focusing on the leftmost Tower. It is growing in size and detail, seeming to him, an apparition. He begins to pray. His voice grows, and Abdulaziz sees that they are all going to be martyred. He joins Atta in the verse, which becomes a chant. They are bobbing their heads and chanting in unison, louder and louder. A building whizzes by on their left, and it is too late for anything now. A moaning wail can be heard in the compartment behind them, and Atta is screaming at the top of his lungs as he jams the throttles to their stops.

The humming sound, the sound of the jet aircraft, grows and changes shape and echo, and it is clear that it is approaching. The echo slaps from the tall buildings as Rafkin watches Montrane cover his ears. He cannot process it, other than a dawning realization that he knows what is about to happen. It is so loud that he is physically afraid. A muffled *thrum* ripples through the floor, not unlike standing on the platform as the Lexington Avenue subway shudders into the station. The rumble grows louder still and blooms into a roar, halting everyone in their tracks, until it reaches a volume he has never heard before and hopes to never hear again. The sound alters all perception and then it is *right there.* It attains crescendo, and it is an explosion that shatters the day and the air and everything that came before and everything that will come again.

"Oh my God! What the fuck is that?" someone shouts, just outside his doorway.

"*Yeb vas,*" Rafkin mutters.

Montrane—still in presentation mode—politely begs his pardon.

It hadn't moved much, but it *had* moved. There are very few things that could shake a building of this size. Maybe an earthquake, if it registered around a seven or higher. But this was no earthquake. Rafkin knows precisely what it was, and an earthquake it was not.

He allows himself a stream of gutter profanity, this time under his breath, when he hears the first pure scream, a woman out in the cubicle farm. He makes eye contact with Helen, her eyes grow, and he thinks he sees her lips move but he can't make out her words.

Montrane says, "Okay, just hold on now…" when the single scream becomes a harmony of three, then perhaps a dozen. Some of the screamers are men.

Rafkin stands, breaking eye lock with Helen. Along with several others, he jogs to the windows where they are greeted with the unlikely panorama of snow, so out of place it is eerily beautiful. In an instant, Rafkin understands that the snow is really paper, thousands of sheets and pieces of it. The paper and other debris blow like a dust devil from a ragged hole in the building across the breezeway.

As he watches, awestruck, a large shaft of flaming steel rains impossibly down past his view. He stands at the window, looking up. The last drabs of a satanic orange fireball are perhaps a hundred feet above him, most of the way up the North Tower.

Too high, he thinks.

The black, oily tendrils from the initial blast evaporate up into the ether, giving way to a torrent of heavy smoke pouring from the topmost fifth of the building.

Rafkin is not surprised that an airliner has impaled itself on the Tower. He is surprised that it happened today.

No time for that. He knows what the others do not. Very soon now, there will be another one. He hops up onto a desk, holding his hands apart, palms out. He removes his suit jacket and holds it clenched in his trembling fist.

"Okay, listen up." He waits a beat. A few of the accountants ignore him, as they stand transfixed at the windows, but he has the attention of most of his staff. Montrane is on the phone, loosening his tie, probably calling security. Strangely, Rafkin thinks that it shows his lack of inner discipline. In any case, he holds out little hope of relief. He knows everything there is to know about the security here. His orders dictated that he did.

A glance at the assembled staff shows that half are in tears, and the other half have run to their phones. He can't imagine whom they might be calling.

He uses his finest command voice, modulating for attention.

"We've had the drills. We're going to wait here until we get the word to evacuate," he enunciates, attempting eye contact with as many as he can.

"Just like the drills, okay?"

Rafkin smiles at Helen. She dabs her eyes with a tissue, gamely showing him her teeth. Montrane tosses the phone onto its console and rushes over.

"Stuart? Mr. Rafkin? I can't get through to security. They gotta be going nuts."

"Yes, thank you, Devard."

"We have to get out," Montrane pleads with his eyes. "Now!"

"We wait," Rafkin says, firmly.

Montrane shakes his head. "I was here the last time. You weren't." Rafkin checks his watch. Four minutes have passed since the aircraft struck Tower One. They should have heard something. He gives it another nervous moment of tenuous authority.

At least Helen is on his side. A few strays ignore him and are slipping out through the double doors.

"All right. Let's check out the exits. Mr. Carville? Would you please have a look in the outer offices? Make certain we don't leave anyone behind." The man complies, jogging around the perimeter of the space, banging open doors as he goes. Rafkin watches him and then turns back to the group, as he looks around the suite. Whatever happens…

"Devard will lead, single-file to the elevators, where we will form into groups of ten. Division Heads, take each group as best you can." He loosens his tie and collar, deciding *what-the-hell,* nodding to Montrane, who turns and marches to the exit, trailing the staff in a nervous caterpillar.

So far, so good. If they can stay that way, they should all be okay. Unless of course, Hanjour is on schedule and the Americans have not awoken and shot him down, as he points another 767 at this particular floor or any floor within fifty meters in either direction.

They reassemble one floor down in the skyway, between two banks of elevators that run eight across, giving them a total of sixteen from which to choose. Rafkin is the last of the group to arrive. He is pressed against the rear wall as he sees that all sixteen "down" buttons have already been selected.

Several dings sound as one. The doors to three of the elevators open, invitingly. A community groan ensues. The cars are nearly full. Rafkin looks at the faces of those on the elevators, marking their expressions. A few are in full panic, angry at this intrusion on their escape, but mostly the people inside are calm. Their faces are blank and resigned.

He shouts to Montrane, who is pressed fifteen feet away by the crowd.

"Do what you can." Montrane is nodding before he is finished. His own group grows loud and panicky, drowning out the message, but Devard understands. He stands between the open doors to two of the elevators and begins to silently motion to the women. Singly or in pairs, some unconsciously holding hands, they get into the cars. Perhaps two dozen have made it onto the elevators, and then they are full. Good job, Rafkin thinks, adjusting his earlier assessment of Montrane. There's nothing like a crisis to define the flavor of a man.

A certain look crosses Montrane's face and Rafkin realizes that the humming sound has begun. Again. This time, the engines are whining, maxed out earlier than the first.

Very few of them can take it now. Their faces are loamy and wild, like cattle in the chutes. They are all aware of what will happen this time.

Rafkin spies an actuary named Blum, a man he is forced to have lunch with on occasion. Blum is speaking calmly into a cell phone, one hand cupped over the mouthpiece to make himself heard above the racket. Blum glances at Rafkin as he speaks; Rafkin sees eternity in his eyes. They both know that Blum will never make it. Rafkin looks away. He moves to the westernmost corner of the anteroom where he sits down on his haunches, his arms up around his face in the crash position.

He fights the urge to look at his watch, but it is 9:01. The buzzing engine sounds grow louder still, louder than the last time, even above the screams. The sounds are magnified by their fear, and Rafkin has an insane urge to look out the windows to see the plane approach. He takes his arms away from his face because he can't *not* look, and he sees Helen standing at the far corner of the space, leaning against the wall as if she may faint. He turns his head to shout reassurance, but his words are torched in his throat as 10,000 pounds of plate glass blow out in a heaving slurry of glistening shards and superheated vapor. The sound is so vast that it is nothing but a giant buzz inside his head. He watches, numbly, as Helen is sliced to ribbons by the flying arsenal of ruptured concrete and shattered glass.

Three-tenths of a second pass.

The world erupts into a blinding avalanche of light and noise. Sixty- thousand pounds of Jet A from the center and wing tanks have accepted the fatal spark. The explosion sends the structure shuddering on its pilings.

Rafkin is senseless, stunned, deaf as a post. He hears nothing, but rather *feels* a long and immense sucking sound. Smoke fills the area for an instant, only to be whisked in a rush back through the holes. Carried along with the smoke, a dryly humorous gent named Bill is vacuumed through the spot where the walls and windows used to be. His plaid sport jacket billows out behind him. Rafkin thinks, incoherently, that the jacket will break his fall, sort of like Mary Poppins.

Finally, he is horrified. Those filthy Arab *gavno* went early. They didn't tell him and now he is a dead man.

An indeterminate time has passed since the explosion, and the death of Helen and Bill. It could be seconds, or several minutes. In any case, Rafkin thinks the building is moving.

In another life when the building was whole and he was wasting away his secret life, the Towers did in fact, sway. Like all tall buildings, they were designed to do just that. The steel members would flex a foot or two to the lee under the stresses of a stiff wind. Occasionally, a pencil would roll off a desk, an amusing trick for a newcomer.

This was not that. The floor danced like it was melting, and he knew that could not be so because the fire was above them. If it were that hot, he would be dead and so would everyone else. But Montrane was screaming, so he could not be dead, and the floor was not melting, but it was moving.

It was…*moving*. The way a floor would, if it had been covered inches thick with thousands and thousands of slimy insects. He had seen that on television sometime or other. That is exactly the way it moves. The association pleases him until he recognizes the symptoms of shock.

And, he had known the second plane was coming.

He looks down at the floor again to confirm the vision. Oddly opposing ripples run through the tiles and he wonders how long they have before the entire fucking thing comes down. Oh, would they be dancing in the streets of Mecca and Medina!

A lesser sound occurs, relative to the explosion of the jet fuel. It is a huge sound, nonetheless. He looks up to find that the ceiling also, is moving. It caves, spilling plaster and ceiling panels, twisted iron, insulation, and other crap—there is even a human being.

A man in eleven-hundred-dollar Patek Philippe drops through the hole where the ceiling used to be, flailing his arms as he falls with the rest of the debris, and he hits the floor with a sickening smack. Rafkin thinks he landed on his head, but he cannot be sure. The man is still for a moment. He moans. Someone kneels next to him, whispering softly into his ear.

There is a scream, louder than the rest. It is Marianne, the woman Helen had been speaking to outside his office. He remembers her name!

She is on fire, as are several others. Jackets are tossed about them, smothering the flames. Rafkin turns away from the horror of their screams. He is surprised and comforted with a cool rain, realizing the sprinkler system has been activated by the blast. It lasts only for a moment, and then the drizzle of the water abruptly stops. He understands that the pipes of the sprinkler system have been severed, either by the aircraft itself or the resultant explosion. If the fire is allowed to burn...if the vertical support columns fail, one after another, the weight of the upper stories will hammer the rest of it flat.

Just as before, there are three open elevators on the west wall where Montrane was standing, except two of them are different. Two of the cars that were open before are gone. Their doors are ajar, he can see the grease-stained walls behind where they used to be, looking like the missing teeth of a giant, mocking the crowd in the skyway. The cables have been severed. He tries not to think of how it must have been for the people on the elevator.

Montrane is still in action. He is working to fill the remaining cars, as if nothing has happened. Briefly, Rafkin feels ashamed at his own temporary blackout.

"Hold them open!" Montrane shouts, and is met with the roar of panic as they rush into the cars. "Three is enough. Let's get everyone in now!" Rafkin meets his eyes over the heads of the panicking crowd. As he does, the entire skyway shifts sideways, knocking him off his feet.

The stairs, then. The elevator shafts would be death traps. The flames and smoke would use the shafts as the world's largest chimney, for they were the closest and most easily accessed route to oxygen. The fire would find the oxygen. It would reach out and find it no matter what stood in its path. As if to confirm this, a twelve-foot tongue of flame shoots from one of the missing holes. It licks along what's left of the ceiling then snakes back down the shaft like a serpent.

Rafkin feels pain in his feet. He looks down to find that his shoes are missing. That, he can understand, but how on earth had his socks disappeared as well? Would they not have to come around the ankle to…*brush it off.* It would be a simple thing to lose focus now and be killed with the rest of them. He ignores the pain from the blackened cuts on his feet as he cups his hands and shouts to Montrane, "The stairs! It's the only way!"

Montrane has one foot into the elevator. He will be the last man out. His dark brown skin is covered with plaster dust, making him look like a matinee zombie. Montrane shakes his head. No. Rafkin waves his arms and shouts insistently, but Montrane turns away from him, and then he is inside the elevator. Rafkin holds eye contact as the doors close. The lights change on the display panel. They are gone.

Rafkin is left in the shattered space with three others: David Traxel from his office, a young Cantonese vendor, and the corpse of the man in the expensive suit. He sees that the man's head has burst like a pomegranate. He looks away. The air smells of soot, human smells, and destruction. Time is strange. He can't decide if Montrane just left on the elevator or if it happened some minutes ago.

Rafkin knows the vendor. His name is Kang, and he brings pastries and such on his cart, every morning. Kang wears bright yellow Nikes and one of those do-rags on his head.

Traxel is not handling it well. His eyes bulge, straining the sockets. Rafkin can see every last vein in his head and the puffy white spittle on his lips. Rafkin realizes that they are awaiting instruction.

He hears a faraway thump occurring regularly, like the backbeat of a drum, strangely timed and echoing faintly off the walls. Another loud bang splits the air, coupled with a strange popping sound.

"We'll take the stairs," Rafkin says, and Kang nods in assent. Traxel shakes his head no. Just as he always thought, Traxel is a sheep, wagging his head from one decision to the other. Rafkin turns on his heel, heading for the stairs.

The air is cleaner in the stairwell. Rafkin takes this as a good sign. It must mean that the fire is taking its feed from the outside air, for now. They pick up a straggler two floors down. She joins them in line down the stairs, saying nothing. There is nothing to say.

The ones and twos turn into a crowd as he passes into the sixties. Refugees. Rafkin turns back, checking on Traxel and Kang. Traxel looks up the stairwell, and Rafkin can see that the back of his shirt is gone, entirely. There are hundreds of tiny dots of blood beading from the soot-blackened flesh. From the front he appears completely unmolested. His tie is neat and correct. Rafkin looks at his watch and sees that it is now 9:26.

He increases his pace.

By the time they reach the thirties, the whole thing could be a fire drill. People wearing more tones of gray than he thought existed, troop side-by-side, bumping past a knot of firefighters, every so often. The firemen are on their way up. Rafkin can't help but see them as courageous, though in his intellect he damns them as fools.

The lights are shining normally, illuminating the thick yellow industrial paint in the stairwell. He performs a routine back-check of his charges, only to find that Traxel is missing. Most likely cowering in some doorway, waiting for the firemen to pick him up and carry him down.

Rafkin resumes his descent.

There is sameness to the escape. The farther they get from the seventy-eighth floor, the more normal people appear. They have heard things, no doubt. But they haven't seen it.

It is now 9:42. They reach the mezzanine, a loft-like foyer to the Tower with an acre of open area one level below, leading to the street.

He joins the small queue heading down the escalators, without looking back to check on Kang. The floor below is littered with broken glass and chunks of unknown material. There is a dead woman, shrouded in a fireman's heavy overcoat. She lies in a tangled heap, five feet from the bottom stair of the escalator.

Her butterscotch hair billows out from under the coat, spilling out onto the floor like an oil slick. Rafkin steps carefully to the side.

At the Church Street entrance, a knot of clearly senior fire officials stand huddled together, gesturing and barking into portable radios. Thump. There it is again. Rafkin has not heard that sound since the Skyway.

A streak of dark light flies vertically downward behind the firemen. It is a heavy object and it piles into the courtyard outside the windows with brutal force. A man in a white peaked cap turns briefly at the sound, and then resumes his conversation.

Rafkin walks in a daze toward the men, the sound, and the Church Street entrance. In a moment he can see the fallen object. He can see what has made that awful sound over and over for the past twenty minutes.

Another human being. A man, who may have been in his forties, or his twenties, or his sixties, lies in broken angles at the edge of the courtyard. His skin is strangely intact in places, hideously burst in others. His crisp white shirttails hang out, singed at the hem. *They are jumping*, Rafkin thinks. *They would rather jump a thousand feet to their deaths than be roasted alive in the fires.*

He leans over and vomits curtly, without warning or shame.

As he rises from his position he can see—in a wider view of the courtyard —several, no, dozens more of the jumper's brethren. Some of them face the sky, and as he looks at their faces he vomits again, dry heaves, as he staggers away toward Liberty Street.

*

He is somewhere else now. He is Stuart Rafkin and he is going home, as the glass crunches under his feet. There are few people about. Strange, he thinks; there should be thousands. As he passes Canal Street, he sees a small group of citizens pointing up at the burning Towers, while taking pictures with a video camera. He passes a man with a Joffrey Ballet cap and a Sony Palmcorder.

The man's face twists into a caricature of fright. Rafkin quickens his pace as he faces forward, only forward. He does not turn to see the object of the man's dismay. The rumble is back. He knows what will follow.

Rafkin breaks into a trot. He hears the rumble grow, larger than the one when the plane hit. He is no longer trotting; he is running, though he thought himself too weak to run. His hair is standing on end, and he is running for his life, seeing an occasional panicked soul as he passes. They are scampering into shops and buildings, but he will never stop until the titanic sound stops. He begins to feel the flick and sting of smaller particles of debris striking him in the back, along his legs, neck, and shoulders. The debris is growing larger...then he feels the wind.

Rafkin cannot fit into his head the size, the scope, and the sound of the wind. It is as if a typhoon has suddenly been snatched up from the Indian Ocean and dropped onto their heads. He is blind. He cannot see. His senses are reduced to feel and taste, the taste of smoke and ash; he gags as he thinks of what the ash might contain. He strains to see the ends of his arms pumping windmills in the vortex. The wind is wild and, oddly, it is warm, the warmth of a Caribbean breeze.

But it is the tan and ochre color of the desert homes of the villains who summoned it.

He slows gradually, trotting, then walking, weeping uncontrollably as he sits down in the road. He is sifting through his childhood, remembering all his faults and weaknesses, his private triumphs. He is in his mortal coil, knowing he will survive, but wishing now that he would not. He sits and weeps, and in the midst of the wind, he decides that he has burned his life in vain.

*

Stuart Rafkin clings to the suit jacket under his arm, staggered on the sidewalk outside a small brick-front West Village apartment building on Cruse Street. He is a tangled shard of a man in early middle age, sandy brown hair with streaks of strawberry blonde, all of it covered in ash and dust. Looking to his left, over the crest of a rise he can see where the Towers stood.

The smoke is gargantuan—the hallmark of a nuclear detonation. It billows up and up and to the east, perhaps to settle at sea.

Rafkin climbs the four cobbled steps, and he is inside. Closing the door behind him, he moves rapidly into the living room. He tears at his shirt as he walks, popping the two remaining buttons, angrily throwing the rag onto the floor.

For some reason, he is wearing shoes. They are wingtips and they aren't his. He has no idea where he got them, but it must have been from the building; therefore, he must remove them. As he kicks off one wingtip it tumbles end-over-end and hits a magazine rack, causing it to topple, spilling his copies of *New York Magazine*, *Newsweek*, and various financial rags. A small blue-and-white Georgian urn tumbles to the heart-of-pine floor—shattered.

Rafkin glances at it, numbly, kicking the other shoe away, and then he rips off his belt, making a thwacking sound. He drops his slacks to the floor, catching one pant leg around his ankle, causing him to stumble. This weakness infuriates him. He grunts loudly, forcing great amounts of blood into his head. He finally throws his shorts against the wall and paces, walking in circles around the living room, rubbing his hands around his shoulders.

After a time, he sits down on the sofa. A moment passes. He believes it to be several minutes. He stands, again, and goes into the kitchen where he procures a heavy tumbler filled to the half with vodka. He adds a splash of tonic, squeezing some fresh lemon into the mix. He goes briefly into the bedroom. When he emerges, he is wearing a pair of tennis socks and comfortable loafers. He is otherwise undressed. On the television, an attractive brunette screeches excitedly into the camera, detailing the world-shaking events of the morning.

Rafkin hears none of this. He watches the scroll across the bottom of the screen in a catatonic state—a new, and not entirely unwelcome sensation. He stirs the drink with his finger, tapping his loafer unconsciously.

The newscaster, with the pall of smoke as backdrop, says that there are as many as fifty-thousand dead in the collapse. Rafkin blinks. The view turns to the Pentagon in Washington. Another aircraft has plowed into E ring. The damage there is superficial, they say. It doesn't look superficial to Rafkin.

He switches stations frequently. From the reports, Jarrah has failed. His aircraft—United 93—has crashed into a field in some backwater in western Pennsylvania.

At least for Jarrah's sake there will be no recrimination. He is—if the Arabs are correct—in Paradise, being serviced by his virgins. Rakfin's own metaphysical coda is hazy. To him, Jarrah simply no longer exists, or is roasting in something along the lines of Hell.

He shakes off his stupor in the course of an hour or two. His hands have settled. He feels capable of holding a conversation. Mixing another, he goes into his bedroom where he takes a cell phone from a shoebox in his closet. Each phone is used for one person only. This particular phone has the number for Muhammad programmed into its memory.

There is no answer. Muhammad is most likely celebrating, joyful in this massacre of the Americans. Rafkin places the phone down gently onto the table.

For all his bluster, Muhammad did not know much. He probably knew about the Towers after Rafkin did—heard and seen on television. If Feliks had any sense, Muhammad wouldn't have known a thing about today's strike.

As he shouldn't; Muhammad is follow-up.

There is a separate phone for Feliks. One for each contact, easily disposed of. He automatically punches the speed-dial…then hangs up before the first ring. First, he must think.

Feliks.

He showers at length, dressing in navy slacks, a rich cotton pullover, and the loafers. The act of dressing has helped to clear his thinking, and he returns to the living room, raising the volume on the television.

Nineteen years, four months, and twenty-seven days. The time he has spent in this country as Stuart Rafkin. Seven thousand days.

And, he was finished. Or thought he was, until the spring of 1999 when Feliks approached him to tell him it wasn't over.

It would never be over.

He had done as ordered, shepherding the Jihadists in through Montreal, arranging the safe house for Muhammad and his men, acquiring the floor plans for the Trade Center. They'd believed that Rafkin had some inside track, working in the Towers as he had. They had not believed him when he told them the blueprints and schematics were available on the Internet for all to see.

Then they had attacked early, on the eleventh. They had known he would be there. Surely they knew.

He tried to recall if he had recognized anyone in the Grand Foyer or out in the tumult of Canal Street…

He hadn't seen anyone he knew. He was sure of it.

The historical record would reflect the loss of Stuart Rafkin in the destruction of the World Trade Center, September 11, 2001. The death toll would be forever incorrect. Off by one. Rafkin sipped at his drink—and made a decision.

CHAPTER 2

GOMEZ WATCHED THE CLOCK, willing the hands to hurry. The phrase *anywhere but here* rolling through his mind like a mantra. Trying to figure a way out. Perhaps if he set himself on fire? He was reaching for his plastic lighter when he heard Porsche Cummings calling his name, strict and strident. They wanted him in the minefield.

"And now Special Agent Gomez will discuss the unique difficulties endured by our Latino agents!"

He rose, delighted to be released from the constrictions of the tiny plastic chair. A chair designed for Oompah-Loompahs and Hollywood leading men. He moved to the head of the class, smiling at the teacher, Ms. Shook.

Shook was going for the Medusa look. A brunette rinse in tight, ropy curls, as if she'd washed her hair in night crawlers. Bait hair.

They were in the Howard School, he and Cummings, as representatives of the Commission. A kind of half-assed task force promoting racial diversity in government—officer-friendly duty for agents whose area of specialty had outlived its convenience. A kind of graveyard.

He adjusted something, stalling, recalling that movie where the little shits came out of a cornfield to disembowel anyone over the age of twenty-five.

He'd faded for a second there. Cummings was staring at him again. He turned to face the class. Every grubby little hand was raised.

"Are you from Mexico?" inquired a youngster, politely.

"I am from Oakland," he replied.

"So you're an American!"

"Yes." A wrinkle appeared, creasing the child's forehead. It took a moment, and Gomez willed him on.

"Then what makes you any different from me?" the kid blurted.

Gomez smiled and tipped the boy a wink.

"That isn't the point," Cummings stressed. She stalled out, speechless. You can fool the first and second graders. After that…

A bright-eyed runt in lavender Oshkosh with gold piping rose from her seat. She had a ninety-dollar haircut, her jewelry worth more than his .45 automatic.

"The undocumented Latino immigrants in this country are willing participants in their oppression by allowing the government to deny them universal health coverage." Her communiqué complete, she sat down, pulled an enormous tome from her desk and began to read. Gomez rolled his eyes, wondering if he could trump up some Mickey-Mouse charge against the girl—better yet, the parents.

Someone yelled from the back, "Are the towel-heads coming to kill me too?" Shook bit off Gomez' reply, teeth flashing, like taking the head off a bat.

"What were we told, Madison?" She approached the offender, whispering into her ear. The girl's eyes brimmed with tears, wagging her head as she left the classroom. Gomez watched, feeling a headache coming on.

Shook was dressing them down, railing about insensitivity. A boy in the front row was smearing something onto the underside of his desk. His lower lip drooped stupidly, tongue hanging like a curious pink slug. The back row was fast asleep. Gomez smiled weakly, as if his executioner was running late. Shook stepped directly in front of him, shielding someone, perhaps.

"Why don't we thank the FBI for sharing with us today?"

The children rose to mumble their thanks. A uniform, sterilized robot. They reminded him of Komsomolskaya, the Soviet youth organization that had brainwashed generations of Russian children until the finale in '91. They were pasteurized, homogenized.

There was, however, one little girl in the rear, silently watching Shook and Cummings, like she was plotting something. Gomez caught her eye. Her tongue darted out, ever so slightly. There is hope.

The door closed with a thud, leaving him there with Cummings. She was cute when she was angry.

He tried to get out in front of her. "At least they get to skip math," he said.

"You find this amusing?"

"Well…"

"I would think that someone with your background would appreciate the effort."

The bell rang. Gomez was pleased.

He lit a cigarette the instant they stepped over the curb, whipping out the pack like a gunslinger.

"It isn't that. It's just the *drumbeat.* Wears me out sometimes."

"Ten years," she said. "It's been ten years since the Union went down. Nobody cares anymore. This is the duty now."

"Don't you ever…"

"This is the duty," she repeated.

"My personal feelings have not, and will never, play a role in how I carry out my assignments." Gomez knew that Cummings, also, had not joined the Bureau for this, but she was young. She had her career to look forward to.

"I'm twenty-eight. Three months will pass. Don't take it out on me just 'cause you don't have the Russians to chase around anymore."

She had him there.

Gomez reached the side of his Ford, key ring hanging loose in his hand.

"I'm sorry. Truly. The Commission isn't my idea of relevant, but you're right." He rattled the change in his pockets, happy to be leaving. "Hey, this diversity business is a good thing. *I'm* diverse. Right?"

There was no point to it. She'd driven away.

He stubbed out his smoke and gunned it out of the parking lot, past the sign with the blocky pedestrian children, bits of gravel shooting out from his tires. There was no paperwork when you were assigned to the Commission. And the end of the day came early. He checked his watch, free from the prying eyes of Shook, the *Oberfuhrer*. Eleven forty-nine. Lunchtime.

Into the drive-thru of the place with the orange clowns. He preferred the orange clowns to the yellow. The yellow clowns didn't put enough salt on the fries; the lawyers had gotten to them. He ordered the fried fish sandwich in consideration of his latest diet, whipping the Ford into an empty space and throwing it into "park." The car stereo was programmed to news-talk, so he turned up the volume, tucking a paper napkin into his collar and tossing the wrapper onto the floorboard.

The callers wanted blood—before the snows flew. Not a single laser-guided bomb had been delivered anywhere in the world on behalf of the Three Thousand. People were losing patience. Rumors sprang up, were caressed and emboldened. There was talk of impending chemical attacks and the nonexistent security at water treatment facilities. Airline pilots wanted the right to fly armed. Tough to blame them. A Russian airliner had exploded in mid-air. Seventy-six dead. President Putin said that terror could not be ruled out. Russia was under the crush of Chechen Muslim rebels. Western Europe knew they were next.

The candlelight vigils mounted.

Gomez knew some of what was going on behind the scenes—the biggest manhunt in history. Ninety percent of the Bureau had been re-tasked to hunting down funding sources and detaining large numbers of suspected terrorists all over the country.

Gomez spent his days waxing the dolphin.

"Ten years," Cummings had said. KGB and GRU. Oleg Penikovskiy and Kim Philby. The Hydrogen Bomb and concrete shelters in the backyard. There would be no more chasing of spies—men in burlap suits with steel teeth and diplomatic passports, trying to blend in and pretend they were commercial attachés. He smiled as he thought of their hairstyles; People's Bowl

Cut Number 1. Their trousers coming up three inches short of style; white gym socks glaring in the moonlight. Then the other side just...went away.

He'd driven up to the City on his first day off after the Eleventh. The train was too crowded, too noisy. He needed his thoughts. He'd arrived to find hundreds of cops from all over the country hanging around, looking to help. There just wasn't anything to do.

The talk-host mentioned the color-coded alert thingy. Today it was a sort of burnt-orange. What a designer might call Paprika. There was that. He made an unconscious motion with his thumb and forefinger, rubbing them together in the texture of oil and salt from the fries. So this is what the Bureau did with their former lions, mostly men with Russian language skills and cross training at Langley.

The Bureau. He'd never liked that word. It inferred something. Something that was now true. He snorted to himself, thinking that he must have looked silly back there.

He finished the sandwich as he sat staring out of the windshield, absently picking at the fries. Incomplete. He threw the Ford into reverse with a notion of rolling right back through the drive-thru for another combo, when he became aware of a peculiar sound. A stirring in his trousers—his new Bureau-issued cell phone. It had come programmed like that and it was starting to piss him off. He answered, listened for a long moment and said, "Okay, Larry. Twenty minutes."

*

Traffic was light, so in eighteen minutes, Gomez sat in Larry Kessler's office at the Hoover Building on Constitution. The chair was a refreshing change from the tiny plastic job at the Howard school.

"How's the Commission workin' out for ya?" Kessler asked him, with a nasty grin. Kessler looked like a six-foot marshmallow that someone had punched in with a baseball bat; warmed, but not quite to the point of melting. He was a large unmade bed. His hair was fine yellow flax, thinning at an alarming rate, and his eyes were sort of caved in and crinkly. Gomez figured him for three, maybe four heart attacks before the big one got him.

"You mentioned something about an assignment. Something else. Let's talk about that."

"Yeah, well, I'm being rude. This is Miss Viisky from the Ministry of Agriculture. From Russia." Kessler waved carelessly at a young woman sitting to one side of his desk. She had the wary, tired eyes of the Slavic hordes, possibly her only flaw. She wore a pair of 501 jeans and she had thin, smooth wrists, he noticed, and her hair was a deep lustrous black—the black of a Siberian coal mine. Gomez had nodded his greeting when he came in, thinking she was administrative personnel or another agent. He smiled blandly, shot his cuffs. Waiting for the dope.

"She's presented us with a problem. I thought you might be the guy to help us out."

"How so?" Gomez lit a cigarette, tucking his Styrofoam cup between the legs of the chair as an ashtray.

"Aw c'mon," Kessler whined. "I just got this gig. Don't go giving me some cheesy code violation."

"Leadership challenge," answered Gomez. "Don't sweat it." He tapped an ash into the cup, missing a little. "Maybe you should get to the point."

Kessler made a show of getting into a huff, aware, Gomez thought, that he had whined like a ninny, in front of the girl. He stood and began to rearrange the knick-knacks on his credenza.

"Anyway, I'll let Miss Viisky fill you in."

Viisky took her cue.

"I am here to concern farm products," she said in a husky voice, thick on the vowels, drawing her words from the back of her throat. She trilled her r's with style and her jaw jutted ever so slightly. St. Petersburg, maybe. Something like that.

"I am ordered observe and report on certain activities have come to attention of Ministry. Irregularities in ports of Murmansk and Arkhangel'sk."

Viisky smiled at Gomez. "There is less arugula arriving than is reported shipped by your companies."

Kessler banged some papers around. Viisky stared at Gomez. He saw concealment in her eyes and then it went away.

"Okay, I'll bite. What's arugula?"

She hesitated, looked at Kessler. "Like eh…green salad item."

"Ahhh."

Gomez thought maybe she knew as much about arugula as he did, which was zero. So she was a bureaucrat. He had a sudden urge to tell her some of his old Soviet jokes; maybe the one about the comrade scientists and the billy goats? Perhaps later.

"Also, there is less cantaloupes arrive than is reporting by your companies," she continued, adjusting her sweater, hands prim on her lap. Kessler and Gomez glancing at each other at her mention of cantaloupes. Faces like slabs of concrete.

She continued. "Our governments wish for cooperation with these vegetables."

She didn't look like a bureaucrat. She was wearing those weird German shoes, something like sandals with a closed toe. She swept her hair back around one ear. Nervous, and hiding it well. Kessler stole a grubby glance, like he wanted to start chewing on her.

"I would have assistance in navigating directorate of ports and exports. There are Russian imports officials who will need questions. *Serious* questions." She grew solemn and Gomez almost laughed, for a moment there she looked like Count Dracula.

Gomez turned to Kessler.

'So what do you want me to do? Just cook up some papers for her and give a heads-up to the Port Authority?" Viisky smiled at him tentatively. "She speaks better English than you do."

"Blow me," said Kessler. "Sorry, miss."

"The fact is, we're manpower deficient," Kessler said. "I've still got to come up with another forty agents for this Homeland Security deal. You speak Russian."

Gomez stood. He leaned over next to Kessler, speaking into his ear in a near whisper, "I can barely remember how to count to ten in Russian. How about sending me over to the Pentagon?"

"How about you become the head of the Commission?" Kessler said. "You can make training videos for FNGs. I'll get you some pasteboard and you can paint rainbows and shit on it."

"Yeah, yeah, yeah. All right. Got it."

Viisky dragged some papers from an attaché. "This is this documents from your Ministry of State."

Gomez had been badgering Kessler since the twelfth, knowing it was futile. Kessler just didn't have the pull. Viisky shoved her papers toward him, eagerly. Gomez had his hands jammed deep in his pockets, head lowered, resigned. Kessler cracked a compassionate smile, a look that Gomez was seeing more of, and that was wearing thin.

"Look, I gotta go to you with this. There isn't anybody else."

Gomez nodded. There was no one else because the younger agents were in the throes of the greatest moments of their lives, just as Gomez had been, tangling with the Soviets. And the veteran agents, his peers, were either smart enough to be in management, like Kessler, or they had cashed it in and were doing lucrative private security somewhere.

In fact, Gomez had a friend, a guy named Hinson whom he had worked with for a year in L.A. Hinson had called and offered Gomez a position. Small hours, big dollars, and bullshitting with the boys about the old days. He'd just about decided to call Hinson out in la-la-land and take him up on it. He could be banging starlets and roller-skating in Venice by Christmas. Of course, it was more likely that he would be watching surveillance cameras during the day and reruns of Gilligan at night. Life for Gomez no longer held the possibility of starlets.

"Guess what?" Kessler was saying. "It's over. They hit us and now they're gone. All those F-16s are punching holes in the sky for nothing. The cow is out of the barn."

Gomez smiled and patted him on the shoulder. "We'll see."

He turned to Viisky.

"Okay let's go."

It was a short walk to his own seldom-used office. Gomez fired up another stinker as they sat down.

"What is this Commission you speak of?" Viisky asked.

"It's nothing."

"I ask only," she said, "because if you are assisting me it may require large slice of time."

Gomez decided he liked the accent—darkly appealing, like the Bride of Stalin, if you were into that sort of thing. Her eyes were set too far apart; not much, just enough to hint at some Asiatic blood. The distance gave her an aura of omniscience. Unsettling, unless you thought she was on your side.

"For arugula?" he asked. "I'll tell you, and you decide."

It was pleasant, really, meeting the old enemy face-to-face, long after the battle was over. Coming to grips with what had happened, knowing that you'd won. He leaned back, looking out the window for a moment, while she fidgeted. It would be easy to lord it over her, the victories of the Blue Team.

Gomez was Blue Team. And Blue Team had done just fine.

"This Commission is complex?"

He could lie. Tell her he was the tip of the sword, chasing wild-eyed terrorists with suitcase bombs through the mean streets of D.C.

"You are still the adversary of Russia?"

"Not really. I'm more of an educator. I do symposiums, lecturing schoolchildren, things like that."

Viisky blinked, clearly surprised. So was he. Actually, at the end of the day when Gomez thought about what he was doing, he was stunned.

"Our priorities have changed since we destroyed you," he said.

Viisky didn't take the bait. "Yes. But the world has not."

The phone rang. Gomez hooked it onto his shoulder. It was Kessler.

"Hey, doesn't she look like that Jessica babe on 'Survivor'?"

"I don't watch that crap."

"After she lost the weight, I mean."

"How about I go up to Shanksville? Stare at the hole in the ground?"

"She's pretty smoking hot is all."

Gomez hung up.

"If you have not time," Viisky said, standing, "I need this proper man." She blew a strand of hair from her face, tired from the travel.

"I apologize," Gomez said, "please have a seat." She looked ragged, jumpy, and tense.

"When did you arrive?"

"I come on British Airways. Just hours ago. Most comfortable."

"Aeroflot taking a break?"

"The flights are not appropriate times," she said coldly, her eyes narrowing. He should not have said it, provoking her like that. Still, it would have been a waste, a beautiful girl dying like that on one of Aeroflot's bucket of bolts. She turned her head and sighed, uninterested in gamesmanship.

Gomez' bearing changed, becoming more correct, military. He decided to stop fucking around.

"That 'arugula' crap was pretty thin."

She placed her hands on his desk, appraising him plainly. "Please forget this trickery," she waved a hand, considering. "I am first important to know what variety of man you are."

He made good eye contact, leaning forward in the chair, speaking slowly in a voice that had dropped an octave.

"If you are who I think you are, you can take one look at me and know exactly what I am made of."

She nodded once, very quickly, a head-fake, then stood and closed the door to the office.

"What," she asked "do you suppose happened to this *Volk Vyydraat* we placed to your country in 1970s and 1980s?"

"How could I forget?" Gomez said quietly. "Volk Vyydraat. *The hiding wolf. The sekret snake.*" He lit a cigarette on the back of another, firing the smoke through his nostrils—a Latin dragon.

He turned to face her. "The sleeper agent."

Chapter 3

"*TEN THOUSAND?*" Gomez blinked hard at the number. He held an image: hordes of Cossacks in knee boots and shapkas, goose-stepping over the border. The Red Team had kicked their ass, after all.

"You must be joking."

The corners of her mouth turned up into a beneficent smile. A question occurred to him; he had a tingling and it was the beginning of an answer.

"They're still here?"

"Did you think we flew them home on Aeroflot? With this surplus finances?"

"The threat changed. There was the Gulf War, but…" He drifted back in.

"We caught a bunch of them," he said, but then corrected. "At least at the time we thought it was a lot." He ran his fingers through the remainder of his hair. "I think the figure was somewhere around three-fifty."

Of course that had been over a span of two decades. If what she was saying was true, it meant that Bureau Counter-Intelligence and the shadow agencies had rounded up roughly fifteen illegals a year—a baker's dozen. Meanwhile, the Soviets were sending in five hundred. If the public knew about the three-fifty they would shit their national pants, but *ten thousand*. My God!

"Not all of records are complete," she continued. "Many peoples engaged in program are dead. Some of them, eh...naturally. It is best guess we can have." She shrugged. "There was academy. Well, do not mind. Anyway, it is what happens now matters."

Gomez tried to recoup, gain some ground.

"You know about the *Dezertirs*," he said. "The ones who decided they liked it here."

"Hmm, yes, we knew."

"I'm not talking about defectors. I mean the ones who pulled a fade. Just decided they liked it here and melted away into society."

"I understand."

She produced a pair of reading glasses from somewhere in her clothing, perching them on the end of her nose. She was a sudden accountant, the IRS giving you the bad news. A file was next, some thick pile of documents bound in red. Gomez thought about her age and the reading glasses and decided it was bullshit.

The glasses were theatre.

"I have three hundred, sixty-four defectors. Forty-two dies of general causes or accidents. Car smashes, such as that."

Gomez was barely listening. He was studying her, sifting through the seven most common signs of a liar.

"...of your *Dezertir*, and many come home. To Russia, or to satellite country they were born from, but most to Russia," she concluded, looking up at him as one who is to deliver news of something incredible and has had the time to process.

Gomez closed his eyes, addressing her more formally.

"And how many agents stayed here, remained loyal to their country, and are now, with a fair degree of certainty, operational?"

She shook her head. He'd been too fast for her.

"How many are still active?"

"Two hundred." She paused. "We think."

It made sense. As a matter of fact, he recalled a CIA report which was circulated in the mid-1990s that posed the very same question. To wit, what *about* all those guys? The Soviet agents still in-country after the Union went down. It would be like the astronauts stuck up there during a nuclear winter.

Both CIA and FBI were aware of the Soviet penchant to destroy from within and had, of course, instituted their own sleeper program, albeit with nothing like these numbers. There were maybe thirty, forty guys. The report would be sitting somewhere in records, collecting mold.

The smoke was beginning to sicken even Gomez. He stood up and opened a window. "One of them has become a threat," he concluded, pacing. "More than one?"

"This is true," she admitted, biting her lip—a gesture that in another moment he might have found fetching.

He looked out the window to buy some time. His internal sensors were banging away like Bill Clinton on an intern. Something was happening here. Something momentous, and he felt sluggish and slow, out of practice. Too much time spent dicking around in elementary schools, shuffling hollow paperwork, when out of the blue he's chatting with some siren of the *Sluzbha* about long-lost sleeper agents.

"Okay. You have identified a problem with an agent of the former KGB who has lived in my country for many years. You have decided to tell us about it, enlist our aid, even." He stopped his pacing and sat down again, brow creased, hands under his chin, waiting. "If you're telling us, it can't be good."

She reached over, fishing a cigarette out of his pack on the desk. Took her time lighting it. "I cannot tell you entire truth," she said, finally.

Gomez stood and walked to the window, trailing a plume of smoke. He was thinking of the Swallows.

They were the most natural espionage tool in the world. All countries used some twist on the theme, just none more effectively than the Soviets. A female comrade with a pure socialist pedigree would seduce the lonely American serviceman or foreign-posted diplomat. His head bursting with secrets and the uniform inability to keep his dick in his pants, he was an easy mark. More information had been lost to the Red Team that way than Walker or Pelton.

Of course, the Swallows were not your average Lyudmila, a bearded lass with a weightlifter's thighs and a mat of back hair.

Gomez had seen actual Swallows. They were invariably intelligent and oozing with sex. Kind of like Ms. Viisky here.

"The United States of America," he said, "does not give a rat's ass about you people anymore. We won. You lost. It is over." He made a show of stubbing out his butt as exclamation. "Eleven days ago, we suffered a horrific, cowardly attack. Every man, woman, and child in this country is out for blood. Terrorist blood."

She listened. Lips parted, exhaling smoke.

"You therefore, are a has-been. You understand the phrase? We have awakened to the threat of Al Qaeda. If you want me to help, you are going to tell me all of it."

She sighed, making the file disappear into the depths of her attaché. Taking her time about it.

"Is most complex," she said.

That was easy. He was being played, by an amateur.

"First you are pleased to know I do not tell all of United States this thing. Only you."

"Because they don't care? Or because you don't want them to know?"

"Perhaps both. I would not know." She smiled.

"You are SVR." It was not a question. She shook her head too rapidly, and Gomez thought he had gotten up to five of the seven signs when he lost count.

"I am Nationale Polizei. FSB."

The rough equivalent of the State Police and State Bureaus of Investigation. Regular coppers on a national scale. She had stared straight ahead as she said it, and Gomez decided that they should have had another rehearsal.

"I am more of a…" she paused, searching for the word. Then she had it. "I shoot the troubles."

I bet you do, he thought. Eyes alight as she said it, fully understanding the double meaning. The woman knew more than she was letting on. The way she said troubles. Like an invitation.

"Wouldn't this be something for SVR? Or GRU?"

She finally met his eyes. "It is matter of *available*. I am available."

Gomez was reminded of when his first wife would tell him that she hadn't really been working late, no, she was out with the girls. Conversation and margaritas. A lie to cover another, larger lie.

"So, whatever," Gomez said aloud. He would figure it out eventually. He leaned in close, detecting the smell of cigarettes and lilacs. "What is the threat?"

"Here is deal. Russia has no money. You know this. So, technology exists now to bring oil from Taymr peninsular—you know this as Northern Siberia— to sell on world market. *American* technology." She stole another smoke. They lit up together.

"Problem becomes price of oil," she continued. "All countries in Europe pay ninety dollars each barrel. America pays thirty dollars. We cannot afford ship oil to you for such small price. Russia needs for America to pay ninety dollars each barrel, like Europeans pay."

Her delivery was efficient and concise, despite the direction he thought she was headed in. She must have practiced, or thought about her little spiel all the way across the Atlantic.

"Europeans don't like Russian. They remember Bear. Also, they would rather buy Arab oil than Russian if price is for same. They have oil deal with Arabs already in place. They get many briberies from Arabs. You see? So. Americans do not care who produces oil. They just care how much price. So. Russians need for Americans to pay more price for oil."

Gomez felt like a hot air balloon, the gases expanding beyond capacity, stretching, glowing, and escaping. His mouth was an angry pink slash. He put it together quickly—the sleepers, the oil, and 9/11. The fact that the Soviet Union had, for many years, invested in radical Islam as an ancillary force; a sort of Green Berets or Special Forces to run illegal interdiction missions against the Main Enemy, the United States. A fifth column.

The room was suddenly very small. Viisky noticed this. She hesitated.

"Go on."

"You know this I am saying?" she asked, blinking once.

"I'm listening."

"So," she looked at him nervously, "if…*you must understand*," she said. "You must understand I learn about this only short time ago!"

"I said, *continue*," Gomez barked, pounding his fist on the desk, sending a coffee cup over the edge and onto the floor. The cup bounced hard, settling in the corner, spinning slowly. It was chipped and broken, like an airliner falling out of the sky, perhaps.

The sound was very loud in the small room. Viisky started, eyes fluttering.

"I am here to help you," she whispered.

"I won't hurt you." He folded his hands over the desk, to show her. "But you are not leaving this room until you tell me."

He stood, came around the desk, moving in a way he wouldn't notice, but she certainly did. Her cigarette had burned down to the filter. He took it from her and stubbed it out in the ashtray, giving her a gentle pat on the shoulder.

"So." She visibly stiffened. "Former Soviet armaments clients request assistance in attacking America. They wish to attack America so their God will be pleased. This would be convenient for Russia also—to raise the price of oil barrels."

She lowered her eyes, looking away. Gomez leaned down over the desk, his palms on the edge.

"You knew," he said.

Her toe tapped on the cheap green linoleum.

"You knew about September 11th. About the plot. You let them do it." The room was a horror of stinking blue smoke. "No, you helped them do it." He paced, muttering outrageous profanities.

She stood, color high on her cheeks.

"*Glasnymi chushka Vy*! You are large, giant swine. I will not relax to this abuse!"

"Then get out."

"I am here to warn you! There is great danger!"

"Truly? You're a little late. If you wanted to warn us you could have told us about this on September 10th."

"But we did," she said softly. *"We did."*

That didn't surprise him either-- who they might have told.

Some politician, no doubt. He didn't care about that.

But the room was closing in. He saw that she wasn't finished. He looked at her, nerves singing, knowing what she was going to say next.

"They are going to do this again."

Chapter 4

A SUCKER PUNCH, meant to throw him. It had worked.

"Wait here."

Viisky sniffed, making a move toward the cigarette pack. Thin, delicate fingers, fidgeting with some papers in her briefcase as Gomez passed her, rushing out into the hallway. He was closing the door and did not see her flip open a cell phone and dial.

He edged out sideways, closing the door before someone noticed the mushroom cloud. His change jingled in his pocket as he walked slowly back toward Kessler's office. It was more of a distracted trudge, head down, thinking, and he made a pit stop in the men's room, although he hadn't needed it. Inside, his kidneys felt just fine, so he washed his hands twice, staring suspiciously into the mirror.

It happened all the time. Someone would waltz into a field office to claim that their neighbor was a commiepinko spy, and would the Bureau please arrest them—inquiring, did the FBI still torture people? The lucky agent would then decide whether to harass the innocent neighbor or file commitment papers on the informant.

This was almost the same thing, Gomez reasoned. But he was no longer a field agent, and Ms. Viktorina Viisky was not a housewife in Missoula with a grudge and latent psychoses.

His shoes clicked along the tiles, toward Kessler's office. He opened the door without knocking and stopped cold just inside the door.

It was not the first time Gomez had caught him.

ASAC Kessler was planted at his desk, leaning one way and then another as if he were on the deck of a schooner caught in a hurricane. His pudgy hands gripped a joystick—it was a sparkling blue one with varicolored lights—Kessler's tongue poked out as he manipulated the joystick like his life depended on it. Kessler was playing a flight simulator game on his taxpayer-funded computer.

From the look on his face, he was winning.

Kessler punched a button on the keyboard, pausing the game.

"So, hey," Kessler said, red in the face. "I sent an e-mail down to the Travel Office. They should have an advance check cut by the end of the week."

Gomez had no intention of being within a hundred miles of the Hoover building by the end of the week. His personal funds would have to last. But that was beside the point.

"I've got some passes for her." Kessler reached into a drawer, producing a manila folder. "Everything's in there. I talked with Treasury. You got contact numbers for every major port between Miami and Boston," Kessler leered. "Go easy on the expenses."

Gomez knew what was next. He was not listening, already thinking past this to what steps he might take to secure the sovereignty and security of the United States of America.

"That is some specimen. If I were you, I'd buy a fuckin' truckload of arugula."

"The woman wouldn't know arugula from a peanut butter sandwich."

Kessler stared blankly.

Gomez gave him a moment.

"What'd you mean? She's not with that Ministry thingy?"

"She is FSB, or says she is." A moment passed. Kessler scratched one of his chins, a middle one, looking confused.

Gomez pressed on, "She claims to have information concerning a follow-up attack to the infamy of 9/11." He explained further, skipping huge blocks of the story; the important parts, actually. He especially forgot to mention those pesky Vyydraat.

Kessler's hand slid away from the joystick. "That shit is huge."

"It would be," Gomez nodded, "if it were true."

"You think she's lying?"

Gomez' change jingled. His cigarettes were back in his office with the Tsarina. He was regretting the oversight.

"Suppose for a moment that you're highly placed in the Russian government. Your country is a sewer, okay?" If Gomez had had any crayons he would have drawn a picture. Charades would work, too. The alternative was to speak very slowly, which he did.

"Nine-Eleven happens. And you, like every other political hack, want to profit from the United States of America—*en extremis*."

"Yeah, maybe."

Possibilities were raised. Viisky might be carrying water—a political proxy sent to promote someone's agenda. Since the fall of the Towers, every country on earth was trying to find advantage in the situation. The biggest task ahead was not in finding out who was responsible so the Marines could kill them, but sifting through the sludge of too much information. The French had offered wine…

"You gotta verify," Kessler offered, courageously.

"Right," Gomez nodded. "In the meantime you need to walk this up the line. Use your office. Generate a memo."

"We got these anthrax letters." Kessler spoke of manpower shortfalls, stumbling blocks galore. Gomez raised an eyebrow.

"All the mosques…"

Gomez studied his shoes. The socks matched today., "What if it was something really huge? he said, obliquely. "Where people could get hurt if you did it the wrong way?"

"All the more reason to play it close. We really want to be sure this isn't some clusterfuck," Kessler said, with a straight face. Naturally so, thought Gomez. People like Larry Kessler would be the last to figure it out. "Hey, uh, did you need me for something else?"

Gomez did not. He reached down to retrieve the foam cup he'd left earlier, leaving Kessler with a parting shot.

"You winning?"

"Sometimes," Kessler allowed.

"That's good."

*

There was an elevator close by; Gomez caught it just as the door was closing. He shouldn't be disappointed about Kessler. The Bureau, like everything else in the country, had relaxed. They even had casual Friday. That was really neat.

A "No Smoking" sign in the elevator reminded him of cigarettes. He needed one, desperately. The poisons helped him to think. This reminded him of Miss Viisky. By this time, she'd photocopied his entire file cabinet and was chucking boxes out the window to the waiting thugs on Constitution Avenue.

Not a problem. The White House would sport minarets by the time they deciphered his filing system.

He stared at the floor of the elevator. So, they'd told somebody about 9/11 before it happened. They were…compromised. Not in the old-fashioned way, with slinking spies and the exchange of real Yankee dollars for the plans to the latest death ray, but in the new, modern way, where some autocrat hasn't done his job and the bad guys cream us. So now, the idiots must cover their asses instead of protecting the populace.

Viktorina Viisky—a bombshell with a bombshell.

The elevator hit bottom.

Gomez forgot to get off, lost in thought. The doors started to close again.

It was time to get cracking.

*

Val Sacco had a small office in the dungeon—a place to hide, to peck in solace on his computer. Sacco was a good man to know. Gomez had beers with him. He left the elevator and approached. The door was open, but he would have knocked for Sacco in any case.

"Who's the tomato?" Sacco asked, without looking up from his monitor.

"Fashion Officer," Gomez replied.

"Wow."

In violation of rule and reason, Gomez told Sacco most of the fairy tale Ms. Viisky had imparted. Sacco held onto his mouse like it was his wife's ass on a Saturday night, and then, as the implications grew, gradually loosened his grip.

"I thought you got stuck with that Commission garbage."

"This just popped up. I speak Russian."

"Yeah?"

"Well, I used to. Haven't said a word in ten years."

"Guess you don't need to these days. Tough break."

Sacco spun lazily on his chair. "You should go see Yates."

"You're right," said Gomez.

He could go back upstairs and kick the whole affair over Kessler's head to the Assistant Director. They would rush Viisky up the chain. Meetings would be held. Dozens, thousands of meetings. And if she were truthful, Chicago would melt in the follow-up attacks just as everyone was safely tucked under the covers.

"Don't forget to talk out of both sides of your mouth."

Gomez wasn't listening. He pursed his lips, thinking.

"Verification?" Sacco added, as an afterthought.

"How?" Gomez pointed out.

Sacco tossed his pen onto the desk, running his hands through his hair. "The appearance of an attempt at verification is of equal importance to the result."

"You've been down here too long."

"True."

Sacco was a detailer—the guy who decided to which field office each and every special agent would be sent for the standard three-year posting. There were other influences. Dictum might arrive from on high. An agent might have screwed up a routine matter that happened to catch the eye of the Director, sending him or her to Attu, Alaska, instead of Maui. But by-and-large, Sacco had the power to dictate the course of thousands of lives with the push of a button.

"Man, you gotta tell somebody." Sacco said, emphasizing this. His work gave him a unique grasp of procedure, something Gomez lacked.

"I thought you said I should verify."

"Yeah, that too. But maybe you could just, you know, like file a Contact Report. Nobody reads those anymore. It would take a month before they asked you about it."

"I already told somebody," Gomez pointed out, smiling. "I told Larry Kessler."

"Oh Christ," Sacco muttered. He began to doodle on his blotter. "How is the estimable Mr. Kessler?"

"Dizzy." Gomez looked at the clock on the wall. By now Ms. Viisky had gone through the entire pack of smokes. If somebody on the sidewalk looked up...well, there was a fire department substation a block away.

"One other thing." Gomez employed just the right inflection and body language, and Sacco caught it, as Gomez knew he would. Sacco got up, closing the door to his office.

"Ms. Viisky says they told us about 9/11—*before* it happened."

Sacco paled. "Oh, Jesus Christ, don't tell me that shit."

"Too late," Gomez observed, watching Sacco as he considered the possibilities.

"There will be Special Prosecutors. There will be much finger pointing. Every moron with a GED and a microphone will take a cot in this building for a year." Gomez saw that this last part scared Sacco the most. He was content here in his little cave, lost in his charts.

Gomez saw it, then, real in his mind: Katie Couric asking a cafeteria lady to define the relationship between Special Agent Gomez and the Director. Katie would wear a hairnet, in commiseration. *Both hairnets, blooming white on the screen.*

Sacco must have seen it too. "You're screwed." This conclusion came as no surprise.

"Maybe not. I forgot to tell Kessler the part about prior warning."

Sacco thought about this for a moment. He seemed to have figured out where Gomez was going.

"That's spooky."

"I am less concerned with somebody's political future than I am with my responsibilities to national security."

"Remember that line. It'll sound good at the inquiry. Inquisition."

"I told Kessler. That's as far as I am willing to go right now."

"You gonna verify?"

"I am going to find them and kick their asses." Gomez smiled.

"That's one way to go." Sacco smiled too.

Val Sacco was no killer. But Gomez knew someone who was. While he had him smiling, Gomez asked, "I need a number. I need to find Davidson."

Sacco was a bright guy. He closed his eyes, attempting a watery protest, "He's retired."

Gomez was going to need some help. Sacco was a paper-pusher. He was a month out of a wicked divorce and carrying an Olympic-sized torch. Sacco's wife, as it turned out, had run off with a guy from Cirq de Soleil. An actual clown. Gomez would never tell a soul.

"He may be retired. He isn't dead."

"How 'bout you go to Yates," Sacco said, "and then when he says run with it, you can ask me for Davidson."

"And while this is happening, Al Qaeda blows the shit out of us."

"Security is tight everywhere. You see that little orange thing on television? That new Terror Alert deal?"

"Yes. It's very impressive." Gomez stood. He had a question for Sacco, something that'd been rolling around in his head for a while now. "What do you think they want"?

"Who?"

"The terrorists. Osama, or whatever it's called."

Sacco tipped back in his chair, happy at the change of subject. "You mean: What do they hope to accomplish with this? Heck if I know. They had this asshole on television. He said we have to take a look at our past sponsorship of Afghanistan, all those shitholes. He said maybe it's our fault."

"Yes?" Gomez asked. His smile had vaporized. "Think through that one again." His tone was not friendly.

"Beats the shit outta me. Listen, this thing with Davidson—"

"If I kick her upstairs," Gomez cut him off. "I'll be buried in bullshit for six months. Or, I could just tell the whole truth to Kessler, tantamount to option A. If I do nothing, we're gonna get clobbered and it will be all your fault for not helping me."

"I really like the way you worked that out."

"Thank you."

Sacco was almost angry now. That was a good thing. There were people who needed to be angry.

Sacco folded, forking over the number for Lewis Davidson—the Russian Killer. Gomez trooped back up to his office, Davidson's number hot in his pocket, feeling the thrill of operations. Then he remembered that Viktorina Viisky was not who she was supposed to be.

Chapter 5

THE DRIVER OF THE TAN Chevy Blazer was busy applying eyeliner, shrieking into her cell phone, and eating an ice cream bar as she drifted randomly in the slow lane, just ahead and to the right of them, running northbound on I-495, the Beltway. It was a Dove bar; Gomez could see the wrapper, and for a brief, tantalizing moment he considered blowing her away, but that would require asking Ms. Viisky to roll down her window to avoid shattering the safety glass. His blood pressure was still spiking and he did not wish to speak to her just yet.

A quarter of a mile ahead, the left-hand exit loomed. Gomez saw the driver of the Blazer turn her head. She was making an interesting point over the phone, or was about to cut him off.

He anticipated, toeing the brake, hugging the outer edge of the lane. She missed him by six inches, yanking the wheel to the left, then cutting across three lanes of traffic before bouncing down the ramp.

Viisky looked a little green around the gills. She opened her mouth to say something, then closed it again. The maples and poplars were shedding summer green for sublime yellows and reds, so she busied herself in observation.

Bet they didn't drive like that in Transylvania, or wherever the hell she came from.

There was a Courtyard by Marriott in Bethesda, where Gomez had once attended a symposium on sexual harassment. He pulled into the turnaround, dumping it off for the valet. There was a message from Cummings on his cell phone. Must have been while he was cheating death on the Beltway. He listened as they walked to the doors.

"Hey. I really respect what you older people have done. I just needed to say that, and I hope we can work together on this. These kids need a better future." The message ended with, "You'd better. If you know what's good for you." Gomez erased it.

They approached the front desk. Gomez awarded himself style points; he had managed to utter not one word since leaving the office.

"Mr. Gomez, Ms. Atta. You're on seventeen." The desk clerk buzzed a bellhop, handing Gomez his American Express Gold Card with a freezing stare. He recognized the name.

In the suite, Gomez tipped the porter generously and closed the door. He threw her garment bag onto the bed.

"The Bureau will pay for this."

"I have budget," she said, looking around the rooms, failing to hide her wonder at the luxury of it. Gomez nodded. Not what he meant.

She turned to him, remembering.

"You give me name of this terrorist hijacker."

He opened the mini-bar and cracked a Heineken.

"You are the living equivalent. You had foreknowledge of the event and failed to stop it. You're as guilty as he is."

Viisky crossed the room to pick up the phone. She spoke in rapid-fire Russian, like chewing on marbles. She listened, said, "*Da,*" and hung up.

"Call them back. Cancel the flight," he ordered.

"*Yeb vas*," she said. "I give you one moment longer to behave like gentleman. If you do not…I will fly away like little bird. Her hands fluttered in the air, almost causing him to smile. They engaged in a brief staring contest until Gomez exhaled loudly, like a sperm whale, ending the stalemate.

He should cuff her. Hold her on some unspecified charge. Maybe beat the information out of her. Or he could play it straight. It was an open question as to who would speak first when his cell phone rang, spoiling the fun. Gomez brought the phone to his ear. It was Kessler.

"Hey, Boris. How's Natasha?"

Gomez looked to the ceiling for assistance.

"You gonna get into that?" Kessler asked. "Why don't you just tell her the Bureau wouldn't spring for a hotel room…take her to your place."

"I thought you would have spoken with Yates by now," Gomez replied.

Viisky was waving at him.

"I am most tired," she said, "I will bathe." Must have canceled the flight, Gomez thought, following her with his eyes as she gathered a few things and disappeared into the bathroom. He turned his attention back to the phone.

"I noticed you'd left," Kessler was saying. "So what're you gonna do?"

With the opportunity to take command—to do his duty—Kessler had decided to play office games. To pass the hot potato. The potential of the situation would elude Kessler until an A-bomb landed on his desk.

"I've got her in a hotel in Bethesda. I'll submit the expense report…whenever."

"I knew it!" Kessler crowed. "That is some shiny piece of ass, right?"

Gomez watched the bathroom door, his thoughts not with Kessler.

"That reminds me," Kessler said, "I got a call this afternoon from one of Senator Smeal's hatchet women. They want you to testify in front of a televised Commission hearing, Monday morning at nine. C-Span."

"Bullshit."

"No, it's for real." Not enough Asian-American agents are getting killed in the line of duty. Someone did the math." Gomez closed his eyes. His sinuses were bothering him again.

"They want to talk to you about it."

"I do not have time for this crap."

Kessler was blathering—something about not being able to cover Gomez for the hearing, when Viisky came out of the bathroom, a towel piled on her head. He'd half expected her to be dressed in some silly black ninja outfit with a knife between her teeth, or a sickle.

"How about I just plug a few guys myself? Get the numbers up."

Silence. Like Kessler was considering it.

"Maybe Chou. I really hate that guy."

"Just get me out of it," Gomez said into the phone.

"Can't do it. Anyway, you're golden. You're a minority!" Gomez wasn't listening.

"I'll sort it all out and call you tomorrow," he mumbled.

"Don't forget," Kessler admonished, "you've got that Commission hearing Monday. Smeal is gonna be there." Gomez made a face and hung up.

"Feel better?" he asked, trying to be cordial.

She nodded her head, yes—softening.

He held out his hand like a matador, motioning to a seating area that ran between the windows and the queen-sized bed. She followed his lead, sitting primly onto the sofa.

"I have become hungry."

"Me, too," he nodded, picking up the phone to dial room service. He looked over his shoulder as he spoke into the phone and asked her if a prime rib sandwich and fries were okay. She agreed, pulling a carafe of overpriced swill from the mini-bar and filling a plastic cup. Gomez looked pointedly at the mini-bar, holding his near-empty. She got him another Heineken.

"Thank you, Ms. Viisky."

"What is this *zzzzzz*? You must call me Vischka."

A look of conciliation. Making the effort. It dawned on him that she expected reciprocity, some familiarity in return.

"Okay."

She watched him a moment, then leaned back against the sofa, accepting it.

He took off his suit jacket and tossed it over a chair. That puppy was gonna wrinkle.

"You said you came here to warn me," he reminded her.

She took a sip of her wine.

"I will tell you in my own way, and if you have further questions then you may ask them of me."

"Your prepositions are improving."

"Excuse me?"

"Never mind. Please continue."

She took another sip, curling her legs up under her ass like a cat. She'd changed into loose khakis and a crew sweatshirt, satanic red, with the letters CCCP across the chest.

Cheeky.

"As I told you before you lost your control, I work directly for Feliks. He is large man. Is involved in many important discussions in FSB and sometimes meets peoples of Parliament. He explains to me two days ago that I am to fly to America to locate someone in your FBI. Someone who can become eh, *podstrekatel*"

"A facilitator."

"Yes. Facilitator. Whatever."

Gomez picked up the file that lay on the coffee table between them. Her eyes crawled off toward the window. "And you just happened to get me."

She did not respond, fiddling with her wineglass, getting shifty again.

Gomez watched her over the file, not understanding a word that was written. It was in Cyrillic and he was lost on the first sentence. His verbal Russian was okay, but the written word was another thing. It had been awhile."Go on," he said, glancing through the file. The cover was bordered in scary red and white stripes. More theatre.

"As I have said, Feliks has previously contacted peoples in your government."

"Who?" Not that it mattered.

"Your Director of FBI." Gomez choked on his Heineken. A waste of good beer. Viisky asked if he was okay. He nodded, waving her off.

"Feliks has risks his ass in doing so. Many SVR leaders are involved in Oktober Swan—assistance of terrorists. If SVR know he is telling your FBI Director, they will most surely kill him."

Gomez leaned forward across the table. "When did Feliks tell the Director?"

"Some months ago."

Back against the sofa, his face a blank. Old spy movies notwithstanding, it was not a simple thing for a security officer of a foreign power to pick up the phone and call the Director. Protocol would be followed. Rivers of paper would be generated—Amazons of paper. He suddenly stood, his knees popping, and said to her, "And this is why you are here speaking with me, because we are compromised?"

"Feliks and I discuss this with much lust. That is one possibility, that you are compromised. Or, is that your Director did not believe Feliks, or third possibility, which I myself believe, he is simply an idiot man."

A knock at the door. Gomez motioned for her to stay seated. An ugly blue automatic appeared in his hand. He padded past the bathroom, muzzle flat behind his thigh as he opened the door, allowing the room-service waiter to roll a chrome serving-cart into the room.

The guy picked up on the tension in the air. He nervously thanked Gomez and hurried to the door.

"Hey, buddy," Gomez called. The young man turned, accepting the tip. He executed a little half-bow and bolted from the room.

"Why do you present the firearm?" Viisky asked him.

"Because…" Gomez shrugged, "old habits…never mind."

They were strangely at ease together, she passing the salt, Gomez handing her something at the right moment. He noticed but did not comment. Also, she seemed to prefer American hotel fare to boiled yak.

"How did Feliks find out about it?"

"I do not know."

They ate, content with the silence, Gomez trying to stuff all of this into his head. The sounds of rush-hour traffic were festering outside on the avenue. The whole thing was completely believable. Not only could he see it, someone probably should have seen it. No, that was too far a reach. But still…*Jesus!*

"Did you notify the C.I.A.?"

She snorted out a laugh. "*Please.*"

"I wouldn't have either," he told her, and they held eye contact.

"And you wouldn't, or couldn't, trust standard diplomatic channels," Gomez said, thinking aloud. "So your Uncle Feliks concocted his Arugula story and sent you over to make contact."

Viisky nodded agreement.

"We request Russian language agent from olden days. Someone to understand me."

"I never wanted to understand you," he said honestly. "I just wanted to crush you."

Viisky dusted her hands of the meal, folding her napkin. It didn't work.

"Neverless, you are here," she shrugged. "From your Kessler's explanation, all your Russian speaking peoples are gone. You are last ancient reptile," she said.

Gomez smiled and the set of his face changed. He stood, pacing the room. She was lying, but that was okay. He expected it. He would let it percolate, for now. They had chosen him and somehow gotten through to him. But chosen him for what?

He stood at the window, wiping the corona of steam fogging the glass. Many of the passing vehicles had American flags attached to their antennae. They were driving more orderly than was usual. It was almost as if they were being courteous to one another. The nation had changed, become one. He wondered how long it would last.

"So, despite the warning, we blew it. The Director, his lackeys and ass-lickers…at this point it doesn't matter." The question came to him; it had been coiled in the back of his mind for hours. He knew but had to ask, "Follow-up?"

"Yes. They are going to strike you in two ways, each as diversion away from other way. This is to split you in half. Divide your menpowers." She raised a finger. "Your water treatments, to amuse Al Qaeda. Your petrol refineries, for SVR. These are to be follow-up attacks to this Eleventh. They are going to smack you while you are down."

Gomez wondered how much Scotch whisky was in the mini-bar. Whatever it was, it wouldn't be enough. He sat heavily, feeling the weight of it.

"And what? You think they'll listen this time? That I'll be able to take you to the right people?"

"I should correct this misunderstanding." The barest flash of spark shone behind her almond eyes, "I am not here to warn you. Not really."

"I am here to help you stop them, of course."

CHAPTER 6

VIISKY WOKE HIM AT SIX, looking refreshed and vigorous, unsurprising for a woman in her late twenties or early thirties. Gomez, however, felt as if an enormous grading machine had swept over him in the night. They shared mumbled good-mornings, followed by turns in the shower. He peeked a little, breaking his promise of averting his eyes when she left the bathroom for a mirrored vestibule, clad only in slacks and a lace bra.

"Will we be speaking with your superiors this day?" she asked, glancing down and to the right.

"Maybe," he said, lacing up. "I guess this works out for you in any case."

She looked at him steadily. "I do not understand."

"Nine-eleven will be good for Russia, as will this follow-up deal. Putin will cry for the cameras and make his statement of condolence, but you'll get your ninety dollars a barrel."

She stood and began to pace. They had something in common. "There are some in Security Services who do not wish to see these terrorists commit more of this, eh…"

"Crime against humanity?"

"Yes."

"What about you? What do you think?"

"Is abomination, is word I am seeking," an apology, of sorts.

Gomez went to the veranda and lit up because the rooms were

non-smoking. How about that. She wandered after him, affecting indifference.

"You will help to explain these conditions to your superiors."

He ignored her, staring out at the traffic. "I'll be right back."

*

There was a newspaper machine down in the lobby. Gomez grabbed some slops from the banquette and moved to a table in the rear, away from the salesmen and travelers. The crowd was sparse. The airlines were reporting light loads, weak business travel. People were afraid.

He called Porsche Cummings while his coffee cooled. They were slated for a bout with some high school kids in Anacostia, so he told her he couldn't make it today, how he was heartbroken—crushed, actually.

Cummings was already there at the school. And she was pissed.

"What am I supposed to do here?"

"Tell them you love them." She'd probably already done that, so he added, "Tell them *a Latino* agent loves them."

"Don't you mess me up," she shrieked. A dire warning about the television thing led to a Cummings tirade and ended with something nasty that would never be allowed by the Thought Police. Gomez was shocked and told her so. He flung a couple of slippery promises at her and hung up.

Back to the paper. In a special section of the *USA Today,* they had a listing; seven pages, six columns across, thirty-two down. It was an installment of the names of victims from the Trade Center, Flight 93, and the Pentagon. There were far too many to fit into one daily. Tomorrow's edition would continue the dirge. He tried to read through it. He owed it to them—to at least know their names. After a while he folded the paper neatly into squares and addressed his breakfast.

It was simple, really. Viisky's mission, as he saw it, would be to prevent this supposed Russian involvement in 9/11 from becoming public. To accomplish this, she must warn off the Vyydraat—or eliminate them. Also, she would somehow have to ensure the silence of each and every last Al Qaeda who had knowledge of the plot.

Procedure was clear. He should take it upstairs. If he told someone about Viisky and it didn't happen, his name would be mud. If he didn't tell anyone and something did happen, he would be boiled in oil on the steps of the Capitol. Plus, he didn't know who she was or what she wanted. Not all of it. He had most of it, though.

Well, the last thing he wanted to do was warn them off. The time was now. Catch the fuckers before the op and grind them into the dust. He would deal with the Russians later. First he had to smoke her out.

*

Viisky was on the phone when he returned. She hung up quickly and stood.

"Will you be getting much menpowers to assist us?"

"We are going to the press," he announced. "They are egomaniacs and simpletons, mainly, but they are the perfect way to mobilize the entire country to the threat. If I force the issue with the Bureau, they will confine us to a windowless room in the Hoover Building where they will wring their hands and generate a thousand tons of paperwork from your answers to their silly questions. They will then keep everything secret to avoid a panic, which will work against them. Even if they believe you, they will be so busy covering their asses that Al Qaeda and your pals will have time to level the Eastern Seaboard."

"These are no friends of mine," she said, with a chill.

"Hey, I apologize. Just a figure of speech."

"I accept this apology." They sat for a moment in silence.

"There is one luck already," she said. "Feliks says the demons attack too early. Is why I am here too late to prevent first attack. We had information they were not to take planes until first day of Oktober. Actually, SVR operation was called Oktober Swan."

"You must be joking."

"No, Feliks says old men are happy, once again, to be celebrating Lenin's birth."

Gomez laced his fingers together and sat, thinking. He took a deep breath. "If that's true, it would mean we have some time."

"Yes," she said, smiling. "This is Luck, you see?"

"If Al Qaeda went early, if they weren't supposed to go until One October, that means that the follow-ups were not supposed to happen until when? Mid-month?"

"I do not know. I know only date of airliners." She thought for a moment. "Which, of course, was wrong date."

"These things can't just be thrown together without serious co-ordination between the principals. They can't have planned two complex ops and jump them both off on the wrong dates."

Viisky crossed the room for her briefcase.

"I am eager to begin the helping." She handed him a sheaf of papers, explaining, "Is all of agents still to be existing."

"You don't know which ones are our targets?"

"No."

They worked the phones, consulting her list of Vyydraat that she'd supposedly gotten from this Feliks goofball. Gomez used his cell phone. Viisky called from the hotel line.

"Gonna need a break," he told her, closing the flip phone after a dozen calls. "This is how I see it. From the ones that are still viable—call it a hundred—we've got to locate and interrogate the ones working with Al Qaeda and get them to talk."

He raised his forefinger like a professor, "And those five or ten—*the bad guys*—have almost certainly moved or gone underground. Unless they are completely incompetent, and the one thing I wouldn't call the old KGB is incompetent." He looked at Viisky, gauging her.

She appeared about to say something and then thought better of it. Gomez paced the room. "We'll go with what we've got," he said, bouncing to his feet.

She stood also, and grabbed her jacket. "We go to press now?"

"No, first we get the evidence. We hit as many of these guys as we can. I count around forty in the DC area alone. Most of the rest look to be in New York, which makes sense. We only need one."

"What if you are mistaken? We should go to this press *now*. What if we waste much time and this attacks occur?"

Gomez opened the door to the suite. "I'm not wrong. I'll bet my country on that."

*

They stopped at his townhouse on a sycamore-lined boulevard in Rock Creek, just outside the Beltway. Viisky waited in the car, listening to music on the car stereo, staring with goggle-eyed fascination at the lunch-hour traffic whizzing past. There were an astounding number of vehicles, most of which looked to be privately owned. And the size of them, *Yeb Vas!* The massive SUVs reminded her of the Russian BMP, roughly equivalent to the American Bradley Fighting Vehicle—lacking only the olive drab cammo and 76-mm chain gun. Many of these were driven by women who could barely see over the steering wheel.

Gomez got back in the car, tossing a large black gym bag into the backseat, and slammed the door.

"What is this *urgency*?" she asked, alarmed.

"What?"

"This women. In the Army trucks."

Gomez laughed. "Shopping," he explained. Gave her a cryptic glance, handing her a leather holster. It held a Beretta Cheetah, ten-shot .380 auto.

"You may need this."

She didn't bother to ask if it was loaded.

*

At 1:10 in the afternoon, Gomez stood next to Viisky in an anteroom to the offices of Congressman James Womack of California.

They arrived unannounced and were greeted by a little prick with maroon tortoiseshell glasses that were too large for his face. His hair was impossibly crisp in Yalie Anal, parted on the left with an overabundance tufted on the crown, like a rooster with encephalitis. Gomez eyed him dubiously. He was *really* young. The chief of staff for a prominent United States congressman looked like he was teetering on the edge of drinking age.

The aide noticed Gomez staring at him and caught the meaning of it.

"I'm twenty-six. Magna cum laude, Brown '98. I have a Master's in International Relations. I am a Rhodes Scholar." He sneered when he said it. Or maybe that was Gomez' imagination. Predisposition.

"The Congressman is on a junket to the mountain regions of Chechnya. He sponsored the last Chechen relief package and is determined to see that the aid is not diverted by the Russian government. He will return next Wednesday."

"May I suggest an appointment?" he asked, looking at Gomez' credentials as if they were a turd.

"If I find out he's here, I'll see to it that you're audited for the next ten years," Gomez threatened. His attitude did nothing to facilitate cooperation. He recognized this and softened. "Look, this is a matter of national security." The phrase that paid.

"If you read the papers, you would know it's true," the aide said, looking Gomez up and down. "House Bill 9472." He smiled.

"You fucking whippet." Little bugger just made you want to…

"We arrive on the Wednesday." Viisky intervened, taking Gomez by the arm and heading for the door. They navigated the building in silence, gaining the street and finding his car.

"Who's fucking next?" he barked, settling into the Ford.

"You will do better to use honey," Viisky advised, fastening her shoulder harness, "to catch the bee." She held out a map they had printed off her laptop in the hotel.

Gomez looked at her, shaking his head. He took the map and studied it for a moment. "I want you to make a note next to that bastard's name. When this is over, I'm going to core his ass."

She said nothing, taking in the sights as they took the ramp toward Virginia.

"Womack represents my district."

"From the California?" she realized what she had said and made her correction. "I mean… "

"He is a fucking spy."

Viisky shifted uncomfortably.

"Correct, but these peoples may not recall this themselves."

*

The car was wearing him out. He pulled to the curb as he thought about challenging her—he'd never mentioned that he was from California.

"Give me that." He took the map from her. "This guy here," he said, pointing at a name in the middle of her list, "is ten minutes from Womack—in the other direction. Is there something I'm missing? That we have to go in circles all day?"

"Is too much to see all in one. We shall go to this Bethesda next," she said, mouth set, eyes drifting down to the floorboards.

A moment passed. The woman was really a poor liar.

"Fine. Whatever."

They pulled into a shopping mall. Gomez killed the engine. They got out of the car, walking toward a large neon sign proclaiming ReMax in blazing red, white, and blue. She took his arm. A nice ego boost. They easily looked the part of a couple looking for a darling Cape Cod, with closing at the end of the month.

A receptionist buzzed them right back, in sharp contrast to Womack's little helper.

The realtor was a man in his early forties, improbably blonde with an appliqué tan. He got off the phone, showed them his gleaming caps.

"Jim Adler," he said, cheerily, extending his hand first to Viisky and then to Gomez. His phone lit up again, making a noise like a duck call. He raised a finger, "Excuse me."

Adler smiled like an asshole, mouthing soothing platitudes into the phone.

"Just make yourself comfortable. I'll be right back." He left, closing the door behind him, so as to prevent their escape. Gomez watched him leave. He turned to Viisky.

"That's KGB imagination for you. They're all named Jim."

"He is properly Kostenko Spasski," she said, emotionless.

"Bet he plays a mean game of chess."

Viisky smiled knowingly. "This real Boris Spasski did work for

KGB. Do you know this?" Gomez froze, scanning her for the lie. She was impassive.

"No, I guess we didn't. Figures."

He looked around the office. *Never in your wildest dreams.* Adler's desktop photos showed a wife and three smiling kids around a kidney-shaped pool, all of them girls between the ages of, say, eight and thirteen. When they found out who Daddy was…a thought occurred to him.

"I suppose KGB had a fondness for Jewish surnames."

"Yes," Viisky said quietly. "Americans will think it most unlikely that Jew was agent of Soviet Union. What they did to those people…is most awful." She stared at the window behind Adler's desk, her face a cipher. She would have a lot riding on this. Her freedom at least. Maybe her life. The Soviet Union was gone; the hard-asses at the Lubyanka were not.

"The blonde hair doesn't go with the ethnicity," he observed.

"Is dyed," she said. "A woman can tell."

Adler returned, grinning widely as he took his seat. His cheeks threatening to split, like he'd just been crowned Miss America. His chair was elevated slightly, to give the illusion of command. Well, Gomez could play theatre, too. He stood and was about to drop the hammer, when Viisky spoke first.

"You enjoy your swimming pool?" Her blatant sex appeal took a turn for something else.

Adler's smile drooped for a fraction of a second. He rallied.

"That your hot button? A pool? That's no problem at all." He shucked his jacket and addressed his keyboard. "Tell me a bit about yourselves."

"My husband is from the California." Viisky smiled, switching effortlessly to Russian.

"I, myself, am from Operations Directorate of the *Sluzhba Vneshney Rasvedi Rossii*."

She stood, her eyes burning a hole into Adler. Gomez thought maybe it was a bad time to mention that she had told him she was FSB and, before that, Ministry of Agriculture. Maybe later.

Adler's smile drooped, like syrup running down a wall. He opened his mouth to speak. She cut him off.

"It has been twenty-eight months since your last visit to the National Theatre Company."

Gomez stood off to the side, humming quietly as she shredded Kostenko Spasski, formerly an agent of GRU, Spetsnaz Special Forces and Soviet sleeper agent. Spasski was on a swivel, looking back and forth between Viisky and Gomez. A dog badly in need of a walk.

"What?" he began. "I don't know…" He raised in a crouch out of his seat then plumped down hard, a whoosh of air escaping.

"*Are you so foolish as to think we would forget you?*" she continued, in Russian. Watching her, Gomez felt just a little bit afraid.

"There's nothing to report!" Spasski whined in English, trying to regain his composure. "What do you want from me? I'm a realtor for Chrissake!" He changed tactics, stood, and made a show of being offended.

"I have been rotting here in this country for nineteen years. I was Spetsnaz before you were born." Viisky pulled the Beretta from behind her jacket and planted the muzzle on his forehead.

"You will now answer the questions. If you do not, I will shoot you. Then, I will go to your home where I will slaughter your family—plus, your pets." She looked pretty sincere to Gomez. "Also, I will barbeque your home."

Gomez studied his nails. He could easily imagine how this man, this former Special Forces soldier, could be beguiled by life in America. The one downside to the sleeper operation was that the young men sent here would experience luxury beyond their imagination. It must have looked like a fable. KGB had to have one hell of a time convincing them America was a façade, as they held it in their hands.

By the numbers Viisky had shown him, they had lost more than a few to the imperialist swine. Clearly, Spasski was one of those. He had a family, a home, an upper middle-class income—all the gadgets and comfort that accompanied that lifestyle. Back in Poopigrad, he'd probably never owned a decent pair of shoes.

"My name is Gomez. I am with the Federal Bureau of Investigation. We can arrest you and have you thrown in big-boy prison, where assorted gang members will knock out your teeth before they sodomize you." He paused to let that one sink in.

"They can do this at will." He lit a cigarette, exhaling loudly. "When your trial is complete, your shame manifest, your family disgraced, we will ship you back to the New Worker's Paradise. I am certain there are men in charge of your operation who will be displeased that you have spoiled U.S.-Russian relations."

Gomez tapped a two-inch ash onto the floor. "A reunion would be nice, don't you think?"

Spasski sat, keeping an eye on Viisky.

"What do you want?"

"You are going to describe to me the total content of your communications with the *Rodina* over the last ten years."

Spasski relaxed further, allowing himself a glance out the window.

"Also, you will describe to us any contact you have had with other Vyydraat."

Spasski jerked slightly at this. Gomez was counting on it. If Gomez knew about the *Vyydraat*…

"I haven't really been active for years," Spasski began. He looked at Viisky.

"In the beginning, I was pretty gung-ho. They started me out in Norfolk. My assignment was to report on ship movements; the carriers, mostly. Subs if I could, but that was pretty tough. They kept armed Marines around those babies."

Viisky scowled at him.

"Hey, I tried." He looked at her and shrugged.

"Anyway, I would hang out in bars, places like that. I tried to meet as many sailors as I could. Get 'em drunk. Get 'em talking. Once I received a communication instructing me to have, uh, relations with certain men if it would help me gather information. That, I wouldn't do." The phone warbled again. Spasski ignored it.

"Coke was big then. I used it to cultivate friendships with some guys. My biggest coup was from this guy, a Lieutenant Commander in 'Phibs. He told me about Grenada—before it happened. I gave Moscow two days notice. They told me it helped the Cubans shoot down a few helicopters."

In one rapid motion Gomez reached over, pinning Spasski's wrist to the desk. Without delay, he held his burning cigarette to the meat of Spasski's hand, grinding it out on the veins.

Spasski howled like a pussy. A wisp of burning hair drifted across the desk, making Gomez' eyes water.

"I said the last ten years, dickhead." The intercom buzzed.

"Was that you, Mr. Adler?"

"No, I hit the thing by accident. Thanks, Amy." Spasski grimaced and looked to Viisky. She was smiling.

"All right already!" he said. "Is that your standard FBI interrogation technique? You guys used to call *us* the barbarians."

"This is not an interrogation." Gomez wondered if the man's American was this seamless in the beginning, or if he had improved over time.

"Okay. The last ten years. When the Wall came down, I was working for Eastern Airlines in Maintenance. I was a supervisor in Avionics. They went tits-up, so I got my real estate license. There was nothing from Moscow. I had to make a living."

Gomez shook his head, amazed at it all.

"What?" Spasski asked.

"Nothing. Please go on."

"Yeah, okay. So in '96, I got a notice. Dead-drop instructions. I was married. We just had our third. Anyway, I met him and he told me that it wasn't over. He said to consider myself still active, that they would be in need of my services. He told me to get involved in the D.C. party scene. Try to get close to some politicians."

Viisky asked him, "And you did this?"

"Sort of. That takes money, and KGB—I mean SVR—certainly didn't give me any." He looked up at them, "I saw one once. I mean, he didn't know who I was."

"Who?" Gomez asked.

"Some Congressman from California. I forget his name. Something Waspy, I think. Anyway, I knew who he was because I saw him smoking a cigarette."

"Go on," Gomez said, knowing where this was going.

"When you make Spetsnaz, you get initiated, just like anywhere else. On the last night of training, a couple of guys from instructor command come and get you while you're asleep. They cut about a three-centimeter gash into the meat of your hand with a buck-knife, like a little '*T*.' It's supposed to represent the Sword of the Party."

Gomez was thinking about his lighter again.

"You know how the KGB is the Sword and the Shield of the Party? Well, we called ourselves the Sword. We don't need no stinking shield." Spasski laughed at his own stupid joke.

"So I'm at this soirée deal in Georgetown. I see him talking to some people and on the back of his hand I see this scar. I could tell what it was from ten feet away." Spasski smiled. "So that's how I knew." He sat back, pleased with himself. "A lady at the party told me he was a Congressman from California."

"Did you speak with him?"

"No."

Gomez walked around the desk to stand behind Spasski, lest he get comfortable. Thinking about the coincidence of how the two guys they met today had been some of the few Vyydraat that had actually met each other. Viisky was leading him, clumsily.

"Ever meet with another agent of the Sluzbha?" she asked. "In the last couple of years, I mean."

"There was a guy one time." He laughed, a nervous croak. "My control officer sent me a fax. You believe that shit?"

Gomez rubbed the back of his neck. Actually, he did believe it. He was getting a first-hand lesson on just how bold they'd been.

"They sent me this fax telling me that a guy would be coming by from Manhattan Bond to sell me some stocks. I had to buy from him. No questions asked. Before we left the school, they told us they would try to facilitate agents earning a living without spending too much time working at it. In other words, I would patronize certain stores and buy things from certain people, so we were sort of self-sustaining."

Gomez nodded, nauseated.

"Tell me about this broker. Did you physically meet him?"

"He came to my house. Normally that didn't happen. You weren't supposed to talk to other Soviets. KGB wanted to compartmentalize, except for a list of places where I'm supposed to shop. They update it every once in a while."

"Tell me."

"Yeah, sure." Spasski pointed at a water cooler in the corner of the office, "You mind?"

Gomez signaled that it was all right. Spasski filled a coffee cup with water from the cooler, Viisky hovering over him.

"He didn't say more than five words to me." He shrugged at Gomez.

"The paperwork was all filled out, ready to go. He just showed me where to sign and I cut him a check. It was all Blue Chips; GM, Delta, shit like that. At first I didn't know if I could afford it. I still have it. Getting a pretty fair return, too. Actually, I need to find him and sell. This terrorism business is gonna hammer my shares."

"How do we find him?" Gomez asked.

Spasski looked at Gomez curiously. He still didn't have a handle on this whole deal. On who was what, and so forth. "You're the FBI. How the hell should I know?"

Gomez resisted the urge to smack him. He saw that Viisky also was considering something.

"What was his name?"

"Hold on a second." Spasski made a move to reach down into his desk. Viisky lunged forward, cracking him across the bridge of his nose with the Beretta. Spasski cowered, hands up around his face.

"Relax you crazy bitch! I'm just getting his name for you!" There was a thin, red scrape across his beak.

Gomez held his hand out to stay her.

Still looking warily at Viisky, Spasski opened a lower drawer and pulled out a file, dumping it onto his desk.

"He signed it right here on the back page of the folder." He held it up for Gomez to see. "It's got his name, address, and phone number."

In case Gomez was blind, Spasski said it aloud.

"Stuart Rafkin."

Chapter 7

BACK IN THE CAR, Gomez carried a copy of the stock certificate hastily burned on Spasski's office equipment, as well as the list of KGB-approved vendors. The front bench seat was sufficiently roomy and Viisky sat with her legs folded under her like a Swami. Gomez watched her from the corner of his eye, wondering if she had ever been a ballerina.

That would be a plus.

"ReMax my ass." Muttering under his breath. He thought of something.

"What about the honey? And the bee?"

"Each subject is different," Viisky replied. "You know this, of course. Kostka was interested merely in this selling of property."

Gomez nodded, thinking of Spasski. He didn't seem all that surprised that an FBI agent and an SVR sorceress just happened to show up in his office.

"He didn't strike me as a man in the middle of an operation."

"This, also, is my assessment."

"We do know that he still reported to the Sluzbha, unlike a lot of guys who defected or ran away."

"We know he is full of shitting. Is afraid not to file reports. He has changed from Captain of *Spetsnaz* to arrogant, lazy American."

She'd called him a Captain. She knew more about Kostenko Spasski than Gomez had been led to believe. It would be a heck of a neat trick to memorize personal data on a hundred and ninety of them.

"We're not all arrogant, you know."

*

Kessler called at six-thirty, asking if Gomez was ready for the C-Span hearings on Monday.

"What's to prepare?" Gomez asked honestly.

"Nothing, I guess. Wear a blue shirt. No mayo or shit on it." Kessler coughed into the phone. "What's up with the balalaika babe? I'm supposed to know what you're doing, in case someone asks. Tell me some bullshit."

Gomez glanced over at Viisky as he replied. "I've uncovered a conspiracy between a shadowy Al Qaeda terrorist cell and some former Soviet sleeper agents, to poison our water supply and destroy our oil refineries in an effort to cripple our economy and advance their reign of terror."

Viisky stared straight ahead, riveted on some faraway object.

"I intend to stop them. Miss Viisky will assist."

There was a protracted silence on the line. Then, "what does arugula have to do with freaking terrorists?" Kessler asked.

"Nothing at all," Gomez replied. He held the phone away, looking at it. He then looked at Viisky. She was still facing forward, stoic. *Jesus*!

"I like it," Kessler said. "Just don't let it keep you from that hearing on Monday."

"I'm all tingly."

*

They gave up at ten-thirty, puddling back to the Marriott, picking up some fast food on the way. Viisky took two bites and was about to throw it away. Gomez stopped her, using her sandwich to wash down his own Double Quarter-Pounder, with cheese.

They entered the suite, Gomez heaving his black gym bag onto the bed and zippering it open. She went to the mini-bar and poured herself a glass of wine, holding it up to Gomez as a question.

"Yeah, sure," he said, hanging fresh clothes in the closet. "At this rate, we'll be defending a wasteland."

"You said this yourself; we will need the luck."

"Right. Luck." He finished hanging his clothes and carried the gym bag around to the side of the bed. It hung low with the weight of something heavy. He tried to stuff it under the bed. It wouldn't fit. He stood and carried the bag around to the entertainment center and crammed it into the space behind the television and the wall. She handed him his glass without questioning him about the bag.

"At this rate, it would take a month to go through your list of names, and even then I'm not certain we would find the one man we need."

Viisky threw off her shoes, coiling up on the sofa.

"Why not to use me?" she asked.

Gomez nearly dumped his drink on his lap. He gulped, unable to disguise his nature.

She smiled, continuing, "Take me to this television. I will explain what is happening with oil places and water places."

He shook his head. "It's too complicated. We need the drama of dragging in a real live KGB man who's lived here for decades, hiding in plain sight. I don't want people disseminating. I don't want the media turning you into the subject. They'll have you on *Access Hollywood* inside an hour. I want them shocked."

They sat in silence for several minutes; Viisky pored over her printouts lying open on the coffee table between them. Gomez splayed his arms across the spine of the sofa. He tilted his head back, thinking.

"Pick twenty," he said. "Just pick twenty of them. Tomorrow we'll do a whirlwind. We go in, pester 'em for five minutes and go hit the next one." He watched her, a lock of hair dangling in her eyes as she thumbed through her files. "Our instincts had better be sharp."

"*Mmmm*," she said, as if she were paying attention. "You have said these men are having moved or change identity?"

"Yes, of course. That's our biggest problem. We have to count on the possibility that one of the guys on your list knows something of the follow-ups. And our subjects are probably *not* on your list."

Viisky leaned forward, enlightenment in her green eyes. "Pay attention to me now," she barked.

Gomez sat up, knowing what would come next. She was as subtle as a T-34 tank.

"This man that sells investments to Spasski? The Rafkin?

He is not on this list."

Chapter 8

THE DOOR TO 2A flew open, nearly tackling Rafkin into the wall.

It was his downstairs neighbor, Paul.

"Oh my God, Stuart. You worked in the Towers!

"Not anymore," Rafkin said. "Haven't been near there for months."

Paul wore low-cut, hip-hugger jeans, men's clogs, and a black cotton shirt, screened with a depiction of a cartoonishly muscled man posing in a grape orchard. Open buttons revealed Paul's thin, hairless chest. He did something with art and traveled a lot. Prosperous—and frantically gay. He reminded Rafkin of a magpie from the Prospekt, his mother's old apartment block. Maria Luganov was her name. She had the habit of knocking on the door at odd moments, such as in the middle of a family argument. Peccadillos sustained her. He wondered, briefly, if she was still alive.

"Did you lose people?"

Rafkin brushed Paul off with a wave. The question was the new status symbol, except for those for whom the answer was yes, and true.

Paul looked him up and down, eyeing the hunting clothes. He studied Rafkin, the corners of his mouth dimpling.

"There's always me."

Rafkin smiled and patted him on the shoulder. He was eager to be on the move. "Fuck off," he said softly, without malice.

"That's what you always say." Paul pouted, hips swinging as he continued down the stairwell. Rafkin saw a little smile.

*

He bought a latte from a café on Seventh Avenue. The best part was the milky froth on the top, and he took small sips as he strolled past the more public ministrations of Atta. He hadn't believed it, even as he left the Skyway for the long trek to the lobby, even as he tumbled into his apartment, thankful for his life—they had done it, and he had helped them do it.

He drifted to the south, toward the destruction. His coffee was cold and he held his jacket close, though the sun pushed hard against the morning chill.

He had very nearly bolted on the afternoon of the eleventh, packed a small bag and caught the subway toward the airport, some flimsy notion of the Caribbean in his head. The Mujahadi who knew his name and his face would all be killed in the follow-up attacks, and Feliks was too old to catch him, so Rafkin could finish his days in the sun, fishing and drinking rum.

But the airlines were grounded and, even as he thought of renting a car and driving to the Mexican border, he knew that he would never make it.

The borders were said to be closed. For real this time. The Guard was patrolling the airports. Soldiers with machine guns were rushing to every station, and fighter jets swept the skies, bristling with live missiles and orders to shoot. It could be days, weeks even, before international travel was possible. So he went back to his apartment and waited.

Hours were passed with pad and pen, drawing concentric circles inside the names of the people who knew what he had done. His life became a witless stew of sleepless nights and wasted days, wandering his apartment, staring at the constant coverage on the television, transfixed by what they were now calling 9/11. He kept discarding the Arabs as mere fanatics. He kept returning to Feliks.

A possible explanation struck him. Feliks was Vydraat and felt betrayed, left here in America to rot. The Arabs came along and wove a tale of Islamic/Russian harmony. Feliks had lost his mind, blinded by his inbred hatred of the West. Feliks had been paid off by the Arabs and their oil money. Feliks…

Or, Feliks wasn't Russian at all.

The thought stunned him. And it was right there, this simplest explanation of all. Feliks knew the words; he knew the old dead-drops and how to contact Rafkin. He told Rafkin that he had been in contact with other Vyydraat.

But what if he had lied? The more he thought of it, the more it fit. Feliks spoke Russian. He looked Russian. Feliks *is* Russian.

But what if he was not? What if he was a nationalist? A betrayer…from Arabia? One of the breakaway republics?

He rounded a corner at Moyer Street, skirting a cart vendor, nearly bowling over a red-haired woman in a patriotic sweater. She was in her twenties, nervously rocking a pram with an infant inside. She was speaking with a television reporter, and she sobbed openly as she thrust a photograph toward the camera. Rafkin slowed and then stopped, folding into a crowd that had gathered to watch. He leaned against a replica gaslight from the turn of the century, the standard covered with hopeful messages and those pathetic photographs.

The cameraman crept forward in a crouch, cables trailing behind him from a van, zooming in tight. It was a shot of a young man on a beach somewhere, gooning for the camera—the dead husband.

The fop with the microphone wore a tan trench coat like newsmen from the thirties, and the woman assured him that her husband was still alive. She'd had a dream in the night. She was an emotional hemorrhage, insisting that Jeremy was lost somewhere, wandering Lower Manhattan. What if he had gotten amnesia? A terrific knock on the head. It was possible.

The baby began to cry and the woman was crying hysterically also, like Russian women at weddings, and Rafkin could take no more. He eased away from his position against the pole and drifted off, unaware of his direction.

The young woman had reminded Rafkin of his mother. Not really alike, except hair color, age, and general build. His mother was a young woman still, in 1982, when they told her he'd been killed in a training accident in Odessa, on the Black Sea. Rafkin never thought of her at all.

The sociopath had suggested a Lebanese restaurant in the Arab quarter. Bensonhurst, no doubt, with a six-hour meal and that annoying, endless chanting. Rafkin would sooner slit his wrists. Every Arabic restaurant in New York would be crawling with FBI and other American policemen. It was not a good week to be an Arab in Manhattan.

*

He arrived cautiously from the west, fifty minutes early, approaching the canopied entranceway to a men's club in SoHo. He had come half-circle, through Tribeca and throngs of forlorn people, into his home district. Everyone thought Rafkin lived in SoHo; the people from his office, the Arabs, even Feliks.

He left the name Patel with the bruiser at the door, slipping inside. He'd selected the club for the volume of its music, as well as the general public's aversion to such places. The club was strictly homosexual.

Three minutes later he emerged into the day. A sporting goods store loomed across the street—a broad, two-story structure fronted with filmy green plate glass.

He dawdled in watercraft for a time on the second floor, purchased a pair of paddles, and listened politely as the sales clerk raved at his selection. Rafkin had not the slightest idea what the man was talking about. Purchase in hand, he secured a seat on a bench made from a two-seater kayak. It had the benefit of a direct, high oblique on the entrance to the club across the street.

It was 9:35. The meeting with the sociopath was scheduled for ten o'clock. Rafkin was to hand over the keys to a self-storage unit in Vineland, New Jersey. The garage numbered 211.

Inside were the weapons they would need to execute the follow-up attacks to 9/11. Stuart Rafkin knew exactly what weapons were in the storage unit. He had put them there.

Gun shows were the best. He'd searched for ads in gun magazines. Went to places like Raleigh and Memphis where he wore cammo clothing and a ball cap. He could spot the desperate dealer in the crowd. He would provide false identification and be on his way to New Jersey with the firepower Feliks demanded. The other instruments proved much harder to procure. But there was always a way in this country, and the way was always money. Twenty thousand dollars received at a postal box had facilitated his purchase from a National Guard sergeant in upstate New York.

The avenue grew calmer as people found their way to work. Ten o'clock came and went. The Arabs had good reason to assume Rafkin was dead. Still, it would be good operational security to make certain.

And so they did. A pale Toyota Sienna rolled to the curb at 10:23. Rafkin knew it was Muhammad before he emerged, crossing the hood to speak briefly with the driver, who nodded and waved an arm, then rolled slowly westbound to the corner where he turned right and disappeared.

Muhammad did not hesitate. He bounced past the bouncer and he, too, was gone into the hollows of the club.

The Sienna turned left, and was back out in front more quickly than Rafkin would have anticipated. They had checked out the club beforehand. This did not concern him. If he'd been seen, Muhammad would never have gone into the club alone. They well knew who Rafkin was.

This was a confirmation. Making sure he was really dead.

Rafkin thought about it. The Chinese boy, Kang, was the last familiar face he'd seen in the stairwell. Kang would be unable to confirm or deny if Rafkin had survived the collapse. And who would ask? When days had passed, perhaps a week without contact, they would assume he had been lost with the others.

Muhammad stepped back onto the curb, prissy fat, looking eastward for the minivan, which arrived in a moment. Muhammad again rounded the nose to speak with the driver. Muscle, Rafkin thought. There would be another in the rear, perhaps more. The windows were illegally tinted. Dumb, but effective.

The bouncer eased from his position on the wall, approaching the van to move them along. Muhammad waved his arms, gesturing to the bouncer. The driver also waved his arms, at whom, or what, Rafkin could not determine. If it were up to Rafkin, they would have left them all back in the Middle Ages.

The driver of the minivan looked directly at him. He'd stopped his waving and was smoking a cigarette. It gave Rafkin a start until he realized there was no way the man could see him, let alone know who he was.

Muhammad waved the van off. He began to walk. They were leaving. Stuart Rafkin was not at the meeting because he was dead, and Stuart Rafkin was watching Muhammad swing his arms to an unheard beat as he made his way up the street…thinking of American marksmanship. If the police didn't get them before the first, he would have to hunt them down and kill them all himself.

CHAPTER 9

"THIS ISN'T GOING TO WORK." Gomez rolled his suit jacket into a ball and pitched it onto the back seat. The thought of a hanger popped into his head…might be in these clothes for a while. He stopped at the side of the car, staring at the red roof of a taco shack, not seeing it. Too many possibilities were sending him to distraction.

"You are hungry?"

"What? No."

A black Hummer rocked him, coming within six inches of smearing him across the road. The door handle was yanked from his grasp. He watched the Hummer recede, thinking evil thoughts. Viisky got in, brushing her hair back with her hands and straightening her blouse.

They had truly made the effort, motoring around the Beltway at warp speed—Viisky navigating poorly with an open map on her lap while Gomez shattered all sorts of municipal traffic codes.

They'd drawn a big, fat blank. Fourteen names had been scratched off the list, without result. Not a single man was active. Most of them had degenerated into beer-swilling, baseball-watching suburbanites. The most interesting one was a guy, Vyydraat, who was hospitalized with cirrhosis. He would not live.

"We need that guy Spasski was talking about. The guy 'not on your list.' We need Rafkin," he said to her, or perhaps to himself. He turned in his seat. "How accurate are these names?"

"I do not know." They looked at each other and their eyes met.

"When are they going to hit us?"

"I do not know. I have told you this already." She'd blinked, or not. Maybe she had no idea. Maybe she had an agenda.

He slammed the door and drove away.

*

An hour later, found Gomez cursing, rolling slowly through a parking lot in a suburban shopping center, past the dry cleaners, a check-cashing place, and one of the ubiquitous Vietnamese nail salons.

"Did you see that hag? I had my signal on first and she took my fucking space!" He gritted his teeth and gave the woman the finger as they lurched past.

Viisky got into the moment.

"There fucking is it! There is lot for parking!" she pointed to a primo slot right in front of the Winn-Dixie. Gomez slammed it in like his hair was on fire.

"This place is similar to me," she said. "Which is this place?"

"Sit tight," he ordered, leaving her looking lost and lonely. "Back in a flash." He left his jacket on the backseat, crossing the parking lot with purpose, the holster exposed on his hip.

*

Viisky had mastered the art of dial surfing. She'd settled on a hip-hop station out of D.C., when she looked out the window to see Gomez crossing the parking lot. His eyes were like gun-slits in an armored car. His shirttails were bunched up around his belt and he'd forgotten to look both ways.

He had Kostenko Spasski by the ear and was dragging him, shoes skipping on the asphalt, one hand pinned painfully behind his back. She quickly turned to hit the unlock button. Gomez yanked open the rear door, heaving Spasski onto the seat like a sack of beets. She picked up on his play, drawing the Beretta and training it on Kostka, who looked at the two of them miserably, wide-eyed and sweating.

"Oh God, it's her again. And that stinking gun!" he whined. Gomez slammed the door on him and hopped in. "My girl's got soccer tonight. Sandy's gonna shit kittens!"

Gomez leaned over the seat, belting Spasski across the chops. Backstroke.

"Shut your fucking mouth," he said unnecessarily. "And you…" he said, pointing at Viisky, "Turn that shit off before I shoot somebody."

"But I am *like* this music."

"Him…or you." She smiled and reached over, silencing the drums. Gomez hit the child locks, burning rubber in reverse, hand pedaling the wheel, accelerating quickly toward the interstate.

"I learned the ear thing in Catechism," he explained. "Works every time."

Viisky grinned as if she understood. She batted her eyes, training the Beretta at an imaginary spot between Spasski's eyes. "To where do you take him?" she asked.

He had the feeling she was going to go with it, no matter what he had in mind. "New York," he said. "The scene of the crime."

*

They looped onto the ramp at Visser Street onto I-95—The Road to Perdition.

"You have said two days."

"I've changed my mind."

She smiled, watching the scenery, and Gomez saw that she was in her element. The mooning from the back seat faded, like a siren heading off in another direction. "It'll take us four or five hours to get to the City, depending on traffic."

They should have flown. But the airlines were still FUBAR, plus there was the delay involved with declaring both his firearms *and* his carry-on Russian sleeper agent. This way he'd have wheels. Maybe if they'd stuffed Spasski in the overhead?

Even then he might have done it, if not for the balance on his American Express card. It was a bit squeaky just now. They would be calling soon, or sending a couple of American Express gorillas to break his legs.

Gomez tapped the brakes, slowing for a 740i crawling in the right lane. The driver was screaming violently into a headset, causing him, momentarily, to forget to speed like a lunatic.

Gomez whipped around, noting the license plate which read ILBURNU. Thirty going on sixteen. He considered popping the blue bubble onto the roof and pulling him over, but the stupid thing was in the trunk.

His fingers tapped the wheel. A better fantasy materialized. He could accelerate to ramming speed and put the little prick right over the guardrail—into the Potomac. He sighed.

Instead, he addressed Spasski over his shoulder, "So, tell us of your role in the butchery of three thousand American citizens."

Spasski began his ineffective protest, blubbering messily in the back seat. Gomez noted the look of utter disgust from Viisky, staring at Spasski like he was a meal. Gomez gave her a winning smile.

She had, however, let the gun drop into her lap.

"Pay attention," Gomez told her. "Keep the gun on him. He may be soft. Then, again, he may not be."

The BMW blew by, doing well over a hundred; a big drag-vacuum rocked the heavy Ford. Gomez could see the silly headset cord dangling from the driver's ear.

"Guess he's off the phone." To Spasski, he said, "By the time we get to New York, you're going to tell me everything...one way or another."

Spasski turned his head away so they couldn't see. He stuck out his tongue.

They slowed behind a line of traffic queuing to the Harbor Tunnel. A hundred yards from the tollbooths, they could see the BMW parked at the side of the road. Gomez smiled. A Maryland State Police interceptor was parked in front, keeping the prick hemmed in. As they rolled past, Gomez snapped off a salute to the Trooper, who saw him and executed a little bow.

He was mildly disappointed. It would have been better for all involved if Beemer Boy had knifed into the bridge abutment at 110 miles an hour. The Fire Department could hose off the concrete and that would be that.

They paused at the tollbooth. Gomez threw a fistful of random coins at the basket. Some of them went in. The LED counted down rapidly. It stopped with a noiseless thud. The ticker sat stubbornly on seventy-eight cents. The gate remained closed.

"I need three quarters." Gomez waited a beat, looking in the rearview at the cars piling up behind him. "Anybody?"

Viisky shrugged. They both turned around to stare at Spasski.

"You want me to pay the fucking *toll*? Why don't you get out and pick one up off the ground?"

Gomez glanced at Viisky. She planted the muzzle on Spasski's forehead. They were getting good at this.

Spasski held out his hands. Viisky uncuffed him long enough to allow him to fish his pockets for loose change. He came up with an even dollar and handed it over.

"There's an extra quarter in it for you, dickhead," Spasski spoke to the window.

"Pardon me?" Gomez asked politely. "Are you speaking to me?"

Spasski saw the eyes in the mirror. "Yeah, just kidding."

"Just so you're aware," Gomez began, "I can turn you over to the gents at Hoover anytime I choose. They are not in the best of moods. So right now, I am your best friend."

"This is incorrect," Viisky cut off Spasski's reply. "You have no friends and do not deserve any such. You are foreign agent in America that has just been attacked." She cracked her window, smoke whistling through her nostrils in a cloud.

Gomez nodded his approval.

"You are agent of country who does no longer exist. Now you betray old country *and* new country. You are man of shit."

Gomez saw no need in torturing the poor slob. He'd volunteered for dangerous duty and been rewarded with a decade of practical abandonment. They had ordered him to stick around...just in case. He looked at Viisky and tried to decide whether it was she or Spasski who was the patriot. Maybe both...or neither.

This stuff was sometimes fun. They would scare the shit out of Spasski, get him in a pliable mood, and he might even know something. Gomez scratched his head, absently, with one hand.

"Shoot him. In the leg, I guess."

Viisky was positively delighted. She racked the slide, turning in her seat.

"Just nick him a little," Gomez cautioned.

"I am enjoying this way of policing!" she laughed, bending to her work.

Gomez smiled. Just two partners, keeping the streets safe for the taxpayers. Right! She was no more a police officer than his Uncle Trujillo, who was currently ironing sheets in Soledad, serving twenty-five-to-life for cutting some *puta* in a dive bar in Compton.

Gomez had turned back to the road when a resounding boom went off. The sound was huge in the confines of the car. *Jesus Christo*! She shot him!

"Are you out of your fucking mind?" Gomez screamed at her, trying to keep the car on the road and at the same time tilt the mirror down.

Spasski's mouth hung open. He was the color of sushi. He didn't speak per se; he just made a choking sound that could have been, "oh no, no, no…"

In the mirror Gomez could see a tuft of foam stuffing, sticking up about an inch from Spasski's package. Gomez reached over and yanked the Beretta out of her grasp.

"We're trying to terrify him. Not blow his brains out!"

"This is problem?"

Spasski was definitely crying now.

It took a minute for everyone to simmer down. Viisky was looking pointedly away, watching Maryland slide past. Gomez checked the mirror again. Spasski had curled into a fetal ball. He was thinking of femoral arteries and exploding gas tanks when it occurred to him—how the hell could she have missed from four feet? Which led to a reciprocal thought...what kind of pistol skills would be required to plant one that close to Spasski's jewels? What *confidence* she had!

Gomez' phone rang, cutting the atmosphere. A voice could be heard through the car, scratching from the cell phone.

"What about Marcus Hook?" said Gomez, his brow furrowed into a scowl.

Viisky was still turned stubbornly away.

"I'll call you when I get to the City." He hit the End button.

Clearly, Viisky was curious. Women and cats. He let it ride.

Finally, "who is on this telephone?" she asked grudgingly.

"I'm setting something up." How much to tell her? The trick was to draw them in, not give away the game.

"Just because I'm not following procedure doesn't mean I'm not going to defend my country." He checked the mirror. Spasski was quiet, at least. "Did you think I was going to stop them all by myself? Just me and you?"

She turned back to her window. Gomez thought he could smell wires burning.

They drove that way through the balance of Maryland, through a brief, dull corner of Delaware and into the Garden State. Gomez thought the autumn scenery was more lovely the closer they got to New England, if you could look past the guardrails and vomiting smokestacks of the chemical plants…

Spasski awoke somewhere near Trenton. He had reconsidered his position.

"You know I had nothing to do with 9/11."

"And?" Gomez shrugged. "So what?"

"I can give you names. Maybe even addresses."

Gomez raised his eyebrow at that one.

"You'll do that too."

Spasski leaned forward a bit on the rear bench seat. He spoke quickly, "I have a list of about fifty guys from the University."

"The University?"

"That's what we called it. Sometimes just the Yankee Academy."

Well, that figures. "Vyydraat?"

Spasski wagged his head like a beagle. "And their instructors. They didn't use their real names, but we all knew somebody from here or there. Word got around." He paused.

Gomez wondered what in the world could be going through Spasski's head, now that he was in a situation that he had been trained to avoid—and had—for almost twenty years.

"I wrote the names down when they were fresh. I'm not a stupid man, Mr. Gomez."

Gomez didn't think he was.

"That was prudent. Very sound. Nonetheless, we now have all the names, courtesy of Ms. Viisky." He looked at her and she smiled, batting her eyes demurely. They were back.

His hole card shredded, Spasski was silent for some time, most likely considering his options.

Gomez gave him time. Something would come to him.

"Hey!" he pointed to an enormous white bucket atop a 150-foot neon sign. "You guys want to stop for the Colonel?"

Spasski said something in the negative. Gomez heard him gagging softly.

"Colonel Osternenko?" Viisky asked, at a loss.

"We'll wait, I guess." Gomez was disappointed, but then he thought of that place on 54th Street where they made the most excellent organ meat Calzones.

Gomez thought of something and asked Viisky, "You do this often? Snatch and squeeze?"

She seemed to understand his meaning. "They sometimes survive. Sometimes they do not." She looked pointedly at Spasski. His head lay against the doorframe, languidly playing with the handle.

"There is a place outside the ring road in Moscow. It is a *Boloto*. A...how do you say it?"

"It's a swamp," Spasski said from the rear.

"Yes. Is swamp!" She mimed happily.

"Well," Gomez cleared his throat, "we don't do that kind of thing in America." He was speaking to Viisky more than their prisoner. "Have no fear, Mr. Spasski, you'll survive."

Spasski snorted and choked out a laugh.

Viisky's mouth turned down into a frown.

Gomez let it go.

Brooklyn Navy Yard, Port of Baltimore, Baypoint refinery and Cherry Point were already covered, or so Davidson had told him. They were still working on Marcus Hook. He would call back when they got to the hotel.

Gomez' ass was getting tired. He wanted coffee. He looked in the back, asking if anyone needed to use the potty. There was no response. They were fast asleep.

Grabbing Spasski…bet she didn't expect that move. Gomez lit a cigarette and rolled on through the decaying cities of the Northeast.

Chapter 10

THE RIVER ROAD—a two-lane demilitarized zone between Lower Manhattan and Hoboken, New Jersey. Gomez had driven this route before, getting the usual thrill from the view of the Manhattan skyline a quarter mile to the north across the water.

Now, the view was recoil. They stared to the left, where the Towers stood when the month began. It was dark, and the spotlights cast towering vertical crystals of light from the rescue pit of Ground Zero. Pockets of smoke lingered above the gap, probably dust from the debris removal.

The fires had been out for a week.

Knots of people gathered along the safety rail at the edge of the road on the Jersey side, standing close in consolation. Friends and neighbors, relatives of the victims—complete strangers, Gomez supposed.

They would have made better time had they come across on 495 from 95, then they would have taken the river farther north, at mid-town near Central Park. Instead, he got off early at the Ferry Street exit to Jersey City. Gomez wanted to see…needed to see.

The Hudson boiled below, the skyline fading off to their left rear quarter as he turned onto the entrance to the Holland Tunnel. Spasski was awake. He was impossible to ignore.

"C'mon man, have a heart. I gotta piss."

"You can hold it for twenty minutes," Gomez said heartlessly, as he had thirty minutes ago. Just when he thought he had seen it all.

They traveled on Broadway, past ascending street numbers with the devastating gap on the left, north toward midtown. Viisky's head was moving as if it were on a spring. Gomez almost made it. He'd been to this hotel before, but he blew it and had to ask directions from a bag lady on 7th Avenue.

In the hotel, Gomez flipped on the tube and turned to a local news station. Here it was real. In Washington it was pro forma, the bullshit flowed and the pundits talked about counseling on a mass scale—for the terrorists.

Here it was personal. Nobody on television said it right out loud, the word *nukes*, but Gomez certainly was thinking submarines, rockets, B2s with MIRVs, and he was sure; so were a great many others.

Viisky, actively silent after her little target-practice incident, now chattered away like a little bird. Gomez thought she looked worried, wound up on bodily fluids. Conversely, Spasski grew solemn, a man whose execution was imminent. He'd found a magazine somewhere and was doing the crossword.

"Tell us more of this Rafkin," she demanded.

Spasski appeared drawn. He hung his head. "Hey, that's all I know. I met the guy once, four years ago. He could be dead for all I know. Or back in the Union."

"Rafkin works for this bondage company, correct? They are from New York. Correct?"

"That doesn't mean anything," Gomez said, as he unpacked his overnighter. "They have branches all over the country. He could be anywhere." Shit. He forgot to bring socks. This reminded him of something.

"I'm sorry we left without your clothes."

"I have valise in car. In the boot." She smiled. "Still, could this man Rafkin not be here? In this Giant Apple?"

"Wait a minute. How'd you get a suitcase into my trunk?"

"Is not important."

Spasski rolled his eyes at Gomez.

"Lady, look. Manhattan Bond is like, one of the biggest corporations in America. The name means nothing anymore. It's like the St. Petersburg Symphony, okay? They're never in St. Petersburg, are they?"

"Yes, I see." She turned toward Gomez. "They are situated in Moscow." She drew her upper lip over her lower, a gesture that got Gomez a bit riled up. He felt the need to reward her effort.

"That doesn't mean we shouldn't pursue it," Gomez said. "Their offices have got to be in New York. I'll bet they can tell us where Rafkin was working last. Hell, he might even be here!"

Spasski made a snorting noise. Gomez caught this "First things first," he said, a little more sternly. "I have to make a few calls. Get yourselves situated. Call for more towels, whatever."

He slipped into the sitting room, a moment's relief from the traveling circus. He drew the bifold dividers and plopped into a divan. The guy at the desk had upgraded them when he saw Gomez' FBI creds.

"We want payback," the desk clerk had said, turning his smile off like it was on a dimmer. "Kill some for me." Gomez had nodded, thinking he might just do that.

He could hear Viisky moving around in the bedroom and wondered if she had already strangled Spasski. He was having trouble forgetting the shape of those 501s. Right!

He called in to the duty officer at Federal Plaza, informing them of his official presence in the city and his intention to conduct an investigation. He somehow got the details of this nightmare tangled up with an old case—some drug asshole on the Ten Most Wanted list. How clumsy. He felt better about the whole thing, but he wouldn't feel anywhere near comfortable until they drew them in and wasted them.

He left a message with Kessler, who wasn't in. Mumbled some codswallop into the voice mail and quickly hung up. Then he retrieved the piece of paper he'd gotten from Val Sacco.

Sacco hadn't wanted a record, so he'd scribbled it on a scrap of paper. Gomez peered at it, scratching his head. He dialed, poking his long, thick fingers carefully on the keypad.

Davidson—the Russian Killer—claimed that he only had a moment. He was having a late dinner with the Mayor of Philadelphia. Gomez looked at his watch…11:30. It was possible, but Gomez thought that the old man was probably sitting in his den watching television—alone. He thought that maybe Davidson still believed in keeping up the image.

"I got the message from your guy Sacco. Talk to me."

"You haven't spoken with Val?"

"I said I got the message. And you'd better be right about this girl. I have vainglory to consider. This could make me look like a crazy old man, trying for one last shot at the title." Arrogance, Gomez supposed, was one key element of Davidson's past success. He just hoped the old man still had it.

"Val tells me we're making progress," Gomez said.

"The refineries are the easy part. How in the hell we're going to cover those treatment plants is another story."

"I realize it's a lot of ground."

"Which is why you have to do your job and do it right. Don't fail us."

Gomez' job, of course, was to find them before they got to the targets. To find them and bring the full might of the country down on their evil heads. Davidson's rhetoric had stirred him. It could not be helped. It was in his nature.

"Here's how it's going to work," Davidson explained. It was not a defense, per se, but more of an exploratory committee.

"We shouldn't underestimate them," Gomez said. There had been too much of that.

"You think so? Coupla punks with box-cutters. Won't happen again, you mark my words. You saw what those people did on that Newark flight…Ninety-three. They got lucky on the eleventh. They won't get lucky this time.

"You were right not to go to them," said Davidson. He meant that Gomez was right not to have pushed. Gone straight to the Director and sat through all the meetings. "Those idiots would have held a press conference."

Gomez rubbed his jaw, "Yeah."

"All right. Here's how it's going to work," Davidson held forth. He had a few wrinkles that Gomez thought were quite brilliant. Gomez could hear him light a cigarette or cigar. It reminded him to do the same, whether he needed one or not.

"Gimme Sacco's number again." They discussed details for a while and hung up.

Gomez put the phone down, rubbing his eyes. The Blue Wall was up. The weight was off—some of it, anyway. Between Sacco and Davidson, they would assemble a few guys to sniff around, fan out and cover the approaches to the targets. Finding enough people wouldn't be a problem. People would listen to the Russian Killer.

It had been quiet in there for a long time. He walked through the divider into the bedroom. Spasski had found a deck of cards and was sitting on the bed playing Russian solitaire. The handcuffs gave the game an interesting physical variant. Viisky was reading Fodor's *New York*. She glanced up at him, smiling. He watched her for a long moment. She had skin like standing cream…and those eyes. He looked away. Really rude of him, staring like that.

Someone had turned out the sleeper sofa while he was on the phone, and he sat down, addressing Viisky. "Uncuff him," he said, jerking a thumb at Spasski, who shouted and said, "Solitaire! I fucking did it!"

"You are sure?" Viisky asked.

"He's not going anywhere," Gomez said, handing her the keys.

A small part of him wished Spasski would go somewhere… anywhere! He and Ms. Viisky could discuss the ten-millimeter hydrashok over a nice bottle of grape juice. She turned the key. Spasski was uncaged. He rubbed his wrists the way freed criminals did.

"I'll cut your balls off if you run," Gomez said.

Spasski grinned, thinking euphemism. Looked at Gomez and dropped his smile. Maybe not.

Gomez turned to Viisky. "Tomorrow afternoon we'll see if we can hunt down your Rafkin. Okay?"

"I have hunch, as you say."

"Too much TV." He smiled at her. "Let's grab some winks."

They stood, eyes lingering.

"I will sleep in this equipment," she said, pointing to the sleeper sofa—leaving Gomez to cuddle up with the hairy, smelly former agent of GRU. He made a face. She could keep an eye on Spasski from one side, leaving Gomez to bar the door. It made sense. Less than he could hope for, but logical.

*

He sighed and went into the bathroom to change out of his rumpled suit.

When he returned, in blue FBI sweat pants and his teeth tasting minty, Spasski was already out, asleep in the clothes they had nabbed him in. Viisky was lying angelic under a single sheet on the pullout, hands folded on her chest, like a child praying. He gave it one last venal thought and turned out the lights.

He'd find Stuart Rafkin for her. Then what? She had some big, brass ones to assume Gomez would do as she wished. Surely she had orders to get rid of him. *Shooting the troubles…*

He padded quietly into the sitting room. The hotel had a cable modem and a rickety old P.C. on the small desk facing the window. He summoned Google, typed in the word "refinery," and read about oil refineries until his sinuses were blocked. Something was going to have to be done about this Internet deal. Your average Abdul could quantify defenses, learn about hours of operation; heck… could print out a map with driving directions from Sphincter, Syria, to the gates of the Baypoint refinery in Bayonne, New Jersey. And get a good deal on a rental car while they were at it.

He found sixty-seven major refineries between Maine and Miami—more than he'd expected. Still, they were invariably fenced in, with hidden electronic security and armed patrols. The oil companies knew a thing or two about terrorism.

The security at the water treatment plants was disturbing.

One thing at a time. He logged off, then did a few quick push-ups to shake off the drive. He couldn't manage much; he was already tired and no longer twenty-five.

Back to the bedroom where he snuck between the sheets, hanging as far over on his side as possible without falling out of bed. Talk about sleeping with the enemy!

Almost immediately, he thought he heard something, like bashing a squeaky toy with a pipe wrench. Spasski ripping one. Gomez covered his nose with the sheets, breathing through his mouth.

And before he fell asleep, Gomez wondered why Davidson still had not spoken to Sacco.

CHAPTER 11

THE BIKE WAS HEAVY; it held the road well. In his inattention, Rafkin had it up to seventy-five before he realized his speed and backed off the throttle. He'd been thinking of Feliks—what it would mean if Feliks was not who he said he was and Rafkin had done this unspeakable thing for the wrong people and the wrong reasons.

He was coasting now, through the outskirts of Paramus, a community of industrial parks and older neighborhoods. The town had a medium-sized Arab population. Muhammad and his compatriots would blend in. Rafkin parked on a quiet street four city blocks from the house.

It was a recce, he thought, preferring the American term even when he was thinking in Cyrillic. A block-and-half away, on a cross street, he noticed a convenient alleyway that ran behind the single-family homes. A welcome accident of civil engineering.

He took advantage, sliding silently into the shadows of the alley, away from the streetlights. He counted off numbers, skipping the odd until he was behind the house. He squatted down on his haunches in the corner of the yard, behind some sort of tool shed.

Idiots. There should be a camera atop the shed, covering the alleyway. He sat for a full five minutes, waiting to be discovered by a motion detector or video device. The worst case would be a dog.

A Doberman or Rottie would be an unappealing proposition. But Rafkin didn't think the Al Qaeda were dog people.

Nothing. No security measure to warn them of an intruder. For his purposes, this was good. For the fate of the Jihadists, it was very bad indeed. He spat a little pool into the dirt beside him. If the enemy were careless, he would not be.

He waited an additional five minutes, peering through the binoculars, taking the time to fire off a half-dozen photos of the rear approaches. Cheap cardboard shingles sagged over drooping frame construction. It was built hastily, in the midst of the boom. There was a tattered awning over a full storm door leading to a daylight basement, and he stepped under it, looking in. He saw nothing, stepped back, checking his flanks. They were not known for their mercy. He stepped back around to the side of the house and made his way in from a hillock on the side, pressing his face to the glass.

Rafkin found that he was looking into a kitchen between some upper cabinets, hovering almost over a sink. An oven exhaust light shone, casting the kitchen in a soft glow. There was no movement. Padding cautiously toward the front of the house, he stopped to unlatch a gate on a chain link fence and passed through. He walked normally, yet softly, around to a bay window in the front. The sill was just above eye level. He could see into the living room if he stood on the tips of his toes.

Through the bay window, he saw three men sleeping on the floor. There was another in an easy chair, an afghan strewn about his upper body…an afghan on an Afghan. He took a step backward and looked up at the second story of the structure. Two bedrooms and a bath, he thought. That probably meant another four upstairs, for a total of eight. He added two more possibles, to be on the safe side—men that could be sleeping in an unseen room, or perhaps there was a basement. It was a lot, he knew.

He'd seen enough. He trod back the way he had come, hugging the side of the house. He took a last look backward glance and crossed the lawn toward the alley. Even if they heard him now he could easily run to the bike, hop on, and be gone in a heartbeat.

Rafkin was passing the tool shed and mentally cursing his predicament when the shovel hit him in the face. He'd sensed motion in front and turned at the last instant, catching the brunt of the blow on the right side of his jaw and his drooping right shoulder. A whistle, as the shovel connected with his right thigh. The thought that Muhammad was a lefty flashed by in a nanosecond. Through the haze of pain, he tried to remember the lessons of hand-to-hand. He was still on his feet and that was good.

"I warned them!" Muhammad crowed. The pig was in his nightclothes, greasy hair flying and the smell of putrid sweat fouling the air. He held the shovel in one hand, gripping it halfway up the shaft. Rafkin backed away a step. Muhammad waved the shovel, railing about causes and revolutions and religious domain. Rafkin was watching the shovel.

He needed time. He held up his hands, palms out.

"You idiot! I came to warn you. Feliks has turned against us."

It was excellent ad-lib bullshit, Rafkin thought. Especially with his brains scrambled. Muhammad paused.

"What of the telephone?"

"The Jamaicans had none. I went to the same place as always but…" Muhammad thought a moment at this, and nodded. Rafkin said a quick prayer to his god of convenience.

"Inside. My men will provide first aid for your injuries."

Rafkin agreed, panting—bent over, hands on his knees. The last place he wanted to be was in the house, surrounded by a swarm of unsociable terrorists.

He hesitated and Muhammad's eyes grew small. He would never leave the house alive.

"Yes, thank you," Rafkin said. Muhammad held out his hand for Rafkin to lead the way. Rafkin stumbled, gripping Muhammad's shoulder for support. He got his other hand onto the shaft of the shovel and drove the tip directly into the underside of Muhammad's jaw.

The pig was stunned, yet held on with a mighty grip. Rafkin tried to head-butt him, managing only to further strain his shoulder. But Muhammad was slow. Before he could parry, Rafkin kneed him in the groin. Missed the genitals, he thought. Still, it had some effect. Muhammad began to pinwheel comically backward, still hanging onto the shaft, snorting like a water buffalo. It was no ballet of violence, just two men in their forties, struggling fiercely.

Rafkin was in far better shape. It took its toll…Muhammad lost his balance and backed away a step or two. Rafkin stepped forward and simply shoved him in the chest. Muhammad's center of gravity failed him and he toppled to the grass like a great, fat whale. He lay half on the macadam at the edge of the alley, emitting a sickening wail.

Rafkin breathed deeply and, placing his foot on the distended belly, he yanked the shovel away. They were silent for a moment, Muhammad seemingly ready to burst with a heart attack and Rafkin looking the worse for wear.

Rafkin looked around the alleyway, thinking that surely someone must have heard. He looked down at Muhammad, deciding how he should proceed.

Muhammad knew what was to be. "Your mother—"

"Perhaps," Rafkin wheezed, and he brought the spade down like a pile driver. He missed a little, the blade skipping off bone, catching Muhammad just below the chin and shearing off two inches of fat and flesh. A dreadful wound opened in his throat. Muhammad opened his mouth to scream. Rafkin stomped on his face, his boots digging into the flesh around the mouth. Rafkin looked and estimated he'd cut the head about halfway off.

Muhammad gurgled, trying to speak. Rafkin had to shut him up before he woke the entire neighborhood. He raised the shovel again and brought it down with everything he had. He'd connected cleanly this time. Miraculously, the head was lolling slowly from side to side, the eyes very wide and pleading. No blood or other fluids came from Muhammad's mouth, as it always did on television.

Rafkin was curious about this. He knew nothing of anatomy and the subject, for some reason, held a sudden fascination. Maybe it had to come through the esophagus? Surely there were fluids in the head?

Still, nobody from the house had come out to investigate. He looked up at the stars, raised the shovel one last time and drove it downward with tremendous force. He had used the power of his legs this time. He felt the blade stick the dirt behind Muhammad's neck. He felt his gorge rise and forced it to recede. Muhammad was as dead as he deserved to be. Rafkin tossed the shovel on the ground next to the pieces and staggered away.

He reached the motorcycle and climbed on, wincing. His body was on fire. The altercation must have taken no more than three minutes. How had none of Muhammad's comrades joined him? He must not have told them he was going outside. Still... thoughts crowded in...worries of physical evidence he discarded as meaningless. He had no prints or other identifiers on file. Officially, Stuart Rafkin was dead. How would they react? Leaderless, they might be captured by the Americans. They would squeal like women.

He worked the Honda through traffic, articulating his turns precisely until the turnpike appeared.

Ninety dollars a month stored the bike in the back room of a struggling garage with an empty bay in the back. Worth every penny, considering the geezer had never asked him his name. An alcoholic with shocking nose hair and more than one dread disease, lived in a one-roomer above it. He pocketed the keys and slipped inside the gate.

*

Rafkin dropped his clothes in a trail toward the bathroom, glancing at the time as he placed his watch on the nightstand. Had it really taken that little time? Half past two. It felt much later. He stepped into the shower for the second time in hours, lathering vigorously behind the ears. Scrub the genitals and the anus. He wanted to wash Muhammad off in a way more meaningful than evidentiary.

The soreness was developing and there was an unwelcome warmth in the right side of his face and neck, burning down into his shoulder. His leg hurt as well. How that had happened, he couldn't recall.

His bath towels were from the Sharper Image; thick, fluffy terrycloth to make him feel clean and brisk. Now the act of drying his body merely hurt. He discovered a sickening bruise on his hip, starting above the point of the pelvis and blooming down the side of his thigh, spreading a bit across his flank.

He went into the kitchen where he pulled half the roll of paper towels from its holder to dab the blood off, then crumpled the paper towels into a ball and jammed them into the wastebasket. He applied anti-bacterial cream to the open scrapes and covered it all with gauze, taping the bandages crudely to his skin.

Around his eye and neck, he applied some foundation—just a little, to make it less obvious. The make-up was old and rarely used, but he managed. He walked back into the living room, fighting the limp. Then, he found if he walked his way through it, he could appear uninjured.

Wearing only boxers and an old pair of shower shoes, he tilted his head back against the sofa, ran his fingers through his drying hair, and tried to think. On its surface, the death of Muhammad was a catastrophe. He had lost the advantage of surprise, his greatest asset. They would be more careful now.

He thumbed the remote. A morbidly obese woman was having surgery to correct her self-inflicted ravages. In the commercial, a conga line of three couples danced through a kitchen, juggling bottles of wine as they cooked spaghetti. A remixed sixties song played, with all the stuffing sucked out of it. The twaddle droned.

The Vyydraat had a unique training method for men like Rafkin. In the seventies and eighties they would take the class to Chechnya or Romania where a small town was constructed, similar to the way Hollywood made Wild-West sets. Always far from the cities, always stocked with dissidents, gypsies, and other undesirables.

Rafkin had arrived by train, on his twenty-second birthday. He was given a machine pistol and two hours. For backup he had a combat knife, which at this very moment was in his bathroom closet—a souvenir, as it were. The knife would be used should the trainee run out of ammunition, or find himself in a tight spot against a dissident who thought he had a chance.

He'd gotten all four, the last one with the knife. One hour and three minutes. It was like falling off a bicycle. He was back on, after twenty years. He felt like a real man. A man who brooked no argument.

Late-night TV. He grew lost in the story of a dishwater blonde whose wretched husband had left her for a teenaged girl. The husband lied and cheated, stealing more from the wife than she could bear. *Lifetime.*

He walked into the kitchen to make himself a cup of tea, favoring his leg. The tendons of his thigh felt like a drawn bow—still keyed up. The quart of adrenaline that shot through his body was slow to metabolize. It was now almost four.

Feliks would have a man hunting him. Someone Feliks could count on, possibly even Vyydraat. He should have thought of that before. He hadn't meant to kill Muhammad, the opportunity had simply presented itself. So, following the thought...despite everything, Stuart Rafkin smiled. The path to freedom was open. Feliks he would save for last—for his betrayal. But first, a place to hide. Seven thousand days was long enough.

The dawn seemed very far away at a quarter till five, and he left the apartment wrapped in his terry bathrobe, shower shoes slapping the landing. He descended stiffly to 2A, rapping softly on the steel door. He gave it half a minute...knocked again, this time more firmly.

The door opened. Paul peered out behind the chain, heavy-lidded and tousled, dressed in winter pajamas with a swirling floral pattern. Paul said nothing for a time. He studied Rafkin's face until he saw what there was to see.

"Are you ready for me?" Paul said, still sleepy eyed.

"Not that. Maybe later." Rafkin's eyes slid away. He straightened, staring coolly at Paul. "Right now I just need to be with someone."

"Let's get you inside. You look awful."

Chapter 12

THEY WERE UP BY SEVEN; Spasski, Gomez, and Viisky bumbling into each other in conflicting rituals. Gomez was foiled in his hopes of another glimpse of Viisky in her undies when she came across him peeking into the mirror sideways, sucking in his stomach.

"It makes you have experience," she said, not unkindly. Gomez wondered if that was a good thing.

A call to room service brought a hearty American breakfast. Eggs and bacon, muffins for the modern woman. Viisky asked the server if this was the Presidential Suite.

"We call it that if a big-shot comes to stay with us. Otherwise it's the 'Saratoga Room.'"

"You have important peoples visiting?"

The server nodded. "Last Friday," she said, "Senator Heidi Menniss brought…a friend. They were touring Ground Zero."

Viisky lit up, eyes greedy. "Oh we love her in the Sov…in Russia!" She adopted the pose of a bodybuilder, flexing her biceps and bowing her arms. "She is *strong woman*."

Gomez lifted a brow, eyeing the tiny muffins before he laid into the grease. "Maybe you can take her back to Russia with you," he said between mouthfuls of toast dipped in yolk. "She would look good in a Lenin beard."

Spasski tittered, a jangly, croaking sound. He was working on his fifth cup of coffee, but he made no move toward the food, too much of it, laid out nicely on a sideboard.

"Yes, I see," said Viisky, icicles in her glare. "This means you *fear* her. Her great strength frightens you."

"I fear all politicians. Especially the ones I vote for." Gomez waved his hand to dismiss the conversation, beckoning Viisky to the table, "Eat. You'll need it." He smiled at her.

She held it for a long time with a smile of her own and sat down, going straight for the muffins. All this eye sex was driving him nuts.

Spasski stood at the window, quietly sipping his mud. They'd let him call his wife last night. He'd asked Gomez for the favor, to assure her he wasn't on some lost weekend odyssey with a pair of stripper twins. The woman had seemed pleasant enough, but not entirely buying Gomez' story of her husband as a Federal witness. What a heartbreaker.

Viisky was tidying, tossing things in the garbage and buzzing around the room, despite Gomez' advice that there were people for that. She just gave him another of those smiles and kept at it. Whatever.

Gomez addressed the copy of the *USA Today* he'd found dumped outside their door. Today's issue had the second installment, beginning with the letter G. He carefully entered them onto his notepad. To do it alphabetically would be an injustice, so he combined them with the names from yesterday.

Dillard, Adams, and May; Waisman and Sisolak—the little kids from the planes. Gomez' face was impassive, his secret heart concealed.

He only had room for a sampling—one in five, maybe. He wrote carefully, his head down, feeling pained that he didn't have room for all of them. There would come another day.

He had, by now, filled three pages in his chicken scratch. Viisky looked over his shoulder to see what he was doing but didn't comment.

They had to wake Spasski when it was time to go. He was crashed out on a wing chair, thrashing and blubbering in his sleep.

Nervous little bugger. They got to the street at 8:50. The car was brought around a minute later. Viisky got in the rear, explaining that it was a better way to keep an eye on their prisoner.

"Prisoner?"

"Yes."

"He's a witness."

"Is possible."

*

"Plenty of time." Gomez swung down the Avenue of the Americas, marking the mood of the street. Wound like a clockspring, was his first impression. People were more intense than usual, which was saying something, and he noticed small acts of courtesy. Men allowing ladies first through graciously held doors…things like that.

Viisky saw him in the rearview. She flashed him one of her patented sex-kitten smiles. She was just nervous. Gomez looked away. They saw it, too.

They were getting closer.

A plate glass window covered with plywood in the front of a street-level attorney's office. Jagged shards still lay in pockets along the sidewalk, and Gomez wondered if they were from down here or from the Towers themselves. He looked at Viisky in the mirror. She was tough to read. Larger hunks of concrete and other debris became visible as he turned onto Church, where whole sections of buildings were missing. Just…gone.

Puffs of spent diesel wafted back in waves from yellow and orange dump trucks, stretched out in the morning mist. They rolled up their windows to blot out the sound of idling engines. There were still a few ambulances standing by, their drivers at idle. He pulled off to the side, the left front tire crunching over some unseen rubble.

"This is the Zero?" Viisky asked. Gomez thought she sounded a little shaky. Spasski said nothing.

After a while they drove off.

*

A white Honda Odyssey fell in behind them on Broadway. Gomez watched it in the mirror, continuing east instead of reversing course. He had noticed that the right front tire on the Odyssey was a little low—two lowbrows in the front seats.

They ran into a detour a mile down the road. Gomez drummed his fingers on the wheel. They were waved through and in five minutes rolled up in a lot under Rockefeller Plaza, the home of MSNBC.

It was clean and quiet, the smells of new carpeting, electronics, coffee, and ink, as they were led from the reception area to a closed-door conference room to await Karyn Macklin.

Gomez was not always assigned to the Commission—that was a new, unpleasant development. He was, with his language skills, Counter-Intelligence.

*

After Gorbachev came and went, Sacco snuck him into Investigations.

Gomez had been working a thing in the Hamptons, four years ago. The taking of a socialite whose husband was one of the original dot-commers. New money, blown easily. Gomez had, at first, thought the kidnappers were Red Mafiya, from Brighton beach.

Turned out it was just a couple of immigrant brothers—nincompoops. In any event, Karyn Macklin had discovered that the husband was uber-leveraged. He was broke, slithering under his creditors. Macklin met Gomez in a pretentious diner and told him that the other media were going to run with it.

The kidnappers would know there was no ransom to be had and the woman would be killed. Macklin told Gomez to hurry. Gomez and two other agents were setting up the fake drop. They were already holding onto a tip, so they decided to go with it.

They busted in.

The brothers chose to fight. Gomez had to kill both of them. The woman was already dead—chopped up and stuffed into garbage bags in a closet in a back bedroom.

But Karyn Macklin had done the right thing.

In the spirit of reciprocity, Gomez gave her a few things from time-to-time. Like tipping her to the identity of the first female Director, ten hours before it became public.

Also, she was fair and tried to show two sides to an issue. He liked her a great deal—so much so that he'd pursued her personally. She'd told him with pitying eyes that he wasn't her type and would never be, unless he changed his anatomy.

Sitting here thinking about it, Gomez felt the frustration. It could have worked.

He said to Viisky, "Back in Spasski's office you said you were SVR. I thought it was FSB." She paused, glancing at Spasski. Gomez was pretty sure Spasski was asleep.

"I am assigned Operations Directorate. In Sector of Middle Eastern Relation. You will recall that Soviet Union had many allies in hordes of Arab lunatics. Crazy peoples." She made the international sign for a madman, rotating her finger at the side of her head.

"But not you or Feliks. Not with Al Qaeda."

"No."

Ten minutes passed. There was a knock, and someone entered. Gomez hadn't remembered Karyn as being so effeminate…or so tiny.

"Hey, folks. I'm Cameron Nguyen, Karyn's personal assistant and executive facilitator." Nguyen was whip thin, in button-down Lacoste with the top three buttons ajar. He wore tight flared pants of some synthetic material, like rayon. They shook all around except for Spasski who was lounging, slumped at the far end, his head on the edge of the marble table.

"Ms. Macklin is in conference," Nguyen told them.

Gomez leaned over to Viisky in a whisper. "That means she's taking a dump."

Nguyen was not amused. He brought himself to his full height, scowling at Gomez. This had no effect. He looked appraisingly at Viisky. "You want the nickel tour?"

"Yes, we would love this!" she bubbled. Gomez glared at Nguyen and got a smirk in return. They stood, Nguyen guiding them toward the door. Spasski needed encouragement, which Gomez provided by rapping his knuckles on Spasski's head.

"Hey, watch it!"

They trooped down a long, bland corridor, Gomez thinking that maybe he would have preferred sticking his tongue into a light socket. Viisky chattered away, her eyes popping. From what he could make out, she was inquiring if Nguyen had met many movie stars or other assholes. Nguyen was smiling, ushering her around like he owned the place.

Gomez got a good look at Nguyen's shoes. *Holy God!* He hadn't noticed them at first. Euro-trash, like Viisky's, but they were perforated plastic with the toe curled upward and they were of a luminescent orange. Like...clogs...on a Dutch girl from outer-space.

Gomez thought about interrupting, to remind them they were here to save the world. He decided they probably wouldn't understand. Viisky saw him shaking his head in a *brrrr* motion.

"Are you quite okay?"

"Just fine, thank you. This is really great."

They were led into the studios. The air had that peculiar smell given off by powerful electrical equipment—lightning, or ozone. There were people in casual clothing hustling back and forth, waving reams of paper and screeching on the telephone as background. In the center, a man and a woman sat on a raised pedestal, reciting half-truths and innuendo from a teleprompter.

The male anchor straightened a pile of worthless papers, turning it over to the female, Ashley Bubier. Gomez recognized her. Bubier was mechanically pretty, the kind of smooth blonde stick-figure you were supposed to find gorgeous—a technical knockout. Gomez estimated her age at nineteen. He thought she belonged in the mall, getting her tongue pierced.

Bubier read an item, some early morning titillation on the Hudson River. A man, rather the head of one, had been discovered in a plastic bag bobbing a few yards from shore. The bag was from Henry's, a local grocer. The head was Arabic in appearance. Misplaced vigilantism could not be ruled out.

At least they were talking about something Gomez could understand. He stared hard at Viisky and almost asked her if she knew anything about the head in the bag.

Nguyen led them directly behind the anchor desk, in view of the three active cameras. Viisky blushed, skimming her hair out of her eyes as they had their six seconds on television.

Spasski, too, had caught on. He was mouthing vulgarities at the winking red light. He raised his hand, preparing to flip the bird to five million viewers. Gomez grabbed him and twisted his arm behind his back, facing the camera with a goofy smile. He hustled Spasski discreetly out of the way.

They gathered at an exit underneath a red "on air" sign. Gomez had had enough.

"I appreciate this, Chance. It's been fascinating. We need to see Ms. Macklin. Please," he added, as a sop.

Nguyen did not like Gomez, he could always tell, and he did like Viisky. He stood too close to her for Gomez's liking and gave Gomez a look that at another time might have been cause for flying chairs and broken glass, resulting in possible letters of reprimand.

"Hold on a minute." Nguyen left them standing there in the darkened corner of the studio.

Loose change jiggled in Gomez' pocket. Viisky grew aloof. She lifted her chin and was about to say something…something about his behavior toward young Master Nguyen, no doubt.

He reasserted. "We do not have time for that crapola."

Viisky backed down, closing her trap. Nguyen was back.

"She'll see you now." He held out his arm for Viisky.

"Excuse me, Chance?"

"It's Cameron."

"I'm sure it is." Gomez pointed to the shoes, "You get those babies in Amsterdam—or Mars?"

Nyugen's face turned a lush shade of purple. Gomez decided that he had let his ass show, but that was one of his strong suits.

Viisky sulked. *Oh brother.* That pout. The incongruous dusting of freckles. Later.

Ngyuen motioned for them to follow. They arrived in a reception area outside Macklin's office. A pair of sleek mahogany doors opened and out stepped Karyn Macklin. She had moved up in the world since he had last seen her. She was most certainly not a man.

She stood about five-ten, only an inch or so of it in the heels. Her face was all severe angles, like a stealth fighter. She had lustrous, straight, blonde hair, the highlighted tips resting easily on her shoulders. Formidable. A woman who could kick your ass.

Gomez sucked in his stomach and said hello, aware that Viisky was watching him closely. He rose, leaving Spasski lounging rudely in the middle. Viisky was on the left, where she belonged.

Macklin invited them in.

"You two can wait out here."

"But…"

"I won't be long."

Viisky was displeased. Spasski mocked them both with a dismal *ha-ha-ha*. Gomez told him to shut his hole.

*

Macklin's office was dark, heavy leather; very clubby. The walls were dressed in a rich walnut wainscoting. It wouldn't surprise Gomez if she fired up a pipe.

"You got the tour?" Macklin sat perpendicular to Gomez, reading a script. Head down, glancing sideways at him as a teacher might to a promising student. He had no doubt that she could absorb her file and provide him sufficient attention at the same time. Gravitas did not have to be feigned in Karyn Macklin.

"How'd your piece turn out?" he asked, referring to the Assistant Director thing.

"You never saw it?" she asked with a slight curl of a smile. "You'd have laughed. It was pap." A tap on the keyboard. A reminder. "But it was important pap. I'll send you a disc."

Gomez crossed his legs, flicking his trousers. She saw that he would draw her out. She tossed the file casually onto her desk and faced him, undivided.

"Who are your friends?

Spasski might be his friend—a shallow acquaintance, someone to go bowling with. Viisky was as much a friend as a dagger in the night.

"The woman is with the Russian government." He left it at that.

Macklin lofted an eyebrow, "And?"

"His name is Konstenko Spasski. He is ex-Soviet Intelligence. His driver's license will tell you that he is James Adler, a real estate agent from Potomac Hills, Virginia. He's a leftover from the Cold War. They apparently didn't find him worth bringing home."

"Really."

Gomez cracked his knuckles.

"So what?" Macklin said. "You have him. You're capable of containing him."

"There are others."

Macklin sat back in her chair. Her hand grazed the keyboard.

"This might be something for one of the news magazines. We could put him on NightWatch. Not right away, of course. We're kind of busy these days. You remember? The greatest attack on America since Pearl Harbor?"

"It's related," Gomez said, "to 9/11."

She stopped tapping.

"They're going to do it again."

Gomez laid it out. He allowed her the heart of the thing, with a few of the parties confused. There was a connection between some colleagues of Spasski and Al Qaeda. They were going to conduct the follow-up attacks to 9/11.

He lied, just a little. He didn't want to give her anything she could take off and run with. Macklin expected this. She was not new to the situation. But Gomez did a better job of dissembling than your average slavering politician. She didn't digest it all, not right away. She was smart, but he wasn't giving her enough.

"Your bosses?"

"They're very busy."

She pulled back from the table. "I'm still thinking news magazine. I don't see that this is simple enough for sound bites."

Macklin wanted immediacy. She wanted the whole thing on a platter, aware that Gomez was not willing to give it to her. He gave her a little more, enough to keep her reaching. He told her about Stuart Rafkin…about his suspicions of Viktorina Viisky and her effort to lead him to Rafkin.

He also told her that Kostenko Spasski was, for all parties concerned, inconsequential.

"So he's a prop," she deduced, meaning Spasski. Her eyes focused on something not there. Gomez saw the look and knew he would get what he wanted.

"That's exactly what he is."

She grinned, liking the way of him. "How much of this do you have?"

"Almost all of it," he allowed. "There are still a few loose ends. I know the outline. I know who my targets are."

She toyed with a letter opener at the side of her lips, unconsciously intimate. It was really a shame, he thought.

"It's too twisty. You have to give me something we can use."

This was refreshing. But he had things to do. He leaned forward, invading her space. "Figure it out, Karyn. This time I'm going to use you."

Chapter 13

KOSTENKO SPASSKI was a silhouette, sitting across from Ashley Bubier on an overlarge chair in an available studio. They dimmed his overhead like he was a mob stoolie, or congressman.

For contrast, Bubier had a softbox glistening down on her like the brush of God. A flattering hair light shone from the diagonal, reminding Gomez of the sun setting on the ocean. It was a fittingly campy image—the forces of darkness and light.

Bubier was breathy, touching her hair as she warmed Spasski up with softballs. His eyes never left chest level. Spasski had asked for, and gotten, a rum and Coke before he would agree to do the interview.

Gomez thought Spasski was asleep, until he saw a drool bubble hanging from his mouth. Someone walked up to pat Spasski's face with a towel.

Gomez leaned against a wall next to Karyn Macklin. "Some of your colleagues seem to have a confusion of loyalties."

"They see it as objective journalism."

"Whose objective?" Gomez asked.

Macklin smiled.

"I have a question for you," he said, watching the dance on stage. He repeated the question he'd asked Val Sacco…the one about the terrorists and their motivation. Gomez was conducting a little experiment.

She ran a finger across an eyebrow. She knew what he meant. "Well, it's either an attempt to validate an under-realized society, *orrrr*, they're trying to stand up to the imperialist aggressions of an arrogant superpower—that's us—who disenfranchise all the little peoples of the world."

Gomez felt his pressure spike before he saw the twinkle in her eye. Macklin was just teasing. She smiled and placed her hand on his arm.

"I really appreciate this."

"You can have my condo. My embarrassing stock portfolio, too."

"No, just the tape. Besides, this is too big. We'll hand it over to the other networks." A twinkle. "After a day or two."

Bubier was finishing Spasski off. Her head bobbed faintly, acknowledging the weight of the moment. Her hair was a masterpiece of intemperate curls. Ashley Bubier, the artiste. She leaned in close, using her accessories.

She wanted to know how it was for him, when the CCCP died. "It must have been devastating!" she cried, lips quivering.

Macklin stormed the stage, admonishing Bubier to stay on script. They'd cooked up a dozen index cards with leading questions, designed to get Gomez's message across without the histrionics.

"The man needs *closure*!" Bubier protested.

Gomez studied Bubier as she swerved back on script. Well, a lamppost has its purpose, too. To hold up the lamp. Macklin gave a shake of her head. She would cull the tripe later.

"She's almost twenty-two," Macklin said, refusing to make eye contact. "She gets a 9.6 share. Pure gold. Don't worry, they'll be watching."

Bubier addressed Spasski as "Boris." The same menacing alias would flash in text on the screen. Between the drama queen and the humbled spy, they managed to convey the message that there was a great danger. It wasn't over yet. Nine-eleven was just the opening salvo. The threat was real.

Gomez would let Macklin know when he had the details of the second wave of attacks and they would warn every household in America.

"This is unbelievable," Macklin shook her head.

"Did you think they were finished?" Gomez asked.

Macklin looked away. "I guess not." She barked an order, figuratively snapping her fingers. The equivalent of an Indy pit crew appeared, rolling things this way and that until the cameras, lights, and makeup were all in order.

Macklin pointed to Viisky, who had been shoved in a corner, out of the way.

"Her turn."

Macklin made a series of gestures like a third base coach. Someone directed Viisky to a chair where makeup was applied.

"She won't need much," Macklin observed, her elbow brushing Gomez. He wiped his brow. Those damned stage lights.

"Cue her," he heard Karyn say.

Viisky mounted the stage. She let her head hang low as Spasski had, perhaps thinking it was some American social covenant. She gave them the details in much the same way she had in Gomez's office four days ago. Gomez watched her very carefully, trying to classify her attitude. He settled, finally, on defiance.

She mentioned Russia eleven times. She said "my country" often, as she described the link between breakaway elements of the SVR and the Al Qaeda terrorists. Hers were not the actions of an officer trying to conceal damning information about her mother country.

*

Nguyen re-appeared as they gathered near the exit. He had hovered around the set, acting as an usher, telling people which way to sit, how much orange clown makeup to apply. He took Viisky's hand, whispered something in her ear as if Gomez weren't there. He paused in front of Spasski, who looked like he might spit on him. Ngyuen lowered his hand and left, clogs clacking across the studio.

Macklin caught Gomez's eye. She had seen him watching Viisky. "Do you want to see it after I've cut it up?"

He waved her off. "I'll let you know."

*

Rafkin found himself disoriented, in unfamiliar sheets. A pattern of wallpaper he did not recognize. He could hear a man's voice, a pleasing contralto in another room. He was with Paul. He remembered why. The killing of Muhammad. The necessity of haven.

"I can't believe you didn't tell *anyone*!" Paul said, passing Rafkin a mug of good coffee. Paul sat on the edge of the bed, patting Rafkin's leg.

"After a while it becomes second nature," Rafkin allowed.

"It's almost like you're like an actor."

"I suppose."

Upstairs in his apartment, Rakfin donned a pair of heavy, loose blue jeans and a T-shirt, under a faded parka. A heavy carton came down from the hall closet. He dragged it to the doorway, putting weight on his right leg and feeling the burn of his injury there. He took a set of personal documents from their hiding place and stuffed them into his jacket pocket: driver's license, credit cards, and social security card, all under the name Scott Tinker. The last item, which he clipped under his jacket, was an NYPD detective's shield.

He slipped back out, avoiding Paul. Craning left to merge into the traffic, he looked back. Paul was watching through half-open window treatments. Rafkin wondered if Paul was going to be a problem.

The Hertz car rental agency was an efficient operation; Rafkin drove off in a dark blue Lumina, chosen for its common appearance. One cannot carry a four-foot sniper rifle on a motorcycle…not in New York. If there really was a Detective Tinker, he was going to owe Hertz a great deal of money.

The Lumina coasted to a stop a block away from the Paramus house. Muhammad had surprised him. That would not happen again. He watched the house from a position half-a-block away that provided good concealment and shade from the surprisingly warm fall sun.

Policemen are always a possibility when one leaves a severed head in the backyard. Rafkin breathed a sigh of relief. There was no sign of police activity. He had given it a fifty-fifty chance that a neighbor or passerby had discovered Mohammed's corpse and called 911. But it had been dark, and Rafkin had left the grisly pieces in shadow at the side of the shed. So what had they done with the corpse? Muhammad was a fatbody, not easily managed. Had they disposed of it, or was it stuffed into a closet upstairs?

Rafkin waited, thinking of Paul. The man was so easy to manipulate. Rafkin had told him that he was an agent of Mossad, the Israeli intelligence arm. Paul had found it all very romantic, as Rafkin had known he would. Now Rafkin had a place to hide, temporarily. Then a decision would have to be made about Paul.

At 3:07, an old Civic rolled slowly between the sycamores. Rafkin glanced at it briefly and then sat up with a start, realizing that it contained four Islamic friends.

They must have come from the alley. He was fortunate they had chosen to pass the house from the front. Idiot! He knew full well the car was kept parked in the rear. He had brushed against it the last time he was here. There was nothing to be gained in that. He started the engine and pulled out of his hiding space, reminding himself to stay sufficiently to the rear.

They drove together, the little Japanese compact with its four villainous occupants, with Rafkin trailing in tow. The Civic made several rudimentary moves designed to shake a tail, turning left three times in as many blocks and completing the box on the same avenue from which they had begun.

Rafkin held back, allowing them to complete one circuit without him. He saw them shoot through an intersection. Again he waited, until they had almost reached the next stop sign, then fell in behind.

Ten minutes later they left the working-class neighborhood for a sector of industrial parks, pocked by gloomy vacant lots. Weeds grew high. Paper and other garbage lay strewn about the streets and sidewalks. Soon, the compact slowed for a hundred yards. They turned without signaling, coming to a stop in a gravel lot. Rafkin pulled over, slipping beside a trio of cars at the side of the road. One of them bore a faded orange "Abandoned" sticker on its starred windshield. The others, he assumed, didn't wish to be recognized.

The building was a cracking stucco edifice, brush-painted a garish purple and blue. Eager, desperate weeds climbed the cracks. A blinking neon sign advertised the name: Bangers II. It stood alone for a square block among the overgrown empty lots, and the crumbling walls struck Rafkin as sad and cheaply maudlin. An unpainted whore. It would look better at night.

The Arabs got out and the two men in front entered the building first. Those that had been in the rear lingered, smoking and watching the sidewalk. After several minutes, they, too, walked toward the entrance and disappeared from view. As Rafkin crossed the avenue, he pulled the hood of the parka over his head. The heavy clothing would help to conceal the scratches.

Rafkin handed the galoot at the door ten dollars, pausing for a moment, allowing his eyes to adjust to the darkness. Rickety tables were packed tight and he sidled his way toward the rear of a room roughly thirty meters square.

He ordered a fifteen-dollar vodka tonic from an overweight woman with breasts like cow udders. He was aware that this expenditure was mandatory.

The Mujahadeen sat four across, along an elevated wooden runway, upon which a girl of perhaps sixteen, coiled and wiggled her naked body. She moved as if she had ingested some illegal substance or other, and the Islamites goggled at her as if she were belly dancing in the bazaar. She was heavily made up and far too thin. Heroin did that.

The four men were smoking up a storm and guzzling the watery alcohol to match the rest of the wastrels. Rafkin noted the conspicuous lack of a Koran or prayer rug. He rose, leaving ten dollars on the table. The waitress attempted a sloppy kiss. Rafkin ducked, smiling his apologies.

On the way out, he stopped in the men's room and urinated, out of necessity. A full bladder would be inconvenient in a few minutes time. He looked at himself in the mirror. He was ready. Muhammad had not been an accident.

He was confident the men inside would remain for at least an hour. He required less than that, perhaps as little as thirty minutes. He got in the rental car, retracing his route. This time, he parked directly in front, between two of the sycamores. They were a brilliant yellow in the heart of the season.

Simple was good. Rafkin knew this much from training, and he walked with purpose up the concrete walk, noting a lack of proper yard maintenance. It helped that they were pigs. He was not a common killer.

He conducted a short, thorough study of the street. Americans never left their homes, so busy they were with television and video games. Satisfied there was no one about, he knocked hard on the peeling paint of the front door.

A young man stood before him, he'd swung the door wide—something Rafkin would never have considered in their position. In his early twenties, he could have been a college student in his Adidas and stonewashed jeans. He was clean-shaven, and it struck Rafkin that they had all shaved their beards.

The boy opened his mouth to say something, probably thinking Rafkin was selling something, or a neighbor in need of a favor.

CHAPTER 14

THE WHITE ODYSSEY was definitely tailing them. The passenger had a head like a partially shaved coconut—a good reference point. Gomez looked in the mirror as they went down into the parking garage. The Odyssey didn't follow.

"I exhaust of these rooms," Viisky pouted. Spasski flopped onto the queen-sized bed, his arms folded behind his head. He was asleep in moments.

"That's a sign of depression," Gomez observed without any feeling for the matter.

She shrugged, "*Who gives a gavno*?" They wandered around, artificially busy. Gomez drifted into the sitting room. After a minute she followed and approached him.

"You were anti-spy, then? You loathe us, during this Freezing War?"

"Yup."

"Hmmm," she said, thinking about it. "You have been married?"

"Once, a long time ago." Actually, a paltry three years, just enough to heal most of the battle damage.

"How are you so sure of this television? In Russia, the television is still controlled by the old men."

"I wasn't," he said. "Just playing the hand I've got. It's a safety valve. If for any reason I feel we're going to get hit, I'll call Karyn and she'll pull the trigger. She'll go public with all of it."

She put her hands in her lap, her eyes sliding away. "You like this woman? This news woman?"

"She's a lesbian," he said.

Viisky cocked her head to the side. The sun glanced off a mirror, catching the line of her jaw.

"It means she likes to sleep with girls."

"Ahhhhh."

An intense vision popped unbidden into his head. Both little Miss Viisky and the Macklin babe. *Hmmm.* Vishka could maybe wear a tiny leather police costume—the kind with those long boots—with Karyn as the astonished French maid, complete with bib and feather duster. Karyn would be Nannette. Viisky would star as Babbette. How on earth he could think of things like that at a time like this was amazing to him, but at the same time he thought it might be a good sign concerning virility and middle age.

They sat at the table nearest the windows, guarding their thoughts. There were fewer taxis compared to the last time he was here. He wondered, randomly, what would happen to the New York City tourist industry.

"Don't you have to contact this Feliks clown? Give him a status report or something?"

"Twice I have done this." She looked out the window as she replied. Gomez said nothing. She'd left his sight only to go to the bathroom.

"I have spoken to him that you are a good man."

"Thanks a lot."

Her smile grew tentative. Gomez lit up, and she followed. Their fingers touched across the ashtray.

"We *must* find this Rafkin," she said, smoking intensely.

Gomez waited. Her face wasn't as wide in profile as he had originally thought. She lacked the square, cinderblock head of the true Slav. She was a goddess, actually.

"Just how important is it to find Mr. Rafkin?"

Her color was high and he wondered how far she was stepping over the line. "Very much so."

"When should we find him?"

"Very soon."

It was similar, he thought, to asking his ex how much chaos she had incurred at the mall. Dragging it, tooth and nail.

"Today? Tomorrow? How soon is soon?"

She stared at him and she had *the look*; he knew she was going to tell him something incredibly important. Then he saw Spasski's stupid mug loom behind her shoulder.

"*What's up, fuckers?*"

Spasski was hammered. He must have done it quickly; they'd been in the sitting room for less than half an hour. Gomez remembered the mini-bar. He gave Spasski a hard look and went into the bedroom. A count of the minibar came up four short—Chivas miniatures. Figures, he would go for the good stuff. He wondered again if snatching Spasski had been a mistake. Viisky would come around anyway, without all the pressure. He sighed and went back to get Spasski.

Viisky had him pinned in a corner. There was humor to be found in this, for the right sort of mind.

"Let's put him in the bathroom. He can't do much in there."

"Allow me to do this." She grabbed Spasski by the hair. Gomez heard a squeal as she shoved him into the other room. Gomez hurried ahead into the bathroom where he swept all the toiletries off the sink into a towel. He tossed the whole bundle onto the bed, quickly, while Viisky drove Spasski ahead of her like a cowpuncher. She pressed the door closed with her whole body and wedged a chair under the doorknob.

"He isn't going anywhere," Gomez observed.

"He is pain in my bottom."

Gomez rubbed his jaw, wondering if he had lost the initiative. They stood facing each other in the bedroom. Now…how to pick up where they had left off?

"I will be changing into more comfortable." Viisky slinked off to the other room. Gomez mopped his brow. He had a bad case of cottonmouth, for some reason.

He foraged under the nightstand, finding the directory for Lower Manhattan. The public had a perception that the Bureau had some sort of mega-database, a whiz-bang-super-government-sized Lexus-Nexus, where they could access the most arcane details about anything in the universe at the touch of a button. People were not really that hard to find. Gomez liked the Yellow Pages.

He found Manhattan Bond under Investments, and with a pencil marked a few numbers at random. Names like Bayview and Lincoln, Harlem and TriBeCa. He had been to New York many times but really did not know the area well.

There was a listing for the Lower Manhattan branch office in Number 2, World Trade Center. He stared at it for a long time.

The office in TriBeCa, then.

A woman answered on the second ring. He identified himself and was told to hold for management. The recorded ads came on, upselling him to Putnam A shares. Viisky chose that moment to appear in the doorway. Her East German slacks and blouse lay strewn on the floor behind her. In bra and panties, she was slimmer, more perfect. Mere clothing did not do justice, Gomez judged.

He made no effort to avert his eyes. She turned, retreating into the sitting area, unlatching her bra and letting it fall to the floor at her feet.

The telephone was buzzing in his hand. Hello? It was the district manager from Manhattan Bond. His name was Jay-Neil Simmons, and he sounded a little like Al Haig taking over the country when Reagan got popped. Gomez asked him about personnel files. Where were they stored? Who had access?

Jay-Neil dribbled some garbage about privacy laws and SEC regulations. Gomez fixed the image of his Vichska in her birthday suit. He held it, gleaming in the forefront of his mind, where it would remain for all time. Manager-boy finally shut up.

"So, you're saying that you refuse to cooperate with the FBI on a matter of National Security."

"No, not at all. Blah, blah, blah…" *What if she were to stay, after this was over?* He could never trust her.

"Listen up, Chuckles. Unless you want me to secure a search warrant and march down there with the TV cameras, you're going to tell me how I can find a broker of yours that once worked in the Tidewater, Virginia, area, who we now suspect to be in New York."

"I'll have to hook you up with HR" Jay-Neil caved. After a bit of bluster and rooster puffing, Gomez was assured that he would receive a call from human resources within the hour. He set the phone gently onto its cradle.

One hour. That was a lot of time. Kingdoms had fallen in an hour.

He found her in the sitting area, lounging on the chaise, a glass of something red in her hand. He pulled a Heineken from the mini-bar, making a note to send his expense report over the hotel fax.

The television was on, tuned to MSNBC. Gomez thought he knew why. He walked to the highboy and turned the sound down to a murmur.

"Why is the taping not broadcast?" She sipped at her wine, watching him. He liked the way she pretended. He liked her act.

"She'll run it when I tell her to run it," Gomez said. He noticed that the panties, also, were gone. Her legs were crossed, just barely. An invitation. That one last little thing…

Her brow crinkled, she propped up on one arm, pointing to the television. "Explain this Lexus please."

Gomez turned to watch the commercial. Three yuppies sneered at each other over their squash rackets.

"It's a car," he explained, because no car was shown in the car commercial. "You see how smug everyone is? That means the car is expensive."

"I mean, how do you say this *Lexus*? What is word?" Viisky managed to arch her back.

He thought about making something up, then shrugged helplessly. He stared at the tiny down of her arms…the stray goose bump…the incongruous sprinkling of freckles. He forgot his manners and did not offer her a blanket to keep her warm.

"I am much confused," Viisky said. Now *that* was a pout.

"Well, we can't have that." He walked over to the wall and lowered the thermostat to a brisk sixty-five. Thought about it, decided that Russians—or people from other northern regions—might be used to the chill. Better knock her down to sixty.

"Why do you go to this press if you do not bother it? Is this problem with your superiors?" It was indeed. Another matter for another time.

"I intend to capture the enemy, not warn him off. I don't want them slinking back over the border." He took a pull on his cerveza, eyes on the prize. "If we time this right, it will harness the power of the people. I think you know what happens when the Americans are motivated."

She was staring at him with some pretty heavy lust in her eyes. No man could miss that. Although he knew it to be a ploy, he couldn't help but wonder. Could she be faking it? Could even *foreign* women be that deceitful?

"Our terrorist friends will know we have them. They'll see it on TV and hear it on the radio, just like everyone else. But I don't think it will stop them from going after the oil. It's too fat a target. If we're really, really lucky, the ones we miss at the ports will go after the water, anyway. They may not even figure out that there will be no one there. Except us."

"In my country, we would do the opposite. We would defend oil at all cost. My government would say this oil is more of value than water."

That statement, more than anything, helped him regain his composure. He was reminded that they stood on opposite sides of a vast cultural plain.

Gomez glanced over at the entrance to the bedroom. Spasski was singing a Czechoslovakian drinking ditty, loud enough to be heard through the bathroom door. He crossed over to her and got down on one knee, his face inches from hers. She was a perfect "C." They had that upward tilt, even lying flat like that on the chaise. He noticed the freckles, then banned them from his mind.

"I noticed you didn't mention Stuart Rafkin at the studio," he said casually. An afterthought. Viisky blinked. Not really, not an actual blink, but a metaphysical one.

She recovered and said, "I wish to capture him. To not frighten him away."

Again, he thought she had done a lousy job of it. Viktorina Viisky was an amateur.

"You are such handsome man." Her voice was like polished glass. "You are more cultured than Russian men." Either way, he was screwed.

"I think…" his cell phone rang, startling him. It was the sound of a choo-choo train. He had changed it during the drive back and forgotten. Viisky brought her lower lip over her upper, like she couldn't have the lollipop. Gomez shifted uncomfortably, rearranging his trousers. The third ring seemed louder, more insistent. He lowered his head, the big one, thinking furiously. He stood, understanding that if it never came to pass, he would hate himself forever.

"I'd better get that."

CHAPTER 15

HE WOULD GET THAT Jay-Neil idiot for this. Simmons had said within the hour, not twenty stinking minutes. Probably the first efficient thing he'd ever done. Gomez was gonna get him.

He passed through the divider and picked up his phone, continuing on to the bathroom. He wanted a third party in here, in case he changed his mind.

There was business to take care of. He pushed the chair to one side and opened the door. Spasski was sitting on the commode, eyeballing Gomez with a blank stare, like a farm animal.

"Wake up, butt-cheese."

"Excuse me?"

Gomez looked at the phone in his hand, "Not you. I was speaking to… this is Gomez."

"Oh, yes sir. It's Kevin Nagle. With Manhattan Bond."

Spasski stood up and made a hand gesture behind Gomez's back.

"I understand you're trying to find someone in our organization."

"His name is Stuart Rafkin. His last known location is in the Tidewater, Virginia area. We know he was there four years ago, but it could be less."

"You mean he doesn't work here in New York?"

"Not that I'm aware of."

Nagle sighed loud enough for Gomez to hear. "Sir, I can only access names and addresses for people working in the TriBeCa office. We've got, like, two hundred brokers, maybe a little more. Manhattan Bond has *fifteen thousand* employees. This guy could be anywhere in the country. Or terminated."

"Or, he could have been in your office in the past. He could be there now."

"Yeah, I suppose that's true. It's Saturday, though. Mr. Simmons dragged me away from my kid's b-ball game. I would have to check with the branch managers one at a time for permission to search their in-house databases."

"Do you have a computer?"

"Of course."

"And a modem?"

Nagel groaned. "This would normally be something for the home office."

Gomez was getting tired of dicking around with the kid. People just didn't want to lift a finger anymore. "So wake up someone at the home office. Get them off the fucking golf course and on the phone. Now." Rattling people's cages was something Gomez was good at. It surprised him a little when Nagle fell away into silence.

"Do I have to repeat myself?"

"You don't know?

"Know what? Listen up, Sonny…"

"The home office was in Tower 2. They used to be in the Parker building in Scarsdale, but…they relocated in May."

How does one respond to that? With an estimated three thousand dead in the Towers alone, it was amazing how small the world had become.

"There are no files. Everything's gone. Everything."

"I see."

Gomez lit a smoke, thinking. "Anyone get out?"

"I think so. I'm not sure. We lost, like seventy or eighty people. A whole bunch of the top brass were in California at a meeting, and it was early in the day for brokers, but…"

"All right, Kevin. Hey, do me a favor. Check your staff anyway. And the HR people of any branch you can get a hold of. I know it's a long shot, but what the hell."

"Yeah, okay."

"It may have something to do with the Towers."

"Are you shitting me?" Nagle blurted.

"Actually, no."

"Mr. Agent?" A third voice had materialized. That little Simmons weasel had been listening in. He must be a real joy to his staff. Probably made them sterilize their keyboards.

"Jay-Neil here." Gomez pictured a chipmunk.

"A couple of people got out. A colleague of mine is among the living. The LM branch was part of the home office.

"Friend of yours?"

"Yes, actually. His name is Devard Montrane. We used to play racquetball every Thursday but he blew out a knee. I don't see him very much anymore."

Gomez rubbed his forehead. "I'm sure Mr. Montrane is a wonderful human being, but to tell you the truth, Mr. Simmons, I wasn't asking about survivors in the spirit of compassion."

"Stuart Rafkin is his boss."

Viisky's luck! That meant that Stuart Rafkin was in the Towers. *How in the…?* What in the heck did *that* mean?

"Do you know how I can find Rafkin?"

"No, the LM Branch is closed, obviously. But I can tell you where Devard lives. I could even drive you there. We're friends, as I mentioned."

"Just the address please."

Jay-Neil recited Devard Montrane's address and home phone number. Gomez ended the call, telling Kevin Nagle to try to find an address on Rafkin, if he could.

Gomez crossed out onto the balcony, past Spasski who was, once again, lying prone on the bed—unconscious this time and not faking it. The doors to the sitting room were closed. Firmly.

He dialed the number Simmons had given him. "You have reached the home of…"

It was a gay greeting. A pre-9-11 greeting. It was voice-hole.

Crap. Now what? He had the link and the link was too busy to connect. Okay. He would try Montrane every hour on the hour until he reached him.

Viisky came out from behind the partition, dressed in cargo pants and a turtleneck. Gomez thought that the heavy clothing was some sort of sign. "Keep out," for example. He felt his heart go over a cliff.

"He's been sleeping in those clothes," Gomez said, jerking his thumb at Spasski. "How about you go out and get him something to wear. I'm not very capable at that type of thing." Gomez had calls to make. It would be better if Viisky didn't hear whom he was calling, and what he had to say. He hooked his wallet out of his hip pocket, but she refused the cash.

"I have budget. I have explained this to you." She was a little cool, but at least she wasn't polite. "I will leave you now to your investigations. Do not burden with me, Sir."

Uh-oh. Polite, with a touch of the martyr. He would have to fix that…later.

Viisky let herself out without a backward look. As a precaution, Gomez roused Spasski and sent him, groggily, into the sitting area. He told him to close the curtain, adding a dire threat as the cherry on top. Spasski staggered out dutifully, not really trying anymore.

Gomez went back out to the balcony. The view was quite spectacular. He was tired of such close quarters. One enemy spy he could handle—the other was growing tedious.

A moment to think. He scribbled on a napkin…Rafkin, Spasski, Viisky and Uncle Feliks; Davidson and Sacco, Macklin and Kessler. Well, a week ago he was ready to hang himself in the closet. Now, he found himself teleported into the most critical situation in the history of the universe.

His phone held four messages. One was from a woman named Rachel, an occasional date. She must be single again. He deleted it without listening to it. The next two were from Cummings and Kessler, respectively. Deleted. Kessler was growing into one of those management types who think they're your father, calling you on the weekend. Have to shut him down pretty soon. Then again, Kessler may come in handy. Have to think about that one.

The last was from Davidson. Situation static. Guys were still rolling in from various law enforcement agencies up and down the East Coast. Gomez thought again that if Al Qaeda struck out in California or on the Gulf, they were royally boned.

He called Davidson and got *his* voice-hole, leaving a lengthy message in regard to Macklin, sharing some ideas he had on the media angle. He told Davidson that he would call in the morning.

He dialed Montrane's number again, waiting as it began to ring. The skyline of Lower Manhattan hung in a balance of haze and peculiar beauty. It didn't look so messy from this vantage.

*

He thought of the millions of people down there, going about their business. There were children being conceived and unions dissolving. More than a few of them were going through the motions in quiet desperation. Crooks of every stripe were gearing up for a weekend's enterprise. Lovers met for the first time. Children played.

My country, Gomez thought. *This land is my land and I'm going to nail you fuckers to the wall.*

He tried Montrane again. On the fifth ring, the familiar tin voice spoke. It seemed to be his day for that. Sometimes you got people. Sometimes only the robots were home. He hung up without leaving a message and lit a cigarette, sipping distantly on his imported beer as dusk descended on the land.

Chapter 16

THE MOB IN THE hotel bar was largely native, judging by the Yankees caps floating around…and a few of the Mets. People were drinking, but there was little of the horsing around and jocularity one would expect in a saloon. They must have wanted to get out, to interact in one of the few ways they knew how; to see and to feel that not everything was gone.

Vishka was at the bar, beguiling its tender. The bartender had a smart-alecky smile. Gomez didn't like the looks of him. Viisky tossed her hair, laughing at something he said. She was taking her time about it.

The second half of a late-season double-header flickered from the two small televisions hanging above their heads. The game was muted. Instead, a big screen dominated the room, tuned to CNN.

Todd Pratt banged a grand slam. No one noticed. All eyes were on the big screen where a morose CNN correspondent was shouting at them by sat-phone.

It was a city scene, European in flavor. Grim houses surrounded grim streets and the grim faces of grim, dirty peasants. The reporter stood amidst fresh carnage. Bloody, tattered clothing lay on a dusty road. The fingers of a corpse poked out from beneath a faded blanket.

From what Gomez could gather, Chechen terrorists had ambushed an element of the Russian army in some shitty border town. The studio reappeared, where it was rumored that the 101st

Screaming Eagles were deploying out of Fort Campbell, Kentucky, for points Mid-East.

Things were tough all over.

Gomez popped a pretzel into his mouth, one eye on the television. He and Spasski sat waiting in a corner booth, observing the local wildlife. Spasski mumbled something to Gomez that he didn't catch. He made no effort, watching Viisky make her way through the crowd, the tray held tightly in both hands like it was the lost treasure of the Romanovs. The tray held several shot glasses and a fifth of Stoli—must have cost her a hundred bucks. "She had budget," he remembered.

Viisky laid the tray on the table and sat down with the first smile he had seen since she left to get Spasski some new threads.

She had strolled in at 6:30, overburdened with shopping bags, quietly pleased with herself. Neither of them mentioned the temptation in the sitting room.

Viisky filled the shot glasses. "Nosdravie."

The two Slavs whacked it back in a blink. Gomez nipped about a third of his, setting it back down on the table. You can't save the world if you can't see it. Viisky eyeballed his glass with disapproval.

"We need to talk about him," he said, jerking his thumb at Spasski, who was rapidly re-loading.

Viisky nodded as the server appeared, a puffy young woman who spent too much time in the sun. Tanning booth, Gomez thought.

"What can I get ya?" Her skin reminded him of something. It was…sailcloth, he realized. He had been thinking about Hinson out in LA and running headlong into semi-retirement. Gomez had three sailing magazines on the coffee table in his condo.

The server's name was Chantal, as it turned out. Gomez ordered all around, burgers and fries. Chantal glanced at the bottle and left.

"I don't think I can let him go," Gomez said, watching Viisky intently.

Her lids fluttered. She glanced at Spasski. He was sucking down his third, or maybe fourth shot of firewater.

"Why is this so?"

Gomez sighed and sat back against the leatherette. Another pretzel.

"At the time, I thought we would go to the press and spill the whole thing. Then I could kick him loose. He would have served his purpose. My thinking has changed on this. Now I'm going to have to keep him until I tell Macklin to air the interview. Or, until this is over."

"What am I? A freaking potato chip? I'm sitting *right here!*" Spasski cried.

"I see," Viisky was tense. And that was good, Gomez thought.

"Why do you not reveal this interview now?"

"As I told you previously, I would rather catch them. Better yet, kill them," he added. "That would be fine, too."

That was the trap for Viisky, Gomez realized. She was forced to press on the media angle. He thought he knew why.

"Why do you not tell your superiors? This would be my plan."

"They don't believe this is a legitimate threat."

"But surely you can try this again?"

"That would be the same thing as airing the interview now. My superiors, as you call them, would jump in front of the first camera they could find. They would blow it." He wasn't kidding about that. "This would be equal to warning them away, effecting their escape." He had purposefully injected some chicane logic into his presentation. She had followed every word. And her accent was slipping. Or maybe that was his imagination.

"So. You must control this media?"

"You got it."

Their booth was nestled in a crevice of the bar. Small drinking tables with high stools were sprinkled randomly in the open center. Gomez heard a guy at a nearby table say, "Not for nuthin', I'd like to bash his fuckin' head. But I got kids, know what I mean?" The two mooks bust out laughing, surprisingly loud in the full room. They would bounce back.

Gomez returned to Viisky.

"Two choices. I can continue as I am, and if I understand things correctly, then Stuart Rafkin is not only assisting Al-Qaeda, he is the key to finding them and…capturing them."

He paused for effect. She had never said it as fact—that Rafkin was the guy. She lowered her eyes. Taking the bottle from Spasski, she poured herself another. "Or, I can blow the whistle. Then we're done."

"You are certain this is not, eh, this cowboy rodeo?"

Gomez drained his first shot. By his count he was at least two behind. "That, of course, is the question. I am interested in your opinion."

"I hope they mess you up good," Spasski said. The man did not even piss Gomez off anymore. He was just sort of there, like a pet goldfish.

"Have a drink." Gomez shoved the wudka across the table at Spasski. Viisky twirled a napkin, twisting it into ever-smaller spirals.

"If is my decision, I, of course, involve my directorate chief and other peoples of command." But she knew nothing of Davidson and Sacco, nothing of their snooping around. Gomez was going to keep it that way.

"Is not for me to speculate," Viisky said. And then, being a woman, she did.

"In Russia, we are having only four to five big ports of oil. In America, is different. You have many smaller locations for the importing of this oil. So, if the terrorist vermin succeed, they will do less damage here than in Russia." She shrugged, "Is not questioning for me." Gomez noticed that she had not answered the question. She may have recognized his eagerness. She was a sharp cookie.

Chantal arrived with the burgers. Spasski sniffed at his and poured another drink. Gomez ordered a beer. He would switch to the Heinis and eat every bite of his burger. The key to drinking is eating. Viisky, it seemed, knew this. She piled it in on top of the late lunch like she hadn't eaten in a week.

Gomez had half a mind to call Karyn Macklin and tell her to spill the whole thing and then tell Davidson that they were wrong;

it was just too risky—they couldn't cover. Security around every port in the country would be trebled by Monday morning. The bad guys would walk away.

Spasski told them he had to use the men's room. Gomez did not doubt it. The restrooms were down a narrow corridor at the opposite end of the entrance. Had he wished to escape, Gomez could run him down easily. He let the man go pee in peace.

Viisky had finished her burger and was demurely wiping her mouth with a napkin.

"Where'd you get the one in your stomach?" Gomez inquired. He was referring to the scarred-over bullet wound he had seen when she had given him the striptease upstairs. Viisky finished chewing. Buying time, he thought.

She looked away. "Was in warehouse in Smovelensk. Criminal peoples, eh, the Mafiya, has stored the fruits of their smuggling enterprise there."

"And the one in your thigh?"

"This is actually accident. I shoot myself on gunfire range." She faced him now, her color came up high in her cheeks. She must have felt it. "Is embarrassment. Very foolish to shoot oneself, is it not?"

Gomez looked away, giving her time to get it together.

Policemen, and women, do not get shot *twice* by the age of thirty. The odds of that happening are slim to none, and slim just left town. Especially in Russia, where they didn't have the gun culture.

In a minute, Spasski returned from the men's room. The front of his pants displayed droplets of…something. It could have been water that splashed when he was washing his hands. Gomez watched him make his way to the back of the booth. His eyes stayed closed just a little too long when he blinked, and he practically fell over Viisky as he climbed into his seat.

Viisky tried to recover.

"He is here too long. He cannot tolerate his vodka so well as a true Russian." To prove that she could, she filled her glass to the tippy-top, then slammed it down with a long *ahhh* at the end. Gomez smiled. He still liked her.

She stood and curtsied, so out of place and with such sublime grace that Gomez thought he had entered another dimension. She smiled, speaking in crystal clear English.

"Please Sir, where might I find the lavatory?"

Gomez cocked his head to the side, completely at a loss.

"Is very first English I learn," she told him. She breezed off, headed for the bathroom.

Gomez shook his head, looking over at Spasski, lying with his head on the table. He played with the label on the bottle, trying to fit Spasski into the mix. Remembering how Spasski hadn't seemed really surprised to see Viisky. Scared, yes. Not surprised. The way Viisky had taken him through a dozen losers and bums in an hour and then zoomed in on Spasski.

He poked Spasski in the ribcage. "What's your story? They asked you to do it but you wouldn't? So they got Rafkin to do it?"

Spasski moaned, unintelligible. Gurgling.

Gomez whipped out his phone to dial the number in Jamaica—the number for Devard Montrane. Got the robot. He listened through half of the same voice message when his phone made a noise like a hippo snorting. Call waiting. It was Sacco.

"You see this shit on Fox?" Sacco asked, without preamble.

"I think it's on every channel," Gomez said, yawning. He'd been watching sporadically out of the corner of his eye, scanning some sort of harried police activity on the closest television to the left.

The crawler on the screen said, "Live." It was at a bad angle, a helicopter shot, but the bartender jabbed the remote, cranking up the sound. Every head in the bar swiveled toward the action—a crazy shootout at some mall in the burbs. Could be more terrorists. The cops had the place surrounded, waiting for Tactical.

Chapter 17

THE ISLAMITES exited their vehicle, moving as a pack into the entrance of Nordstrom's department store at the River Mills Mall in Nutley, New Jersey—an hour from Bangers II. Rafkin nearly peeled off and counted it good when he thought he saw a man in the back seat of the Honda turn his head to look behind them.

Rafkin circled the lot, battling eager shoppers for ten minutes until he saw a suitable opening. He pulled into the third slot from the end and parked, with the engine running. He drained his third bottle of Poland water down to the last half inch of swill and cut the top off with his knife. He urinated until it was near overflowing, setting it down onto the passenger-side footwell.

When he'd entered the house in Paramus, he'd found a mess of beer bottles and packaged food containers. The boy had screamed, begging for mercy as Rafkin marched him down the hallway, impaled on the combat knife. Rafkin thought it was a shame how they betrayed these children and stuffed their heads with drivel. He'd wrinkled his nose in disgust and caught motion on the right peripheral. An older terrorist, thirty-five or so, sat in a dirty green recliner next to a fireplace. Rafkin recognized him as the driver of the van in SoHo. The driver smiled tentatively at Rafkin, half standing to greet him, holding a magazine and a bag of potato chips on his lap.

Rafkin had taken six long strides, a snarl slipping out. The man's half-smile changed to recognition as he dropped the magazine, turning to reach for the Skorpion submachine gun propped against the mantle.

He'd almost made it. But Rafkin never slowed and raised the knife high over his head, bringing it down like Jack the Ripper, burying it deep into the man's neck just at the beginning of the curve to the shoulder. The driver had struggled to get his hands around Rafkin's neck, but Rafkin was stronger and he drove his thumbs into the ribcage.

The driver had shouted something about religion, grunting with the effort, and Rafkin kicked him in the balls. The man made a high-pitched squealing sound, so very like young girls at a rock music concert, and he sat down hard in the recliner. He grasped not for his mortal wound, but clutched the arms of the chair like a particularly nervous flyer.

Rafkin had wiped the blade on the driver's shirt. "You will kill no children this day, or any other," he said, then slapped the driver in the face, a wicked smack, and once more as the life left the driver's body, along with his will.

Rafkin had searched, then. The house was quiet; it had no feel of occupancy , yet he pulled a small caliber pistol from an ankle holster as he climbed the stairs. He'd hoped for some indication on a computer, or the written word, but he wasted thirty minutes sweating, and panicked until he slammed the last door, knowing that Feliks was a ghost.

Just as Feliks thought Rafkin lived in SoHo, Rafkin had always met Feliks in public places. If he couldn't find Feliks…he was risking his life for nothing. Once again, he thought of running—home to Paul and infinite comfort. Paul would cluck over his scrapes and bruises and they would talk about escape.

Instead, he drove back the way he had come. His luck held. The Civic was still there in the gravel lot at the strip-club, though what they could be seeing that they hadn't in the past hour, he could not imagine.

*

Rafkin's stomach growled. He had had nothing to eat since breakfast with Paul. He factored his hunger, as well as fatigue and his aching bruises, the estimated skill of the remaining Arabs and other variables, trying to decide if he might take more of them here, in such a public place.

His tactical situation was poor with too many civilians and too many obstacles. There must be a thousand cars parked in this sector alone.

Should he confront them, they would have the advantage of spreading out and using the cars as shields so the others could creep up behind him and shoot him in the head. Or, they would use the knife. Rafkin feared the knife.

He allowed another ten minutes, then pulled out of his slot and down the lane toward the terrorists' vehicle. He parked again, this time to the outside of their car. He would follow them when they came out.

Twenty minutes passed with no sign of the enemy. But there they were, in P.J. Willickers, grouped together in a perfect bull's-eye, sucking down chicken wings and margaritas. Rafkin thrilled at his fortune, ticking off the positive factoids in his mind: low wind, close range, silenced weapon—ensuring initial confusion. Subjects were unaware, seated, making very small motion. Better than Paramus, with its parked cars and low hedges. It was more than one could hope for. They were grouped together like a ten-ring.

A waist-high iron fence surrounded the patio. Painted flat black, it rose to the shoulders of the targets, exposing only their heads. To shoot at the torso—the center of mass—was his preferred target. But it was out of the question. The odds were too high that he would hit the iron. A ricochet could carom and kill a child.

Another plus, the tables closest to the terrorists were empty, while the balance of the area was flush with early diners. The Americans were staying clear of Arabs.

Out of the Lumina, he performed a series of stretching exercises, drawing an odd look from a passing family. They had no idea who they disdained.

The Dragunov was both the hardest to acquire and the easiest to assemble and use. In three minutes he was ready. Satisfied, he sighted on the targets. A server plied them with refills, a pitcher in each hand. The barrel rested nicely on the window frame, allowing traverse.

Rafkin looked through the scope. The sight picture, with its lack of strollers and housewives, was satisfactory. He could get off two, possibly three rounds before they scattered or returned fire. The server was back, standing next to their table with one hand on her hip, saying something to them and holding her head back in laughter. Tip time. He had better hurry. The ass end of a Nissan Pathfinder jutted out enough to obstruct his view of the man on the far right. He lowered his weapon and saw movement at the table. One of the men stood, leaning over to say something to his compatriots.

Quickly now, with great urgency, he reached over and lowered the left rear window, diving clumsily into the back seat.

Reset, and...there. The perfect sight picture. Assignation of target order. Take the hardest shot first. One–two-three-four. Far right, then the far left. Take the one in the middle as things heated up and save the standing man for last. If there was a mad scramble of motion, simply blaze away into the middle, hoping for a lucky shot.

The man in the soccer shirt turned and abruptly walked away. Off for a piss. Rafkin felt a drop of perspiration leak into his eye. He wiped it off with the back of his hand, ruining his aim entirely. Exhaling hard, directly upward, to push the beads of sweat out of his eyes, he readjusted. He got it under control. The men at the table began to stir, and Rafkin understood they were waiting for the other one to return. Centering the reticule on the first target—cross hairs on the nose.

Phhhht. The Dragunov was a whisper. More a matter of will than direct pull. What a fine trigger. An instant later, Rafkin heard a dull, faraway plink on the wrought iron. He had missed utterly and completely. Inhaled at the wrong moment. He re-sighted. The man in the center raised his face skyward, as if looking for rain. The man on the right turned and scanned the parking lot before he was even aware of what was happening, some instinct commanding him.

Rafkin fired on the man in the center and once again he heard a sound, a half-second delay after he pulled the trigger. This time, it sounded as if he hit the brick wall behind them. Then he saw the blood. It sprayed from the throat of the man in the center. The bullet had passed clean through. He saw, rather than heard, the man gagging convulsively, and he thought of Kennedy and the Zapruder film.

Rafkin felt his hands shaking. The man who had left chose that moment to return. Rafkin took in the sight of him shouting; it wafted over the distance to the car. He fumbled the bolt, got it together. One in the chamber. *Phhhht.* He was aiming for the torso of the man who had relieved himself and he was fairly sure he missed but saw that he came close enough for the man to hear the round pass by his head.

The man from the rest room—Rafkin could see now that he had a mustache—drew a pistol from his jacket. It happened so quickly. The man from the restroom placed the pistol against the head of the wounded man and calmly shot him in the head. His hand jumped—that is how Rafkin knew he fired—and the dead man toppled over, chair and all, onto the concrete patio.

The Americans were jumpy. They had seen their Towers fall. They were quick to react, flattening like a marigold field touched by a sudden breeze. People dove under their tables and cowered. A few brave souls ran for it, hurtling over iron chairs, knocking down tables on their way to the exit.

Rafkin held his fire. The targets were blending in. The man who executed his comrade stood stock still, oak among the melee, his weapon hanging down at his thigh. He appeared to be staring directly at Rafkin. He gestured to his friends. They were aware that the enemy sniper covered the street entrance. They took off through the doors leading to the interior of the mall.

Rafkin breathed for the first time in forty seconds. He had eliminated a total of four out of a probable seven. The first siren had yet to sound.

What if he could get the other three? Right now. He might be a little late for Paul, but only fashionably so. That would do it. He would kill them and call Feliks to meet him someplace where he would kill him too, then he could tell Paul of his plans for their escape.

He lowered the Dragunov, out of view of the shoppers streaming through the parking lot. They were oblivious of the blond man with the rifle hanging out the window of a blue Chevrolet.

The answer was simple—effortless, really. His chi, karma, his essence, or whatever the latest label, it all meant the same thing; he was rolling.

From the belly pouch of his sweatshirt he removed a laminated ID card and a badge, each secured to a thin metal chain. Rafkin hung them around his neck. Before closing the trunk, he grabbed a Mossberg Cruiser, a twelve-gauge combat shotgun, stuffing seven shells into the chamber. He pumped it twice, headed for the entrance next to Willicker's, shouting police jargon from television.

Rafkin thought he would not wish to see his face in a mirror. He hit the pavement, going for broke.

Chapter 18

RAFKIN TRIPPED going in, his heel catching the rubberized entry pad in full gallop. He regained his balance, wheeling through the big glass doors. They had not quite closed from the last clutch of fleeing shoppers, and he hit them hard, assisting the servos with his shoulder, ducking as he crossed the threshold to merchandising heaven.

Crouching proved to be a wise move. He heard and felt the whipcrack of bullets whining over his head to punch into the glass as the doors closed behind him. Several sprinters' strides and a short roll took him skidding across the glossy floor. He slid to a stop on his stomach behind a concrete container of ficus, a plant that had gone out of style about the same time as the hammer and sickle.

Somewhere, an architect deserved to be sacked. The interior of the mall stood as a monument to bad taste. More is better is more; more of everything is better. Rafkin lay between a bad rendition of Roman ruins, colliding gaudily with California Mexican. Really, he thought, there are some things money can't buy.

On second thought, the interior designers were to blame. The portable elements of décor were atrocious, namely the ficus pots. They were the size of boxcars or commercial cattle troughs. Swirling African designs in distended plaster covered the sides. They stood twenty feet apart, marching all the way to the far end of the mall, which he could not even see for its distance.

It was a shooting gallery. The savages were positioned in the shop alcoves to either side of the entrance, roughly sixty feet up the row. They had defiladed with a quick step backward into the recesses of the stores and could lay down crossfire on the approaches. Anyone entering the mall was in for a bad time.

The man on the right was a tenuous vision. Rafkin hadn't seen anything at all, of the third surviving enemy. He'd gotten a good look at the man on the left. It was Akil, primary target. Akil was personal bodyguard to Muhammad, accompanying him whenever Muhammad and Rafkin met. Akil was the one who scared Rafkin. He was the leader and would hold his fire. He would wait. He would know better.

Without thinking, Rafkin raised the shotgun and loosed several booming blasts in the general direction of his adversaries.

Suppressive fire. Cover and conceal. Reposition; keep the enemy unaware of your intentions. He remembered that much. It came back to him instinctively, and he marveled at the brain's ability to recall such scattered mental debris. He was alone and feeling it.

Rafkin forced himself to relax. Use your training. Take the man on the left by any practical means; secondarily, move on the other two. Don't let them flank you. He coughed, rather loudly, drawing a burst of clattering automatic fire from the left.

The Skorpion was a disturbing development. Akil must have had it hidden under his coat. Rafkin had thought it would be pistols all the way. It was time for a plan. He found he could lie supine behind the planter with a minimum of four feet of cover behind the toes of his boots. He belly-crawled as far as he could, to the right, without breaking cover. They would assume he was still in the center.

Rafkin heard shouting in their guttural, throat-clearing tongue. He took the opportunity, poking his head out on the right side of the planter, exposing himself to the nose and no further. It would take one hell of a shot to hit an eight-inch circular target, flush to the ground as he was. Of course, if they saw him, they might figure it out and rush him from both sides. Akil and his Skorpion arriving suddenly on the left, was an unappealing proposition.

Rafkin looked up. The pig on the right was in relief, bathed in the display-box lights of a men's clothier. A nine-millimeter, or maybe a .45 dangled from his hand. Ten shots? Could be up to fifteen if it was a .40. The man had wasted six or seven of them when Rafkin came through the door and when he had coughed.

The pig hurtled gibberish across the corridor to Akil, who overrode him, or so it sounded. Rakfin's neck began to ache. He lay his forehead down on the cool marble. Their shouting faded. Rafkin lifted his chin from the floor. He had excellent visibility all the way up the right-hand side of the corridor.

There was a complication. In the B. Dalton, next up from the clothier, a police officer crouched behind a rack of cookbooks and self-help hokum. She weighed a minimum of 200 pounds, towering nearly five feet tall. She was puffing like a beluga, eyes wide with fear or panic. Rafkin focused his energies into the center of his forehead and tried to send the knowledge over to her that there was a threat in the Banks store next to her. He could not tell if she received it.

He stood, yelling *Allahu Ahkbar*! in hopes of confusing them. Wheeling left, he emptied the shotgun in a howling frenzy across the top of the planter. Dozens of pellet holes appeared magically in the stucco, but the target had the presence of mind to flatten himself against the doorway. Rafkin was exposed for almost five seconds. He was paying no attention to the other two. He was waiting for Akil to venture a peek.

Rafkin saw motion on his right. The cop emerged shakily from her hidey-hole. She assumed the Weaver stance with her left shoulder against the jamb. She leveled her pistol at Rafkin. "*Hold it right there, police!*"

Could she not see what was hanging around his neck? Was she blind? Rafkin grasped the policeman's shield by a corner and stretched it out on the chain, showing her. The policewoman closed her eyes and the bang of her pistol stunned him—the Arabs were firing as well, banging away as plaster chinked off the face of the planter.

Rafkin hugged the floor. He would wait her out. The shotgun was at port arms, flat on the floor. He could have killed her easily. But he wouldn't. Couldn't.

Akil had no such compunction. From the left corner, Rafkin saw Akil raise his arm as a burst stitched the wall behind the cop. She went down, a crimp of pain on her pasty moon face. Rafkin skittered behind the planter before Akil could shoot him too, calmly stuffing in fresh shells. Reloaded, he slithered over to his extreme left. He emptied the shotgun at the façade of a nail salon. He saw the sign as he stood and fired, incredibly exposed for an incredibly long time. They were talking again—getting organized.

Then there was silence…relative silence. He could hear the cop sobbing softly to herself and praising Jesus. He took that as a good sign. He looked over at the clothier. The man on the right, the one that was just there, was gone. Maybe he had sprinted up the line while Rafkin was engaged with Akil. Maybe he was trying to flank him.

The cop still whimpered. He must remember to watch her. She had shot at him once, and he meant to disabuse her of that notion should it strike again.

Pain, he thought. Her face was the color of masking tape. Better than shock. Their eyes met. Rafkin again showed her his badge. She blinked, shaking her head, as if to say she was such an idiot.

There was a broad, dark stain on the drapery of her pants. Shot in the ass. It made sense, really; her body was eighty percent ass. She spoke rapidly into the radio gadget on her shoulder, and, silently, Rafkin pointed his finger north, toward their new position. She nodded vigorously and he was off, crabbing from the Old Navy, across the diagonal into a Justice for Girls, where he took up position behind a stainless steel rack of halter-tops.

There was a sound, a quiet sob, followed by another. He swiveled his head slowly, scanning the rear of the store. Women and children, perhaps two dozen of them, huddled around the dressing closets. There were doubtless more inside the closets themselves. Not enough room in there for everyone. It struck him then that he had not seen a soul during the gunfight and subsequent maneuvers—only the terrorist swine and the policewoman. The shoppers could not have all made it out in time. Now he understood.

They were taking cover in the rear of the stores. Rafkin counted six, pleading to him with their eyes, and he held out his detective's shield, boldly grinning. A bug-eyed woman whimpered like a child. The woman next to her placed her hand over her mouth to stifle the awful sound. She looked at Rafkin and smiled.

It had been a bad idea, chasing them in here. There were too many civilians, and he felt it, the power receding. He could see his death, and then he drew from his confidence. The feeling passed.

It was time to move.

The first of the sirens howled as he left the halters behind, skidding across no man's land to the cover of another planter. The siren split into the sound of two or more. The cavalry was coming.

*

Miriam Golden crouched behind the counter of the Cinnabon franchise, her eyes just above the lip of the glass. What kind of luck was this? She happened to be here for one of those Big Buns she liked; they were $3.95, an outrage, but they were really delicious. She'd planned on taking it home and making a cup of decaf—the regular repeated on her—and then she could have her nap watching that jerk on *The Price is Right.* He always put her to sleep, unlike the old guy whom she had watched for years and just loved.

Terrorists! Right here in her mall!

Miriam was not alone. They were five in all, trapped in the Cinnabon when the shooting started. Some middle-aged man who looked as if he might have a heart attack, was sitting on the floor in the rear of the store behind the big side counters. There was a severe woman in a charcoal suit, obviously some kind of executive. Miriam thought she looked like a pencil sharpener. The little girl who worked here, she had not seen since the whole thing began. The Puerto Rican guy next to her was talking on his phone. She could tell he was Puerto Rican by that pantyhose thingy on his head.

*

With the coming of the sirens, Rafkin realized the magnitude of his error. He should have never pressed it this far. He should have left them after that silly restaurant. The problem was no longer just the Arabs.

He should run for it. Right now. Hit one of the side exits, grab Paul and be at LaGuardia within the hour. But the police were sure to capture the Arabs. They would buy advantage with their exposure of Rafkin. Hobson's choice.

To hell with it. The power had yet to desert him, and it would be difficult to reach another exit without having to fight his way through the enemy. Rafkin smiled back at the woman and hauled ass into an Ikea store, thirty yards up the line.

Something to the right gave Rafkin pause. He saw movement behind the counter in the Cinnabon. Citizens, three or four of them, and they were perilously close to Akil.

He saw the ambush clearly, poked his head around the corner of the Ikea entrance, seventy meters south of the food court. Akil was to the left, half his body exposed around a scaled-down version of the Corinthian column, five meters aside a fancified taco stand. Another one huddled deep on the right behind the glass counter of an establishment called Chicago Pizza. The heavy glass of the warmers might protect him. Rafkin would have to blast his way through. Akil and his Skorpion would be lagging in the center rear, deep in the shadows. He would wait for his moment, see which way Rafkin was going and then strike. Rafkin would just have to be faster.

The one on the right, then. Fire from the hip as he crossed the gap to close the distance. Immediately turn to the one on the left and then react as the point man broke cover. Rafkin constructed his plan, deciding on a count of three.

*

Sid was gone, for three years now. His heart just gave out one day, and Miriam missed him sometimes. Not always, but sometimes.

One of the few items left from his estate that she hadn't sold or junked, was the revolver Sid kept in a cigar box in the closet. He always said it was for the race riots, when they would be crawling up the lawn with machetes in their teeth. She thought he was full of shit then, and she still did.

But when the Towers fell, now that there was a real threat, well, she hadn't survived Sid by being stupid. She loaded the gun with one of those round plastic bullet thingies and carried it with her whenever she left the apartment, which was not often. She could hear them jabbering in Arabic, unfortunately so like the Hebrew she had been forced to learn as a girl and had mostly forgotten.

The Puerto Rican man had a knee on the floor. He was speaking intensely to the business lady and waving his hands a lot. Miriam began to think she did not want to die here in this silly mall for wont of a cinnamon bun. She'd had three meager years of peace without Sid's badgering, and there were things she wanted to accomplish.

She risked another peek. The policeman with the badge hanging around his neck was down on one knee in a furniture store. She thought there might be a terrorist on her right but she couldn't be sure. All she had to go by was the noise when they fired those terrible weapons. The one she could see, the ugly man with the mustache, leaned in the recesses of a doorway, maybe twenty yards from the policeman on the same side of the mall. The policeman would be unable to see the mustache man. Miriam was turning to tell the Puerto Rican kid about the danger and that maybe there was some way they could shout a warning, when the policeman broke and began to run across the atrium.

*

Rafkin advanced into the corridor, fully exposed, pumping buckshot furiously at the man behind the pizza counter. The tactic seemed to be working. The pizza guy ducked, held down by Rafkin's fire. He had only to make it to the other side…

Rafkin felt the heat in his back before he heard the discharge of the weapon. He sensed the man behind him and knew his move was fatal. He'd thought Akil was far back, down the middle.

He fell, dropping the shotgun as a ricochet skipped and punched through his foot. Pain, hot and blinding, burned into him until it felt as if his entire left side would burst into flames. He dropped hard and flat, onto the cool of the floor. The shotgun lay a meter away, like a promise. He grabbed for the weapon as the pizza man moved on him, walking warily. It was too far. Rafkin's foot was shredded. He was going to die here. The dirty little pig approached, pistol extended. Akil had been just a little too well concealed. His seven thousand days were one thing—to have the brilliance of the future revealed to him so close before death; it was beyond unfair.

*

Miriam yelped as the policeman was shot and the business lady was at her side, yanking a dainty little pearl-handled automatic from her bag. The Puerto Rican came next, wielding a dubious pistol with some lettering spray-stencilled across the grips. He rested the thin little barrel across the top of the counter, as the terrorist from their right appeared, walking carefully toward the fallen cop.

She squinted down the sight, pointing with the little notchy thing on the end. The slinky bastard wouldn't stand still. It was making things difficult.

Miriam could see him hollering something in Arabic at the policeman. She licked her lips… and pulled the trigger. Six hundred foot/pounds of recoil blew her backward, plastic shoes skidding across four inches of linoleum, yet she stayed on her feet, heels digging in and scratching crazy scuff marks across the floor. She'd broken a heel.

The others opened fire. Miriam shrieked with delight. Now, having experienced the violence of firing the weapon for the first time since Sid passed—God rest his soul—she grew instantly confident. "*Oh, you meshugannah sons of bitches*," she muttered under her breath, ripping off five quick rounds, yanking the trigger in rapid succession.

Astonishingly, one of the bastards screamed and fell down. Miriam was sure it was she who had hit him. She cackled—*this beat the hell out of canasta with Eleanor and that dingbat Pearl Gladstein, who was always complaining about some new ailment or other like she was eighty-five, when she was only seventy-three*—and after fumbling a little, she found the thing Sid showed her on the side of the revolver.

She released the catch, dumping the smoking brass out onto the floor.

She didn't know anyone who had passed in the Towers. She was too old, and all her people were gone, but she had not been this angry since Pearl fucking Harbor. The guy next to her was yelling in that awful Spanish and blazing away like Steve McQueen in *Bullitt*. She turned to him and shouted as loud as she could to be heard over the racket, "Who's got ammo?"

*

Akil saw the policeman go down with a minor wound, the shotgun a meter from his outstretched hand. He crept out into the food court, as Behrooz approached the fallen infidel. Akil began to relax.

His smile evaporated, becoming instead, a look of puzzlement. Behrooz had been a mere five meters from ending this when a flash of light crossed his vision. He was told the New Yorkers would be unarmed. Americans had many guns, yes. But not in New York.

*

Miriam finally figured out the speed loader. She spun right and fired. The barrel leapt upward in recoil as she aimed with great care. She was old and weak, causing her to pull the trigger instead of jerking it. As a result, she was firing with accuracy, unlike her fellow New Yorkers who were chewing up a great deal of plaster and plate glass with little to show for it.

The guy from the back showed up, looking a lot better. He introduced himself as Steve as the lead flew and the others glared at him, but Miriam missed all of this; she never bothered to look, smoke drifting laterally out of her Colt. Steve joined the battle, grabbing a handful of cinnamon buns and proceeding to throw them at the terrorists while shouting a rainbow of curse words.

Miriam saw the one with the mustache making a break for it.

She let him have it. A round or two went into the Mexican place and bowls of taco chips and spicy salsa flew as if in some Yucatan tornado. Her hair frizzed out in a static electrical halo behind her head. She rested her arms on a stack of fresh cinnamon buns, smearing sugary toppings all over her coat and she looked just a little bit insane.

*

It was the old woman who drew his greatest ire. It was always the Jews. They should have driven the aircraft into Tel Aviv and Jerusalem. Akil would have welcomed the war that followed. The woman was older than his own mother. She was firing a weapon that Akil himself, coveted. It was a Colt Python, he knew, .357 magnum, its six-inch barrel giving it accuracy uncommon among handguns. And it was heavy. Seven kilograms fully loaded. More cannon than pistol. It was a wonder the weight of the barrel alone didn't tip the Jew woman over onto her head.

He backed away into the alcove. The Jew had deadly accuracy. He could actually feel the heat of the bullets as they passed by his ear and clothing. He was missing badly at this range. They were low on ammunition in any case. By the time Behrooz' body hit the floor, he knew the situation was lost.

Taweel, also, had seen that they were outnumbered. He dashed over to Akil, gamely loosing a number of rounds at the enemy. His bullets blew a variety of two-pound buns into the air, where they spun like clay pigeons.

The New Yorkers reacted. They turned like a line of dragoons, burying the walls behind and around them in lead. The old woman screamed like a savage as she fired, the great, flat crack of her Colt drowning out the smaller caliber weapons. Akil glanced at Taweel…the exit in his eyes.

*

RAFKIN LAID his head onto the cool of the tiles, looking to the sky. The ceiling of the mall was a domed construction of wire mesh and turquoise glass, similar to a greenhouse or atrium. The light was a reflection. The sun had refracted off the glass as his saviors had raised their weapons. He felt the bubble, closing around him. It barely hurt at all.

Chapter 19

"YOU ANYWHERE NEAR that fuckin' mall?"

"No," Gomez replied. "Hell, I don't know." He had to hold the phone away and *shush* Sacco several times so he could stay abreast of the happenings on the screen. From what he could gather, the chaos in the mall involved some shady Middle-Eastern types and a pair of undercover cops. There was word that the good citizens of New Jersey were armed and trading powder with the terrorists. Sacco loved the idea. Gomez was not so sure.

"I'm kind of in the middle of something," Gomez mumbled, snatching a glimpse of Viisky's legs. *Russian my ass, like she's from Hollywood or something.*

Sacco hesitated. He was leading up to something, "Here's the thing. Davidson says fifty guys is enough, but I just don't see how we can cover these ports and the treatment plants with fifty guys. You have any idea how big a water treatment plant is? And there's like, nothing there. Two rent-a-cops sleeping in a guard shack. A cyclone fence you could cut with garden shears. A teenager could drop a gallon of rat poison in there in about five seconds flat."

If nothing else, Sacco had livened up. Gomez had begun to worry about him. There's nothing like World War III to bring a man up from the abyss.

"They would need something bigger than that," Gomez said. "It would have to be a tanker truck, something like that." A beat of silence on the line. Sacco was edging toward revolt, Gomez thought. Hard to blame him.

The picture on the screen showed an impromptu press conference outside the mall. A bald, haggard cop addressed the media with the mall in the background. There were a minimum of two dozen microphones shoved in his face. A second cop stood beside him, squinting into the lights.

Sacco was saying, "I don't know how long we can keep the lid on this thing. Davidson says he knows all these guys. He swears 'em to secrecy, but eventually, somebody's gonna find out."

"It was just in case," Gomez said. "I wasn't asking you to defend them, just check things out."

"You decide yet whether this thing is for real?"

Gomez lit up, "I know it is."

"Then you have to tell them," Sacco said, meaning it was time to take the matter upstairs, through the normal chain of command. "If you have some evidence, something to show 'em, it's time to blow the lid off."

"I need until Monday. That's thirty-six hours. Tell Davidson the same thing. I have a couple errands to run up here, then I'm coming back to DC."

"Just remember, I'll have to start with Kessler. By the time I get past him to somebody who'll do something, it could all be over."

Gomez was keeping one eye on the tube. That mall deal looked like a helluva mess.

"This is the heart of the matter," Gomez said, stalling Sacco. "It's going to take some time to get an official presence covering those facilities." His thinking in the first place—duty.

"I've been thinking about the Russian woman, obviously." Sacco wasn't convinced. "You have any idea when?"

Gomez knew what he was asking—when Gomez would know when. "Not yet."

"Yeah, but when?" Sacco pressed.

"I'll let you know."

A buzzing erupted in the crowd around the bar. People had left their bar stools, an act that under most circumstances would require a meteor falling into Central Park. They bunched up around the big-screen, getting the word. The armed attackers in the mall had been positively ID'ed as Arabic.

"Looks like we got a run on Arabs," said Sacco, not sounding broken-hearted.

"Yeah?"

"Something else might tie into this mall thing," Sacco yawned. "Some chick is jogging this morning—apparently there's this road runs right alongside the Hudson. She finds this head in a bag. No body, just the head. Talk about comedy."

Gomez did not reply. Viisky had returned from the *ladies* and sat down gingerly on her side of the booth. She could hold her liquor. Not what he wanted.

"So, anyway, she finds this head in a Henry's bag. Bureau Intel says it's a terrorist. The Arabic expert says the head belonged to Muhammad al bunga bunga or whatever. We had a file on this piece of shit. They got a Paramus address. Apparently, he's the public face for some big deal in the Fatwahti al Hussein, an offshoot of Iraqi Al Qaeda.

"Yeah, I saw the head thing," Gomez replied. "So between that and this mall thing and what you told me..."

"You thinking vigilante?"

"What do *you* think it means?" Gomez asked, holding up a finger to Viisky, to tell her he would only be a moment.

"Could be," Sacco said. "They're cleaning up their standby assets, or punishing the ones who were supposed to go on September the eleventh and didn't."

"Or Miss Viisky is telling the truth, and the Russians are sweeping up their stray Arabs. They've got more to lose."

Sacco chewed on that one for a minute. "Still could be a vigilante," he said. "Some nutbag going after Arabs. It wouldn't surprise me, with the Towers and all."

"A vigilante would have to get damned lucky to happen on this Muhammad character," Gomez said. "Paramus has about thirty thousand Arab-American citizens. It would be more likely that he'd nail some innocent American who happened to be of Arabic descent."

There was a pause on the line. "You know, for a minute there, you sort of sounded like Senator Smeal." Sacco sounded worried.

Gomez mentally slapped his forehead. *Good God!*

"It's true, though," he said. "We shouldn't make the mistake of lumping every Arab-American in with these scumbags." The pit was growing deeper. Sacco would never let him off the hook.

It *was* true, though. Gomez said he'd call back.

He folded the phone. He had not expected his investigation to last forever. Still, he was satisfied that he had done what he needed to do. He wouldn't hide it. He would tell Kessler and the Assistant Director and OPR and whomever else, that he had done what he thought necessary, without overburdening the Investigations Division.

The barroom grew quiet. Gomez noticed that Spasski's head was lolling in a pool of something that looked like vomit. Could be bar nuts.

An image of Ashley Bubier appeared on the screen, thrusting a microphone into the face of the bald cop. A drunk yelled out something lewd and was told to shut up.

"Can you confirm any civilian injuries?"

"I think we got lucky on this one," the sergeant said. Bubier asked again about casualties. She was palpably disappointed. There would be no grieving relatives to ask how they felt, after their loved ones got cut in half by a machine-gun.

"We've heard there were New Yorkers in there, shooting it out with the terrorists. Can you confirm that?"

In the background, to the left, an intense uniformed copper held his hands apart the width of a large submarine sandwich. He was speaking to someone off-camera. "So it's this old bag, right? She had a cannon the size of my di…" The guy had turned away, thankfully. Gomez could have told Karyn Macklin. That's what you get when you go live.

While the spokesman struggled with Bubier, a plainclothesman rushed up, unmindful of the banks of microphones sticking up like a microphone garden. The bar was utterly silent, and they heard him shout, big as life on national television. "They got that Rourke kid out back of the food court. Blew his heart out. We gotta get that fuckin' helicopter over the woods behind the mall."

The plainclothes guy ran off. The spokesman looked back at the cameras. He began to speak and looked like he'd forgotten what he was going to say. He changed direction, speaking about the heroism of Officer Stokes and Detective Tinker.

The hand-held swiveled, targeting a sandy-haired man with an Eisenhower jacket around his shoulders. He was being led from the scene. The lower legs of his trousers were soaked in blood. Detective Tinker, presumably.

The sergeant turned away from the podium. A hand-held caught him sitting on the curb, his face crumpled in his hands. The camera zoomed.

"Is terrible," Viisky said. She looked like she meant it.

Spasski said, "*Ghung*?" Shit-faced.

Gomez couldn't decide what to make of any of it. The faces in the bar went back to their cocktails and lies. The news was over, Gomez saw. The ballgame too. The Mets had lost to the Braves in extra innings. TBS was running the James Bond format, where they show every one of the movies back to back. Spasski was interested. He leaned his chin on the table, watching alternately with one eye closed and then the other.

"We will now play game," Viisky said, eyeing Gomez and changing the subject. Her color was high, eyes a little glassy. Getting there, Gomez thought. He just hoped he could keep up.

"Is called *Stoi!*" The game was very simple, an absolute requirement since each player would be blind stinking drunk within five minutes of the outset. Gomez brought his wrist close to his face. Nine-thirty by his watch. They had been in the bar for just under three hours. She should be hammered by now.

Chantal came over to the table to see how they were doing. Viisky demanded another bottle—a good sign.

"Jason should have never given you that one," Chantal replied. She fingered a chain around her neck. "What'd you do? Promise him a little something?" Viisky gave her that look that can only pass between one woman and another.

Gomez found his creds. He slapped them on the table.

"Federal Bureau of Investigation." He had run the words together a little, smoothed out the syllabic breaks. "I am interrogating this man." He poked a finger over at Spasski, who was listing heavily. Spasski must have heard Gomez refer to him, because his head snapped upward, like a trout hitting a jig.

Chantal looked at Spasski dubiously, "I don't think so."

"Do you have children?" Spasski was fully awake, and leering. He must be seeing something that Gomez did not.

"No."

"Of course not," Spasski hid a belch in his hand. "You're a beautiful woman. Your skin is like butter."

"We've already killed that one," Gomez said reasonably, pointing at the bottle. "What's the harm of another?"

"You're staying here?" Chantal asked.

"These Saratoga Rooms!" Viisky crowed. Chantal left, muttering something out of earshot.

Gomez studied Viisky like a painting. She was about to say something. Suddenly, she brought her hand to her mouth, "Oh! Where is *pussy*?"

Gomez was confused. What the…? Then he got it.

Spasski had disappeared completely, tipping over prone into the fetal position on the seat of the booth. *Spasski* was the pussy. Gomez raised a finger, pointing downward. The confusion evaporated and they began to laugh.

"Where'd you get that word?"

"I watch the television while you are on phone. Cartoon Network."

"Ahhh."

Chantal returned with two large water glasses filled with a clear liquid.

She grabbed the dead soldier from the table, laid it sideways on her tray. "That's it. No more."

Gomez thanked her with a pair of twenties. He slipped his hand into that of his Vischka; his little pumpkin. They sat in silence for a moment. She made no move to pull her hand away, growing serious as she studied him. He returned the look and they were, for a brief moment, lovers, dining in moonlight on the Seine.

The booth shook. Spasski sat up. He was a drunken monster, wild-eyed, hair akimbo. He pointed at the television. Sean Connery was preparing to receive inferred fellatio. Kim Novak bent toward Connery, who seemed to feel he deserved it. Novak leaned farther. Cut to commercial. "A license to kill. Get it? She has a fucking license!" Spasski was sort of laughing and sort of crying and his hair looked like spiders were weaving webs in it. He was attracting attention from the people on the stools around them.

"Get a hold of yourself," Gomez said, without much enthusiasm. It was time to get him back to the rooms.

"She'll kill you too," Spasski was no longer laughing. He was maudlin, weeping. "She's a fucking *ubijca!* It means…"

"I know what it means," Gomez said. He dismissed Spasski, and the word *ubijca*, which he knew to mean assassin. Viisky had told him at various times that she was FSB, SVR, and that ridiculous arugula thing. Now Spasski said she was an assassin. Gomez did not think she was any of those things. He was pretty sure she was a terrorist.

Spasski moaned. Gomez gave him a shove. His eyes clouded and he tipped back over, his head banging hard against the wood trim. It would leave a bruise and add to his headache in the morning. Gomez did not look at Viisky. He watched Spasski, whose face was mottled, the color of a pomegranate. Gomez worried briefly about strokes, aneurysms, and he chided himself for his thickness.

A license. He knew how to get to Rafkin.

Chapter 20

"IT IS THE EXHAUSTION that I feel," Viisky slurred. It was about damn time. Gomez was feeling kind of topped-out himself.

"Now," she started to giggle, "how to carry shit-for-brain?" Good question. He sure as heck wasn't going to carry Spasski all the way to the elevators. He saw Chantal standing at the bar. She had her hands on her hips, glaring.

Gomez thought for a moment and kicked Spasski as hard as he could underneath the table. The old man had insisted on *mas futbol*, so he knew to draw the kick from the muscles of the thigh and lower back. Spasski squealed a little and jerked up into a sitting position.

"Wha? Okay, okay, I'm okay." There was a bruise forming where he'd bonked his head on the booth. Gonna be a beauty.

"Time for nighty-night." They each took an arm and marched him through the doors.

In the elevator, Gomez said to Viisky in lumbering Russian, "What did Felix tell you to do with the Vyydraat when you found them?"

She smiled at him drowsily, not answering. She closed her eyes and leaned her head against the wall. The bell dinged, announcing their floor.

They threw Spasski onto the pull-out. Someone had been kind enough to put chocolates on the pillow. They would be flat and mushy in the morning. Gomez didn't want them to go to waste.

He reached under Spasski's head to retrieve the chocolate and she was on him, wrapping her arms around him and planting kisses on his stubble. She murmured sweet nothings; in Russian, they sounded like an executioner's song. He guided her over to the bed, holding onto her with one hand while he pulled back the coverlet with the other. Not entirely gently, he plopped her on the side closest to the door and covered her up. She did not resist.

Thinking it was a little warm, he went into the sitting area and turned the thermostat back down. He smiled, remembering Viisky on the chaise. He went out onto the balcony and lit a cigarette. It tasted sweet and nasty with all the vodka, so he flipped it over into the street, recalling a quintessential New York phrase: *Tastes like assholes.*

Ten minutes passed. It would take an air raid to rouse her. He opened the door and crossed the room to the foyer, where he had seen her stash her laptop in a cubby in the wall. He picked up the machine, carrying it back out onto the balcony.

The battery had a good charge. The startup screen came up and it was of course, in Cyrillic. There were a series of asterisks in the box intended for a password. She had clicked on the option to maintain her password on startup. Really dumb.

Gomez stared at the screen, befuddled. Viisky was being kind when she told him that his Russian was excellent. He had learned the language as a tool with which to defeat his enemies, not as a social device. And reading a language was always much more difficult than speaking it. He would do what he always did. Begin with the beginning.

The start menu worked like his own, and he slid the cursor around, having some difficulty with the trackball in his condition. The symbol for *Word* was also the same. He clicked on it, introducing a series of files. He sighed and began to click things at random. Hoping that they were in order of most recently accessed, he went through them one at a time, opening them and finding all sorts of gobbledygook.

The first file contained a mish-mash of maps, ranging from Boston to Port of Baltimore, centering on the coastal areas. There was an addendum to each, covering what seemed to be logistical folderol. The second was a lengthy list of names, the one she had shown him in the hotel in Maryland. On it went, and after a time, he slipped into a fugue state. Staring at it, not quite knowing what he was looking at, or for.

Eventually, he went back to the maps. They did not look like water treatment plants or oil refineries, which should have giant reservoirs and massive tubes set up like log flume rides.

The first diagram was a building, square in design. Wide corridors split rooms approximately equal in dimension. Gomez counted thirty rooms total. He multiplied by what he thought was the number of floors, which was two. There was a suite of what should be offices, tucked into the near corner of the building. A small portico terminated in an equally small plaza. There was a circle at the terminus and the draftsman had done a quick slash of what would reside there. It was a flag.

So it was a government building.

Gomez didn't think the treatment plants would have a flag out front. He didn't think they were even federal facilities. Nor would they want to advertise their existence. Water treatment plants were targets of opportunity for vandals, long before the terrorists had come onto the stage.

It was the large outbuilding that he had noticed, peeling off from the main structure. He flipped back to the main page. A room of the same size sat apart from the main building, similar in every way to the outbuilding, with one exception. There were big, double doors, like the kind you would need if you wanted to move in heavy equipment—or maybe, pallets. Shit. He couldn't figure it.

How could there be more than one sizeable terror op going on at the same time? If there were, then Al Qaeda was going to be even more effective than he'd thought. But maybe there could be. What a month ago would seem outrageous and beyond bizarre, was now something people could look at and somehow accept. A pair of thousand-foot buildings being rammed by loaded airliners changed a lot of perspectives.

Gomez closed *Word* and *Adobe.* He was about to do the same with the whole stupid machine when he realized there were icons—just like American computers!

After cursing himself, he reviewed the icons, of which there were few. It was very easy, and plain as the day is long. One of the icons held the name *Lebed Oktober.* October Swan. Fucking melodrama. It opened without a password, and again he wondered if Viisky was more clueless than he with computers.

There were tabs, and the few he looked at were hopelessly long, page after page of writing that he could never decipher. He opened the tab on the end. The tab was labeled *Liaison Paboyne.* Gomez thought it meant something like "action liaison" or "working friends."

The name at the top was Vladislav Rubicoff. Beside the name was an address and telephone number in Chesapeake, Virginia. Gomez would bet his shirt that it was Stuart Rafkin. Viisky hadn't lied when she told him she did not know Rafkin's latest address. Maybe. Probably. Below was a paragraph or three that looked like a bio, of sorts. Gomez ignored it. He really didn't care.

Spasski's name and bio were next, conspicuously separate from the main list of clowns they'd used back in DC. And there was a third name Gomez did not recognize. Boy, he couldn't wait to meet yet another Vyydraat.

He went inside to get his cell from his jacket pocket. Smelled like jet fuel in here. He hoped it was Spasski.

Back out onto the balcony, he tried Kessler first. It didn't seem right to wake Davidson. He would let Davidson know after he had Rafkin.

The phone rang through to the message beep. Gomez set the hook, letting out just a touch of line, informing Kessler that he was onto something that related to the Eleventh and Al Qaeda. He would keep Kessler informed all the way. He would almost certainly need assistance. He held his fingers crossed behind his back for most of it.

Gomez cocked his head, thinking. Something he'd missed. The laptop was still sitting open, an invitation—the synapses fired in his addled head. He realized what he had just seen and ignored, probably because it was too much.

He put down the phone and walked back over to pull up the list of files under "Recent Documents." There were a dozen or so, but it was the bottom three that had caught his eye and had taken so long to register. The files were labeled in bold and italics. They were not in Cyrillic. It was a language few Americans recognized, but many soon would.

The files were in Arabic.

Chapter 21

FELIKS PULLED UP to a stoplight. The fiasco at River Mills sent him into a rage so profound that he pounded on the steering wheel with his fists until a button popped from his crisp white shirt. He didn't notice that he was emitting an animal growling sound and cursing in two languages, until he gained control. He was breathing heavily. He looked at his hands atop the wheel. They were liver-spotted, shaking mildly. Not something to be trifled with at his age. This would not be a good time for a stroke.

To his left, motion caught his eye. A frumpy woman in a powder blue Taurus couldn't help but witness his tirade. She had disturbing orange hair, and she held her hand to her mouth in a ridiculous display of shock and titillation.

Feliks' eyes burned into her. She pissed him off, with her hair and her stupid Taurus. Feliks mouthed the words "*stupid bitch.*" Not the best words for lip reading, but he knew what it did to women. Smiling a wicked smile, he began to scream it at her.

She leaned back against her door, arms up around her face in defensive posture. "*Stupid bitch, stupid bitch, stupid bitch.*" She may not have understood what Feliks was saying, but she did understand that he was insane. She looked quickly both ways, then blew the light.

The light turned green. Feliks accelerated and remembered an adage: The cleverest plans do not survive the first moments of battle.

He looked in the rearview to check the condition of his blood pressure. A few drops of saliva glistened on his chin. He wiped them off with the collar of his ruined shirt. If he didn't catch another red light he could make it in an hour.

*

Akil ducked as the helicopter shot low over his head. There was no need; it was just a helicopter and the woods provided fantastic cover. He looked up to see a canopy of green, something like ten meters of vine and leaves. He walked quickly through the oak, cherry, and many other species of trees that he couldn't identify and didn't give a shit about. The helicopters reminded him of something…an eight-month exercise with the Sheik in Pakistan.

He admitted to himself that he had gotten used to the creature comforts here. Eight months of sand and dust had seemed like a thousand years. On reflection, he might not be as ready for Paradise as Taweel and Behrooz had been. But who gave greater weight to the cause? Better Taweel than he. He was needed.

Akil was thirsty. According to his Swatch, he'd been walking and jogging through the forest for over an hour. He had not heard the sounds of the helicopters in some time. He tucked his hands into his pockets as he walked along the side of the road and looked up just in time to see the Cadillac roll up behind him.

*

Feliks was a man in the 1930s sense of the word—before women conquered the Western world. He was tall and thin and a snap-brim fedora would not have looked out of place…an umbrella, even. He was an English gentleman, without the accent.

They'd driven together, saying little, to the house in Paramus, where they'd found the dead boy and the dead man in the living room. Getting low on foot soldiers. Akil had followed Feliks in his '92 Mustang, with what was left of Mohammed in the trunk. Feliks made Akil park the Mustang in the rear of the carport, in case someone had taken note of it. It was now almost four in the morning.

He was on the phone in a spare bedroom he'd converted into an office. Talking to the girl, Akil thought, as he waited in the den.

Akil had a surprise for Feliks, something that was sure to make his stock rise. He knew something the girl didn't.

"Amazing. It's all going to work," Akil spoke in New Jersey American, natural enough, for that was where he had gone to school on a student visa, which had expired seven years ago.

"Not yet it isn't." The old man joined him on the sofa. "You shouldn't be here."

Feliks banged his pipe out against an ashtray. His thick, gray hair was in place and, as Akil answered, he stood up and backed into another room, motioning for Akil to come with him. Akil thought Feliks was reliving the spy days and saw himself as Kim Philby.

Akil pulled a pack of cigarettes from his denim jacket, his hand steady as a rock. Feliks looked as if he wanted to tell him not to smoke—hypocritical, under the circumstances. Feliks lit a pipe. A rich, woodland aroma filled the rumpus room.

"I was going to go to the mosque in Passaic," Akil said. They shared a smile. Neither mentioned what a bad idea that would have been.

Feliks picked up a remote from a pile of them. They were heaped there like an assortment of magic wands, and he tuned to CNN. Together they watched a replay of the press conference outside the River Mills Mall. This was a signal that Feliks knew all about Akil's adventures.

Feliks did not inquire as to the health of Akil's comrades. "I get the impression you intend to survive."

Akil did not respond. He was aware of Feliks' reputation. Akil kept his hand in his jacket, tight against the grips of his pistol. Feliks might think that all was lost and wish to tie up loose ends.

"I have been hurting the Russians for a long time. I like to think I played a role in—well, never mind." Feliks coughed; a wet, rattling sound.

Feliks paced, his slippers making a rasping sound on the carpet.

"I thought I was finished, to be honest with you. Until this… opportunity came along."

Akil listened; a skill he learned in Pakistan with the mullahs. One did not, at twenty-seven years of age, interrupt when an elder in the movement was speaking.

Feliks seemed to have come to some conclusion. He rapped his pipe into the ashtray and resumed pacing, patiently. "I have served for fifty years. This is my last chance." Feliks was on the verge of something. As Akil listened, it dawned on him that he—not Feliks—held all the cards.

"Let me ask you, do you think at my age another chance like this will come along?"

Akil allowed the silence to grow.

"I thought not." Feliks reached for the remote, turned off the television. "We must continue. Do you understand?"

Akil nodded and then made his play.

"I want the money."

Feliks did not react. Akil was impressed. He watched the old man process. He considered killing him, feeling capable of it. But there were problems with that. Feliks might not keep the money here; probably he did not. It was in a bank somewhere, or in cash in some secret hideout. Even if it was in the house, he might never find it. The sad fact was he needed Feliks—as Feliks needed him.

Feliks squinted over his pipe.

"Fine. You are corrupted. I have no problem with that." Feliks didn't even look disappointed. "You can have it. All of it."

"How much is left?"

"Two million." Feliks smiled. It came off as strained. Feliks was a purist. He really believed that one day, all the world would worship at the feet of Islam.

Akil had not expected that much money. It was a magnificent turn of fortune when he found that he could not sleep, went out into the yard and found the head…

"But first, you have to help me finish this."

Akil was already nodding his agreement. It was a fair price.

"Where will you go?" Feliks asked.

"Someplace cold."

"Someplace warm then?"

"No, you idiot. Someplace like Greenland…Iceland, a place where they won't look for me." He didn't have to explain to Feliks just who would be looking for him.

Akil was still wired from the debacle at the mall. Akhmed and the policeman were the first two human beings he had killed. It was still not out of the question to kill the old man. Right here, right now.

"I just don't see how it can be done without more men."

"Oh, there are plenty of men. We haven't sat on our behinds while you were in Pakistan, you know. There are always more."

"Just so you understand, I won't go down with them. You can have your victory. I'll take mine." An arm's length respect was building between them, akin to a father and the son who has chosen a different path, and is successful.

There was work to do.

"Go get the head…and the rest of it," Feliks ordered. There was an uncomfortable, measurable pause.

"Don't tell me you got rid of it?"

"What if I had been stopped? The police…"

"You brought the rest of him in the trunk of your car," Feliks pointed out.

"Yes." Akil had been frightened. He had not told the others about the murder of Muhammad. They were ignorant peasants. They could panic.

He'd put the head in a box on the front seat and drove for an hour until he found a suitable dumping ground. But he'd kept the rest of it. Feliks would know what to do. He always did.

"Where?"

"The Hudson. They'll never find it." The old man had had years to practice intimidation. It was all in the eyes.

"They've already found it. Now forensics will get it and we'll be lucky if they don't identify him by tomorrow."

The old man rubbed his gray stubble thoughtfully. He was aware that Akil had designs on command responsibility, now a reality with the death of Muhammad. Akil was tough and practical—traits, Feliks suspected, that were fruits of his stupidity. All points in his favor, for when they identified the remains.

"Very well. Drive around back."

*

Akil dragged the corpse past a tall privacy fence on the side of Feliks' closest neighbor, opposite the fir trees. He did not see, was unaware there existed a gaggle of electronic monitoring devices, cameras, motion sensors, and spotlights. Toward the detached garage, there was a lonely circular pattern where a pool must have once stood. Akil didn't know it, but beneath the pattern lay the remains of Feliks' wife, Marie.

Feliks had cut her throat in 1987. Nosy bitch. He told the children she'd run off with another man. Eventually, they'd somewhat believed him—not that they stopped by on holidays. Now, he would get to re-fertilize. Feliks coughed, a rickety croak from all the smoking. Akil pretended not to notice.

They buried the torso, arms, and legs of Mohammed beneath some hydrangea encircling a rotting hot tub on the back deck. Feliks made Akil chop the pieces up with an axe in the garage, mainly for his own amusement. Also, it made for a smaller hole; less time wasted digging.

The dismemberment didn't seem to bother Akil. They scrubbed the garage floor and returned to the living room.

Dawn began to rise through the single window. Deep circles were visible under Feliks' eyes.

"How did they find you at the mall, then? Chance, is it?"

Akil savored the moment. This had to be worth some points. With Rafkin alive, the original plan was back in play. The only change, of course, was that Akil would get the funds.

"Forget the police. The police couldn't ..." Akil couldn't think of a clever metaphor. He was tired and had the bodies of his comrades banging around in his head. He decided to just say it.

"It wasn't the police. It was the Russian."

CHAPTER 22

RAFKIN ARRIVED in darkness. Through the window of the cab he could see shades of gray and blue and a purplish swirling mist that reminded him of the blood of insects. It was very early morning.

His arm was in a sling. His right foot was swollen like a gourd and his rib cage felt as if a giant was squatting on him. He felt logy, medicated. He shook off the sling to discover that his arm was not broken after all. But something else was. Ribs, he thought. He could feel something crunching around in there.

The morning mist gathered about his ankles and he felt a stab of fear.

Akil had seen his face. Feliks would know it was he, Rafkin, who was eliminating his soldiers. Feliks would never stop. But he was, for the moment, free. He had Paul. There were options.

He hobbled up the cobbled steps, dragging his foot in clip-clop fashion, like a wounded horse. He liked the sound the cobbles made and he hoisted himself back down to the landing then clip-clopped his way up, once again.

It was time to run. He would not bother to kill Paul. By the time Paul reported anything, if ever, he would be out of the country. In any case, Stuart Rafkin was officially dead.

He hesitated at the door. He should get back into the cab, run off to the airport where the planes were now flying. But then,

Feliks would do what Rafkin knew he was going to do. All of those children would die and Rafkin would have been a dupe in the process. That was something he didn't think he could live with.

Paul pulled the door open almost before he had finished knocking. Paul gave Rafkin a wry glance. It was nearly dawn. Paul had seen this sort of behavior before, but he could not see in the purpling dark that Rafkin was injured. Rafkin saw the look and understood. Paul thought Rafkin had been out all night, tomcatting.

"I'm not like that," Rafkin said.

*

Cleaning his wounds was a painful, somewhat lengthy process. Paul blanched when he removed Rafkin's sneaker to see the saturated athletic sock. Rafkin sent Paul out of the bathroom, aware that some part of his foot was missing. It felt peculiar. Not painful really, just different.

Rafkin peeled off his sock, starting at the calf. When he got to the end, he found over half of his big toe and the entire, mangled second toe were lying in the sock pocket he had fashioned. He paled, feeling his gorge rise.

The feeling passed. He wadded up the whole mess, tossing it into the wastebasket. There was a roll of cotton bandage and Rafkin hurriedly wrapped his foot before Paul saw the gore. He taped the whole thing together poorly, as a husband would wrap his wife's Christmas gifts.

Paul returned, looking better. The dawn was cracking through the window behind him. Paul was backlit and appeared somehow powerful, although Rafkin knew he was not.

"I saw you on television," Paul said. It was obvious that Paul was very worried about Rafkin. He didn't spring it, like a trap. "They kept showing this old lady, over and over again. They said she was shooting at the terrorists. You were walking behind her. I had it on Tivo. I played it again and again. It was you."

"Yes," Rafkin replied, watching Paul's eyes. Paul was being very cool about the whole thing. Rafkin could see it working inside him—this man appearing, this secret agent from another land. For Paul, and men like him, this must be the equivalent of a young girl and her fantasy of a charming prince, arriving on a unicorn to take her away from the madness.

Rafkin sat back onto the edge of the tub, relating the events of the mall. His delivery was perfect, just the right amount of understatement.

Paul leaned forward, eager for the details of the escape, and Rafkin did not begrudge him his enthusiasm.

"They bought it," Rafkin said, remembering. "I had the detective's shield on a chain around my neck." He let the pause linger, watching Paul's anticipation build. " I looked like a cop. It wasn't difficult to fake the pain." He leaned his head back against the wall.

Paul touched him on the knee. "Guess what I've got?" he said, excited.

He did not wait for Rafkin's response, rushing into the bedroom and returning a moment later with his treasure. He shook a bottle, dangling it in front of Rafkin and rattling the contents.

"Percocet, baby!"

"Careful with the wine," Paul advised, shaking two pink tablets out, placing them in Rafkin's open palm. "Two is your max. I want to hear more."

Rafkin swallowed the pills, watching the gleam in Paul's eye.

"I was lying on the floor," Rafkin said. "It was pleasantly cool. There was the most beautiful skylight up in the ceiling." He looked wistfully at nothing. "I don't know how they knew the shooting was over, but all of a sudden there were dozens of cops. You know those guys in those silly black outfits?" They chuckled.

"I think they were disappointed they didn't get to kill anyone. Anyway, I just tried to stay still, not saying a word. I was on a stretcher. They threw me in an ambulance—have you ever ridden in an ambulance?"

"No."

"It wasn't bad. Lots of pillows, warm blankets; I guess they have a blanket warmer in there in case you're hypothermic or something."

"Mmmm."

Paul let Rafkin detail his story without interruption. The pills were taking effect. He was mellow…more than mellow, he was glowing. With the success of the day, the escape, the feeling of hearth and home, and the freedom he had here, he wanted the moment to last.

"I didn't know what hospital it was until I left. They wheeled me in and a nurse looked at me. I think she could tell pretty quickly that I wasn't in any danger. They brought the woman cop in too; I saw her go by on a stretcher. Hope she's okay."

"That was really nice of you," Paul said, "to think of her like that, when you were hurt yourself."

Rafkin reached over to refill both their glasses from the bottle on the coffee table. His ribs felt like a bag of broken glass.

He wondered how he was going to get the weapons out of Vineland.

"To be honest, I thought they would have exposed me before then," Rafkin smiled. "They told me the mayor was coming to see me. Guiliani." His grin widened as he remembered.

Paul scowled, and opined on King Rudy, "I think he's a big dummy."

Rafkin laughed.

"The ER was in a circle. Someone must have been badly hurt because most of the staff went rushing out into the entrance, yelling like they do on *ER*. I waited until there was only one man out in the reception area, then I walked away—right through the front door."

Rafkin's pause was perfect.

"That's brilliant!" Paul said, turning to look at Rafkin in admiration.

Paul made tea, a vomitous brew of organic herbs and suspicious-looking weeds. Rafkin could not deny him, so great was his relief, and he choked it down. They spoke of other things for a time. Finally Paul got to the point.

"Tell me about Israel."

Rafkin said nothing for a second.

"I was born in Haifa. It's a port city. The largest in the country."

"That's not what I meant. Tell me about the people. A city is made up of the soul of its people."

"My people are proud. And tough. We're surrounded by these Arabs who wish only to kill us." Stuart Rafkin, of course, had no interest in Israel, or its people. He'd never been there, had no desire to go. But it was better than the truth.

If they left the country together, Paul would have to know the truth. Rafkin really did not want to eliminate Paul. But Feliks was still alive and Rafkin still didn't know how to find him. He had planned on going to Vineland to move the weapons, but he was hurt. Maybe Paul could do it for him—a surrogate.

Paul was concerned about infection. He treated Rafkin like a movie star.

"Why can't anyone know?" Paul would love to broadcast the whole affair. He could stand at Rakfin's side as the cameras rolled. The world would know of Stuart's heroics. "America is on your side."

"Can't happen. There would be international repercussions."

Paul digested it. Rafkin watched him carefully. This was the moment. The first one, anyway, and such moments become easier after the first.

"There is a man. His name is Feliks. He claims to be Russian, though he may be from one of the Republics. I was in contact with him, thinking he was a friend, but now I'm not so sure." Rafkin decided to see how far he could go.

"I must capture this man. Or kill him."

Paul's eyes widened. He blushed and Rafkin knew he had him.

"I need your help," Rafkin declared. "I have to get my rental car out of the parking lot at the mall. I couldn't take it last night, for obvious reasons. There are certain items inside. The police can't find them."

Paul returned Rafkin's stare. He answered with feeling. "I'll do anything."

Chapter 23

GOMEZ STEPPED out onto the curb at 6:40 on Sunday morning. He headed up Broadway, up the Great White Way—maybe. He really didn't know where or what the hell those places were, but it had a touristy ring. He could be in Hell's Kitchen for all he knew. He felt the alcohol burning off after a single city block. A nice bonus.

Terrorist threats, phone calls, Kessler, hotels, Sacco and Davidson, and every other damned thing…it was all starting to run together. The physical proximity to Viktorina Viisky was interrupting his sleep patterns. It was becoming difficult to work through his suspicions of her while she was three feet away. Those eyes….

People were out, even at this early hour. He enjoyed watching them, buzzing around like they were on the floor of a vast ocean, the gray buildings towering above them, radio masts and satellite dishes poking through the surface like periscopes. The few birds that had survived the pollution and stray gunfire twittered artfully.

The key to this cluster was Stuart Rafkin. He needed to spend some brain time on Rafkin.

He passed an older couple, walking together on Seventh Avenue. The old woman was humming. The man's sweater was buttoned haphazardly and she was attempting to fix it, poignant in her efforts.

He realized that she was humming along with a larger sound. There were other voices, many voices, rising together in a prosaic moment of human harmony. The sound grew; it had a rich, evocative quality, and Gomez felt the hair rise on the back of his neck.

Curious, he followed the old couple as they waddled in the direction of the singing. He crossed 46th, stopped, and found himself at the verge of a small parking lot, adjacent to another at the rear of a Gothic church. He knew he was in the area of Times Square, which meant St. Patrick's Cathedral. This must be it.

The air was clean and still, an oddity for Manhattan. The usual profanity, in a dozen languages, was conspicuously absent. Gomez looked up at the spires and the granite, the kind of building that would never be built again, enjoying the moment.

The parishioners began to let out. As the last of them straggled off, he looked up to see a priest standing at the edge of a hooded alcove, smoking a cigarette. From a distance the priest appeared to be very young, and as he finished his cigarette, he looked up directly into the eyes of Gomez. The young priest smiled, they shared a look that passes when two people of like kind meet and know each other instantly, and well.

The priest's name was Rivera. Gomez's first impression had been a little off. Rivera was not so young, probably in his middle thirties. Gomez was informed that this was actually St. Mary the Virgin. St. Pat's was a half mile off to the east.

Rivera wanted to know if Gomez had been at early mass.

"No."

"I didn't think so. You're not old enough and you don't look like a tourist." He hunched his shoulders against the chill and, without a word, he turned and ambled into the rectory.

Gomez followed.

Rivera hung his outer vestments on a coat hook in his office. There was remembrance in that. Gomez remained standing so that he could more easily run away, should Rivera try to get him into the confessional. He looked up, thankful that thus far, the entire ceiling had not caved in when God saw who had entered His house.

"There's this girl," Gomez began.

"I might have guessed."

"It isn't what you think."

"It never is," Rivera said with a worldly grin, and they both laughed.

"Would you like some coffee?"

"Please."

It turned out that they were from the same neighborhood in Oakland. Time was passed remembering the old sights, sounds, and smells. The girls they once knew.

"So how did you...?"

"The whole priest deal?" Rivera leaned back, scratching his head.

"Think of it like a corporate gig. Only with God as CEO."

"But the church."

"Yeah, I know. The Scandals." Rivera thought for a moment, and then appeared to have found his words. "Say, for example, you're middle-management. Your company is in big fat trouble. You stay, while others scurry away like rats. In the end, when the company survives, you look like a hero."

"So you're ambitious."

"Just a little," Rivera smiled.

"But that's not the only reason."

"Don't be ridiculous," he scowled. For a moment Gomez was six years old again, cowed by a man of the cloth.

"God called me when I was still a child. It's the only thing I ever expected to be."

Gomez digested this for a moment. "It was the same with me."

Gomez got the coffee pot from the burner. He told Rivera the whole story, beginning with Viisky in DC. It took most of an hour to go through Spasski and Stuart Rafkin, the threat against the nation.

Rivera was a good listener.

"I will pray for you."

"I was hoping for something a little, how should I say it? A little more *immediate*."

"What do you want? Like a guaranteed miracle?"

Gomez looked away. "If it isn't too much trouble."

Another, older priest came in briefly, glancing at them. Probably thinking marriage counseling. He pulled some vestments from a locker and left.

Rivera wanted Gomez to do the praying himself.

"It's been awhile."

"It doesn't have to be out of a book or anything like that. Just think of someone besides yourself who could use some help."

"Okay, there's a friend of mine. Val Sacco. He's having some problems."

"Ah, Valentine of Rome. Patron of love and lovers, happy marriages."

"His wife ran off with…an actor."

"I see. Well, Valentine is also the patron saint of plague, epilepsy, and greeting-card manufacturers. So it could go either way."

"These Saints get kind of loaded up, then."

Rivera swung his chair around until he was facing a Dell desktop, typing while he spoke. Gomez saw that it was a directory of saints and their patronage. The wired church.

"We need a saint for you. It won't be difficult. There are saints for everything. Cities and countries, for fainting spells, beekeepers. My own namesake, Saint Jerome, is for abandoned people. A good saint. Gimme your first name. I'll tell you if I've got a hit."

Gomez smiled. "If my parents named me after a Saint, then I was fourteen years old and it was an act of desperation."

"Did you know there's a patron saint of arms dealers?"

"That's certainly different."

"Adrian of Nicomedia. Bad luck for him. You don't get to choose."

Gomez asked, "How about Islamic terrorists?"

Rivera said nothing. He swiveled around, elbows on his knees, looking at Gomez, who said, "So, given your calling, how do you view the terrorists? You forgive them?"

Rivera looked up at the ceiling. "That'd be a tough one. Satan has blinded them."

Gomez thought he would perhaps do more than that. Disembowel them, maybe. Stomp on the entrails.

He pointed out that they weren't stopped on the eleventh.

"Then there was a purpose to 9/11."

"What possible purpose could there be?"

"How the hell would I know?" Rivera looked a little peeved. He went back to pecking on his keyboard. Finally he came up with one.

"Okay, got it. How about Eustachius?"

"Go on. What did old Eustachius do?" Gomez asked.

"One of those whose sainted name was chosen wisely. A Roman general in the army of the emperor Trajan." Rivera was playing it, leading up to the punch line.

"Eustachius is the patron saint of hunters."

*

There were busy sounds coming from the Cathedral, people filing in for the next mass. Gomez pointed out that this was getting perilously close to "God is on our side." They discussed the matter from differing metaphysical points of view, and after a time Rivera handed Gomez his card. It was time to prepare.

"Won't you stay for eight o'clock?"

"I wish I could," Gomez said. "There's someplace I have to be."

"Of course there is."

They shook hands just outside the door to the rectory. Gomez, in turn, gave Rivera his card along with a suspicious promise to attend mass in the near future.

Gomez turned to leave, watching Rivera disappear into the recesses of the rectory. But instead of exiting the way he had come, he hung a left and entered the cathedral.

American Gothic was his first thought, but no. That wasn't it. An older design, including midnight-blue stained glass atop the towering central cathedral. It was breathtaking.

And it was full, or almost full, thirty-five minutes before Mass. Gomez thought, once again, that with 9/11, everything had changed.

He found a pew very near to the exit, feeling exposed. He leaned with half his butt sticking out on the end, just in case. Edgy, still thinking he might burst into flames at any moment...he began to pray.

From his childhood Sundays, he remembered nothing. So he made it up. He prayed for his mother, now dead eleven years, from an uncommon blood disorder. He prayed for the victims of the Pentagon, Flight 93, and the World Trade Center. He prayed for Kessler and for everyone else he knew, all of whom worked at the Bureau, as he had no real social life. There was even a prayer for Spasski and for Viisky too.

In the middle of it, an old woman passed through his place on the pew. Trying to leave, she banged her knobby knees against him and he nearly swatted her in the head, or damned her to hell in the middle of St. Mary the Virgin Catholic Church.

But he caught himself, just in time.

And when he was done, he felt better.

He stood, fumbling the genuflection badly. Looking up, he saw Rivera standing underneath the third Station of the Cross, watching him. He felt a glow of warmth and comfort overcome his doubt and cynicism.

Walking away, Gomez looked back once at the spires. The confessional had been avoided, at least. It was just a childhood bugaboo. But the thought of confessing his sins still gave him a bad moment. *It's been thirty-one years since my last confession.* That alone would require some nimble footwork. The list of sins...the "impure thoughts" part would keep him in there for a month.

But wasn't he, Gomez, commanded personally to populate the earth? This led to thoughts of Viisky, and in that moment Gomez felt very near to God indeed.

He was puffing a little by Eight Avenue. He stood at the edge of the street, waiting. A hack came along and he got in, giving the man directions toward Lower Manhattan.

The cab driver said something about the activity at Ground Zero. All the overtime those guys must be racking up. Gomez answered with a soft "Yup" and a grunt. The guy got the message. He went back to his steering.

*

Sacco called with the response to Gomez' request. If it were true that Rafkin's cover was that of a stockbroker, he would have had to take a test and be issued a license—by the Commonwealth of Virginia, for example. And if he moved and wished to maintain his status, his new address would be on record. Sacco had, of course, run a driver's license check on Rafkin at Gomez' request on Thursday, but driver's licenses were a dime a dozen. The SEC was another matter. You didn't screw around with those guys.

"Don't know why I didn't think of it before," Gomez said sheepishly.

Sacco replied, "Hey, we're all human."

He looked out the window, smiling at the thought of Spasski cowering back at the hotel. He had told Viisky to get him cleaned up. They would be leaving the hotel at eleven.

He looked at his watch. Ten minutes past nine. Still plenty of time.

They would dump Spasski at Grand Central Station this afternoon. Gomez couldn't stand the thought of another six hours in the car with the two of them. His whiny wife could pick him up, and they could whine together with their undoubtedly whiny kids. Then he and Viisky would go see about Mr. Stuart Rafkin.

The trip took twenty minutes. It started to drizzle as he got out of the cab at the entrance to the Ellis Island Ferry; something he'd always wanted to see. The Statue of Liberty hung in the distance, barely visible through the fog. He told the cabbie to wait while he walked up to the ticket terminal.

The ferry wasn't running. The statue was closed for repairs.

It didn't matter. Gomez had been thinking it through in the cab and he said to himself aloud, "She's not Russian. She's trying to *blame* it on the Russians."

He lit a smoke. "Time for the big boys."

His step grew lighter. It was almost ten o'clock—time to go back and grab Viisky and Spasski. They could be done with Karyn Macklin in time for a late lunch. Gomez could be in California in a week.

The cabbie was gone. Gomez cursed him, but there was nothing he could do. No other taxis were in sight, so he continued down the ramp, onto the sidewalk, without breaking stride. He was surprised at how invigorating all this walking was. He made a vow to take evening walks after this was over…tighten the old gut.

He drifted through a residential neighborhood. The feeling he had of being cleansed passed into mild fatigue as he searched in vain for a cab. The wool jacket was getting to him. He stopped in the overhang of a bodega and tried the hotel on his cell phone. No answer. Maybe they had gone down to the bar for breakfast. He shrugged, continued to walk.

By a quarter to ten he was downright tired. He stopped to mop his brow. The temperature was in the high sixties. It was enough to wear you out if you were active.

He had decided to find an intersection and call in a cab to pick him up, when he heard the sound of a car rolling slowly behind him. He turned to see the light-bar of a blue and white.

He stopped, waiting for the cop to approach. The guy was young, in his twenties, and he slammed the door behind him as he walked up to Gomez.

"Can I see some ID, sir?" he asked.

"Feds," Gomez advised him. "I'm carrying, of course. I'm gonna reach inside my jacket for my creds." The cop's expression did not change.

"Don't think so, pops." The cop's hand rested on the butt of his weapon. "Lock your hands behind your head."

"Yeah, sure." Gomez did what he was told. The cop opened his jacket, hooked out the automatic then the flat ID wallet. He told Gomez to wait where he was, as he returned to his cruiser with the gun and the badge.

Gomez hung fire while the guy called him in. Maybe now the country would get on the ball, with three thousand dead innocents and a national institution vaporized. It was time to take official notice of suspicious young Arab males wandering about.

It was time to offend somebody.

The cop returned shortly, handing Gomez his things, explaining, "Somebody called in. Said some guy was cruising the neighborhood. He might have been an Arab. Sorry about that."

"Don't be," Gomez told him. "But next time, call for backup." He smiled. "Hey, can you give me a lift?"

The cop drove him toward the hotel and they bullshitted about baseball, avoiding the topic of Islamic terrorists. Gomez finally asked him how the city was doing.

"I don't know about anyone else," he turned to look at Gomez, "but I'm extremely pissed off."

Gomez's cell rang. He looked at the display, recognizing the number of the hotel. She could slap Spasski around all she wanted. He pocketed the phone without answering.

The cop mentioned something about the quarter of a billion dollars paid for Rodriguez, by the Yankees, and the phone rang again. She wasn't going to let go. This time he answered. His face tightened. He snapped the phone shut with as much disgust as possible, looked out the window and said, "Aww, crap."

The cruiser stopped across the street and Gomez thanked the cop, who asked Gomez if he wanted him to stay. Gomez told him to take off. Why get involved in all the paperwork?

He caught a glimpse of Vishka's lustrous black hair as she turned in profile. She was standing in the gutter, speaking with a paramedic. Gomez thanked the cop again and closed the door.

"This is gonna suck." He took a deep breath and walked into the intersection.

*

An ambulance and police car blocked the northbound lanes. People milled around the scene, gawking at the sheet-covered body in the road. Forty feet past the body there was a city bus, white with a blue stripe on the side, and a mural depicting Ashley Bubier holding a product to combat yeast infections. On further inspection, he could make out the bus driver, talking with his hands to a policeman, about ten feet to the left of Viisky and her paramedic. The EMT sat in the ambulance, reading a magazine.

There would be no need for heroics. Just like the Eleventh. They must be getting frustrated.

The light turned green. He made his way across the intersection, his eyes on Viisky. She noticed him about halfway across.

She formed a smile as she saw him. As his expression became evident, she fidgeted with her collar, dusting her hair, looking off down the boulevard. The smile slipped away.

Gomez barged in on the paramedic, holding out his badge. The guy was saying something about witnesses and the police. Gomez ignored him. He appraised Viisky coldly. "Tell me."

"We are going to this Zero. To view destruction." She looked away. "We have both wanted to see, you see."

Gomez glanced over at the lump. The sheet covered about ninety percent of what was left of Kostenko Spasski. His feet were exposed. One ankle lay propped up on the curb, revealing the lurid yellow socks that Viisky had purchased on her excursion the day before. The socks were ground-in filthy, as if they'd been worn for a month. A lonely Topsider lay crumpled about a yard away from the feet. Spider-lines of blood were spattered across the sheet, roughly where Spasski's head must have been. Pollock.

"Go upstairs. Lock yourself in the room. Do not use the telephone. If I find out that you have, I will ship your little ass out of LaGuardia on the next flight to points east."

Viisky pursed her lips. She was about to say something, then thought better of it.

Gomez grabbed her arm as she turned to go, "Diplomatic crap." He held out his hand. She reached into her purse, handed him a thin leather wallet. He leaned down close to her ear, "And your cell phone." She grew diffident, but she pulled out her phone, giving it to Gomez. He stuffed it into his jacket and turned to the paramedic. He ignored her snooty little march into the building.

The EMT was jolly fat, with a Wild-West mustache, an older guy who'd seen more than one of these. He blathered on about the injuries to the victim, something about craniums and massive internal injuries, culminating in gallons of blood loss.

Gomez half-listened, looking around for the laziest cop. He needed one who had an aversion to paperwork and procedure. One who wouldn't interfere when he pulled the rug out. The paramedic said something amusing. He chuckled. Gomez shooed him away. He went to talk to the cop.

The cop's name was Gary, classic NYPD flatfoot. A perfect little pot belly, like a volleyball stuffed beneath his shirt. He had those baleful eyes and dark ringlets of the perpetual worrier. He accepted Gomez' presence without question, glancing at the Bureau creds with the eyes of a Bassett hound.

"Guy didn't look. He was from Maryland. Go figure."

"Guess it didn't work," Gomez mumbled to himself.

"What didn't work?"

"Never mind. What other witnesses do you have? Besides Ms. Viisky."

"Coupla people. They all have the same story. This Adler character was looking right," Gary turned and pointed north.

Gomez, on hearing the name Adler, thought the cop was talking about someone else, and then it registered.

"...he never did turn. The bus driver laid on the horn just as he fell into the street." Gary also spoke with his hands, "Bammo. That's it."

"So, no ME?"

"Nah," the cop replied. "They'll do it at the slaughterhouse."

There would be no medical examiner at the scene, hence no need for any further questioning of the witnesses. The autopsy would be done later. Spasski was already a statistic.

"What's the Fibbies want with him?" Gary jerked a stubby finger over at the corpse.

"Mr. Adler was a witness of mine. He was traveling with me and Ms. Viisky."

"Oh, shit."

"Indeed."

They lit up together. "I'd like to be the one to tell his wife. If that's okay," Gomez said.

"Be my guest." The eye-luggage crinkled. Gomez had volunteered for the biggest shit-job of them all.

"Good luck," Gary said, handing Gomez his card, escaping to his cruiser. Gomez looked first up one length of the road, then down the other, studying the place where Kostenko Spasski's life had ended.

There must be relatives still alive somewhere in Russia… perhaps his mother. They would never know. Pedestrians walked past more quickly.

The little scene was fading into ignominy as quickly as it had developed. Maybe not everything had changed.

Maybe Spasski had killed himself.

Cars passed, filled with people on their way to Sunday social engagements, or out to the Island for a last run at the beaches. He stubbed out his cigarette and walked into the hotel, wondering what he would tell the wife and kids.

Chapter 24

CHECKING OUT over the phone; in a stroke of luck, his American Express held and didn't explode into a thousand plastic shards when they ran it through. He watched Viisky pack, the hotel phone held to his ear. A cross voice on the other end of the line.

"Karyn? We've got a little problem."

Macklin was displeased to hear of Spasski's death. Yes, it was more than a little problem and *yes* he was asking her to hold off for right now.

Macklin's voice grew in intensity, sounding like a thunderclap in the small room. Viisky was making a sour puss as she packed. She still didn't like the threat of Macklin.

The car was brought around and Gomez stuffed a few bucks into the hungry palm of the valet. He merged onto the West Side Highway, a full city mile from the hotel, before she finally spoke.

"To where are you taking me?"

Gomez gave her his best look of withering revulsion. She looked out the window for a moment and then turned back toward him.

"He steps into the lorry! What am I to be? His shitting mother?"

Gomez eased past a pizza supply truck.

"Who's next?" he spat. "Rafkin? You think they won't do the same thing to you?" He let it go at that. She harrumphed, staring out the window again. Gomez was tempted to look at his watch, to see if she could last thirty seconds before running her yap. Instead, he clocked it in his head. *Nine, ten, eleven-*

"What is this *next*?" she hissed. "You are...you are supposing as if this is fault of mine!"

Gomez now knew what she would look like when he left the toilet seat up, or washed white sweaters with red underwear—on hot.

"We'll discuss it later." Give her time to recognize the precariousness of her position. Either way, he was not interested in going around the maypole about it.

It was not an accident—neither the bus that killed Spasski, nor the fact that they had gone to him in the first place. She had not picked him randomly off her list. In fact, she hadn't mentioned her precious fucking list at all, from the moment Gomez snatched Spasski and told her he was going to New York.

What Gomez thought was that Spasski was supposed to do something for Viisky and Feliks. Whatever it was that Rafkin had done—procuring weapons maybe, or facilitating someone's entry into the country—Spasski had refused, and paid the price.

That was what Gomez thought.

*

Sacco had come up big. Gomez had an address, different from the one Rafkin had put on his driver's license. He slid through a right, looking in the rearview to see if the tail was still on him. He'd watched the Odyssey glide away from the curb after them, leaving the hotel. He couldn't pick them up now, but they were back there somewhere. These guys were pretty good.

There was almost enough room, and Gomez engineered the big Ford into most of a space, nicking the rear quarter panel of a little cream Lexus coupe as he double-parked in the fashionable West Village amidst the trendy junk shops and eight-dollar latte vendors.

Gomez smiled. It was a grim smile—the ghost of Spasski mocked him—but the thought of the yuppie sniveling and moaning about a dime-sized dent in his little death trap lightened his mood. Bastard shouldn't have taken up two spaces.

He produced a small white placard from the glove box and propped it up on the driver's side of the windshield. It read "FBI—Crime Scene," with some official looking mumbo jumbo, and an authorizing signature at the bottom. The signature was the hard part, boosting it off the Internet from a copy of the Declaration of Independence.

He got out stiffly, rounded the hood and leaned into her window. "Wait."

She glared at him, all squinty-eyed, making it easier for him. He jogged around to the back of the building, confirming the lack of a rear exit. It was an end unit; a tiny alleyway ran beside it, a vertical row of windows on the alley side. If Rafkin was on the first floor he could jump out of the window. Gomez tossed a butt into the hedge and went back to the car, to the slowly steaming Viisky.

He'd rather have a confrontation with someone at his side, even if she was the enemy. They both had the same basic motivation concerning Stuart Rafkin. In a weird way, she was his back-up.

"You can come. But if you lay a hand on him, I'll rip your lungs out."

It wouldn't hold her. But he'd confiscated the Beretta.

As he got to the door, Gomez saw that behind Viisky, a hundred yards down on the east side of the street, sat the Odyssey—an idling threat. The two goons were not visible from this distance. Hopefully they were still inside, where they needed to be, instead of following him in. Maybe he could have Viisky deliver some vodka…

The building was early twentieth century brownstone, once the home of a single wealthy family, now broken up into apartments. It had attractive copper awnings in lieu of shutters. Gomez felt it was the type of building he would wish to live in were he a New Yorker.

A pause at the foot of a winding iron staircase revealed that it looped gracefully upward four stories, and Gomez could see all the way to the top to a tastefully added skylight. He checked the names on the mailbox; a four-across unit hung on the wall inside the front door. Viisky mimicked him, cocking her head.

"This is the Rafkin?"

"Yesiree," he said, and began to climb the stairs.

He was winded when he got to a small landing on the fourth floor. He sucked in his gut and strove to breathe evenly. It figured that Rafkin would want to be on the top floor, but you'd think they could afford an elevator.

"I will like my weapon now."

"Sorry, toots."

"You say it yourself. Kostka was in the depression."

He considered it. Rafkin might be some super-ninja warrior dude. The back-up wouldn't hurt. If he had a real team, they would go house-to-house, conducting Q-and-A's—smother the place with presence. All he had was Viisky. He should give her the Beretta. Then again, she had killed a man, not three hours ago.

"He's not here anyway," Gomez's personal sonar was telling him the place was unoccupied. It was a talent he thought everyone had. He clenched his fist and began to pound on the wooden door. Waiting insufficiently for a response, he pounded again, in a technique designed to aggravate and unbalance the respondent. He ignored Viisky, except for a glimpse he stole of her chest. She, too, was breathing hard after the climb. Exquisite. He battered the door again, to no effect.

A door popped open on the floor below them. A man emerged, gripping the railing and leaning over to shout up at them.

"Must you *pound* like that?" Early-thirties, wearing a half-open peasant shirt and his lips were compressed into a thin, red line. He had one of those gangsta do-rags shoved back on his head as he continued to whine like the wrong girl had caught the bouquet.

Gomez could see that he was shoeless and spoke in a voice that was almost, but not quite, effeminate. His hair was dirty blonde, thinning poorly; it hung in a mess around the sides and stuck up in expensive designer clumps. Gomez felt that he could achieve the same hairstyle for free by lying in bed for two days without washing his hair.

He leaned over the railing.

"You know the man in this apartment?"

"No, not really. I think he works a lot. Who are you?" There was a sheen of perspiration on his thin, hairless chest. Maybe he had been exercising.

"Fire department. We've had a report of a code violation."

The man wrinkled his nose. Gomez was wearing his rumpled suit and Viisky looked like a model in Claiborne and Taylor. Well, whatever they looked like, the fire department was not on the list.

"Is the super in?" he asked. The man laughed.

"There's no *super* here. It's a quad brownstone in the West Village." He made a scoffing noise. "Where do you think you are? Queens?" He had lisped finally, at *Queens*.

"Thank you for your time," Gomez told him, annoyed at the standard Upper West Side attitude of provincial superiority. He remembered that many of the firefighters had lived in Queens. He lit a cigarette, as much to annoy the guy as to satisfy any chemical demand.

"There is no *smoking* in this building."

He said the word "smoking" as if it were sheep fucking, or the laying of land mines.

Gomez flicked the burning cigarette down past him into the foyer. The man stared back…and wilted. He scuttled back into his apartment.

Gomez winked at Viisky. He produced a set of high-tension burglar's picks from his jacket pocket. He had an electric pick gun, a rake, purchased when he was young and still fantasizing, but it was in the hall closet in his townhouse where it wouldn't do anybody any good.

He'd never actually done this—picked a lock—but he still remembered his training; three weeks on "black bag" nonsense at a CIA co-op facility in Chincoteague.

Viisky watched, hands on her hips, as he fiddled with the locks, first the top lock and then the far easier doorknob. Gomez felt perspiration on his brow. You had to do these babies one at a time. If Rafkin were inside, he would have set up a flamethrower by now, or maybe a nice machine-gun nest. But he wasn't. Rafkin was an intelligence officer, not some drunken hillbilly holding his mother-in-law hostage.

Gomez took his time. The top lock gave him quite a hard time; it was an expensive pin tumbler. He defeated it anyway, after eleven tedious minutes. He drew his weapon and shielded Viisky with one arm as he shouldered the door open in a rush and… they were inside.

The door opened into a living room with eggshell walls, a dark leather sofa, and wing chairs surrounding an area rug. The wall adjacent to the entry was authentic yellow brick, probably late nineteenth century…an attractive feature.

The tables were blond maple, in the late '80s Swedish Modern that had since been passed over for the preposterous new Urban Industrial.

Together they crept across the living area into the kitchen, divided from a breakfast nook by a half-wall of faux painted Grecian white. Viisky, unarmed and unhappy, waited in the kitchen area while Gomez stormed the rear of the apartment, one room at a time. He came back without a word, holstering his automatic. Viisky looked bored.

There was a small green table in the kitchen area. Gomez sat down, extracting his notebook. He began to take notes…stalling. He was stumped.

Viisky wandered around the living area, eventually making her way into the bedroom and disappearing from view. Gomez finished his notes and stood, following her path into the bedroom.

He found her rooting carefully through a dresser, tucking things back the way she had found them. Gomez made a mental note to ask her how to fold a tee shirt, an engineering wonder he could never seem to master. Perhaps later.

"Fetish?" he asked.

She gave him a dirty look and continued her search. No way she knew what a fetish was. Or did she?

Gomez checked out the bathroom. Rafkin's toiletry items were arranged with military precision in a chrome medicine cabinet. The white porcelain sink was dazzling to the eyes. Nothing unusual in that, if you were a deviant commie-pinko spy. Gomez' own bathroom was home to millions—possibly trillions—of exotic bacteria and other creepy organisms. He considered it his nod to the environment, allowing the little guys to flourish, without threat from deadly cleaning products. Medications and colognes were tipped over, knick-knacks upended. Nothing of interest was to be found. Gomez swept his arm across the shelf of a flush-mounted maple cabinet, making an unholy mess of things. Might as well leave a message, just in case he came back.

Out in the bedroom again, he saw that Viisky was through with her search. She crawled out from under the bed, where she presumably had been looking for a hidey-hole of some sort.

"Anything?" he asked her.

"Nyet. I mean *No*," she said. "Is possible he keeps weapons and communications equipment in other location.

"He's gone," Gomez told her.

"Yes. Is most obvious, is it not?"

"I mean he bolted. Took off." This lack of cognitive resonance would be more appropriate if they were married.

"I mean that Stuart Rafkin, or Ivan the Terrible, or whoever he is, has left the building."

"That is the Elvis, is it not?"

Gomez took a deep breath.

"I mean he has escaped. I mean that Rafkin has either left the city or is in hiding." He decided to bait her, "Or, and this is the one that worries me, he is on his way to Port of Brooklyn or Marcus Hook. Whichever target he intends to destroy."

Viisky blinked, and worried a nail.

"Is not yet time," she said, and for the first time since he'd met her, she looked truly worried.

Gomez stared. He was close to breaking her.

They went back into the living area. Gomez got down on his hands and knees to rifle through a television cabinet. He turned to Viisky. "Why don't you go down and speak with that clown in the apartment below?"

"He is…clown? How do you know this?"

"Figure of speech." He stood, his knees popping like howitzers. "It is unlikely that he doesn't know Stuart Rafkin. This is a small building. Close quarters. They would have met." He picked up a statuette and looked at it briefly. "Therefore, he is lying. You need to speak with him to find out why."

"You will stay here?"

Gomez nodded. "He doesn't appreciate me. You may have better luck." He smiled at her for the first time since finding Spasski in the road.

"Use your feminine wiles."

"Explain this wiles to me," she smiled back. A little joke to soften the tension.

"Never mind. Wouldn't work on him anyway."

Viisky held her chin in one hand.

"I will use the intimidation, I think." She was glowing as she left. Maybe she was kidding.

They would have to come back here, Gomez decided. Tomorrow morning he'd spill the beans and they'd bring in the forensic professionals. No man lives in a vacuum. The word would get out. They would find him, most likely too late.

There were other signs that Stuart Rafkin had headed for someplace less threatening to his health. Gomez found no toothbrush or razor in the bathroom, nor were there any of the usual clues of recent activity. The coffee pot was dry as a bone. There was a thin patina of dust on every surface he touched, counter-indicative of the behavioral patterns Rafkin had established in his bathroom. He'd missed Rafkin by a lot. A week, maybe.

It didn't matter. He was gone and that was that. Time to hand Viisky over and the let the meetings begin—dozens, thousands of meetings. The State Department would want to get involved, no matter which republic she was from…Sphincterbad, Typhoidistan, whatever.

The phone rang. At first he thought it was Rafkin's home line, but then he remembered…he'd changed the stupid thing again. The ring tone was now a Souza march—The Battle Hymn of the Republic.

Porsche Cummings was screeching at him before he finished saying hello.

"Who do you think you are not to return my messages? I don't care what kind of shit you did—"

"Call back when you can control yourself," Gomez said evenly, and hung up.

Now, then. With Viisky out of the way, he went back into the kitchen and approached the refrigerator. He had first noticed it when he sat at the table.

There was no sun fading on the side closest to the window. The panel had been replaced. He produced a pocketknife, which he used to pry at the molding between the refrigerator and an upper cabinet. It came away easily, revealing an aluminum panel attached to the sidewall of the casement with four screws. He selected the Phillips head attachment of his knife and unscrewed the panel.

It wasn't much. No carefully updated diary with a thesaurus of code words and maps with X's on them pointing the way to the White House. No bazookas or suitcase A-bomb. What it was, was a start.

Behind the panel, strapped to the back with tape, were two cell phones. They looked to be of older manufacture. He wiped them off and tried to power them up. Dead, both of 'em.

He stuffed them into his pockets, making a note to have Sacco hand them off to Technical Services.

He strode over to the brick wall to peer through the open window. The white Odyssey sat where he had last seen it. As he watched, a hand shot out from the passenger side window and flicked a cigarette butt onto the pavement.

Gonna have to do something about those guys.

CHAPTER 25

VIKTORINA VIISKY rapped her knuckles on the door to the flat of the fruitcake. Gomez was under the mistaken impression that he was with the circus. Vischka knew better. When they stood on the landing, she had easily seen that the man was homosexual. Doubtless, some type of artist or other miscreant. No matter. She would have no trouble from him whatever his proclivities.

"Leave your storm trooper at home?" Paul inquired. They both glanced up briefly in the direction of Rafkin's apartment. A moderately loud bang could be heard, then something like rippling metal.

Paul leaned with one arm on the jamb. The other held the doorknob. She peered into the apartment behind him. "This flat is your home?" she asked, smiling like a co-conspirator.

He nodded. "May I ask what the fire department is doing upstairs?"

"Is codes immigration, I'm afraid. As this man said."

Paul continued to smile. "It's *violation,*" he spoke loudly, enunciating the way people do when dealing with the idiots in customer service. "Can I see some identification?"

She fumbled through her clutch and then smacked herself theatrically on the forehead. Gomez had not returned her ID wallet after absconding with it in front of the hotel.

"I am so sorry. Have left identification at the…*mmm*, the Bureau for Fire Brigades!" She gave him an ingratiating, silly look.

"Uh huh." Paul scratched the bridge of his nose, folding his arms across his chest.

"In America," he lectured, "People don't have to answer to the Fire Department. I'd bet a dollar you don't even work for the city." His mouth tightened triumphantly. He was about to close the door. She held out a hand to stop him.

"Please," she said, pouting. It couldn't hurt, "I am not to do you harm. I must find this upstairs-man." She leaned forward, dropping her voice almost to a whisper, "He is in much danger."

Paul was swayed. Stuart had warned him, but it was probably exaggeration. This was, after all, so very exciting. To have this element of European intrigue and danger attached to Stuart... well. If this got any better, Paul was going to pop.

"You can come in," he allowed. "Just for a sec. I have a show at one."

The sounds of destruction died out as the door closed. They sat on the sofa and Paul offered her refreshment, which she declined.

The apartment was the most beautiful she had ever seen. It had acres of walnut, discreet artwork in all the right places...just the right tone. Very masculine.

"So, when is the last time you have seen this Rafkin?"

Paul crossed his legs, leaning back on the suede sofa. "What? Is he some kind of criminal? I need details."

"Do you know the location of his toils?"

"What is that supposed to mean?"

She searched for the words, "The working place. Where he has job."

Paul uncrossed his legs. He thought for a moment. There may have been a twinkle in his eye. "He's barely ever here. I think, no, I think he's a criminal. The Mafia, do you think?"

"This is most serious matter."

"Okay sure. I really don't know the man." His face turned vaguely lecherous. "But I wish I did."

She knew it. In Russia and the satellite countries, even today with all of the Western reforms, it was still common to imprison a man like this. They would haul him off to Dzershinsky Square. He would not be so clever after that.

"Do you know the type of his automobile?"

"I don't think he has one."

"Has he a mistress?"

"I surely hope not."

"I am becoming annoyed with you."

"And I," Paul stood, "don't believe you have the authority to persecute me! Who the hell are you, anyway? Some freak from the IRS?"

"I am with the Fire Brigade, as I have described."

"It's time for you to leave."

"I overflow with questions."

Viisky stood, glowering at him. Paul wilted, yet he held his ground, pointing toward the door, chin held royally aloft. "I'll call the police. The *real* police." She tucked away her notepad, carrying eye contact with him all the way to the door.

"*Nekulturny gomoseksual'nyjj feja*," she said.

"Slut."

"Shithead."

"Cow."

Viisky couldn't find a word. Paul waited.

A light came on in her eyes.

"Pussy."

"*Yeb vas*," spat Paul, slamming the door in her face.

*

Paul stomped off to the rear of his apartment, still annoyed at the chutzpah of the little foreign girl. And her shoes sucked. Nice bag though—had to be Choo. He entered the bathroom, into Italian tile and brushed nickel fixtures. The shower curtain was a tasteful nude, a Roman female. He drew the curtain.

"They're gone, lover."

Rafkin climbed out of the tub, stumbling and almost falling when he applied his weight to his bad leg. Paul gripped him under the arm.

"Do all Russians have such bad taste?"

"They're Russian?" Rafkin frowned. He was grim, worried.

"Just the girl."

"How do you know?"

"I spoke to the man in the stairwell. He grunted in American."

Rafkin sat down on the closed seat. Paul was animation itself, jittering around the small bathroom like a marionette. It dawned on Rafkin that Paul was enjoying this.

"You're sure?" Rafkin said. "Tell me. You're sure the man was American?"

"He was a moron. A big, knuckle-dragging Sasquatch.And I think they're doing the nasty."

Rafkin was nervous. An American and a Russian? Together? It could mean that Feliks had tipped off the FBI. Very bad news.

Feliks had never been a man to trust. It would not shock Rafkin to learn there was also something in place to kill the woman, and possibly even the FBI fellow after they took care of Stuart Rafkin.

He tuned back in.

"...no doubt destroying your apartment. The slut said she was with the Fire Department." Paul snorted his disdain. "Not bleeding, likely."

"No. Not likely," Rafkin agreed.

They waited for an hour. Paul went into the living room to peek through the curtains. The man and the Russian girl were standing next to a white Crown Victoria. For some reason, the beast leaned over the trunk of a sweet little Lexus convertible that was parked next to them. As Paul watched, the guy did something to the Lexus and then the woman said something to him. Maybe they thought the coupe belonged to Stuart.

Paul padded back to the bathroom.

"They're still here, but I think they're about to leave."

"We wait. Give it at least thirty minutes," Rafkin said. "Paul?"

"Hmmm?"

"Do you prefer mountains or beaches?"

*

They spent the next half-hour or so discussing places they knew. St. John's was Paul's favorite, and of course Key West, but Stuart said they must leave the country altogether.

They were leaning toward the Turks/Caicos, a place neither of them had ever been, when Rafkin said, "Would you go and have a look?"

Paul, again, went to look through the window. The Crown Victoria was gone. He went back to tell Stuart.

They made their way into the living room, Rafkin leaning heavily on Paul for support. Paul arranged some pillows on which Rafkin propped his leg.

He returned from the kitchen with two balloon snifters. Rafkin took a sip. Courvoisier.

"I need to make a telephone call." Rafkin adjusted his position. His discomfort was painful for Paul to see. "In my apartment, there is a secure phone." He explained its location and method of access.

Paul buttoned the top two buttons on his shirt and retrieved a screwdriver from a kitchen junk drawer. He trooped off to get the phone. He returned a few minutes later without the phone, but with a look of consternation. "It's gone. That jerk tore the whole effing place apart."

"They may come back. If they do, they'll send someone more… emphatic." Stuart paused to let that sink in. "They will question you as to my habits, my likes and dislikes, things of that nature."

He, once again, grabbed Paul by the elbow, this time with some force. "You must not give them the slightest indication that you know me. If you do, they will haul you off to a place you really do not want to be."

Paul feigned a lascivious leer, "Ooh the salt mines! What if I enjoy it?"

Rafkin shook Paul's arm, drawing his face to within three inches. "Quit screwing around. They could be coming to do something other than kill me." He let that sink in. "The Russians are somewhat lacking in the social graces, if you must know."

Paul smiled, planting a kiss on Rafkin. "Don't worry, baby. I'll handle them."

Paul wasn't going to understand.

*

They used Paul's cell phone. If Paul had a wiretap on him, it was over anyway. Rafkin was soon rewarded with the voice of Feliks. He wasted no time.

"Who's the girl?" Rafkin dropped all pretense of courtesy.

Feliks was shocked. He'd heard Rafkin had been killed in the Towers. He was greatly saddened, but had no knowledge of any female agent in America. They should meet.

Rafkin gave the phone back to Paul, pursing his lips, thinking.

"Is this bad?" Paul asked. "I mean…does this mean something really bad is going to happen?"

Rafkin patted him on the shoulder. "Sit down."

Rafkin took a deep breath. Paul couldn't stop fidgeting. Rafkin took his hand, "How spontaneous are you?"

CHAPTER 26

"ANY LUCK?" Gomez asked. He took the slate steps two at a time.

"He is in need of insanity doctor," Viisky spat, joining him at the car. Gomez almost wished they were in Diarreahstan. He could leave it up to Viisky. She would get information from Paul in the non-American way, without Miranda and legal protections. The *Sluzbha* way, with a bag over the head, hot knives flashing.

"Why didn't you do him like Spasski? Cut out his tongue."

"Enough of this *tongue*! It is the suicide."

Gomez thought it was time to cuff her. Let the boys in DC handle her.

He had enough to go to Yates.

Actually, he had enough on Tuesday morning, five minutes after Viisky spun her web.

They could have a forensic unit in here by Monday afternoon, Tuesday at the latest. They'd scrub the apartment, canvass the neighborhood. Gomez did not think they would find Stuart Rafkin. He had an interesting thought, that maybe Stuart Rakfin was dead. He asked Viisky, *pro forma*, "So he doesn't know Rafkin?"

"He claims no."

"What's his name?"

"Is Paul Nealy."

Gomez marked it in his notebook. He'd have Sacco run the guy through the computers on the off chance he was somebody. That, and Sacco would get the cell phones from Rafkin's refrigerator cache.

The Lexus coupe had been moved. The stinking creep must have gone somewhere in the hour and a half Gomez had been inside. Lexus-boy was back; he'd jammed the coupe over the line into the street. *And*...he had stuffed his little aerodynamic bumper about three inches from Gomez' space.

Gomez almost got into the car. But the pull was too strong.

He had an idea. This was natural; ideas were what he was paid for. He held the door for Viisky. Too late, he remembered that she was probably Count Dracula and he should have not afforded her the courtesy. Whatever.

He circled the coupe like a cheetah. As he neared the trunk—his intended target—he caught motion in the windows of the apartment building and looked up just in time to see Paul looking through the curtains.

Gomez waved...and found his mark. It sounded like the point of a nail scraping along a window. He was smiling when he got back in the drivers seat and started the engine.

Viisky looked pointedly at the keys in his hand.

"Why must you ruin this? Is lovely auto."

"Therapy."

*

Down Second Avenue, onto the VanWyck Expressway; he was getting good at this. Still, these people had too many expressways.

The midtown tunnel was dank and gloomy, with no end in sight. He asked her if it reminded her of home. Viisky did not speak, which was fine by him.

He thought about Paul, and the notion that Paul never spoke to Rafkin. Gomez thought that unlikely, but possible. People today didn't interact in they way they had in the past. The proliferation of electronic media had seen to that. Times change. Nevertheless, he was running on fumes.

Only one more card to play. A weak one. A duece of clubs.

He asked Viisky for a pen. She reached into her purse, and Gomez immediately thought *bayonet,* but she came out with just a pen. He really should cuff her. He was getting too old for sudden movements; his heart could explode. He rewound his voice mail, wrote down the address that Scott Nagle had left that morning.

"Map." She slapped it into his hand. Seems he'd lost the edge he'd had earlier. He juggled the map, notepad and pen, balancing the pyramid on his lap while he drove. This time Viisky didn't offer to navigate.

This next stop would be made simply because he was here, in New York. Rafkin was gone and Gomez could not imagine a scenario in which any personal information would help to find him.

In fact, it was almost certainly too late to find him. But they were in the neighborhood. Sometimes you picked things up where they didn't belong.

*

Devard Montrane lived in the center of a quiet block in the Jamaica section of Queens, in a thirties-era Craftsman with those tapered front porch columns that were making a comeback in new construction—altogether a cozy, middle-class home. Gomez got out, rounding the car to the passenger-side window. He gave Viisky a boiling glare and told her to wait. He didn't want her killing any more witnesses. She had just launched into her screeching reply when he turned on his heel and marched up the freshly painted steps.

The door opened on his third knock. Montrane's wife was Jamaican, as it happened. With her, you were an interloper, Gomez thought, as he looked at the woman in the doorway— hands on hips, forcing a smile. She introduced herself as Patience Montrane and led him into the kitchen where a mild-looking fellow, presumably Devard, sat with his legs propped over a folding chair.

The legs of his flannel pajamas were hacked off, to accommodate the burns.

"Thanks for this," Gomez said. "Being a Sunday and all."

He looked down at Montrane's legs. They were swaddled up like a mummy and reeked of some hideous salve, reminding him of when he scraped his knees as a child, and his grandmother would smear him with her stinking poultice.

"No problem. We're not big church-goers," Montrane said.

"Me neither," Gomez replied.

Patience saw her opening and broke into the gap. "You can see why we weren't answering the phone. I'll bet we got thirty voice-mails from those devil reporters. Not counting this morning."

Gomez asked, so Patience shared their story. He learned how she had called and called, a thousand times, trying desperately to reach Devard on the morning of the eleventh. She had gone to her mother's house to await the bad news, knowing in her soul that her husband was gone. And when Devard appeared, in the form of a call from Mercy hospital...Patience was reborn.

She remembered that call with reverence, gripping Montrane's hand like it was the world's largest diamond.

Montrane spent a few days in the burn unit; until it was determined his injuries were not as serious as originally thought. A week of impossible boredom punctuated by excruciating pain, prefaced his release on Wednesday. Three days ago.

"The wheelchair's a pain in the ass," Montrane opined. He was around thirty-five, dark complected, with a short, homemade haircut. He spoke in quick, rabbit-like sentences, with the busy accent of a native New Yorker.

He looked to his wife before he spoke.

"I guess you want to know about Stuart."

"I do."

"Get you some coffee?" Montrane looked again to his wife, Patience.

"That would be fine."

Something was strange. They weren't surprised to see him—like it was a natural event to have a Special Agent of the FBI barge into your house on a Sunday morning, or any other morning. Gomez felt like an alarm salesman.

Patience poured them each a mug and set it down on the table, pointing out the cream and sugar.

Montrane shared a look with his wife. "Patience always thought Stuart was a prick."

"Was?"

"Well, he was dead."

"You're talking about the Towers?"

"I was in his office when they hit. We were together. I took a bunch of people down the stairwell from the Skyway. He balked. It wasn't like I was gonna tell him which way to go, right? I mean, I was the overseas guy, not a fuckin' fire chief."

Patience glared at him, then softened. A second honeymoon.

"Stuart and three other people—that idiot Traxel was one of them, and some Chinese kid—they all went down the A stairwell." Montrane closed his eyes.

"He looked at me. Right before we split up. He looked right in my eyes, and I knew he was gonna die. Or I was." Montrane opened his eyes slowly, coming back from it. Something he would do for the rest of his life.

"I'm not really an Overseas Manager. It's just a convenient title. I'm actually more like an expert on the Nikkei. Sometimes, anyway," he laughed, a self-deprecating little shuffle.

Gomez said nothing. He didn't need a notepad for this.

"Stuart was a transfer from somewhere. I forget now."

"Virginia?" Gomez offered.

Montrane raised an eyebrow. "Hmm, maybe. Virginia or Maryland, somewhere down there. Yeah, that could be." Montrane thought for a moment.

"Anyway, a guy in…you know what? That's it. It was Ray Neidel from Tidewater. He called me up and asked me if I would take this guy. Rafkin was moving to the city and he wanted to stay with the company. These guys are predisposed to knocking around a lot, so you want to keep the good ones if you can. Neidel told me how terrific Rafkin was and all these big cases he brought in." He smiled at Gomez. "Brokerage guys have a tendency to exaggerate."

Gomez returned the smile. "So Rafkin shows up, when?""

Montrane thought about it and looked at Patience, instead of up at the ceiling or into space.

"In 1998? Something like that. So he shows up and he's my boss in like, eighteen months."

"He stole my husband's promotion. He's a very arrogant man." Montrane had a fan in Patience.

Patience made Gomez uneasy. She kept looking at him like she'd caught him at something. She left the table for the sink, fooling around with the dishes while she listened in. Montrane waved at her to forget it. Gomez thought she never would.

"What was he like?"

Montrane drained the last of his coffee. "A little weird."

"Weird how?"

"I don't know. Quiet, I guess. You have to understand that the business is about charisma, and you tell these guys…" he smiled at Gomez again.

"Sorry. Habit."

"They had better give you a branch now," Patience said. "You almost got killed for that company."

"I did not," Montrane protested. "How in the hell did they know some maniac in a jumbo jet was gonna ram the building?"

The exchange sounded to Gomez like an encore, and not the first.

It was time to become proactive.

"Did Rafkin ever work out of his home?"

"Sometimes."

"Was he married?"

"Not that I'm aware of."

"Tell me, if you would, any and every personal detail about him that you can think of."

"I don't know much, to be honest with you. We weren't social."

Gomez waited. Patience looked him over, suspiciously. "Okay. He was single, I think, about forty, maybe forty-five. Six feet, reddish blond hair, clean-shaven. He sometimes wore reading glasses. He lived somewhere in SoHo. I don't think he had a car; he was like, a regular New Yorker. He wanted to pork Helen Pardue. I know that much. He was always staring at her. She probably would have done it, too. She stared back, a lot."

"Do you have access to any documentation on Rafkin? Personnel file? Something we could use to track him down?

"No, man, everything's gone. Obviously." Montrane stared across the kitchen at that. "You might find something in the electronic stuff, but that's just data."

Gomez gave him a moment. Then he said, "Okay, quickly now. Close your eyes and tell me about Stuart."

Montrane dutifully closed his eyes. Gomez waited. Montrane must not have heard the part about quickly.

Ten seconds passed.

"Man, I just really did not *know* the dude. Know what I mean?"

Gomez exhaled. Patience returned to the room and he caught her eye. He didn't need to ask, she pre-empted him.

"I never cared for him," she sniffed.

Gomez stood. What a monumental waste of time. Patience smiled, genuine for the first time…pleased to see him leaving. He shook her hand and then Montrane's. He told them he could find his own way out.

He paused at the door.

"I've gotta ask. You're not curious as to *why* we're looking for Mr. Rafkin?"

They looked at each other, Devard and Patience, like Gomez was an imbecile. Like maybe he really was a reporter who had snuck through their defenses, with a journalist's deceit.

"Dude," Montrane said. "We called you."

Patience explained, "Are you guys not on the same page? Devard was yelling that Stuart was on the TV. I told him that son of a bitch was dead, but sure enough, there he was, big as life—all hurt outside that godforsaken mall. They was carrying his ass out, and I'll be damned if they weren't saying he was a cop who shot it out with Arab terrorists.

"I thought Devard was gonna stroke out on me," she added.

Gomez did not hear her last comment, or the concern in her voice. He was out the door.

A blackwall Chevy squatted behind Gomez' car at the curb

outside the Montrane residence. Two obvious plainclothes detectives leaned into the windows, trying to romance Viisky.

They spoke in unison as Gomez marched past them, holding up his creds.

"Guy said he recognized one of the shooters from last night."

"They full of shit or what?" said the other.

"Get the fuck off the car," Gomez ordered.

Viisky was bubbling on about the cops. Well, bloodsucking killers were human too. She had enjoyed the attention.

It registered as background noise as he took the streets in an increasingly reckless fashion. The stereo was off. No rap this time. Gomez was a bit surprised that she was still there when he came out of Montrane's. Not that he cared one way or the other. He stuck the blue plastic bubble on the roof and hammered the accelerator on the L.I.E. He quickly had it up to ninety, using every pony he had—heading south.

CHAPTER 27

GOMEZ BLEW ONTO the Highway of Smoking Wreckage at three in the afternoon.

It was a windy day; the car rocked occasionally and they could see the blush of the turning leaves fluttering from the trees along the parkway. Gomez' thinking cap was on overheat, ready to launch off his head like a bottle rocket.

Things were becoming clearer since last night in the bar, since finding Spasski dead in the road—after his little visit with the Montranes.

It had taken him a hair under five days to figure it out. Not too shabby. But then, he was *supposed* to figure it out.

The revelation from the Montranes was the last piece, like a hundred-ton iron ingot sliding smoothly across another. The last piece falling into place.

If he had this straight—if any of this made sense—it would mean that he, Gomez, was trying to find, capture, or kill Rafkin, who was trying to kill the Arabs he had mistakenly assisted. Gomez was also trying to kill Feliks and the Arabs, before they achieved their aim. Viisky had already killed Spasski; now she was trying to kill the Arabs, Rafkin, and maybe Gomez. Rafkin would probably like to kill Viisky, who he thought was his equal on the other side, and who also was trying to kill the Arabs. The SVR guys tailing them would then kill Viisky, Gomez, Rafkin, and any stray Arabs that had survived.

Good Lord! Explaining this to Kessler would be like explaining the workings of the female brain to a penguin—in Chinese.

A five-hour run to the District. Viisky's attitude would make it feel like a week. She sat there, hunkered like a stone. Like her batteries had been removed. She had not moved a muscle since Queens.

She saw a Hummer blow by and was agog. "This is the Army jeep! But it is yellow!"

"Yep. Bet you guys don't dress up your…whatever the hell it's called.

"BMP."

"Yeah, BMP." He remembered them, a big Russian box with unreliable mechanics—like an armor-plated conversion van.

"Do you get bonus rubles for every one you kill?"

"*Iintensivnaya nenavist. yada yada yada.*" More caterwauling in Russian.

Perhaps he should try a different tact, less confrontational.

Or not. "Don't you have to check in with Feliks?"

She did not answer; she was smoldering and he could see that she did indeed need to call in. Score one for Gomez! The notion of calling in struck him, as it did on occasion. He hit Kessler on the speed-dial.

"What? You stuck inside the commie chick?"

"There's going to be a terrorist attack. The follow-up to 9/11." Gomez reminded himself to speak very slowly. "We got bad guys."

"Tell me," Kessler commanded.

"The guy I told you about? This Stuart Rafkin? His name ain't Rafkin."

Gomez related most of his doings of the prior four-and-a-half days, rounding over the sharp edges, omitting intricate chunks entirely. He did not give the location of the attacks and Kessler did not ask. He didn't bother with the fact that Stuart Rafkin was exterminating Arabs. He also failed to mention Ms. Viisky's role in the matter, or her identity. That would take a little longer.

"I see," said Kessler. Gomez doubted it.

It was getting close to the time when Kessler would start badgering, asking why Gomez had not kept him updated. Gomez changed the subject.

"Also, I am being followed. There are two Sluzbha thugs in a white Honda minivan. They've been on me since at least Friday evening. There is a strong probability that they will take action against Ms. Viisky, and possibly myself, should we get to Stuart Rafkin before they do." Gomez thought he could hear the vacuum tubes warming up in Kessler's skull.

"I thought he was dead in the Towers, "Kessler said, pulling something out of thin air.

"Maybe. Probably. I really don't know."

A measurable silence ensued…Kessler trying to process. All that thinking, and the only thing Kessler could come up with was, "Goddammit!"

"I would appreciate it if you wouldn't blaspheme," Gomez was feeling pious, after his ten minutes in St. Mary the Virgin.

"You know the Russians are gone," Kessler said. "Have been for ten years."

"There is a Russian intelligence officer sitting next to me," Gomez lied. He still needed Viisky to find Rafkin, and maybe Feliks. He would expose her later.

"I am so confused," Kessler said, sounding it.

"I'll explain later. The only thing you need to know right now is that cleanup in New York. Have the boys up there whitewash this Adler thing and make sure it goes down as an accident. Two…" He looked over at Viisky. "I'm going to play a little game with my tail. If anything happens you'll need to clean that up as well."

"Where are you right now?" Kessler sounded like he was taking notes.

"I-95, passing Wilmington. I'll drag 'em all the way in before I make a move."

"All right, look," Kessler said, "the New York thing is easy, but don't make a big mess with those guys on your ass. On second thought, why don't you just drive right up to the office and we'll pop 'em there?"

"I think I want to keep them. They'll just send more."

"Your call."

"Yes it is."

*

Viisky turned toward Gomez. "Why do you not tell him of the Macklin?"

"I will decide when to make it public. *I* am on top of the situation, not Larry Kessler." Also, he thought, Rafkin won't get them all. I have to expect the attacks to occur just like they planned. She wasn't there for the Montranes' revelation.

"You keep forgetting. I want to catch them," he said.

"You are wrong," Viisky told him. She was blushing. "There is changing of minds. Now bad SVR wishes to eliminate the remaining Al Qaeda. They feel mission is completed." She added, "Oil prices already go up like giant balloon."

"Feliks told you this?"

She nodded.

"You have got to be shitting me."

"I do not shit."

There were times when Gomez found her use of the language appealing. There were others, such as now, when he just wanted to strangle her. "Do you have any aspirin?"

"No."

The sign for a public rest area appeared up ahead. One mile. "Whose side are they on?" he pointed with his head over his shoulder, to the Odyssey directly behind them. So much for covert.

"Pleasure? I do not know what you are saying."

"They're Russians," he said, deciding to bait her. "Real Russians." Like Stuart Rafkin, who was honest to God, real live Volk Vyydraat. *Unlike you*, he did not say. Still she sat looking out of the window.

"Enough of this bullshit."

He peeled off the ramp leading to the rest area, past all the signs promoting restaurants and gas stations, making sure to signal in plenty of time. He didn't want his tail to miss the exit. They parked in the convenience plaza. Gomez handed her a twenty.

"Get me some aspirin and a large coffee, will you? I gotta use the men's room." He pointed to a brick outbuilding.

"Certainly."

He watched her for a moment as she disappeared into the plaza. What a gorgeous day.

He'd noticed that the Sluhzba goons had parked directly behind him, one row removed. Twin shadows silhouetted in the afternoon sun. Gomez walked up to the minivan, whistling a tune from *Rocky VIII*, the one where Stallone beats the crap out of the big blond Russian. They wouldn't get it, but he did. That was what mattered.

"Hey, jack-holes!" Gomez smiled and waved as he approached.

To their credit, the Igors in the Odyssey did not overreact. The one in the passenger seat shared a wry glance, his hands moving out of Gomez' view. The driver, a man in his forties—probably the leader—stepped out of the car and leaned over the roof to grin at Gomez.

Gomez shook his head and clucked his tongue. The driver wore new stonewashed jeans, the kind that were tight around the ankles, like ringlets. His sneakers were brilliant white, a recent purchase. His bowling shirt hung over his belt in an extraordinary display of bad taste. Worst of all, the haircut was the same bowl-job they had been wearing since WWI.

They had cable and McDonalds, and all manner of Western influence. Still, they looked like Moe from the Three Stooges.

"What's up, bud?" The driver had the kind of English you might hear in Kansas or Nebraska. Gomez stood there for a moment, looking back and forth between the two of them. The driver's move had the effect of splitting the targets, dividing Gomez attention. He addressed the driver over the roof of the car.

"IDs. Hand 'em over."

"*Yeb vas.*"

Gomez sucker-punched the passenger, square in the mouth. The man grunted and his hands shot to his nose. Gomez looked up over the roof as the driver's hand slid into the minivan. *Gun*, he thought. A third of a second later he looked down, into the smiling, bleeding face of the passenger. Like a magic trick, he held a large automatic pistol, pointed at the little mole on the bridge of Gomez' nose. The driver's hands reappeared, holding nothing at all. Pretty smooth.

"You guys practice that?"

Gomez was looking at the driver as he said it, and he hit the passenger again, a wicked, straight-arm left. This time the guy did not recover so easily. Nobody can take that. His head was back against the headrest. Gomez thought that he might have dropped the gun into his lap.

He was wrong. The passenger's hand shot out and grasped Gomez around the wrist. Gomez would have hit him again, but he couldn't be sure about the driver.

Thinking it out, he saw Viisky carrying a styrofoam cup in her hand, eyes hooded like a viper, sliding in an arc around and behind the driver.

She was not stealthy enough. The driver felt the motion and turned. He'd seen her.

Gomez smiled at the passenger, looked back at Viisky and she read him, easing around to within six feet of the driver at his back. She held her free hand tucked in her jacket pocket. Gomez had not returned the Beretta. She wouldn't need it.

The driver closed his eyes, as if to say how unnecessary this was.

"Can't we all just get along?"

"Maybe I enjoy it," Gomez said. The pressure on his hand grew. He was becoming annoyed. He dug his thumb—the only free digit—around and into the joint of the wrist, forcing the passenger to release as the pressure point was violated. Gomez reversed the axis and now held the other guy's wrist, thumb and all, in an excruciating grip. Just like training. Fruity, but effective.

The driver glanced back at Viisky, unperturbed. Gomez did not like the way he looked at her. Like she was a fat, juicy turnip.

"She's not on our team."

Gomez rolled his eyes at the word *team*. It sounded like Jay-Neil, cajoling his staff into pushing more product. "I am aware of that."

The passenger's eyes watered. Tough little guy. Peripherally, citizens could be seen, ducking into cars and pointing. Gomez decided to end it…soon, anyway.

The funny thing was, from Viisky's point of view, this could be explained. She would claim these guys were aligned with the bad element of SVR. They were helping Al Qaeda, trying to prevent Viisky from saving America. But there was no bad SVR—only a bad Viisky.

She backed around another foot, so that she was square at the back of the driver, and for a while it seemed there was nothing else to say. The moment had arrived. The crux, as it were.

Gomez turned back to the driver.

"Simple message. You can follow if you wish. I won't call you in. But if and when we take Rafkin, I'm going to consider Ms. Viisky my personal charge. You let your people know, too, if you touch a hair on her pretty head, I'm going to fuck you up."

He released pressure as he said it. The passenger made a whimpering noise. The driver shook his head and smiled, revealing a hint of iron at the back molars. Gomez took a step backward and Viisky did the same. They got in the Ford and took off.

Viisky set the coffee into the center cup holder and popped the lid off like an adoring wife. Of the scene in the parking lot, she said not a word. She was a sharp cookie.

Gomez drove, enraptured by the colors of autumn. It was really something. In a minute, he realized that his wrist hurt like hell, and his headache was back.

"You get the aspirin?"

"I have purchased something much superior." She shook the plastic baggie out and was studying a bottle of something with renditions of skateboarders and snow-sport people on it. *XtremeHead.*

"Oh Christ. Just…gimme a couple of those, would you?"

Viisky read the directions. Through the pounding in his head, Gomez was excited to see that the reading glasses were back.

She peered at him over the rims.

"Bleeding of the rectum, eyes, ears, and…"

"Whatever, *just*—"

"What is this melting?"

"Hunh?"

"This is great danger! You must not take too many of this in twenty-four hour, or you will experience melting!"

"Gimme that." He took his eyes from the road, reading the back of the stupid pill bottle with its stupid figurines. How can you jump a mountain bike off a cliff if you've got a migraine? Sure enough, on the warning label, one of the potential side effects was complete and total melting of the human body.

"Gimme four," he said, handing the bottle back to her.

*

Three or four miles down the road he saw the Odyssey again, picking up speed in the passing lane—catching up. He dropped it down to a leisurely sixty-five, holding his hand in his lap. It hurt like hell and he knew it would be sore for a week.

"Thanks for the backup," he told her, not knowing precisely how to take her. She had backed him up readily in the parking lot; now she was cold and distant. Maybe they were meant for each other.

"Why do you twist the tail of this tiger? This is stupid."

Gomez's reply bore a hint of threat, "My country, remember? You forget your place. I won't allow your asshole buddies to run around committing agg assault like it's fucking Poland."

She was staring out the window. "They will not kill me, I think."

He almost didn't hear her with her head turned like that. He laughed…a genuine note of disbelief. "You are…" He wagged his head back and forth. Steadied himself. *"They will cut you down like a weed."*

She said nothing, lighting up as she rolled down the window.

Gomez saw the lights of a State Trooper whip by in the opposite direction, headed for the rest area. He had stopped at the last one in Delaware, by design. They would cross into Maryland in about three minutes, and there would be jurisdictional issues. By the time the state bears got their act together, he would be on the outskirts of Baltimore. He busied himself for a time, squeezing his fingers together. Better to keep the circulation going.

"Oh! There is sign for Virginia! Home of much presidents!"

"More importantly, we've crossed the state line. It'll take them a while to coordinate."

"I do not understand."

"I don't want to get stopped by the State Police."

"But *you* are police."

"I committed multiple Class A felonies. In public."

"But are you not larger police?"

"It doesn't work like that."

Her eyes were large with wonder, and he knew that she thought he was teasing.

"Really," he said.

She gave him an odd look and turned back to look out the window. Gomez dry-swallowed two more XtremeHead caplets. Still she looked coldly out the window and Gomez was beginning to feel as if they were already married.

"I mean, you didn't even know those guys were on us."

"Their names are Mikhail and Gregoriiy. I am sleeping with the both of them." As she turned back to the right, Gomez could see her smile, and he felt better.

*

They ran through Aberdeen and Whitemarsh, past the turn-offs for Accomac and Winchester, Culpeper, and Massaponax. Gomez liked the ring of the Indian names. California was all San-this and Los-that. The variety of the American landscape thrilled him and fed fuel to his patriotic light.

Larry Kessler called about an hour after their encounter with the Stooges.

"Status?"

"Leave em'. These two I can handle."

"Can't do it."

"Do not be such a *sissy girl*," Gomez grumbled. He looked over at Viisky, thinking of the automatic PC apology. Finely honed Pavlovian instinct.

"Oh, that's just great," Kessler was saying. "I can explain that I didn't curtail the illegal activities of two known foreign belligerents because it might seem like I was a sissy girl. That's just fucking great. Maybe you can tell Senator Smeal that what we really need in Federal Law Enforcement are less *sissy girls*."

Kessler's voice had climbed there at the end. Gomez was sort of proud of him. He choked back a snort of laughter.

"Just..." he blew out his breath in a deep bellow. "Do what I ask, okay, Larry? Please?"

Kessler was grumbling something and it was all Gomez could do not to laugh. He told Kessler he'd call him later.

He hung up to face the wrath of Viisky.

Her eyes bored into him like little black diamonds. Gleaming laser beams of molten plasma.

"What is this sissy girl!" she thundered. "I will demonstrate the sissy girl to you, you son of bitches bastard! I will extract your limbs from your torso! I will crush the testicles into small bits!"

Gomez' strength failed him. Tears ran into his stubble, howling in laughter. It was like driving in heavy fog. She beat him with her fists, quick little hammer shots that really smarted. He drifted a-foot-and-a-half into the center lane, correcting before he piled into a family of four. He had his right arm tucked up around his face, barely controlling the wheel with his left.

Viisky landed a nasty combination to his right kidney and the pain mixed with the laughter in one of life's ironically pleasant brews. Her act was failing. She had a smile at the corners of her, oh so wondrous, lips.

He could see that she had pulled her punches. She knew how to do much worse than she had. It reminded him to get a pair of handcuffs. Now would be a great time to cuff her.

Gomez rubbed his forehead, pressing in hard circular motions. She should have lied and said the two bullet holes were from a single incident. It would have been more plausible.

He passed a big Kenwood on the left and said, "The attacks are real aren't they?"

"Have you not been paying attention?"

Chapter 28

VIISKY WAITED in the darkened car in the driveway of a nice two-story brick job in the northwest burbs of DC Her eyes had popped as they passed home after home that, in the Caucasus, would be the residence of the *chekist* himself. All those years, she thought. All those years it was really true about America.

Gomez appeared in the doorway. He was speaking to a woman dressed in a heavy bathrobe, clutched about her like a suit of armor. He held both her hands in his and his head was titled downward at the paved walkway.

She could hear their voices but not the words, and it seemed as if they were speaking very quietly. Gomez hugged the woman, loosely, like strangers will, and then he was walking along a lighted path toward the car.

Vischka brushed her hair from her eyes. Gomez got in quietly. He settled into the seat and fired the ignition. Rebecca Adler stood at the end of her walkway, watching them as they drove away.

*

They arrived at Gomez's apartment at ten. Viisky had her laptop and a single bag; Gomez was lugging his overnighter. He left the heavy gym bag in the trunk; thus, they were able to make it in one trip. The Odyssey had not reared its ugly bumpers since dinnertime. Gomez felt the need to crow about it, "That's *twice* I kicked their ass." He ushered her inside with a small act of chivalry, holding out his arms expansively and taking her luggage from her inside the foyer.

"How was woman?" Viisky asked him.

"Okay." He paused to look into her eyes. "She was strong, actually."

Gomez made them bacon and eggs, and they ate watching the news. Viisky declared that she liked this American quirk of having breakfast at any hour of the day.

A commercial for a rectal cream came on. It didn't go well with the eggs. Gomez looked away. She had her opening.

"Suppose you are working for home country?" she began. "And you are ordered to undertake certain tasks that you find, eh, not so pleasurable."

"Please," Gomez shook his head solemnly. "Just...don't."

Viisky got up to take their plates into the kitchen. She hesitated, watching his back as he sat staring at the television. She changed direction and went down a narrow hallway, into the rear of the apartment.

Her bag was in the smaller of the two bedrooms, a bleak, apartment—white room with no furniture, and nothing on the walls. She opened her bag, taking a few things out into the hall.

In the bathroom, she closed the door behind her. There was a gasp as she turned on the light. It was...*horrible!* She stood there for a moment, gathering herself, and then began to root around under the vanity. Shortly, she found what she was looking for.

In the living room, a very young boy lectured Gomez from the safety of a television studio. Behind him was a scene of the rescue workers digging in the pits of Ground Zero. The two images were morphed together to give the illusion that the boy was standing there in front of the salvage crews. Gomez knew he was standing in front of a blue-screen in the studios they had visited two days ago.

The boy held a Cronkite-gray umbrella, and no rain touched its somber surfaces. Outside, it was pouring. The reporter's name was Blythe. Gomez was surprised that he was out of junior high, but he must be because of all the child labor laws.

In a rambling, twisted spurt of disjointed and nonsensical verbiage, chock full of illogic, he managed to blame every federal agency in existence—there were many—as well as most of the leadership on both sides of the aisle. He wrapped with, "It is incumbent upon us, as Americans, to understand *why* these acts have occurred and to take a long, hard look at our own behavior."

Gomez sighed, lowering the volume with the remote. He sat at his desk, a great mass of old walnut, and began picking at the keys of his outmoded personal computer. He typed in the words "Russia" and "enemy" on Google.

The search spat out eleven-million, three-hundred-thousand entries.

Besides the offers to purchase a mail-order bride, the majority of the articles were devoted to Russia's troubles with her rambunctious satellites.

Their Cold War sponsorship was backfiring on them.

He could barely pronounce most of them. How about this one? Udmurtia. Where in the hell was that? Or Buryatia, Adygea, Kalmykia, or Tartarstan. This would keep the Commission busy for years. Senator Smeal would love it.

Gomez narrowed it down to three countries. Azerbaijan looked pretty good—a majority Muslim country on the northern border of Iran. For a moment he almost felt sorry for the Russians.

Chechnya was a possibility. Again, an Islamic majority and unfriendly with Moscow, to say the least. Their history was long and bloody, consisting mainly of the Russkies stomping the shit out of Chechnya, one century after another.

Speaking of history, Gomez typed in "Eustachius." He learned that his original name was Placidas. He was, as Rivera had said, a Roman general. Placidas was on a hunting trip and evidently saw a glowing cross between the antlers of a wild stag…probably hammered on mead at the time. But the interesting part was when Gomez read about how even after Eustachius was denounced for being a Christian, lost his property and his family, the Romans needed his skills. Trajan recalled him to duty, and Eustachius did his duty.

As his reward, Trajan tried to feed Eustachius and his family to the lions. For some reason, the lions wouldn't eat them. When that didn't work, they were cooked to death in a bronze bull. That had to suck, there. Also, Eustachius was one of the Fourteen Holy Helpers…so he had that going for him.

Chechnya, then. Or Azerbaijan. For what it was worth. He logged off.

Vissky was, Gomez assumed, still freshening up, and he finished scraping the dishes, wondering how he was going to handle the next twenty or thirty minutes. If he had had some furniture in the spare bedroom, it might have given him some options. There was always the sofa, but it beat hell out of his lower back. He rinsed and tossed their plates into the dishwasher, wondering what could be taking so long. He bounced nervously, trying to decide if he should wait out here, or? Crap.

When he saw Viisky coming down the hallway, his first thought was to go for his weapon. Her hands were wrapped in the only two hand towels he owned. He had not seen them for a very long time. She had a secret smile on her face, and she stopped halfway, unwrapping the towels from her hands.

"Where is dust bin?" Coy, with a dash of sex.

"In the kitchen," he pointed.

The towels went into the trash can and she beckoned for him to follow. Against his better judgment, he did. She took a sharp left and stood there, holding the door open for him. Gomez gasped as he entered the bathroom.

Holy God!

It was clean. No, it was sparkling…veritably gleaming. She must have found some bathroom cleaning product somewhere—he didn't know where, because he couldn't recall ever buying such a thing—but there it was. The white tiles of the sink, the tub, and the floors twinkled like a commercial advertisement, the one with the bald guy and the ecstatic dancing housewife.

"I use this towels on my hands to avoid tiny creatures. I hope you do not mind." She smiled at him, looking for some response. "You must now burn towels."

All the white hurt his eyes. He took her by the arm, leading her into the living room.

"Why did you have to go and do something like that?"

"You are not pleased?"

"No. I…*thank you*, I mean it's great!"

They stood there, measuring what was in each other's eyes. Gomez held her gaze for what seemed like forever and he thought that he would never leave her.

"We must take shower," she said, a little hitch in her voice. She cast her eyes toward a window. Gomez realized, thickly, that it was his play. He nodded, dazed, and he let her guide him toward the bathroom. She looked at the length of his body and smiled, her lids partially closed. He felt himself guided on a cloud until he was standing next to the shower. She backed away, fingers slipping from his hand, staring into his eyes as she eased all the way out into the hall. She closed the door behind her.

Gomez stood there, alone for a moment, surveying Viisky's work. He had been alone in the living room for what? Ten or fifteen minutes at the most. He would have thought it would require a jackhammer or an electroplating removal device to reveal the white of the tiles. He didn't know how she'd done it, but the evidence was before him.

He turned on the showerhead and stripped off his clothes. His head felt fuzzy as he tried to understand her. Why had she so lasciviously led him into the bathroom and then just walked away?

He got into the shower and saw that his bar of soap was there and also a bottle of what must be shampoo. It was labeled in Cyrillic. He decided that whatever it smelled like it would please her if he would use it. He normally just used the bar of Zest for his body and his hair. The Zest came in handy when he forgot to buy shaving cream, also.

He was singing loudly and terribly off-key, when he noticed a shape behind the curtain.

She could kill him easily. He was a foolish old G-man, hornswaggled by the simplest of tricks. He stood there, the ball of lather in his hands, waiting.

She drew the curtain and got in—the sight of her took his breath away.

Better than advertised, bullet holes and all. She leaned her head against him. She came up to the center of his sternum and rested her dimpled chin on his chest.

Gomez dropped the soap.

"This won't get you out of it," he said

"Is not to do with Kostka or…any of this." He noticed her chest rising and falling rapidly. There was a glistening dot of water in the hollow of her throat.

Gomez wavered…ran his hand along the smooth, perfect angle of her shoulder blade. This had to be a ploy. Had to be. She was a nubile young thing and he was practically an old man. She was a vicious stone killer. She would get on top while his intellect flowed from his penis. She'd slit his throat like a chicken.

Unbidden, an image of being stuck inside Viisky—what Kessler had said—popped into his dirty mind. He laughed out loud.

"What is humor?"

What if? He smiled, remembering something.

He stepped out, telling her he'd be right back, ignoring the water dripping everywhere. Half the apartment would be soaked within the hour anyway. Into the bedroom, in the bottom drawer of his nightstand, he came up with a pair of heavy-duty Krueger handcuffs.

Back into the bathroom, into the shower, and the echo of a giggle rang off the tile as Gomez closed the curtain behind him.

Chapter 29

HE AWOKE TO FIND his lover gone. There was a missive on the countertop in the kitchen: She would return shortly. It ended with an endearment in Cyrillic. Loosely translated, it said, *"From your little potato."*

They say potato—we say tomato.

At least it wasn't boiled cabbage.

He stretched, hands reaching to the sky, forcibly ejecting all the built-up crud of a forty-four-year-old man, long held responsible for the safety of others. He considered a little jig, but conditioning held out.

The woman was a dynamo!

Singing in the shower…a country tune from the eighties he kept mixing up with a Diana Ross number. *"She's a hot little babushka—babushka! My homicidal Baltic princess!"*

An alternative to the madness popped into his head as he was lathering his beard with the commie shampoo. He would retire from the Bureau, cash in his chips on a secondhand yacht. Viisky could wear a sailor hat, nothing else.

Or a thong. How about three thongs? One for her tasty body, one on each foot! There'd be a great many cocktails, conversation on the poop deck in twilight, making passionate love day and night. Modern yachts had autopilot and all those navigational gizmos—GPS, radar. That way, he would not have to imprison or kill her. It could work.

He looked deeply into the mirror. He was fucking a terrorist. Not his best moment. The toothbrush slowed, he cast an eye at himself, snorting a little laugh. Dripped some goo into the sink. He shook his head from side to side, rolling his eyes.

By eight-twenty he was dressed. Greasing his conscience with a wild fantasy in which Viisky had been kidnapped by the *real* terrorists and forced to pose as a Russian spy, in order to blame the Russians for their complicity in terrorist acts against America. Sort of like OJ's story.

They would kill her family if she did not do as they asked.

He was talking to himself and sometimes answering when Viisky appeared with a box of doughnuts and Dunkin' Donuts coffee. The best in the world.

After they ate, he watched her clearing the doughnut mess, tossing the napkins, wiping the tabletop. This could get out of hand.

Rafkin was gone. Kostenko Spasski was dead in the road. His options were zero. He had run a by-God investigation and now it was over. Three days was enough to convince him.

"It's time for the menpowers."

Viktorina smiled.

*

Gomez called Kessler, wiping a dab of Boston crème from his chin.

"Where the heck are you?" Kessler sounded desperate. "The hearing started at nine.

"Forget that crap. I'm bringing Miss Viisky in. We have to talk."

"Yeah, yeah, yeah, I've already talked to some people. But first you gotta do this Commission hearing." Kessler's voice was climbing. He was sounding more and more like a neglected toddler. "You promised."

Gomez massaged his temples. "I'm running a little late."

"The Rayburn Senate Office Bldg., third floor, A wing. I left your name with the Capitol Police."

"Tell them to put Ms. Viisky on the list."

Kessler said he would.

"And bring somebody from Justice."

Viisky was polishing off her third crueller.

"We have to go downtown to meet with…some people." He could never bring himself to use the acronym. "My other job."

She pursed her lips, remembering, "This is stinky peoples?"

"The Commission," Gomez nodded.

She dusted her hands of the powdered sugar, seeing the reticence he wore like a beacon. "Perhaps they will not need you for this." She looked pointedly at the clock above the oven. She wanted to know—did he still have the handcuffs?

An exhilarating half-hour was passed in a new position, something Gomez had never dreamed of, but that he enjoyed immensely. When they left the condo forty minutes later, Viisky was rubbing her wrists. Gomez hadn't wanted a scene, so he took them off. He could always just cuff her again later.

*

The Rayburn Senate Office building was imposing. Soldiers patrolled with German shepherds, and people were perched on the rooftops with Stinger anti-aircraft missiles, their ball caps on backwards. Plainclothes would be out on the sidewalks, scouring the passersby. Female agents pushed baby carriages; younger agents were dressed like students. They were waking up.

Gomez showed his creds to a gate guard, who found them a reserved space near a side entrance.

"Explain this Rayburn please."

"Some old crook." The doors closed behind them.

Imposing historical documents in gilded frames under deftly placed task lighting. Oils by Frederick Remington dared the Lakota and Sioux to stop the expansion. Viisky's eyes were huge. She must have felt like Gomez would have felt strolling through the Kremlin in 1984. Then he remembered, she was mujahadeen. The paintings were fakes, anyway. The real stuff would be in the National Archives.

He saw that Viisky was afterglowing. Maybe no one would notice.

Twice, they had to ask for assistance before finding a security desk at the end of a windowless hallway. An aide pinned plastic badges on them. They were expected in A wing.

A heavyset Capitol Police officer escorted them. They were ushered into the conference room of Senator Roger Smeal, one hour and twenty-seven minutes after the call from Kessler. The hearings had ended at ten.

The cabal in the conference room reminded Gomez of photos he had seen of JFK and the boys discussing the Cuban Missile Crises, with sober expressions and in shirtsleeves. There were three of them; two looked as if they qualified as bona fide big-boys, and Larry Kessler. Who knew how much Kessler had told them, or of what logic or clarity his tale consisted, but clearly the big-boys were interested. Kessler, at last, had served a function.

"Todd Smint, Chief of Staff," was a blur of motion, the picture of a harried bureaucrat. Smint was a small man, dressed to the nines. He wore matching cuff links, a nice touch. He introduced himself in a very soft voice. Gomez, who had been prepared for Senator Smeal, decided that Smint was genuine. Maybe this wouldn't be so bad. Smint extended his hand. It was like shaking a tuna fish sandwich.

A solid-looking gentleman sat next to Kessler with his legs crossed, poking a stylus on his PalmPilot. Early fifties, good hygiene, confident leadership type, and a studied indifference that told you who held the weight in these parts. He looked like a lobbyist. Gomez did not like lobbyists, although he was hazy on what exactly it was that a lobbyist did. Perhaps this would be his chance to meet one.

He did notice that Kessler was afraid of the guy. Big-time Bureau, Gomez thought. So much of authority was assumptive.

"You look like you came out of my dog's ass," Kessler greeted him, sotto voice. The lobbyist stood, introducing himself as Henry Yates, the Assistant Director of Investigations. Gomez accepted his business card with a nod. Horseshit was going to be tricky.

They were all staring at Viisky. Gomez tried to remember what he'd told Kessler. He finally introduced her as Miss Viisky, with the Russian Ministry of Agriculture.

"She's Russian," Kessler sagely informed them. Gomez caught Viisky's reaction on the peripheral. The corners of her mouth crinkled.

Yates cleared his throat.

"Kessler here tells me you've run into something."

"That is correct," Gomez answered. Nothing more. Kessler was staring down at the polished conference table.

"Well?" Yates shot his cuffs. Gomez stared at Todd Smint. He shouldn't have agreed to meet Kessler here. He should have waited until later, at Hoover. No way was he going to brief Todd Smint. The spin would flow from here like a river.

Kessler jumped in, "I gave Director Yates the basics of yesterday's conversation."

"There's a concern I would like to express before I get into that," Gomez let his gaze linger on Smint. "This is not primarily a political matter." He waved a hand at Smint. "No offense, but I'd rather not share this information with anyone outside the Bureau. For now, anyway."

Smint smiled, a genuinely arrogant smile. He pushed off the desk, rubbing his hands together. Warming up. "We won't get into realms of authority or whether or not it is your prerogative to determine the course of a federal investigation." Smint began to pace, hitting his stride. "An operation involving Islamic terrorists and an intelligence organ of the Russian Federation *can only* become a political matter. After National Security considerations, of course."

"Excuse me….*what*?"

"Look here, Gomez." It was Yates' turn. "Your initiative is to be commended. Considering your….eh, current duties." He'd said that on purpose. A reminder for Gomez. "I think it would be best if you left the political crap to us." He nodded to Smint, who in turn nodded, and Gomez was reminded of Gilligan and the Skipper.

"What do you know?" Gomez asked. Strange really, that someone of Yates' stature would be in on this already. He would be a busy big-boy these days—unless they knew more than Kessler had told them.

"That's not really your question now is it?" Yates smiled for the first time.

Gomez went with the Geneva Convention line of bullshit. "I informed ASAC Kessler of my discoveries with the intention of alerting the Bureau to a potential problem." He looked pointedly at Todd Smint for his next statement. "I did not intend to alert the media."

"Kessler is your immediate superior. You'll report to him," Yates said.

"He isn't, not really," Gomez said. "Commission liaison is Marion Stokes. Putting me under Kessler was a way to keep me in the organizational chart." Gomez glanced at Kessler. He was very, very pale.

Yates said, "Report to Kessler. Do it now."

The last thing they needed was to politicize this mess. Senator Roger Smeal, or someone like him, would let fly with the news that they were going to hit us. People would go into a tizzy. There would be old men with shotguns at every doorstep, citizens with pitchforks lining the streets. Smeal would get a lot of face time on the evening news. And the attacks would never occur.

Al Qaeda would see that they were exposed. They would crawl back into whatever pit they were hiding in until the Americans fell back to sleep. Then they would blow us to kingdom come.

A moment later, the matter was taken from Gomez' hands. A young woman appeared through a door Gomez had not noticed previously. Also, she had a really excellent ass. Not that he'd noticed.

Trailing along behind her, head down a little, arms stuffed with file folders, was Val Sacco. The sides of Smint's mouth curled, a tic that Gomez was expected to view as a *gotcha*. Silly prick.

More garden party stuff, introductions, hand gripping.

Gomez yawned. He looked to see how Viisky was holding up. She was a question mark, confused by his mention of press leaks. He would explain later.

"Why don't we all have a seat," Smint directed. They all did, with the exception of Gomez. Viisky almost made it to her chair and then popped back up like a punching bag when she saw Gomez's play. Gomez looked at Kessler, who turned away.

Yates looked comfortable, at ease. He was a good meeting manager. "Fill us in, if you would, Agent Sacco, on the state of our defensive posture," he said.

Sacco had a briefcase with him. He played with it for a second, got it open and consulted his notes.

"Okay. Starting with Marcus Hook," Sacco said, "SAC Dover, plus ten men are securing the site in shifts. I've got a team in a hotel close to the refinery. We can have them there in ten minutes."

"We would prefer, I think, a broader view," Yates said.

Sacco was out of his element. He looked around the room for help, pausing at Gomez, who stared back, unblinking. Smint diddled with his papers.

"We're good on the East Coast. Slowly ramping up out west. The southern ports are a worry. New Orleans, Tampa, JAX—we could have a problem there. A bunch of guys have already left for the Middle East, so we're gonna be thin no matter what happens."

Sacco had not just spoken to these idiots in the last few hours. Gomez tried to recall the last time he spoke to Sacco. Saturday night? What had Val told Davidson? Gomez had a thought, and then lost it. He was playing too many crosswords at once. It was wearing him out.

"I'm waiting for your approval on the State Police angle we talked about," Sacco continued. "I've got feelers out to every Commandant from Maine to Florida. They know where, but not what the requirement is, other than how many guys and how they need to be equipped."

"Don't worry about manpower," Yates broke in. Easy for him to say, Gomez thought. He noticed Yates did not elaborate. And never would.

"The problem is one of training," Sacco said. "These State guys just don't have the firepower or the training to handle anything other than a couple guys on semi-auto. We do have SWAT teams coming out our ears, so that can't hurt, but if they come at us with more than small unit action, maybe even company-sized, which is what we have to prepare for, it's going to be a bitch to handle."

"I'll give you a hint," Gomez said. "Drop everything but the Northeast." They may as well know.

"I think not," Smint chirped. They were all about authority. Who gets to be Dad. Gomez was closest to the problem; therefore, he was to be ignored. "What happens if they nuke Miami? What do we say when the press finds out we pulled assets away to cover the Brooklyn Navy yard?" Smint made a note on a little pad.

"Ten guys," Gomez said, "for an area the size of Syria."

Sacco looked over at Gomez. He blushed, just a little, and then squared himself and said to Smint, "I really think we need to consider the National Guard."

Smint's ass must have been getting sore. He left his position on the front of the desk and sat down in the chair. Senator Smeal's chair was Gomez's guess. Smint most likely tried on Smeal's suits and made Smeal speeches in front of a full-length Smeal mirror.

"I want to be very clear on this," Smint said. "No soldiers. The nation is already in a state of panic, one that we will not magnify."

Gomez, in a virtual coma by now, began to awaken. And then Smint made *the comment*—the one that validated Gomez' decision to keep Viisky, Rafkin, and the whole mess from these people in the first place.

"It is incumbent upon us, as officers of the Federal Government, to maintain the confident and productive attitude of the nation," Smint said. "Failing that, we must present the *illusion* that all is well. No soldiers. You'll all have a statement to that effect this afternoon."

Yates, who by now was drifting, wrinkled his nose. It went unnoticed by Smint.

"Signed by whom?" Yates asked. He looked a little uncertain. A crack? Could be an ally there.

"The President is coming close to policy on how we're going to handle this new reality. We're not going to force his hand. We are not going to do something that will smear us in shit. There are literally hundreds of agencies, Federal, state, and local, that must all be on the same page before any action is taken—offensive or defensive."

Gomez felt an artery pulsing dangerously. He stood and interrupted, "What would you say…if we just found them instead? And killed them?"

They pretended Gomez hadn't spoken. Machismo worked in a lot of situations, though this might not be one of them. And just maybe, the dynamic had shifted. Gomez leaned forward and held Yate's eye.

"So I guess I'm done."

"You got it."

"That's too bad," he added. "Actually, I don't give a fuck."

Yates inspected his nails. Smint blanched. He stood, moving behind his chair. The testosterone was getting to him.

Viisky showed Gomez a small, tight smile of encouragement.

There can be relief in spilling the burden to others. Gomez was almost tempted to tell them all of it—the whole truth. Almost, but not quite.

"The operation is called Oktober Swan."

"Ahh…"Kessler threw up his hands. It *was* a little goofy…a cold warrior dredging up the Cold War, Russian sleepers, code-word ops. Gomez sighed. He should explain it to them. Just because the Blue Team won, that didn't mean the Red Team would go away forever. Yates and Smint looked to him, expectantly.

Yes, he had taken steps to cover the threatened national assets. Yes, there were other agents that had quasi-official notice of the activities of Al-Qaeda in regard to the anticipated attacks. "No," he told them, "I did not feel it was in the best interest of the Bureau, and the country as a whole, to notify ASAC Kessler. Undue activity, especially the high probability of a leak to the press, would all but ensure their escape." He made sure he had eye contact and punctuated, "They watch the news, too. They'll just wait until we forget about them."

Gomez also forgot something. He forgot to tell them about Viisky—that she was, in fact, a blood-sucking-vampire-terrorist-assassin-killer. That silly agriculture thing was just for grins. He smiled at her. She smiled back, batting her eyes.

"So you took it upon yourself to institute an *ad hoc* defense of the refineries. You, meanwhile, were going to track them down. Unorthodox, don't you think?" Yates looked thoughtful.

"I thought I should to do something to help," Gomez replied, "instead of talking about something that's already happened."

Neither Yates, nor Smint, nor Kessler had a reply to that one.

"I want to nail them. Now. Not when we're hosing blood out of the craters." At the moment, Gomez felt he was ahead on points. Maybe they'd let him continue the investigation, if that's what it could be called. He decided to push it. Blow this thing away.

"The last I heard, Oversight cannot become actively involved in an ongoing investigation." Kessler closed his eyes. Gomez stuffed his hands into his pockets, feeling much better. So much so, that he smiled at Viisky.

"This thing could put the Senator over the top in Oh-four," Smint said, stepping in the poopy. He looked at Yates and blurted, "and I gotta deal with this idiot."

The air left the room. Gomez made a small sucking sound between his teeth. Viisky said *ahh*, very softly under her breath.

"The Senator is a friend of the Bureau," Smint said, trying to save it. It was in the way he said "friend." Gomez had a sudden urge to rip his tongue out of his head. "As Chairman he has the wherewithal to rapidly increase Bureau funding to meet this new reality."

"What has any of that got to do with...*anything?*" Gomez wanted to know.

Yates didn't like that question; it was too close to the heart of the machine. "Who is Stuart Rafkin?" he said, very casually.

It took a moment for Gomez to realize that his finger was still in the air, pointing at Smint. If they knew about Rafkin... why had they let him continue? The answer appeared just as quickly. It was so they had time to cover their backsides. Nothing had changed.

"We don't have time for that now."

Todd Smint came up out of his chair. "I should have you in a Federal Detention Center. It is not your place…"

"I contacted Agent Sacco because I knew he could put some manpower in place. In case we *don't* find them." Gomez aimed a finger at Smint. "In the meantime, we are close to finding out precisely *where* they're going to strike, and potentially, *when,* so that we can kill every last one of them. Now. Beforehand. Not afterward."

Gomez pulled a cigarette from his jacket and began tapping on the table.

"You're not going to light that," Yates said. More question than order. A minor victory.

"No."

"So, again, who is Stuart Rafkin?"

Gomez sighed. The venom left him a little. He was wasting his breath. They were not going to get it. Ever.

"He's dead. So it doesn't matter. Killed in the collapse of Tower Two, if you can believe that."

Viktorina Viisky had not spoken for so long that her voice cracked. She'd virtually disappeared from the room, like smoke. They didn't hear her the first time, so she said it again. "The Rafkin is quite alive."

Her statement left an enormous vacuum. A vacuum Smint tried to fill with the one in his head. "I want her gone." He looked a question over at Yates, who gave him a look that said, "Let me deal with them."

"Fine," Yates said. "I think we can all agree that she needs to go. We cannot have an agent of a foreign government involved in an active counter-terror investigation."

"She murdered an American citizen." Kessler added.

"It is the suicide," Viisky insisted.

Gomez was getting frustrated. "Rafkin was a spy. A citizen of a country that no longer exists."

"I've had enough of this bullshit," Smint sneered. The kind of sneer that says things are more complicated than the rube could possibly grasp.

But things were not complicated, Gomez thought. Things were simple. They want to kill us. We kill them first.

"Bottom line is this," Smint said, "we are taking the position that there is no credible threat *vis a vis* the Viktorina Viisky thing."

"Yes?" asked Gomez. He stood, staring hard at Smint. Yates found something interesting on the ceiling. "Well then. I, myself am *taking the position*…that I am a ballerina."

Kessler blew something through his nose. Gomez tried to light the cigarette, but found he'd twisted it into a worthless ball of fluff. He turned on his heel, grasping for the doorknob.

"Where do you think you're going?" Yates asked, with even less authority than before.

"Men's room."

*

He got lost a few times, navigating this colossus of lunacy. This served to aggravate his mood to the point of implosion. Once, he looked behind him to see if they were coming to get him. Whatever. If they did, they did.

He found his car and got in, slamming the door harder than was necessary, or prudent. He found the pack and lit up. If he could have smoked two at the same time he would have…lit the whole fucking pack with a propane torch. He looked at his watch.

He'd give it three minutes, tops.

In thirty-six seconds, Viisky appeared at the window. She got in and closed the door. Looked at him like a lover will and said, "I also, have needed the use of this men's room."

CHAPTER 30

AN AMERICAN AIRLINES 767 would rotate out of LaGuardia at two-forty on Monday afternoon, bound for the island of St. Kitts—doubtless, with more Sky Marshals on board than paying passengers. In continued irony, a United 767 would leave Newark for Grace Bay in the Turks/Caicos on Tuesday morning. The airlines were taking their first tentative steps toward normalcy.

The afternoon flight was preferable. LaGuardia was easier, and Stuart was itching to get out of the country. They were so close.

Paul's travel agency pal had secured two first class tickets for them, a dividend of Paul's frequent flier miles from his travels to galleries on buying excursions. They would try for the American at two-forty.

"He said to get there as early as possible. There are soldiers running around everywhere." Paul exhaled deeply as he re-hooked the portable phone.

Rafkin wasn't concerned with discovery. His passport was good. The chances that the authorities knew anything about him were remote.

"You're ready?" he asked.

"Yes."

*

They each carried a bag, one of which contained clothing and toiletries. The other was filled with basic survival gear—Paul's laptop, assorted digital media, a host of superfluous vitamins and medications. Rafkin emptied out a briefcase. They would need that one.

They went down the stairs, and Rafkin did not turn to look at his apartment for the last time. He was eager to be on the road. Sentimentality could wait.

Paul made a show of dragging another, smaller bag to the foyer door, letting it drop heavily to the floor. He froze, staring at Rakfin. The bag was stuffed with cash, jewelry, and most important, the names, addresses, account numbers, and PINs to Paul's brokerage accounts. Together with Rafkin's respectable accrual, it was enough to keep them living well for the foreseeable future. Paul brought his Audi Roadster around and they crammed their bags into the inadequate trunk.

"I'm going to miss this car," Paul smiled, a melancholy smile.

Rafkin nodded, thinking back to the people he'd known… Helen Pardue, dead in the Towers…Devard Montrane, almost certainly abandoned to the same fate. Rafkin didn't know for sure, he hadn't looked through the lists of the dead, but he'd seen the empty elevator shafts—their doors opened to eternity.

"Now watch, the plane will crash," Paul smiled weakly. Rafkin led Paul to the car and they got in, with Rafkin at the wheel.

He thought of telling Paul the true story of his entry into the United States, back when the Cold War was real and people feared the Bear. How scared he had been beneath his mask. It would only serve to make Paul feel weak and inexperienced, so he said nothing.

Rafkin's salary had been a fair one hundred-forty thousand, a long way from Sevastopol, but not enough to save any real money. Not in a place like Manhattan. At Rafkin's advice, Paul had the bulk of his assets with Rafkin's former employer. The rest was rotting in a money market at the bank.

Rafkin pulled to the curb. He plied the meter with coins, enough for an hour or so. Back in the driver's seat, he faced Paul.

"Remember. It's your money. You want a cashier's check, not a brokerage disbursal. That would take three days. They may try to put a hold on the funds. Do not agree. They'll drag their feet and we'll be sitting here a week from now. You want the check in your hand."

"Got it."

"Don't let them bully you."

There was new purpose in Paul's stride as he walked to the building. Rafkin could almost smell the humidity and taste the salt and sand of the Islands. It would be a shame, when they got to Grace Bay. Perhaps he wouldn't have to do it.

There was a poster in the window of a street-level travel office. Rafkin paced abreast of it, staring at destinations. He bought a pack of cigarettes from a newsstand, smoking without inhaling. The poster was a helicopter view of a minor mountaintop somewhere in the Mediterranean. Greece, he thought, with the bright blue of a mosque overlooking sloops in the crystal harbor in the foreground.

He watched a young woman struggling with a half-dozen straining leashes…a dog walker. Sometimes they walked the children from the city schools in similar fashion—on leashes. Rafkin realized, with a start, that he would miss this place.

It bothered him, the children. He had done well, he thought. He'd eliminated most of them. But he wasn't finished. He could see that now.

In less than twelve hours, Feliks would attack. First the diversion, then the children. They could be Russian children that Feliks was going to murder. Rafkin's conscience nagged and he thought of calling the FBI, but he was afraid of triangulation.

Fine. There was another way. They would fly out tomorrow. The instant they landed, Rafkin would purchase two one-way tickets to Athens. From there, who knew? But Rafkin would quickly and easily delete the trail Paul was leaving in the bank, and if the connection were ever made it would be impossible to follow.

Twenty minutes passed. He should have gone into the brokerage house with Paul. Forty-five minutes. Rafkin pictured them in there, pushing some index fund or other. Still, he worried. Without Paul's money, he would last only three or four years. He doubted the Caicos government had a need for senior intelligence officers.

Paul's smile appeared on the sidewalk next to Rafkin. He wagged a manila folder at Stuart. "Got it!"

Paul motioned to the poster. "Is that what you're thinking?" Paul was game.

"As a matter of fact, yes." Rafkin could see the clocks on the wall inside the travel office, with the time of day in every corner of the world. It was tomorrow in Hong Kong. In London, they were finishing their sickening English suppers. Unfortunately, it was afternoon in New York. The American flight was out of the question.

"But first, we have to go somewhere less inviting." Rafkin took the manila folder from Paul as he headed for the car.

"We have to go to Vineland, New Jersey."

*

They left the top down on the Audi, despite the chill. It was a product of Paul's feeling that this was a great adventure, where all is new and exciting.

"I thought they had machines for that," Paul said, motioning to an old coot astride an older tractor, a hundred yards from the road, as they blew past.

Paul was out of his element. He was a city boy, through-and-through. Rafkin thought Paul cultivated the rube. The old man waved. Quaint. Paul waved back. Rafkin wondered what Paul would think of Sevastopol, or the *Stasi*, the sekret police of Bulgaria. Paul had a bad moment and he asked Rafkin if they could ever return.

"I don't think so."

"Never?"

Rafkin shook his head. Paul watched him closely. Rafkin thought Paul was shrinking into himself.

"I hope you understand what this is about," he advised. Rafkin's tone was pensive. He wanted to remind Paul that they were not on holiday.

"What is it?" Paul picked up on Stuart's mood. Rafkin had told him they were going to Vineland to meet a man from Mossad—a colleague. Paul thrilled for the moment. Rafkin realized this wasn't going to work, not if he was going to bring the weapons out.

"I have something to tell you."

Paul hit the switches to raise the windows, so that he could better hear Stuart over the draft.

"Earlier, I spoke to an associate of mine…while you were in the bank." Rafkin paused, trying to decide if he could still finesse this. He didn't wish to sentence Paul to death by his own hand, with his own words.

"This can't be repeated. To anyone." Paul took his eyes from the wheel to reassure him. Gone was the little boy look.

"We have discovered a threat to your country. The Jihadists are going to attack again—a follow-up to September the Eleventh."

Paul's eyes grew. His speed dropped to forty-five. "My God!"

"Yes," Rafkin agreed. "They are going after children this time. Elementary schools, we think—in New York and Philadelphia." Rafkin did not know precisely which school. It was a slip that led to this knowledge in the first place, and he wondered if Mohammed had not run his fat mouth, they might have warned him about the aircraft on the Eleventh. And what he might have done.

Paul was properly aghast, but underneath there was a layer of awe and pride at this secret knowledge from Stuart. The spy. His lover.

"Well, aren't you going to tell someone?" Paul seemed to know the answer to his question. He leaned against his door a little… pulling away. "Aren't we, like, allies?"

"It's more complicated than that. Not everyone in your government is a friend of Israel."

Paul pulled into a cutout. He left the engine idling."How long have you known?" There was more than a question there—an accusation, almost.

Rafkin was surprised and a bit taken aback. He'd thought he controlled Paul utterly. Maybe Paul had the fabled American backbone after all.

"I told you. I just spoke to my colleague two hours ago." A car whizzed past, startling them. They had seen very little traffic on this two-lane road. It was almost five in the afternoon. Rush hour, only there is no rush hour in farm country.

"My God," Paul said again. "What could they hope to gain by hurting children?" He fingered a gold ring, staring down at his hands. Digesting.

Rafkin looked out the window to his right. It could go either way.

The Pine Barrens. Aptly named. The car that just passed was the first they'd seen in ten minutes or more. A pale yellow farmhouse sat squat on a knoll to their left, a quarter mile farther up the road. There was silence here, and desolation. Rafkin had no access to weapons, but ten minutes was a long time. He thought he noticed movement in the brush…a raccoon or other small creature.

"What's in Vineland?" Paul's tone had changed. Less deferential and alluding to more common sense than Rakfin had thought. The affected femininity was gone.

"Listen to me. I do not make the rules. If it were up to me I'd inform the FBI, State Police, and every other damned thing." He allowed the frustration to creep into his voice. It was not feigned. "It's not up to me. And it isn't up to you either." The statement lingered.

Paul's indignance softened. Stuart had told him he was an agent of Mossad. He had killed men, just yesterday.

Rafkin didn't want the Islamites to succeed. He didn't want to harm Paul, and he especially did not want Feliks to draw another breath. There was a limit, however, to what he could accomplish and still make it out of the country.

"The weapons are in Vineland."

Paul shifted in his seat. Rafkin could almost see the trust returning. It was a hopeful thing.

"We are going to deny them the ability to inflict damage. We'll destroy the guns—you and I—then we'll notify the FBI before we board the plane."

Paul nodded, imperceptibly at first, then stronger.

"Good enough?"

Paul had changed. Despite his persona, and art-world sophistication, Paul was aware of a threat to his country. Suddenly, he was a two-bit redneck in a rusty pickup truck. "Good enough."

They left the cutout and were miles ahead as Paul studied the road, speaking to Rafkin without looking at him.

"What if we had made the flight? If we hadn't gotten held up at the bank?

Rafkin held Paul's eyes.

"Would you have told me?" Paul turned away from the road. "Would you have told *anyone?*"

Rafkin's heart hardened, and he thought that Paul had just made things easier for him.

*

He had the key card intended for Mohammed. He swiped it through a small metal box at the gate. A light turned green when he pushed a button. The gate opened. He waved Paul through as he hopped back into the passenger seat.

"Where did you get that?" Paul was impressed with Rafkin's spy tricks. It was an attitude Rafkin encouraged, as long as Paul didn't ask *when* he got the key. His story about the phone call while Paul was in the bank would crumble like eggshells.

"It's in the rear. That way." Rafkin pointed to the right of a dilapidated guard shack where there was a rutted trail in the gravel leading to the rear of the facility. It was growing dark and the lights were on inside the shack. They could see a rock and roll hair-farmer reading a magazine, his feet up on the desk.

"You're supposed to sign in," Rafkin said, smiling lightly at Paul's confusion.

"How did…?"

Rafkin shrugged. He tapped his temple with a forefinger, pointing to the gravel trail. Paul complied. The Roadster crunched to a halt in front of 211. Paul got out immediately, spoiling Rafkin's plan of telling him to wait in the car.

It didn't matter. At this stage, Paul knew—or thought he knew—far too much. They had to get to the Islands. Then he could decide.

Rakfin again swiped the key. There was a standard door on the right, as well as a garage door for loading and unloading large items. They entered through the door on the right. Rafkin found the light switch.

It was Rafkin's turn to be amazed.

Feliks had given him a laundry list: M-14s and 16s; RPGs, Car 15s, and hand grenades. The big-ticket item was a 60-mm mortar with four hundred rounds of ammunition. The mortar came from the National Guard sergeant. It had all been breathtakingly easy to purchase.

The room was roughly fifteen feet wide and thirty feet deep. It was filled to the ceiling with crates and boxes. Some of them were clearly labeled, military style. There was a lot more here than Rafkin's contribution—too much to do anything about.

"What is all of this for?" Paul was in shock.

"I have no idea," Rafkin answered honestly.

Paul was beyond uneasy, balancing his fear with an obvious desire to do the right thing. No one wanted to see children harmed. Rafkin made soothing comments, to show Paul he had a handle on it.

*

They pulled out onto the highway, heading north, checking behind to see if the white minivan was still back there. He'd first noticed them as they pulled into the storage place. It was as if they were waiting for someone. Rafkin maintained a steady sixty miles per hour. He didn't want to lose the tail.

"There's the sign. We're only thirty miles to Newark. They'll have hotels all around the airport…"

Paul wanted to call it in. Immediately.

"No."

"We can call the FBI from a pay phone…there are still a few left somewhere. We don't have to use a cell phone," Paul was babbling.

The men in the minivan were not Arabs. Those people didn't have the sophistication of the Americans or Europeans—even the Russians. It was this last group that Rakfin was banking on. If the

Americans were on him it was over anyway. But they were not. The Bureau man and the Russian woman would have had a team crawling all over the apartment building. That they had not was an indication that they were fishing.

That meant the men in the minivan were Russians. Rafkin didn't have time to worry about how they had gotten this close. Something to think about tomorrow afternoon, when they were changing planes.

Chapter 31

GOMEZ SAW STARS arcing across his vision. The blood still pounded in his head, and he willed himself to relax. The old man had died of a massive thrombosis at forty-seven. He turned to Viisky.

"Well, that went okay."

She smiled. "They will pursue us?"

"They can't wipe their ass without another hundred meetings, all of which will be digitally recorded on five separate media for the purpose of wrapping a blanket around themselves. Then when they've had enough meetings, they will spend a month shredding everything."

Thinking about it was counter-productive. They had gotten out of there and were together, as opposed to eating green bologna sandwiches in a Federal Detention Center.

"Your way…is the correct way," Viisky said, and the disgust and frustration dropped from him in a wave. But he wasn't so sure she was right. He remembered Kessler's comment about his dog and the dog's rectal putrefaction. He smiled in spite of his current feelings toward Kessler.

In the meantime, he had a few questions for Vischka. "How can you be sure Rafkin is alive?"

"Feliks."

"Of course."

Gomez hooked around onto K Street in Georgetown…trying to decide where to go. "How is it," he asked, "that you need my help to find this guy? He's an agent of the SVR for God's sake. Kessler gets his panties tangled if he doesn't hear from me for an hour. You know that."

"It is your country. You recall? How can *you* not find him?"

"Answer the question."

"You understand how our Directorate has became somewhat, eh, dismembered, after 1991. Evidently, this Rafkin is located in New York several years past."

"I don't follow you."

"He lies. He lies about this new residence when he arrives in New York."

"Didn't he have a control officer? Someone he had to meet and check in with?"

"Control officer runs away. After Gorbachev."

That might even be true, the part about the control guy. It explained a few things. Stuart Rafkin was a real live Igor, a Soviet spy. They had abandoned him when the Soviet Union died its richly deserved death. It even fit in with the story she had told him about the ex-Vyydraat.

Rafkin had been piddling around on his own for a long time. How does one do that? Left alone to rot in the enemy's camp? Well, it was America, not the Sudan. A guy could get comfortable. Then Viisky and Feliks come along, pretending to be the new KGB. They tell him they have not forgotten. They have a mission for him. This whole setup was pretty slick.

"I don't want to go back to the condo. They have a tendency to get organized when something really doesn't matter. It's possible they'll haul us in so they can keep everything quiet until they know what to do about it." Which would happen about the time their magic carpets were above the Capitol Dome.

Maybe he could find Rafkin and they could hide together.

"You have told the menpowers that you do not wish to press," Viisky said. Why?"

Gomez watched her for a second. That fit, too. "They're just looking for self-promotion. The media need to be used in the correct way." Oh brother, Orwell would be kicking his heels. Better change the subject.

"They're kidding about the murder charges," Gomez said. "But they'll use it if they have to, as a way to keep you under wraps and answering questions. We can't go back to my place."

Viisky agreed. She had reached the same conclusion.

"There is cousin..." she began.

Gomez listened to her explanation. Supposedly she had a relative living in Annandale, a suburb of Washington where the rich and the wannabes lived. It sounded fishy. It sounded like Gomez was going to be taken to an SVR safe house. But then, she wasn't SVR—only pretending to be. So, instead, it would be a terrorist safe house. Maybe he should stop off and grab an afghan, for his head...grow a quick beard.

"Also, I will be in need of new outerwear."

Gomez thought about that for a minute. "I know just the place."

*

The Italian—his first wife—had loved to shop. A redundancy, but on occasion Gomez had been dragged along. He knew of a retail nightmare in the immediate area. He hung a left.

Viisky had fallen hard for shopping. She disappeared into a T.J. Maxx and her eyes were wide with delight and wonder. She was old enough, he thought. As a child she'd probably waited in line for a week to buy some piece of shit cardboard shoes made in a tractor factory in Pinsk. Gomez sat on a bench outside the store, smoking heavily, options banging around his head. Conclusions were reached, discarded, and refined.

The saving chance—the third way—would be if he could somehow find Stuart Rafkin and break a few of Rafkin's bones until he told them where to find the Al-Qaeda. But Stuart Rafkin was gone—off to Russia where they would give him a medal and then shoot him in the head. Bury him in a shallow grave.

If Rafkin were smart, he would be sucking rum slammers on a beach somewhat close to the equator. That would be Gomez's bet. That's what he would do.

He called the switchboard at Hoover. He was instantly routed to Yates' voice-hole… a twenty-four karat miracle. Two weeks ago, Gomez had tried to call in a large Supreme at a Pizza Hut and had to go through four layers of lackey before reaching someone who could operate a menu.

He waited for all the beeping and bonging to stop.

"On the Tenth of October…" He hit the details; everything he had learned from his discoveries in Viisky's laptop. Yates might be the one guy in charge with enough brains, and stones, to do what was right.

Gomez sat on the bench and smoked some more, hoping that somewhere inside Yates there was a man. That Yates would remember why he'd signed up in the first place.

*

Viisky emerged from the store, bedecked in a slew of gaily-colored bags overflowing with tasteful garments for both fall and winter.

"I have experienced great savings!" she gushed. Gomez tossed his butt into the gutter and went to help her get her bags to the car. It could work.

Her purchases were crammed into the back seat. The tires settled…a sure sign of successful shopping. He found that he could not see anything in the rearview mirror for all the packages.

He did not start the engine. He was trying to decide how to tell her that he was running out of cash—the mating male's most dreadful predicament—when Val Sacco called.

"I told them I had to go," Sacco began. "I was gonna shift the paradigm of our defensive posture."

"They love that word."

"Paradigm?"

"Defensive."

"Yeah."

*

They met Sacco in a Waffle House on 410.

"That Smint asshole wants to bag the whole deal. Yates said your idea was actually a pretty good one."

"Kessler?"

"Whichever way it was blowing." They ordered coffee. Gomez told the waitress to keep it coming.

"No way we can let them pull anyone off. There aren't enough men as it is." Gomez stared off into space.

"What if we just called the cops? Dial 911."

"That's not a bad idea, assuming I can nail down the exact date and time. Just remember, it's gonna be in the Northeast."

Sacco looked as if he was about to ask questions. He thought better of it. "Somebody from Exxon/Mobil called in," he explained. This was the apology for giving up Gomez. "They wanted to know what was with the Bureau guys running all over the place. Kessler got a hold of me. Told me they had plenty of guys who wanted to be Detailer."

"Sorry," Sacco added.

"Don't sweat it. I knew it couldn't last. I should know more by now. Which ports. Entry routes. Point of attack. It's been four days."

Sacco announced that they were leaving him in overall command of the guys on the ground. "Yates said it was due to my familiarity with the principals and objectives."

"They think you'll keep your mouth shut," Gomez said. The waitress refilled their cups.

"What if we're over-reacting?"

"Trust me, we're not," Gomez said sincerely.

"Okay, here's what we got. Marcus Hook. Davidson pulled together a bunch of retired guys—and no, they're not all eighty years old. These guys are experienced, so I feel good about that one."

"By the way," Gomez signaled for the check, "when was the last time you heard from him?"

*

In the parking lot, Gomez told Sacco to hold on a minute. He went to his car to get the two cell-phones.

"See what you can get out of these."

"Dare I ask?" Sacco stuffed the phones into his briefcase.

"Took 'em from Rafkin's apartment."

Sacco didn't respond. Viisky gave him a little hug and a few Euro-kisses…two on each cheek. Sacco blushed and drove off.

Before they could make it out of the lot, Gomez heard the sound of a submarine, going deep. *Bawahhhh*… He looked at the phone. The little light was blinking. He had a new message. Kessler must have called while they were inside.

"Uh, hi!" Kessler sounded stilted, nervous. Gomez pictured Yates and Todd Smint, standing over Kessler's shoulder with riding crops.

"The good news is that Director Yates has decided not to pursue formal charges in the murder of…that guy. Ms. Viisky, of course, will be required to leave the country." In true clandestine fashion, Smint could be heard whispering to Kessler. Something fell over, from a desk perhaps, and someone cursed. "Uh, call me."

If this went bad it would be Kessler left standing, with all fingers pointed at him. Probably even his own. Or, Kessler could stand in front of a mirror and simply point at the mirror.

Gomez deleted the message. He tried to determine a meaning, deciding that there really wasn't one. He scowled at the phone, opting to turn it off as they drove. Soon, it would be time to dispose of it. If they were serious, they could track him by a chip in the phone; the one that would, one day, be implanted into everyone's forehead.

Viisky had her maps and files out. She was poking her finger halfway down a page.

"Is twenty-eight Vyydraat remaining. If we…"

"Spare me. Okay?"

She didn't even try.

He only wondered when she would think of the next reason to drag him back to New York. The rest was filler.

Silence. Five fidgeting minutes while Gomez thought about Davidson, and Viisky sulked.

She could not resist. She leaned over the seat, going straight for the bags. The treasure chest. She came out with a lovely sweater and held it across her breast, modeling for Gomez.

"It's really nice."

Gomez was the recipient of a poisonous glare. Viisky went rooting through the bag like a badger. He was spared further effort to compliment when she produced another item—a gauzy, diaphanous…*thing*. Little sparkly plastic beads pasted all over it. She was sort of not letting him see, and at the same time showing it off. Gomez smiled, to tell her it went with her eyes.

"They did explain the necessity of such items. How I deserve this treat in my busy life."

Gomez kept his eyes rigidly on the road, trying to figure out what the filmy thing was. Then he got it. *Accessories.* "You don't have to get all defensive about it."

*

There was a sign overhead, I-495 to Rockville-Frederick. Viisky was waving, oscillating wildly in her seat. Gomez relented, hitting his blinker for the exit. A week ago he'd been searching for just the right color Crayola; now he was on his way to an Islamofacist sleepover. And they were bringing guests. There it was—the white Odyssey, two hundred yards back. Gomez hoped Viisky's cousin had enough pillows. He tossed a jaunty wave at the rearview mirror, then flipped them the bird while he was at it.

Viisky had gotten over his snub of her purchases. "I will instruct my cousin to cook delicious Baltic treats for you."

"Sounds yummy."

They coasted down the ramp. A stoplight at the bottom of the hill offered three directions. He watched them in the mirror still, wondering what they would do. With Gomez at a stoplight ahead, they were exposed.

The white Odyssey then did something strange—it pulled up right beside the Ford. Gomez looked over, planning on some adolescent gesture.

There was a magnetic realty sign on the driver's side door, and the driver was a woman in her sixties. She looked at Gomez like he was a rapist, then pulled away. Right on red. So where were the

Russians? Gomez thought about it and decided maybe he knew where they were.

CHAPTER 32

STUART RAFKIN stepped onto the curb, leaving the apartment for the last time. Paul had demanded they go to a hotel near Newark airport where they could call the FBI from a pay phone before they boarded the ten-ten to St. Kitts. Rafkin had denied him. The apartment was a known entity, unfamiliar to the authorities. It would surely remain so for eleven hours.

Paul's equanimity was important, at least until tomorrow. Rafkin allowed that they would call the authorities when they landed. Paul, of course, had no idea this would be too late. Feliks would attack tonight, after midnight.

Paul reverted to type, mewling and simpering when Rafkin told him he had one last errand to run. "No more spy shit. What if something happens to you? I've given up my life for this. I'm not going to the islands by myself."

Rafkin patted him on the shoulder. "I'm going to meet a Russian."

Something else for Paul to wonder about. Rafkin turned on his heel, leaving Paul standing there next to the fireplace with a glass of wine in his hand, looking lost and alone.

*

Rafkin had told the truth. He stood on the curb, scanning the street as if looking for a taxi. There—tucked behind a FedEx drop box. It really isn't possible to shadow someone after they find out you are doing it.

Rafkin walked to the north, the rifle in a box under his arm. He didn't want to alarm them with the box. It was so obviously a weapon, considering its size, shape, and owner.

He stopped directly in front of the white Honda Odyssey.

The driver's hands disappeared from the wheel, and he held Rafkin's eyes as the passenger got out and approached.

"*Vneshney das pered vy.*" The man's breath stank of garlic and pork byproducts. The memory assailed Rafkin. Seven thousand days. Almost twenty years. The smell was like going home.

"English please. It's been too long," Rafkin said, "and I am not a fool."

"Ah, but you are." The Russian's speech was slow and thick, like bricks being stacked with mortar. An awkward moment passed. "We allow you to see us, of course. You are so stupid to be tricked by the Chechen that we believe you will not notice. So…"

"I'm not the first. He was Sluzbha before you were born." Rakfin was not interested. Besides, the Russian was right.

Rafkin felt small shame. Feliks has been exposing stray Russian agents since Rafkin was in short pants, thereby gaining prestige in the Bureau while he stole things and passed secrets off to the enemies. But he'd saved his biggest play for last.

The driver joined them. His English was markedly better. He introduced himself as Boris. He named his passenger Igor.

"Right," Rafkin said.

Boris ignored him. "We have known who he is for some time."

"Then why?" Rafkin began.

"Who he is. Not where he is."

"I see." Rafkin knew better than to believe anything they said. There must have been another reason they'd let Feliks live.

"The Americans do not understand the scope of the Islamic threat."

Rakfin didn't respond.

"You know where he is. Tell us." The passenger—Igor—took a step toward Rafkin, so close now that Rafkin was becoming uncomfortable. Some things never change. "Tell us. We will kill him for you."

It sounded promising. It would be difficult for Feliks to chase Rafkin if he were dead. Rafkin could flee to the islands. There would be no bleeding bodies of children on the news tomorrow.

"There isn't much time," Rafkin said.

"We know that."

Rafkin looked down at the box in his hands. He should have gone after Feliks first. He'd known in his heart that no matter how many lackeys he killed, there would always be more. He was only one man, an injured one at that.

"There is a suburb of Philadelphia. Abington Township. You'll have to hurry."

Chapter 33

GOMEZ HAD ONCE been inside an actual safe house—on the periphery of a counter-intelligence bust with Davidson in '89. He was younger then, and disappointed by the lack of glamour. They had found no secret panels or revolving bookcases, no racks of AKs or confusing radio gear in the attic. Just four thick oafs in gold chains and dreadful cologne, sitting around watching *Return of the Jedi* on an old console television.

They were unarmed and did not resist. So he knew what a safe house really was. It was just a house—that was supposed to be safe.

He stopped for gas at an Amoco off the exit. A buck-sixteen a gallon. It wouldn't last. It seemed so trivial a thing for everyone to get so worked up about.

"You will enjoy my cousins," Viisky said.

"My nipples are hard just thinking about it."

Gomez realized they were close to Langley, Virginia, home to the people with phones in their shoes. Also, curiously close to where Spasski had lived. Gomez did not think the location of either residence was a coincidence.

They eased into a residential area. Not the Annandale with which Gomez was familiar, where upper echelon government-types like Henry Yates lived. This area was lower-middle class. Lime-green vinyl siding that could stand a pressure washing, and those little plastic cars with their yellow plastic roofs. Assorted, punctured balls were lying in every yard.

A fucked-up Big Wheel lay at the head of the driveway where they parked, lying on its side like it had been T-boned.

"If this is a Russian safe house, then my spare bedroom is Norad Missile Command."

"Pleasure?" Viisky purred. Her way of saying, "Excuse me."

An interesting thought occurred. What if he was about to meet Stuart Rafkin? What if Feliks had him, and they were going to tidy up the whole thing at once?

A towering brute met them at the door. Viisky said his name was Lukasha. He was supposedly Viisky's cousin's husband. Definitely not Rafkin. The giant stared at them for a moment, leaving the door ajar as he disappeared into the house. He didn't even grunt. They were expected.

*

Lounging in a beaten recliner, nursing a bottle of beer with no label and speaking haltingly to Luka, Gomez had something sharp gouging his lumbar. He pulled the cushion, finding a rusty 3/8-inch socket wrench. Asked Luka what to do with it. Got no reply.

Gomez tossed the wrench onto the floor, where the spot of chrome captured Luka's attention. That ought to keep him busy for a while. It gave Gomez time to think, wondering again if he could be doing something more vis-à-vis the Rafkin thing, the bombing of the oil refinery thing, and the psycho-killer girlfriend thing.

But in many ways he felt that he had played it correctly. He still had eleven days to find them—Rafkin or the nest of Al Qaeda, or both. Sacco still had it covered. He could still blow the whistle with Macklin and all would be well. And when it came down to tacks, Viisky would let him know.

The only thing left to do was wait.

He watched his Vishka through a short hall leading into the kitchen. She was a dynamo of a different stripe, flitting around in a flurry of domesticity, rattling pots and utensils, yammering in a vortex of machine-gun Russian. It was a glimpse of what the holidays might be like.

There was much smoking. Luka sucked them down one after another, until the living room was like San Francisco Bay at the break of dawn. Gomez watched, expecting him to crush the butts out on his palm.

The man was something from the Dark Ages. His gracefully sloped forehead gave entree to cavernous sunken eyes. Wiry hair shot out in bouquets from every cranial orifice and his teeth bore signs of vintage gulag. Iron and concrete, the Soviet dentist's best friend. Silent, neckless, he watched Gomez with a wariness bordering on paranoia.

But the Big One—his signature feature—consisted of a truly epic scar, running on the diagonal across the massive skull from his lower jaw up to where it disappeared into his hairline. The scar was subcutaneous, smushed into his features, riding the crest of his nose and the valleys of his cheeks like a topographical map of the San Fernando Valley. Saltine-cracker sized rectangles, six of them, were evenly divided by purplish circles the size of a pencil eraser. It looked *exactly* like a tank tread had been ground into his face—thirty tons or so, if Gomez recalled. Luka, he decided, had once been run over by a T-72 on maneuvers in Afghanistan.

He tipped back, enjoying the warm comfort of home, slouching and grunting while the women chatted. Gallons of slop stewing in the kitchen. The kids, well, the kids he could do without. At the moment a child of ten, a mess of scrapes and bruises, tugged on the leg of his slacks, asking Gomez invasive questions in a patter of Russian and English.

"What's the difference between a burrito and an enchilada? Are you an illegal alien?"

"One day you will drown in a toilet!" replied Gomez in Spanish, grinning paternally and allowing the boy to hold his pistol with the clip dropped out.

Viisky materialized at his side.

"You are enjoying the children?"

There was more to the question than he wished to contemplate. He nodded and faked a happy face, visions of exploding fecal matter dancing in his head. She placed her hand on his shoulder, producing emotions too warm to examine, for now. She was munching on a cut of celery, wearing an apron adorned with a map of Belarus, and a smile so unlike the previous Viisky that he realized it was genuine. This is her, off-duty.

She stood over him, her head down and mussing his hair. As he looked up, he saw what she would look like when she was old, and he was glad.

He blushed and turned to see if Luka was looking. Not. Luka was barefoot, mining his toenails. A hound, the banana-yellow of Luka's corns joined in, licking up the leavings with a deliberate slurp.

"We will be coming here for Christmas?" he asked.

"Naturally."

Gomez nodded. It wouldn't be so bad. He motioned toward Luka, "That looks like a tank ran over his face."

"BMP."

"I'll be damned."

*

They stuck with the charade that Tatiana was her cousin, a relation Gomez entertained with some question. He thought maybe Tatiana was a kind of terrorist-enabler.

They sure *acted* like cousins. The women would pause and clutch each other, laughing in a language known only to the fairer sex. As for them being cousins, well…Gomez supposed they were all cousins.

According to Viisky, they could stay here for several days, perhaps a week. Gomez was doubtful, but did not wish to incur another hotel bill. One more and his AmEx might ignite in his wallet.

"Is dinnertime!"

Gomez, as the male guest, sat on the opposite head of the table as Luka, who ceremoniously slugged the last of his beer, hoisting it up and upending the mug, Viking style. Gomez cringed when Luka reached down to pinch a shot glass in his big meat hook.

Vodka Time.

Viisky caught his concern, funny how they could read one another already, and she smiled.

"No, is fine. Luka is handles his Vodka quite well you will soon notice. He is a…New Soviet Man. No," she placed her forefinger up to her lips in a strikingly coquettish gesture, searching for the right words.

"Luka is *metro-sexual*," laughed Tatiana, smiling broadly and showing Gomez her own fine dentistry. "Is big pussy. It is I who beat him!" She mimed a strongman, very familiar to the way his Vischka had done in the hotel room. Gomez smiled, flipping his shot glass right side up—the signal for Luka to pour him a stiff one. You could go crazy, or you could join them. There seemed to be little choice in the in-between.

He grew magnanimous, sharing his family recipes with Tatiana. Tripe tortillas smothered in a jellied sauce called *guanito* appealed to her. She reciprocated by telling him of the Autumn Festival, when the men of the village would toss a thousand-pound yak—horns, fur, glaring eyeballs, and all—into a pot the size of a minivan, and the children would dance around the pot, and sing their songs. The yak would boil for a month, until it took on the consistency of oatmeal. Only then could the Kollective survive the winter.

"Other cousin has sent some *Guilik*, for the freezer. I was thinking you would not like it."

"Next time?"

"Yes, next time," Tatiana promised.

*

They retired to the living room and Viisky took up a position on Gomez' knee. Something he could get used to. He wrapped his arms loosely around her waist, the better to avoid touching the surfaces of the furniture.

Luka told the tale of the BMP in greater detail, transitioning into other, less humorous, vignettes of his time in the mountains. At one point he grew forlorn, his face crumpled, and Tatiana held his big head in her hands and kissed away his demons.

"Maybe your leaders should not have gone there," Gomez said boorishly.

"To Afghanistan?" It was Tatiana. She ran a cold eye over Gomez. "Perhaps if you had joined us, there would not be such tragedy in the New Republics."

"Really? How so?"

Viisky was making body signals to Tatiana, cautioning her.

"You believe everything your government tells you? And your press?" she spat the last word. "The CCCP did commit many wrongs. The biggest was not in Afghanistan." She appeared ready to say more, but held her tongue.

"Just like home, right? Back in uhh…" Gomez threw it in there quickly, off-topic.

"Grozny," Tatiana said proudly. Gomez did not see Viisky twitch, as she realized what Tatiana had said.

Gomez had been pretty sure of it already. He'd known it was some offshoot breakaway republic, straining at the leash of the dying Russian empire. It didn't matter, really. She could have been from any of a dozen countries that wished harm on the Russians. But it was nice to know.

Grozny. A classic Slavic sewer, and the capital of Chechnya.

"Please," Viisky said. She made the word sound thick and exciting, and Gomez thought that he was falling in love with her.

But Tatiana wasn't backing down.

"You supplied these murderers with the rockets and the guns. Only in this way did they defeat us."

Gomez wondered which side Tatiana was talking about.

"Maybe," Gomez said, dryly, "it was payback for the SAMs and MiGs you gave to the North Vietnamese."

Blessed interruption. The little brat—he looked just like Luka—came into the room and asked his mother if he could have a cookie. She kissed him, then shooed him off to the kitchen.

"What Tatiana is saying is that the Soviet Union had no right to attack the citizens of its own country," Viisky spoke in Russian. Gomez amazed himself by understanding every word.

"*Gavno,*" he said, also in Russian. "Afghanistan was the problem. You were on the beginning of a long march southwest to the Gulf. To the oil." He was talking his way out of a free hotel. He couldn't help it.

"*Think*," Viisky pleaded. They *have* oil. They have trillions of barrels in Tamyr. This is why I am here with you today!" Luka was nodding his head, very slowly. Gomez noticed she said "*they,*" and not "*we.*"

He stood.

"We are here today because a Russian—sent by your government—is assisting Al-Qaeda in an operation designed to murder thousands of innocent citizens of the United States of America."

"This is incorrect," Tatiana was no pushover. "The Muslims have felt the sting of the Russian glove for longer than you have felt terror from the Muslims."

"In Azerbaijan, they have killed and tortured without discrimination," she continued. "In Chechnya, they have done the same and much worse. All throughout the provinces in the south, they have hated us and butchered us for many years."

Tatiana dropped all pretense. "America was on the wrong side."

The three Chechens grew silent, contemplating what had been said. Wondering if they had slipped up and admitted who they really were—that they were not the Russians they purported to be.

"Was big misunderstanding." Luka spoke. Slowly, but with less difficulty than he had before.

Gomez nodded. Then he smiled. And as he began to laugh, they joined him. They laughed until it hurt, and in the midst of it Gomez repeated what Luka had said.

"A big misunderstanding!"

They calmed down after a time. Gomez thought what would have been had Luka held council with Ike or JFK...Kissinger, maybe. What a screw-up.

"So, how do you like it here in America?" Gomez asked, as if he had invited them and created all that surrounded them.

"Is home now," Tatiana replied. Gomez noticed just the tiniest bit of regret in her eyes. "We have Club. There are a great many friends in bowling league. We are happy."

"I am very surprised at the number of Americans who speak our language," Viisky said, still in Russian...trying very hard to change the subject.

Tatiana's eye crinkled, "I have met very few."

"There is Parliamentarian, Womack." Viisky looked at Gomez in her error. He spared her the scowl. "There is Gomez," she smiled, placing her palm on his cheek. "There is fruitcake in New York flat." She looked at Gomez for confirmation.

"Who? What building do you mean?" Gomez asked. "There are actually very few Americans who speak anything but Visa and American Express."

"The skinny man. The man whom you thought was a clown?" Viisky prompted.

"Who? You mean the guy in the apartment under Rafkin?"

"Yes. I upset him with my questions and he spoke Russian in his anger."

Gomez felt it then, a bright tingle. It could have been the warmth of the room, the shot of hooch, the setting of newfound friends. He did not think so.

"What did he say?" He was leaning forward, pressing hard against her.

"I did anger him. He said '*Yeb Vas*' to send me from his home."

Viisky, Luka, and Tatiana chuckled. A sophisticated American, cursing them in their own rough language. "He is *gomoseksual'nyjj feja*." The troika giggled.

"Did he say anything else? Anything at all in Russian?"

Viisky saw the intensity in Gomez; she figured it out in an instant and she said, "Son of shit."

"Let's go," Gomez said, and they tore from the house with barely an apology.

CHAPTER 34

FELIKS WAS RIGHT. It had been no problem at all, adding replacements to the Jihad. Feliks wasn't kidding when he said he had lists. The Imams were only too happy to gather martyrs for the cause. Feliks had dipped into the fund, a little something for the Imams. Akil let it go.

The older ones were wiser; they asked questions, so Akil stuck with the gung-ho recruits who were either born here, disillusioned here, or late of some Islamic hellhole. A simple threat, followed with the revelation that Akil knew where the family lived, usually did the trick.

One man had balked, telling Akil something to the effect that Allah wouldn't countenance these murders. Akil cut his throat and stuffed him into the freezer. He would soon be joined by the Russians.

*

Two of the new recruits had spotted them sitting in a minivan smoking cigarettes, three blocks from the Shi'aa restaurant where Feliks and Akil were preparing their Fatwah. One more benefit of their dirt-poor recruits not having cars.

The younger Russian was praying. Both of them sat on step stools in the back of a walk-in freezer. Akil studied the older one as he rubbed his arms together, stamping his feet against the cold.

The good thing about a knife is that you never had to reload—and it never jammed. Akil demonstrated this essential truth, starting with the one that was praying.

The man tried to scream around his gag, but the older one was strong. His eyes—the only part of his face Akil could really see—showed peace as Akil approached. He did that one quickly.

It was getting easier, especially when he thought of the two million dollars, and the amount of female attention he might buy with it.

The restaurant was the perfect staging area. The owner was a contributor and sympathizer to the cause, one of the many on Feliks' Terrorist Rolodex.

Akil laughed to himself...*Terrorist Rolodex.* Fortunately, the place was closed on Sundays and Mondays. This week, it would be closed Tuesday as well. In fact, it would be closed until the end of time, although the owner did not yet know this.

Feliks was in the main dining salon, shouting orders to the assembled. Akil had wanted a few more—it couldn't hurt—but Feliks decided they had enough. Eleven new martyrs in a-day-and-a-half. Not a bad haul.

They were fresh in more ways than one, though. Akil worried they might not hack it in actual operations. That sword cut both ways. Neither Akil nor Feliks wanted any of them to live, so it kind of evened out. All they had to do was die.

Akil walked over to Feliks, who was sitting in a booth by the shuttered front glass.

"The Russians?" Feliks asked.

"The Diversion?" Akil replied, and they smiled together.

"They left ten minutes ago," Feliks said of the four men whose job it was to be martyred first. Fodder. Feliks had chosen one of them to lead, a scraggly psychopath who'd assured Feliks they'd never be taken alive.

"So did the Russians," Akil pushed his tongue to his upper lip, smiling ironically.

The old man had those wiry, old man eyebrows—something that was beginning to bug Akil. Beneath them, his smallish dark eyes looked like black lumps of coal with a hard, sick light in the center. Akil realized that the attack on the Americans, and the subsequent blaming of the Russians, was a sidelight to the whole thing. Feliks was doing this because he enjoyed it.

Akil was doing it for a reason. He could never go back. Not after eight years in the land of plenty, where he'd never get laid by the platinum blondes or move up the ladder because he was a dirty Arab, and in their eyes a lesser being. He was disenfranchised. Those news people were right about that.

A little rationalization never hurt. Not when you were about to kill several hundred children.

"You said you'd show it to me."

Feliks nodded. He stood, motioning for Akil to follow. They walked past the men, who were all in various stages of preparation. Automatic weapons were being handled clumsily. Akil brushed past a boy whose vain attempt at a beard almost made him laugh.

The kid was trying to load a clip into an AK—backwards. Two men had a laptop out and were fiddling with pieces of the M-60 mortar while reading the instruction manual on the Internet. Akil didn't give a damn if none of it worked. The sooner they were all killed, the sooner he'd get out of here.

Feliks had one condition: that they were all engaged at the time of their deaths. Akil had only to lead them there and wind them up. He would meet Feliks after the school.

Feliks led him to the kitchen. They both glanced at the locked door to the walk-in, then got down to business. Feliks opened a large paper sack. Peering inside, Akil could see the stacks of greenbacks—all hundreds.

"You mind if I count it?" he asked.

"Don't push it," Feliks rolled the bag shut.

Akil jammed his hands into his pockets, staring thoughtfully at the paper bag. "Okay," he said, as if he had a choice.

Feliks insisted on prayer. The new Mujahadi knelt, inappropriately, in front of the bar. Feliks was long-winded and Akil neither understood nor listened to him, standing sullen at the rear of the restaurant, trying not to roll his eyes. When it was done, the men filed to the cars. Akil grabbed Feliks by the arm.

"What are we going to do with the Russian?"

"The same thing we're going to do to his country," Feliks smiled, looking like that old guy in the horror movies.

"Which country?"

"Both of them."

Chapter 35

GOMEZ GLANCED AT THE dashboard clock as he double-parked in front of the West Village apartment: 10:27. He hoped they weren't too late. Viisky looked to him expectantly. He knew what she was thinking and shook his head.

"No menpowers." Not with what may happen here. It was what she wanted anyway.

The momentary distraction caused him to smack into a Ford Expedition, crumpling both their fenders and precipitating a sprinkling of plastic crap falling into the street. The Expedition's car alarm began its robotic keening.

The alarm inspired Gomez. He reached into the floorboard and came back up with a tire-iron—a lean, new, one-spoke model.

He'd ground the tapered end down to a nasty point. The lug end was good for brain bonking. The old four-spokers were a little bulky and hard to handle. Viisky looked at him questioningly.

"In case I ever get a flat," he said. He did not see her scoff because he was out of the car, taking a three-second scan of the street in both directions. His vision telescoped, narrowing on a white Honda Odyssey parked about sixty yards on the North end of the avenue. Gomez thought it was good to have them where he could see them.

He counted in his head; he got to five-Mississippi, when he saw the cream Lexus coupe behind the Expedition. He was at the hood in three long strides. Seven-Mississippi. He lofted an eyebrow, raised his arm with the tire iron…

The left headlamp exploded like a bomb. White chemical powder and tinkling glass came poofing out. The Lexus sounded as if it was having its tail-pipe reamed. Now there were *two* howling alarms.

How incredible, Gomez realized. The Expedition sounded just like Willie Nelson. He grabbed Viisky, hustling her up to the portico. She stumbled, drawing very close to him. She was steamy and tense, looking up at him with those big eyes.

"You have created such surprise."

"I want them looking out the window. People keep their guns in the bedrooms… always the bedrooms." Reflex would have them at the window to see what was going on. Raids don't begin with car alarms.

"They'll have their backs to us when we go in."

Paul's apartment was a direct path up one flight of stairs. Gomez could see the second he went through the entryway that it didn't have the locks Rafkin had and, without pause, he loped six or seven long strides, hitting the door with his shoulder. It creaked and moaned, yet the lock held. Gomez thought that besides bursting a bunch of capillaries, he had just lost the advantage.

Viisky came to a halt beside him. Angry now, and with a flood of prehistoric chemicals pumping through him, he dropped the tire iron, stepped back and hammered at the knob with his wingtip. He dented the shit out of it with the first effort, feeling the pull of a big thigh muscle. The knob hung, cocked at a pathetic angle, so he kicked it again and again until the whole thing caved, and they were standing inside.

Gomez had the other, better iron in his hand. He saw the shirttails of a man running down a narrow hallway toward the back of the apartment. Viisky's nemesis, Paul. The guy he had swapped insults with on his earlier visit. Relaxing on a white corduroy sofa, staggered at degrees to a white brick fireplace, sat Stuart Rafkin.

Got him.

Rafkin dipped his head, the way you would on noticing an acquaintance in the clubhouse after a round of golf. His hands were folded into his lap. He wore gray khakis below a white sweater, and he had a crooked smile on his heavily bruised face. He was unarmed. The little shit that ran into the bedroom, on the other hand, bore caution. Gomez judged him to be way too emotional.

Which reminded him to keep a third eye on Viisky. Shouldn't have given her the Beretta. He gripped his right hand with his left and aimed for Rafkin's nose.

"Place your fucking hands on the top of your fucking head."

Rafkin did so, calmly and with dignity…just as Paul came zipping out into the hallway with a blue bowling bag in his hand. Gomez shifted his aim, settling on Paul, who stopped in his tracks, wind-milling his arms. He had a devious leer on his pretty face. Gomez was tempted to shoot him on general principals.

"Get the bag," he said to Viisky. She scooted around a nice Shaker end table, yanking the bag from Paul's grasp without much effort. Kneeling, she unzippered it, producing a large black handgun of unfamiliar manufacture and, portentously, a half-dozen plump green hand grenades, maybe eight.

Gomez recognized them as the MkIV, a fragmentation grenade made for the Warsaw Pact nations and all the third-world cesspools. They had been produced by the kazillions in the seventies and eighties and passed out like candy to any and all bomb-chuckers of the world. He had, in fact, seen them before. A long time ago.

She held them up for Gomez to see; a see-I-told-you-so.

"Go sit on the sofa," Gomez commanded.

"Fire department huh?" Paul was triumphant, petulant, but Gomez also thought there could be some steel in there. It was the skinny ones who got all worked up. Plus, Paul might have seen one too many episodes of MacGyver.

"You'll speak when spoken to."

Paul sat too close, snuggling really, next to Rafkin. He sort of shimmied over on the sofa, placing his hand on Rafkin's forearm. Gomez saw it, the relationship between Rafkin and Paul. Though he'd thought about that on the ride up here and half-expected it, he did not like it. Rafkin would be using the man. Or, their affection could be genuine. Either way, it would make this more difficult.

"Go down to the street. Deal with those alarms," Gomez told Viisky.

He wanted tranquility, for the racket to die down on the streets before he finished this. "Move my car if you have to." He reached into his slacks and tossed Viisky the keys. She turned and left.

Gomez watched them in the pause, saying nothing. Their fingers touched…aid and comfort. Gomez was not pleased. He'd been hoping that Rafkin was using Paul as haven.

He studied Rafkin more closely. Trim build, blond crew cut, aging well, as some men have the good fortune. He might have been one of those guys who was portly as a child, or geeky looking, but in his forties now had magnetism about him. His cheekbones were flat, high, and Slavic, a feature you wouldn't notice, but if someone told you, it would be instantly apparent.

What to do with the wife? The caffeinated one. With Rafkin he had no compunction. It was decided.

There was a muffled crash from outside. Another. The honking alarms ceased. A moment later Viisky blew in, out of breath, her hair frizzed out like she'd rubbed it with a dryer-sheet.

"I have eliminated this distraction."

Paul glared at her. "Shrew."

"Douche bag."

"Crone."

"Imperialist dog."

"That's enough," Gomez barked. He had never wanted children.

"She's a *tarantula*."

"Is this region having many swamps?" Viisky lifted her brow. She was relaxed, knowing she had the upper hand. It must have frustrated her the last time they were here.

"Like a fucking mink!"

"Minx," Gomez corrected.

"Mink," Paul smiled. He was enjoying this.

"Yeah, whatever. You win."

Viisky cocked her arm to tag him one. Gomez blocked her with his forearm.

"Not yet."

Paul would talk. That was a given. There was too much drama here for him to be left out. You could tell by the sheen in his eyes—like ripples on a pond. The whole affair was a lark.

Rafkin must have been here the whole time. The two of them down here diddling each other while Gomez was upstairs wrecking the place.

"Stuart said you might come back."

"Don't ever doubt it."

"Not you. *Her.* Stuart said she would be a problem."

Gomez addressed Rafkin, "What other weapons? Besides the stuff in the bag?"

"There's a Winchester Super X in the bedroom closet. The ammunition is stored separately in a shoebox, also in the closet." He raised his hands from his head, palms out in supplication. "Other than that…"

A quiet settled. The four of them drifting back in after the entertainment between Viisky and Paul. Remembering why they were here.

Rafkin set himself, looking like he had made a decision. He ignored the others, speaking only to Gomez.

"There is one cell. One only." This gave Gomez a spooky thought. He had never really considered a second coordinated, mass attack. They were going to get lucky with this one, no matter how it ended. Unless Rafkin was lying.

"How can you be sure?"

"I'll tell you where their weapons are stored, the cars they're driving, even the address of where they're staying. Although they're probably gone." He paused for effect. "In exchange for my freedom." He really meant in exchange for his life. Watching Viisky as he spoke, Rafkin knew who Viisky was, and why she was here.

"I spoke with Devard Montrane," Gomez said laconically. Viisky slipped off the arm of the sofa and was rotating around behind him. Rafkin cocked his head and blinked.

"He says he saw you on television. You were a police officer rescuing those citizens from GlenRock Mall."

Rafkin was nodding his head, "I always liked Devard. Glad to hear he made it."

Gomez motioned to the bags sitting by the ruined door. They were covered in plaster dust.

"Disappearing for real this time?"

Rafkin let his gaze settle on Gomez.

"We still could be." He looked at Viisky, then back to Gomez, "You could let us."

"Don't think so, sport."

Paul pursed his lips at Rafkin. Huffy, as if to say, *"Aren't you going to do something about these people?"* His chest rose and fell too quickly. Gomez wanted to tell him to button the damned shirt.

"You're FBI?" Rafkin saw that he would not get a response. "She's not," he said, poking a finger at Viisky. His nails were buffed and polished. Paul's influence, Gomez thought.

Gomez edged back the drapery to look at the Odyssey, seeing no lunatic Russians or betoweled mujahadi on the street. The perimeter was secure…sort of.

"May I have a glass of water? I'll give you everything."

"No," Gomez said. Rafkin's eyes had slipped over Gomez's head.

Gomez turned reflexively in an instant, thinking it was the oldest, dumbest thing he'd ever done.

But it wasn't a trick. A man stood in the doorway, looking like the hall monitor in a particularly messy dormitory.

"Which one of you buttwipes hurt my car!" he squealed. It was the Lexus asshole. Feet spread apart, knuckles on hips. Gomez almost laughed. He'd made the right decision.

"Oh, hi, Richard!" Paul waved to the guy.

"You can be leaving now, Pussy-Man," Viisky barked, as she wandered over toward the doorway. Gomez thought he saw the Lexus guy flinch.

Situational awareness. Gomez reminded himself to stay alert to the threats—all of them. Getting to be too many to count.

Rafkin stood, aware that Gomez was still on top of it. He looked a question to Gomez, who nodded assent.

Rafkin walked to the door. He took Richard by the elbow, speaking quietly and with assurance. When Richard's feathers were realigned, he left, giving Paul a little finger-wave over his shoulder. Gomez did not bother to ask questions.

Rafkin smoothed his hair absently, watching the doorway.

"I was under orders. I had thought, actually, that the assignment was over."

"Where are they?" Gomez leaned forward.

Rafkin kept his eyes on Paul as he answered, "I didn't know." He held one palm out, warding off Gomez' impatience. "I thought I was done. I haven't been tasked since 1990." Paul couldn't stop shifting, not liking the way this was going.

"Stuart is *helping* you! Are you fucking blind?"

"You will close your pie," Viisky growled at Paul.

"Pie-hole," Paul snarled up at her as she advanced across the room. Only Viisky, it seemed, could inspire him.

Gomez wondered how much of this Viisky knew. How much they had told her. He began to feel nervous, less in control of the situation. In Paul he had an emotional wreck with a confusion of loyalties. Stuart Rafkin was an honest-to-God Soviet sleeper agent who had, willingly or unwillingly, participated in the greatest attack in terrorist history.

Then there was his pretty, killer girlfriend, Viisky, the psycho slasher. She was rotating around the back of him, never seeming to allow them out of the sweep of the Beretta.

"That's enough," Gomez said quietly. He racked the slide on the .45, cocking it and gaining the attention and cooperation of all, before it got out of hand.

"But these *puta*," Gomez said, perching on the end table. "These insidious pieces of shit who did 9/11. They had other handlers. Right? Other Vyydraat who they convinced to help them. It's all the same thing. This is follow-up."

"I have no idea," said Rafkin. "Don't waste your time. They're gone," he said, answering the next question before Gomez could ask. "I guarantee it. If they existed at all."

They were gone all right, as were any other Vyydraat who'd been suckered into this thing. But Gomez would bet the only other Rafkin was Kostenko Spasski. And Spasski was busy being exsanguinated at Slumber Brothers.

Gomez paced, angling behind and to the right of Viisky. Her eyes stayed on target.

"So why aren't you gone too?"

"My control was a guy named Oskar. He had a fondness for American girls. He also liked South American beaches," Rafkin smiled, remembering. "He was the last real Russian I ever spoke to. They don't know where I am."

Gomez looked at Viisky. *They do now.* "The head in the river. Yours?" Gomez felt himself settling, after the rush into the apartment.

Paul couldn't reconcile the situation. "This is *not right.* This isn't how the police do things!"

Rafkin, however, understood. "That was Muhammad. He was like…an advance man. He was a pig," Rafkin added.

"How many are left?"

"Of the original grouping?" Rafkin looked up at the ceiling, counting. "Muhammad on Friday. Two more on Saturday and I think, but I can't be sure of three at the mall. I got one. That old lady got another. The news said there was a third, but I only saw the two I mentioned."

He glanced at Paul. There was an inch of separation between them, now that they were talking about killing. Gomez checked—six. Viisky was at his back with her head down touching her chest, like she was praying.

In case Rafkin hadn't figured the whole thing out, Gomez said, "They wanted you dead in the Towers. They've got a regular press kit on you. They were going to spill your name to the media. You were the *fait accompli* of Russian involvement."

That was the heart of it, Gomez thought. It even sort of mattered, the politics involved. He would have to brief someone when this was over.

He checked Viisky again. She was no longer praying, or sleeping, or whatever. Her face fixed on Gomez. Inscrutable. It was amazing how pure and crystalline her eyes were. A Queen-Bee, preparing to eat her young.

Rafkin scratched his head. His face sagged. "I see."

"What do you mean you *see*?" Paul yipped. "See what? Everyone *sees* everything and I don't know what the fuck is going on!"

Gomez lit a cigarette. "I want them. Give them to me."

Rafkin cleared his throat. "This is what you need to know..." He recited the addresses of the warehouse and the house in Paramus, to which Gomez had no intention of going. The warehouse, though. That mattered. Rafkin told Gomez the route from Manhattan to Vineland, New Jersey. Sporting of him. Gomez jotted it all down.

"But you don't understand," Rafkin said. "The Jihad is still out there. It's endless. I only wanted to get the ones that had seen my face." He looked at Paul, clearly concerned of Paul's reaction. "I didn't think..."

"What?"

"It's not the Tenth."

"Speak English," Gomez ordered, tired of this.

"October the Tenth is the wrong date. Do you remember that I told you the original attack was scheduled for October the first?" Gomez allowed that he did.

"Think. They did it in September, early."

Again, Gomez' sonar was blinking. A rush of fear hit his heart. If he was right about where Rafkin was headed with all of this...

"Did you know what anniversary falls on September Eleventh?"

Gomez did not. Rafkin told him it was some seminal event in Islamic lore. Gomez sort of recalled this coming out on the news after 9/11. Not that he cared.

"Who told you about these dates?" Gomez asked, eyes narrowing. Rafkin ignored him.

"I was completely caught off guard on 9/11. You think I would have gone to work that day if I knew they were going to ram a jumbo jet into my office?"

Viisky had slithered over to the right of Gomez. Her arm brushed his shoulder. Gomez thought, any minute now...

"Get on with it."

Rafkin stuttered, working a thumbnail. "I don't know what October the tenth means." He was lying. He knew something, possibly had known for a long time. Even Paul picked up on it. "Could be it doesn't mean anything at all. You know they love to murder people on historic dates."

"They're going early again," Gomez blurted. His mental egg timer, the one that had a-week-and-a-half left, just kicked into reset. How had he been so stupid as to rely on the word of Viisky? His mind flicked instantly, to Karyn Macklin.

"When?" Gomez spat.

"In the year Twelve-Sixteen, a Saladin named…" Rafkin was, it seemed, a history buff. He told the story of the event that spurred the anniversary of September the Eleventh, and some other bullshit that took place on October the First, in the year blah, blah, blah. Gomez wasn't listening. He was busy calculating distances—wondering if Rafkin's directions to central New Jersey were accurate.

"I didn't realize that I was…"

"You were fodder."

A moment passed. Rafkin nodded. "The First of October," he said.

Gomez ran his tongue across his teeth, then lit another smoke. *One October*. It had a ring to it.

Rafkin had his hands clasped together on his knees. He looked up at Gomez and, strangely, it looked like he had a tear in his eye. It changed nothing. Not for Gomez.

Paul said, "Oh you poor man."

Gomez sat, finally. He'd been shifting on his feet for an hour and the old dogs were getting tired. Checked his watch—he could make it to this storage place by one.

It wouldn't be without pain for Paul. He would be taken to Hoover and debriefed, gently but firmly. Hell, they'd probably cuff him. Viisky could give him a few tips. He would enjoy it.

Handcuffs equaled Viisky. Speaking of the imp, Viisky had started to tighten up. She'd gone into the kitchen to get something, and Gomez hoped she wouldn't come out shooting around the wall. He could get caught in the cross. He remembered that round between Spasski's legs. No, she knew what she was doing.

"Gotta go now," Gomez stood, adjusting his belt. "See you later. Gonna go shoot and kill these Jihad assholes."

Rafkin gave it away. He looked like a child who has avoided a serious spanking. He exhaled, glancing at Paul with almost a smile. He thought he was going to make it.

"But first, I've gotta ask you something." Gomez slipped the automatic from its holster, examining the checkergrid pattern on the grips.

"If you really didn't help them, then what are they going to use for proof that you did? I mean, it's the Information Age. Things can be checked out."

Rafkin deflated. It was definitely a tear rolling down his cheek. He wasn't going to make it, after all. Gomez lowered the pistol, twirling it through his finger and evened the front sight on Rafkin's forehead. Rafkin stuttered, wiping his palms on his slacks.

"What is he saying?" Paul pleaded to Rafkin. Paul had been lost through most of the past hour.

"When did you bring them across?"

Rafkin knew better than to lie. He sighed, trying not to look at Paul. Gestured at Viisky, "Whatever she told you is a lie."

Gomez did something menacing with the pistol. Letting Rafkin know how things were.

"I brought them in through Toronto. Two at a time, beginning in July of 1999. You really should work on your border security."

"Spare me the commentary."

"Yes. All right," Rafkin continued. "I set them up in a dump in Paramus. The weapons were slightly more difficult, but not terribly so. I went to gun shows, mostly in the Southeast. The Carolinas, Tennessee."

Paul was aghast. He touched Rafkin's shoulder, wagging his head. For the first time, Gomez thought that maybe Paul knew some of this.

"Phase One was scheduled for One October. They really didn't tell me they were going early. I knew the targets and the principals, of course."

"You mean September Eleventh," Gomez said gently.

Rafkin closed his eyes. In his last moments now, he opened them and turned to Paul.

"What are you *talking* about?" Paul asked. "This is bullshit! Stuart is..." Paul sat back, betrayed. *"You told me..."*

Rafkin smiled lightly, painfully.

Paul began to rock back and forth—self-comforting.

"I had it pretty much figured out when they asked me to help them enroll in the flight schools. I know the idiom. The ins and outs, as it were."

"You dirty *liar*!" Paul shouted. Rafkin twitched slightly. In extremis, Paul's lisp had disappeared.

"So you admit you assisted the 9/11 hijackers," Gomez said.

"Yes, but only as far as..." he trailed off.

Gomez reached into his jacket pocket, for the notepad. The list of names. Getting ready. Rafkin didn't like the looks of it. He cringed at the names Gomez read aloud. The apartment had the air of a trial. Sentencing to follow. Gomez placed a check mark next to two of the names on his list. Might as well get the paperwork out of the way. Once again, he pointed the automatic at Rafkin.

"I want the name, address, and phone number of the chief murdering psychopath. I want..."

"Listen to me! The Russians know. They're outside on the street! I got an address. I was going there tonight!"

"You brought them here," Gomez's voice came from the grave. "You helped them."

"Let me get them! I'll do it for you. I lied. I know who Feliks is. He isn't Russian. He's some kind of terrorist freak. His name is..."

Viisky leaned over Gomez's shoulder and shot Stuart Rafkin in the mouth. Rafkin dropped heavily onto the sofa next to Paul, who shrieked and tried to jump away.

"You will lie no more," she said, pumping two more rounds into the pulp in his head. The whole mess fell, legs tumbling onto the floor, the head sliding down the back of the sofa like a plate of spaghetti hitting the kitchen floor.

Paul's forearms came up in the classic defense posture. He was dribbling and sobbing, holding himself in an ever-diminishing fetal ball. Gomez tucked the list back into his jacket pocket. If she hadn't done it…

He cleared his throat. That sofa would be a bitch to clean. He intuited movement. Felt Viisky advancing, pivoting on his arc and he swung out his arm. Spoiling her aim.

"He's a bystander." He watched her eyes, in case she was aiming for him and not Paul. He looked down at the body of Rafkin. He still thought it was too good for anyone associated with Nine-Eleven. He was muttering under his breath when he heard Viisky speak.

"Do not fill with worry," she said. Taking advantage of Gomez's half-second distraction—she brought the gun up and killed Paul with a single round to the forehead.

"I know precisely where they are."

Chapter 36

GOMEZ SAW IT, then. Like a long, baffled tube. *A silencer.* He thought, *How the in the...?* But there wasn't time to think about how she had managed it. Gomez did his best jitterbug, the twirling part like when the girl is lighter than air on a warm Saturday night—her arm had just begun its pivot toward his face when his wrist connected with hers, spinning the gun away from him.

He thought it was surprise, mostly, that allowed him to continue the move in a three-quarter circle—with Paul's body still in its final, unassisted slide down the sofa to rest beside Rafkin. Gomez had Viktorina Viisky in a regulation choke-hold on her lovely neck.

Gomez couldn't see her eyes. He would have liked to know if she had meant to shoot him, too.

They paused, crouched over, breathing heavily. The Minx and the Mongoose.

"Please to release me," she said softly, in a *tone*...husky and laden with sex.

Such balls she has—thought Gomez, as he wondered which of the many potential meanings it held.

Moving rapidly, he snatched the gun from the floor and threw it onto the sofa. It landed in Paul's lap, unfortunately. The cuffs came off their clip at the small of his back and onto her wrists, without resistance. He told her to sit, like a puppy, shoving her unkindly into a recliner. She wasn't going anywhere. She wasn't through with him.

Gomez stepped over the corpse of Paul, not looking at him like he usually did at corpses—including the two men he had killed. He went back to the bedroom for a fast weapons search. Felt the time beating against his heart.

He found a belly gun in the top drawer of a nightstand. He took it, along with two fully loaded clips of Federal 9mm stuffing the firepower in his pockets. You can never have enough. He checked the closet where the Winchester was resting, just as Rafkin had said it was. A long rifle might come in handy should he find himself in a bind. He considered it, briefly, then decided to discard it, bringing it out to the kitchen where he laid it on the granite for the cleaning crew.

Back in the living area, he glanced at Viisky. She was watching Rafkin intently, like he might want to make further conversation. He picked her up under her arm, making sure to apply plenty of thumb pressure. She was wincing, the pain contorting her when they skidded through the hallway and out into the night.

*

A small metallic device flew up in their faces as they reached the doorway downstairs. Gomez registered movement; he heard a clicking sound as they stepped over the threshold and onto the sidewalk.

It was Richard again, wearing checkerboard flannels, an angora sweater, and the ubiquitous tortoiseshells—jumping out of the doorway at the image of Gomez and a manacled Viisky, with her head down in her trudgery.

Gomez did not break stride. The idiot had a camera phone in one hand, a landline in the other. Gomez though he heard a sound, like *eeeeekk!* when they swept by within six inches of him, at ramming speed. Richard snapped another shot of Gomez heaving Viisky into the Crown Victoria.

"I don't know what you people are doing up there." He had a shrill, accusatory wail, reconciling Gomez's earlier customization of the Lexus.

"I've called the police." Lips compressed into a zipper, "They're on their way. Hundreds of them."

Richard backed away as he lectured, wagging a finger. Gomez realized he must look like the Grim Reaper, or maybe Bob Dole, with his intent and his anger at what she had done. He bared his teeth involuntarily, a kind of razor smile.

"What have you done with Mr. Nealy?"

Richard's suede slippers were wet. It must have rained while they were inside killing everybody. He tucked his arms together in the folds of his sweater as Gomez brushed past him, without response—back into the death house.

He spent three minutes arranging things inside. When he returned, Richard was on the phone again. Gomez motored by with his bowling bag of hand grenades. He didn't realize these suckers were so heavy. He plopped them into the trunk of the Vic.

"You're the same...*person* who's been mangling my car. Aren't you? Hmmm?" Richard asked, as Gomez rounded to the driver's side and got in.

"Adds character," Gomez said judiciously, eyeballing the coupe, an idea forming.

He noticed Richard's license plate. ALLFORME. That sealed it.

He started the Ford, intent on the fuel gauge instead of paying attention to where he was going and he backed up hard, turning his head too late.

He nailed the Lexus at ten miles per hour. Bumpers met, and crumpled. More shattered plastic. "Darn clumsy of me."

"Evelyn!" Richard squealed. Gomez closed his eyes. People who name their cars deserve anything they get. He shook his head, got out, walked around to the passenger side and was in the process of hauling Viisky roughly from her seat just as the first prowl car slid to the curb. The light bar was dark. No siren. They were serious.

A cop got out. Lean, with an athletic build. Not what Gomez needed just now. The cop left the door ajar for available cover. His hand rested on the sling of his holster. Gomez realized he should have thrown a pistol or two on the floor upstairs to make it credible—long enough for him to call it in. Once he was on the road it wouldn't matter.

The cop pulled his gun. He held it down against his hip as he came loping toward the action.

"Federal Bureau of Investigation," Gomez declared imperially, over the squeakings of Lexus-boy. Gomez offered his badge case.

The cop was in his twenties, young enough to not have suffered the institutional pretensions of the Bureau. A relief for Gomez. He needed to be on the road and did not have time for a protracted explanation. Of course, he did have to keep everybody out of the apartment.

The cop had desert eyes, like a cowboy—New York style. The women probably loved him, the uniform and the gun. He stayed focused on Gomez, the obvious threat. He ignored Richard.

"The woman," Gomez said, holding eye contact, "is a fugitive. We've been looking for her in three states." He stepped closer. "She may have been involved in the Towers." Viisky leaned against the Ford, ankles crossed, handcuffs unobtrusive in her pose, like a shoulder model.

"She don't look like no towel-head," the cop opined.

"No. It's like Eastern Europe. Azerbaijan, Chechnya. Places like that."

"Oh yeah? She got wants?"

Good question, thought Gomez. He shook his head in the negative, "This is spy stuff. Counter-intelligence. Sleeper agents."

The cop was starting to buy it, or at least he had the business to realize he needed his friends. His hand eased from the gun, creeping toward his shoulder radio.

"You need to seal 2A," Gomez jerked a thumb at the portico, "and 4A. Keep this idiot out of the way." The cop understood. He was nodding, as he looked at Gomez sideways. He already had the push-to-talk button and was calling in a helping hand.

Gomez left Viisky leaning against the Ford. He could smell the ozone as he walked a-block-and-a-half north to where he had seen the Odyssey. The cracks in the sidewalk pooled with water. He approached from the rear quarter, out of programming, knowing it would be empty. It was.

The driver's-side door was unlocked. Gomez yanked it open, looking inside. They were gone. But a streetlamp had the angle on the front seat, and something reflected orange through the windshield. Gomez reached in, grabbing the keys from where they sat in a tangle in a cup holder on the center console. He locked it. Maybe he would remember later. The techs could go over it for evidence. He clucked his tongue and shook his head. He had almost liked the older Russian.

He walked back toward Paul's apartment, feeling the time like a piano on his chest. He looked at his watch…four past midnight. Technically, the first of October. So, they could hit the targets at any time. Could already be doing so. He slowed his pace, jingling his change.

The terrorists would have two goals: maximum exposure and maximum casualties. They wouldn't do it in the middle of the night when nobody was looking…or videotaping. Then again, they wouldn't go if the streets were teeming with commuters and cops. Find the balance.

Call it dawn.

*

Gomez was still a block away, but he could hear the cop saying loudly and plainly, "Ma'am, please step away. Go back to your vehicle."

Gomez managed a smile. He approached to find Viisky reaming both the cop and Richard in pure devil-Russian. The cop seemed to be amused.

Also, Gomez noticed he had a black leather key ring dangling from his hand. Gomez reached around the back of his car, yanking Viisky out roughly by the upper arm. The cop was taking dictation from Richard—painstakingly jotting down every nub of spittle, every exclamation point. They like it when the cops write down what they say. It was only paper.

"I need that," Gomez told the cop, pointing to the Lexus. He was, if not legally in command, then ipso facto. "Keys," he demanded, holding out his palm. Richard's face turned the color of a can of Coke…winding up like a three-year-old.

Gomez thought about the black bag in the trunk. He muttered something about National Security and stepped very close, invading Richard's personal space. The cop backed up a yard, distancing from the whole thing.

"Shit if I know."

Gomez transferred the bag of grenades to the Lexus. Richard made a peep. Gomez silenced him with a single glare.

The cop asked, "If you don't mind my asking, what's in the bag?"

"Bartlett pears," Gomez said, looking down into the bag. The green tops were poking out. They did look a little like pears. "They'll just spoil."

He heard the cop say, "Selfish bastard," as he opened the door to get in.

The dashboard clock, a cool little digital gizmo, told them it was getting very late. He thought about it, decided he had the time. He would have liked to stay and watch the tantrum. He could hear the cop educating Richard on the pertinent statutes for interfering with a police investigation. It all sounded good. Pretty reasonable. Viisky walked around to the passenger side on her own, the chain slapping against her new belt from T.J. Maxx.

Gomez tossed the grenades behind the bucket seats, where there were six inches of space allotted for maps and things. He didn't want them in the trunk, where they would be worthless when he needed them. And he would need them—felt it coming on hard.

Gomez mentioned something to Viisky, one of his favorite adages, "Given ten hours to chop down a tree, I would spend the first nine hours sharpening my axe." She stared at her window, ignoring his wit. "Abraham Lincoln."

So, think. Preparation. Kessler first. Then the rest of it.

*

Hammering down the expressway, Viisky remote and distant beside him, rationalizing his role in Paul's death. Trying hard to console himself with the brittle truth—that Paul was harboring a fugitive. He did have, in his possession, a pile of Soviet grenades. Not your average knick-knack.

It didn't wash. His conscience nagged.

He felt the allure of the coupe. From the outside it looked like a Kia with gastritis. The cockpit—no other word for it—was designed with mid-life crises in mind. It reminded Gomez of the F-14 Tomcat. Shame it didn't have the 20-mm cannons and ejection seat. He searched the dials, running his fingers across the molded fairings, looking for the bright yellow handle. If necessary, he could punch Viisky right through the roof.

Viisky faced her window, watching the grime of the city slide by. Rather smug, he thought. The gibbous moon touched her face, a lock of hair riding against her cheek. Time to get her in the proper frame of mind.

He slapped her, backhanded, in the mouth. "My country," he barked, loud enough to turn her head. The hard light of defiance in her eyes. "That's for Paul."

It wasn't, though it should have been. She had no right. Like she was fucking Dracula or something. "That man was an American citizen. An innocent."

"No harm will come to you," Viisky said, like she was doing him a favor. "I was thinking you are not this fool."

The *gall* of this woman.

She turned back to her window, her hand caressing her lip. "You knew I would do this."

Gomez lit a cigarette.

"Yeah," his face was a brick, "maybe."

*

The streets were empty in the city that never sleeps. He took the ramp for the Highway of Flaming Debris, walking the Lexus up to the fear factor. Two-and-a-half hours to Vineland, according to Rafkin. More, with the detour.

Gomez heard an intermittent bleat…the cries of a mortally wounded finch. The message light winked. Kessler again.

Instead, he punched in Yates' number, the one he had left on his phone. He hit the speed-dial and was disappointed. Voice hole.

Yates called back immediately, "You jeopardized the safety of the nation." What a charmer.

"I took steps to *ensure* the security of the nation," Gomez responded. "Ever since Ivan died, the Bureau has deteriorated into an increasingly bizarre and inept tool for political ladder climbers. How can CIA not know about 9/11? What are they doing over there? Wiretapping Martha Stewart? How can we not catch these murdering fucks before they get to Logan?"

Yates said nothing.

"The infrastructure is a disaster." Gomez kept on rolling, "Inter-agency communication is a disaster. The working relationship between the security agencies and the executive branch, someone who can make a fucking decision, is a disaster. What I did was bring some quality assets into place before we had a 10/10, as well as a 9/11."

A long silence ensued…an audible blink.

"Even so. You jeopardized the integrity of the Bureau." Yates' heart wasn't in it. He mumbled, "Keep me informed" and disconnected.

Gomez finally reached Kessler on his cell at the office. Another forty minutes slipping crucially past midnight. "You still have that prison cell warmed up for me?"

"Where've you been? I've been calling." Kessler sounded wide-awake. Chipper, almost. They must be figuring it out in DC.

"You first," Gomez said. Kessler had to have something, to be in the office this late.

"You were right. We got 'em," Kessler laid it out. "Four terror suspects were shot to death an hour ago. They were going for Baypoint. That BP refinery in North Jersey. They're spooling up a JetRanger for me at Andrews. This thing may be over before it begins."

"Don't get too skippy just yet," Gomez said. "I need a clean-up on aisle five."

"Oh Christ," Kessler moaned.

"We found Stuart Rafkin. He is no longer with us." He gave Kessler the West Village address. "Also, Miss Viisky murdered a citizen."

"Another one?"

Gomez held the phone away from his ear. He could do without Kessler's whining.

"…her into custody. *Immediately!*"

Kessler was in a rave. He wanted Viisky arrested and imprisoned. No more Russian thuggery. He told Gomez to hang on to her. He could whistle up an agent to meet them at LaGuardia in two hours. Do not drive back. She might claw him to death on the way.

"I'm closer to Newark," Gomez told him. "Make some calls. Have a guy meet us out front at the American curbside check-in. An Air Marshal would be good." He listened for a moment. Kessler's voice grew louder. Viisky could hear little of what he was saying, as evidenced by her glower and position shifting.

Gomez lit a smoke…and interrupted, "You remember what this whole deal is about? The oil, and the water, and things that don't mix?" He turned to look at Viisky. This time she flinched.

"It's today. The first of October."

Kessler stayed true to form. "Tomorrow is the first. I know for a fact because I got a Commission thing…oh poo."

"Do your thing," Gomez said. "I gotta get rid of my date. Then I'm going somewhere else. I'll call in a couple hours."

"Don't you dare leave her side," Kessler commanded.

"See ya," Gomez hung up.

The Lexus was purring now, unlimbered and ready to run. Gomez pushed it up to ninety. Stray droplets smacked the windscreen. That was good. A heavy rain would help with the secondary fires, if he missed them. "Larry Kessler says to say hello." Gomez yawned. What sleep he'd gotten over the past four days was riven with terrible dreams of conflagration, those people jumping from the Towers.

She wasn't going to speak. Gomez was tired of being managed. Time to invert the dynamic.

"It's a whitewash. I am taking you to the airport in Newark, New Jersey."

Viisky turned, aghast. Perhaps they'd heard about Newark in the Caucasus?

"You're going to fly to Washington. They will take you, in your steel bracelets, to the Russian embassy. They won't bother to deport you. They'll just give you the old 'persona non grata' treatment. You'll be in the Federation, sucking down vodka with your comrades by Thursday."

"You cannot!" Instant agitation. She straightened, caught herself. Gomez had thrown the right switch. He had her.

"An Air Marshal is waiting for us in Newark. The red-eye lands at one-forty. Last one out. An agent will pick you up in DC."

"But," she fidgeted, unable to control it.

He yawned again, stretching it, "I'm going to drive down. They're waiting to take me to the Hoover building, where I fill out forms for the next thirty years."

"You cannot! I have explained the evil persons in SVR."

"You have also said, and I'll do this in order if I can remember, you were with the Russian Ministry of Agriculture." He slowed, brought it down to sixty, ticking them off on his fingers across the steering wheel, "You were then an inspector of FSB. Finally, you are SVR." He turned back to the road. Let it stew.

"I am none of these things."

"Didn't think so," Gomez said. And waited.

Viisky didn't elaborate. Still defiant, admitting some, but not all. The wipers scraped across dry glass. The rain had stopped.

"I really thought there was some good in you."

"Pleasure?"

"Never mind"

Tires ticking on the road, Gomez sighed. His clothes were sticky. It felt like he was wearing Saran wrap. He might have the time, but not the inclination to pick her apart, piece-by-piece. Rather, the whole house came down at once. Gotta break her soon.

He spoke softly…so quietly that she would have to strain to hear him. "They got them on their way to a refinery called Baypoint. The dumb-ass driver made an illegal u-turn and got pulled over. The car was packed with explosives and automatic weapons. Feliks should have given them better maps."

He tossed a butt out the window. "Fortunately, the cop ran the plate and called in the world." Her face was a picture of confusion, eyes sad and wide as if there was something she did not understand. Well, all allegiance is temporary. It's a question of where you were sitting at that certain moment.

He knew he was close, so he said, "But they're not the guys. He made that U-turn on purpose."

Her head began to swivel, a dissociative weather vane, back and forth.

"Didn't he? He knew he had a cop behind him, and he knew they would draw half the cops within a thirty-mile radius. He did it…because he was a diversion."

Gomez, of course, knew all of this. Hoping fervently that someone else did. Yates, maybe.

"Because you don't bring in a Viktorina Viisky, you don't have a Stuart Rafkin, you cannot be that *clever*, just to have four morons blown away in a traffic stop." He was walking her through to the punch line.

"Who is Feliks?

She tightened. Turned away, as if he'd bit her. He'd rushed it. Crap.

A flash of iridescent green overhead. The exit for Newark International rushing up on the right. He'd been paying attention a little; he'd slowed down to less than forty in order to time the interrogation.

The Lexus curved along the access road, past the ramp for the Delta terminal, and Jet Blue, and Southwest—the lesser but hungrier carriers—and eventually, they slid to a stop in a cut-out to the right and in front of the first security gate. Newark International. The origination point of Flight 93.

They weren't pretending anymore, Gomez and Viisky. The pretending had ceased with the words of Stuart Rafkin and the news that ten days had evaporated into six hours, and he knew that she knew it.

"I'll give you to the Russians." With the car at a stop he could now face her directly, "You know what they'll do with you."

They would chop her up. Right there in the embassy. Toss the pieces into an acid vat.

"Larry Kessler doesn't know who you are."

Viisky was trembling. Gomez was amazed, given his experience with her, until he realized it had nothing to do with fear of the Russians. Though, maybe it should. It was the betrayal…eating her up.

"What happened to the guys in the Odyssey?"

"I do not know."

"I do. They were *real* Russians. Your buddies killed them because the Russians know you're trying to pin this terrorism shit on them. The fucking of America is just a bonus to the fucking of Russia."

Gomez let it sit, the whole thing dumped on her head at once, and just…roasting her brain. Served her right for thinking she could run a game on him—for thinking he was an asshole.

A man stepped out of the security shack, a radio held to his ear. He had taken notice of this darkened car sitting there, fifty yards from the entrance of a major airport in the middle of the night, less than three weeks after 9/11.

Gomez should get his name. Stupid clown would've let fifty truck bombs through before he put his skin rags away and did something about it. He started the car, leaving his foot on the brake.

"Who is Feliks?"

She faced him. A single tear dripped, like a diamond.

"If you don't tell me, I'll put you on the plane and the Russians will rip your heart out. I'll find out anyway."

He let off the brake and the Lexus coasted up to the shack. Gomez waved his badge. The guard, seventy-five if he was a day, smiled and waved them through. The badge might have come out of a box of cereal, Gomez muttered to himself as they rolled past the terminal.

They both turned to look. They could see two men standing near the entrance in thin blue windbreakers. Very slimming. One of them said something into a portable radio.

Gomez dropped to five miles per hour. Viisky twitched. He came to a complete stop. Viisky's carriage told him that she wasn't ready to tell him everything. He should dump her with the windbreaker guys.

But what if she overpowered them? Hijacked the plane? He laughed out loud, drawing a look from Viisky. That wasn't likely. Those guys took the alert thingy to heart.

A mobile sign machine stood sentry in front of the drop-off. Stern lettering informed travelers of today's' terror-alert level. It was the color of chilled abalone—Terror Alert number two.

If they only knew.

Gomez let off the brake. He kept going, out around the security pylons and onto the main access road leading to the departure area. Viisky was quiet, and he wondered what would have happened had he dropped her off at the gates. She definitely would have given them a fight, cuffs or no cuffs.

He decided that he was right to keep her. She no longer faced the window. It appeared that the war inside her was over.

Her face was unlined, serene. He even thought he knew which side had won.

"It's my guess that you're eh…what's the Russian word for it?"

She let out a long sigh, "I am called *Ubijca.*"

"Assassin?"

"Hmmm, yes. Assassin.

Gomez rolled his eyes, "Fine. Whatever." Taking the loop out onto I-95 South, toward Delaware, he said, "All right, no more screwing around. Who is Feliks?"

So she told him.

"I'll be darned."

*

Blowing through the Pine Barrens, in and out of a one-convenience-store town, in the time it takes to push the plunger on a car bomb.

Gomez caught a flash of chrome grille crouched beside a billboard. State Trooper. He thought of running. Vineland and the self-storage place were twenty minutes ahead. He let his foot off a fraction. Nothing happened. The road was straight and long and he saw no cop car fishtailing out in pursuit—must be cooping.

He checked his notepad. Twenty-three miles to go. Viisky had given up on the window; there was nothing to see out there anyway. Her head was down on her chest. She hadn't said anything in fifteen minutes.

"You would like Washington. I'll bet you didn't know it was once a swamp."

"Is still swamp," Viisky said, without raising her head from her chest. Guess she was awake.

Whipping through the acres of pine like a rocket-ship, eerily dark in the black of two-thirty in the morning, the occasional house blinked a lonely night-light, far back from the road, an earthy silence adding to the mood. Farm country.

She would have never made it over to the Russians, had he dumped her at Newark. She'd have come up with another cockamamie story, which Kessler would swallow whole, thinking he was getting a deal. And in New York or Washington, with her looks, she'd be a media/political piñata. They would eventually release her. A book deal was inevitable, and then she could do contrition interviews on Karyn Macklin's NightWatch. Gomez could see it—perhaps a personal clothing line, the most baffling of the latest in pop culture, the American way.

But in the other American way—the Gomez way—justice had a chance. Unlike New York, and unlike Washington, both Maryland and Virginia had the death penalty. It was even occasionally enforced.

It would become his life's mission. He lit a smoke, praying for jurisdiction in Maryland. Strap her ass into the gas chamber.

Then he thought of Feliks. Feliks would never get that far.

*

A stout hurricane fence encircled the Red Ball storage facility aside a berry patch in Vineland; barbed wire at apogee, cameras rotating on mechanical arms. The only thing it needed was a moat. It was fortress compared to Newark International. Of course, fifty bucks got you in.

He stood at the gates, looking back at Viisky while holding his creds up into the spotlights.

The gates swung open. A guard came out. It was a young woman, seriously ugly, but with great tits and very long braided pigtails. She looked a lot like Pippi Longstocking, without the freckles

Gomez saw a boxy nine-millimeter in a hogleg strap around her thigh. No way in hell it was legal.

"Had any visitors this evening? Young, shifty-looking Mid-Eastern males- carrying detonators?"

"Haven't had anyone in here since nine," the guard answered like it was the most normal question in the world."Sunday night is really slow."

"Listen, uh, Pippi. You know how to use that thing?"

"Call me that again and I'll put one through your brain."

"Great. Okay listen. Here's what we got."

Gomez explained it to her. It was nearing three a.m., the witching hour. There was a slim possibility that someone was in there guarding the cache. Pippi listened politely. He had to stop and go back to the car to ask Viisky what Unit number.

"Is Two-one-one."

They chained the gate up tight, turned out all the spotlights, left the cameras on just in case they got really lucky and the bastards showed up while they were in the back.

Leaving Viisky in the car, Gomez and the guard snuck around to 211. It was in the rear, thirty yards from the other side of the fence, with only the deep woods behind them.

"You stand right here. Point that thing over my shoulder. I'm gonna unlock it."

"I'm Antoinette," she smiled. Her security guard uniform was black rayon. It was very tight. Gomez cast a gimlet eye—now *that's* a woman. He slipped the master key into the lock as quietly as possible...turned the knob, and kicked it. Antoinette swept her pistol across the blackened space like a SWAT team veteran.

They heard not a sound. No tanks or machine guns, no cases of plastic explosive. No twenty-something Arabic males with knives flashing in their teeth. They semi-relaxed, turned on the lights and quick-searched the twenty-by-ten-foot garage. It was completely empty. The only thing of interest was a smear on the back of the door. A closer look revealed more of the stuff smeared on the floor and walls. Packing grease. The kind used for long-term storage of automatic weapons.

Gomez holstered the .45, surveying the empty space where the weapons were until very recently and said, "They started without us."

He whipped out his phone, dialing Karyn Macklin's home number that he'd programmed in at the studios on Friday afternoon. Macklin's sleep voice evaporated as Gomez told her what had happened. He listed the probable targets, one by one…

"Start spreadin' the news."

CHAPTER 37

GOMEZ HAULED PAST the open door, leaving the security guard lagging in the dust. He reached the coupe, heaved open the door and…"I don't know what to do," he said, hand still on the door as the guard skidded up next to him. The tree still stood, tall and defiant, and he'd used up most of his axe-sharpening time. He thought of the dawn that was coming, envisioning the purple glow of the sun backlit by the orange glow of the fires.

Kessler and Yates were making tracks for Baypoint. They should be there within the hour—JetRangers were fast. Along with them would be a bunch of Bureau guys, HRT, SWAT, and the blue and red fucking Power Rangers; Chuckles the clown, for levity.

"You've got your diversion. Everyone's headed for Baypoint." He'd never understood that, how the accident scene attracted all comers, after the damage had been done. He leaned into the window.

"What's the target?" He popped Viisky for the second time. A sweet forehand stroke, hair flying, head rocked back against the leather.

"Hey…" protested the guard, backing off a step.

"I need a map," Gomez told her, his eyes asking her to trust him. She hesitated, still backing up, looking like she wanted to say something. She took off in a jog for her guard shack.

Gomez was still in a staring contest with Viisky when the security babe cantered back, handing him a map. He opened it, knowing he would never get it folded again. There was nothing on the map to indicate the location of refineries, though ports could be determined by the location of large bodies of water—bays, mostly. But what if the treatment plants were really a target? No, just the oil part was real. Symbolism. So, start with that—even though the diagrams on her laptop had looked nothing like an oil refinery.

"It has to be a long way from Baypoint. So the menpowers are effectively drawn away." Now he was talking like Viisky. The guard was watching in the wings, intently. "But not too far away. They won't want to be separated. They're going to want to strike quickly as soon as they hear the diversion worked."

"Why even have a diversion then?" the guard asked. "That means we're alerted and can be there in a coupla minutes, geared up and ready to fight."

Gomez looked at Antoinette in a new way. "Because it ensures that the cops are not there—wherever *there* is—randomly, or any other way."

"Without the diversion at Baypoint we could be anywhere in fifteen minutes. Maybe without the black leotards, but in fifteen," Pippi said.

"You can blow up a lot of shit in fifteen minutes." Gomez could see she wasn't buying it. He sucked on his teeth, shaking his head. It seemed like a lot of risk for fifteen minutes, like there could be another way to divert us. And then Gomez' phone rang; Val Sacco explained the rest.

His name popped up on the display. Gomez answered by saying, "Everybody's awake tonight."

"Fuckin' brutal. Hey listen. I got the lowdown from the boys in Tech Services. That phone?"

"It's four in the morning and I'm in the middle of a wicked CTO." Gomez was too tired to be patient.

Pippi was leaning into the car. He could just see the back of her head. It looked like she was very close to Viisky, like the two of them were getting along. He caught Viisky's eye. She seemed unhappy about something.

"Call me later. Next Thursday?"

"Okay. But there's one other thing. The reason I'm awake is this guy Greg Jimsom called me." Sacco apparently had cultivated key people at the various refineries. Jimsom, it seemed, was one of Sacco's contacts from BP and had called Sacco in a panic. Neither Kessler nor Yates could be reached. No wonder…cell reception was spotty in a helicopter at nine hundred feet.

Sacco had no one else to turn to.

"…about eleven last night. All the guys packed up their shit and left in the trucks. It's kinda sorta bothering me."

"What did you say?" Gomez voice hardened, like he'd eaten a handful of driveway gravel.

"I mean, I had like forty guys in full tactical at Marcus Hook. They beat feet at eleven o'clock last night. The guy in charge was Al Ballew. He won't answer his phone, which is weird. He's real anal. The kind of guy who misses his kids T-ball games for a safety inspection that *he* scheduled. He wouldn't take a dump without orders, let alone pull his guys from a protection assignment."

"Did this Jimsom guy say who Ballew was talking to?"

Gomez needn't have bothered. He knew before the name came out of Sacco's mouth. He should have gone there, instead of dicking around at the weapons dump.

Stuart Rafkin was right. The weapons were gone because Lewis Davdison was Feliks, and it was Feliks who was the traitorous sonofabitch who was dirty, and it was Feliks who was spinning them around in circles.

"Jimson heard the whole thing. He took the call for Ballew." This big, gaping hole was dawning on Val Sacco as he got the tone of the question. He said the name in a very soft voice, as if the name were made of crystal and he didn't want it to break.

"Davidson."

A lot of balloons were about to be popped—big, set-in-stone balloons. Balloons maintained by people who had none.

Gomez told Sacco to get a hold of Yates *fast*—get a hold of everybody fast. Tell them to get a move on toward Marcus Hook. He stuffed the phone into his pocket.

The security guard had turned away from the car, and Viisky had a sour look. Gomez heard, *"What a snot-nosed bitch,"* as he brushed around her to the driver's side and hopped in like Batman into his Batmobile.

He cranked the engine. The guard rushed over and leaned into his window, "You know, you could um, call me Pippi…if you like."

Gomez thought about what a little Revlon might do, and about the fact that he was in a two-seater and how uncomfortable it might be. He thought about firepower and the lack thereof. He looked at Viisky. Her lips were a thin red line. She was gonna blow a valve.

Maybe he should give Pippi the acid test?

"So, what do *you* think the terrorists want?"

"Aw, those fuckers are just jealous."

"Get in."

Chapter 38

AKIL TAPPED HIS FINGERS on the armrest of the captain's chair. He'd hit a quick speedball before they left the restaurant. The greatest career move he'd ever make was in motion. He didn't want to fall asleep at a critical moment.

He looked at the driver, the only man over the age of twenty-five. Akil had his doubts. The cretin needed to die on time and in good order. He was a professor of Middle-Eastern studies at Temple University, and he was frightened—for himself, and for his son.

Feliks had come knocking on the professor's door. Akil went along as physical presence. Feliks was better at intimidation, though. He had this way of looking at them.

Together, they went to the house to take the son, who'd made the mistake of attending a rally in which the keynote was a known agitator and Hizbollah fundraiser. The FBI compiled lists of such people, thus Feliks had access without much difficulty. Not the result of their list-making the Bureau had in mind.

The professor had boldly offered his services.

"I will go in his place. The young cannot be the only ones to carry the burden of Jihad."

"You're right," Akil had replied.

They'd taken the kid, too. One more for the heap.

Feliks had picked the four stupidest ones to go ahead early, driving west on the turnpike. One of them was fifteen. The brightest of the dim, a fanatical kid from Dearborn, Michigan, was told what was required. He'd agreed with great vigor, bobbing his head rapidly. They should all be dead by now.

The fuzzy drone of a news-talk station warned of possible late-season thundershowers this afternoon. An apartment building had burned to the ground three hours ago. Someone was raping women near the Art Museum.

The tone of the announcements changed. The announcer became serious. The terror alert level was still orange—elevated. Akil laughed, "That'll stop us."

There was no response from the others in the van. Maybe they knew.

The news continued, with talk of letters containing anthrax being delivered to members of Congress and the media. The radio guy had this way of speaking that sounded authoritative and casually knowledgeable at the same time. He pissed Akil off. Akil was tired of the news, with their sniveling and whining about the innocent victims. No one was innocent. Not on this earth.

Akil was to remain long enough to make sure of the men assigned to Marcus Hook, then he and two others would head for the school. The professor and son, and the rest, were mere instruments of time.

They would attack with the sun.

Chapter 39

"FIGURE FELIKS HAS this thing timed to the minute. Synchronized watches, the whole shebang." Gomez could feel the Lexus struggling a little with the extra weight. He buried the pedal, northbound on the two-lane macadam of Rte. 55, bound for the Delaware Valley. Thirty minutes at this speed. He rolled down the window, felt the sucking sound of the trees, flashes of green as they whizzed past. Pippi leaned against the door panel, half on top of and crushing a seething Viktorina Viisky.

"Your hair," said Pippi, gesturing. Gomez snuck a peek at the rearview. The hair on the crown, the thinning stuff like tangled dental floss, was standing on end.

"It's the cloth roof. Electrostatic...never mind. Just pay attention to the fucking map." She unfolded another quadrant, now entirely obscuring Viisky's head...staking out her turf. Gomez could sense the steam coming out from under the map. He thought he saw Pippi sneak in a quick elbow shot.

"As I was saying..." He went through the timing of it. How Feliks would anticipate, sending the real attackers on their way even before the diversionary guys were cut down. How long it would take everyone to lose focus on the diversion guys and race to Marcus Hook.

"It's gonna be close."

His curiosity got the better of him. "How does a seventy-year-old man—*a fifty-year Bureau veteran*—get to be a freaking Muslim terrorist?"

Pippi had the good sense to not ask questions. Another point in her favor.

"He's using them." Al Qaeda, he meant. "Isn't he?"

"Perhaps they use him," Viisky answered, a little muffled, under Pippi.

"So that's why he was so good at bagging Russian illegals. He hates them."

"Is more than hate. Is *ya prezirayu!* The word had no English equivalent. Good word.

"We hated them too, but it was more like sport. So how…?" Gomez appeared to be bouncing in his seat, a big Latin bundle of ions.

"He has the parents."

"Oh, for crying out loud." It had to be something asinine like that. So Davidson's parents were Chechen, over on the big boat in the twenties or thirties. The Bureau in those days didn't have anything like the background procedure they did today. Some things were taken as a matter of faith. Even if they knew about his parents, it would have been okay. So he hated the Russians—so what?

He was about to ask how Viisky got involved in all this, when he had a crazy thought. *Jesus!*

Working the phones. First, Kessler again. No signal. He dialed 911 and identified himself while burning through a nasty curve, at a hair under a hundred.

Pushing it on the straightaway, he noticed it was 1:15. Pippi gave him the name of the nearest decent-sized town to Marcus Hook. He was patched directly through to the fire department.

"Roll everything you've got. But not too close," Gomez explained. The Fire guy told him he'd station the ladder trucks in the parking lot behind a Sav-rite, a half-mile from the main gates.

"What's gonna happen if this place blows?"

"You don't want to know."

Viisky peeled the map from atop her nose.

"You are forgetting the mens who are called away from this Hook."

"Huh? Oh, right. Ballew and the Tactical guys." He thought about it.

"Forget it. Feliks sent them somewhere far, far away." Like Neverland. "Why do you care?" Her eyes were melancholy, and for a moment it was coming back to him, the allure of her. Hard to despise her with her face sandwiched like that between Pippi's bicep and the padding of the door.

Gomez had a fleeting image of Pippi without her uniform. All greased up in suntan oil. She was perfectly proportioned, yet meaty. Like good bacon.

"What of the Army Man? At the Army Land?"

Pippi let her weight settle, smushing Viisky back where she belonged; smiling at Gomez.

"That's a heckuva thought." Ms. Viisky had a conscience after all.

He handed the phone to Pippi, letting the Lexus out on a long stretch at 135 mph—no fucking way he could chat. He knuckled the wheel, feeling the fear. If they so much as ran over a rock…

"Fort Dix. Just call information. Tell them you're with FAKT."

"FACT?"

"Federal Ass-Kicking Task force." The *force* part didn't fit.

"Is there such a thing?"

"No, but there should be." He thought he felt a shimmy, scared him senseless. Got control.

"Get the duty officer. Tell them there's a full-blown terrorist assault on the Marcus Hook refinery. We need tanks and shit. Helicopters." He risked a tenth of a second to look at the dashboard clock, "They've got ten minutes." He backed off the gas. Couldn't take it. Eased it down to a hundred. It felt like sixty after the blinding speed of a moment ago. "He's got us totally bamboozled. It's a Chinese fire drill."

"Explain please this fire drill?"

*

The refinery was bigger than he'd imagined. Gomez thought it looked like Professor Floodlediddle's amazing steam engine. Like a turn-of-the-century sweat shop with grease and steam, rusted pipes snaking everywhere. Sacco's guy—Greg Jimsom—wore a white hard hat and was standing in front of a trailer, waving his arms. Gomez pulled up next to Jimsom as his phone rang.

Kessler sounded like he was on the rides at Disney World. "We're on our way to Port of Baltimore," Kessler was shouting, though Gomez could hear him perfectly. "I've been on the phone with Davidson. He said…"

"Screw POB. Screw Davidson. It's right here. Marcus Hook." The line went blank. Gomez stared at the phone for a moment. After a time, he opened his eyes. He followed Jimsom into a construction trailer with Pippi at his side. They left Viisky cuffed to a bumper lug on the Lexus.

Jimsom was a stubby little Swede; he looked like a gym rat with a low center of gravity, and a disturbing mustache that reminded Gomez of Geraldo. The type of guy who thought women liked mustaches.

He spread a map across a central drafting table, explaining the layout, using a mixture of petroleum slang and engineering lingo. Gomez' eyes rolled back in his head. He just wanted to know how many gates there were. He wondered how Karyn Macklin was doing. There didn't seem to be a television around, so he guessed they wouldn't know until it was over.

Jimsom kept glancing at the floor as he poked his map. Finally he got to the point.

"This is it? Two of you?" He tactfully did not mention Viisky. He'd seen Gomez chain her to the car. "I told that Agent Ballew to stay as long as he'd like. You guys can bring the army in for all I care. I'm responsible for this entire facility."

"You may just get your wish," Gomez said. He was thinking about that, hoping the Army guys would get here soon. "I hope they can shoot straight. All these pipes and shit."

"We got a big problem," Jimson said. "There's an arrival. She was scheduled for late last night but they got hung up by a storm off Hatteras."

"Look. All I want to know is where we are, where are the entrances and exits, and in your opinion what are the most vital targets."

"We're here, Jimsom poked a finger onto a dot on the map. Gomez leaned in, feeling the smooth brush of rayon as Pippi leaned in close. He saw the dot, gauging the proportions. The map was about three feet by four. The dot was a pinprick.

"How big is this place?"

"Seven miles in perimeter."

Gomez thought he heard Pippi gulp.

"There is no one thing more vital than another—except maybe the natural gas. If that goes…"

"Something screwy here," Gomez was thinking out loud again. The maps, or diagrams, or whatever the hell they were from Viisky's attaché, popped back into his head on viewing the layout of the refinery.

They were nothing alike. What if Viisky's diagrams were a red herring? She meant for him to see them. They wouldn't be that stupid as to have her dragging maps of the targets around with her, like a loaf of bread.

But they *were* stupid. And arrogant. He remembered the 1993 WTC bombing, when the morons were captured trying to return the Ryder truck. They'd wanted their deposit back.

He was missing something.

"These storage tanks look pretty juicy." Gomez picked a spot on the map. "We're going out along the fence. Get on the blower. Call 911 and tell them to bring every cop in the Valley. When the cops get here, make sure you tell them we're out there."

Jimsom was reaching for the phone and muttering as they slammed through the door. Gomez had a random thought that it might be shift-change time for cops—or close to it; he really didn't know. That could mean they would get double cops. Or none at all. The cops might not be a good idea;

pistols and shotguns against rocket launchers. Not a happy equation.

*

The first two-and-a-half-ton truck rolled up as Gomez was popping the trunk. The boys from Dix hadn't wasted any time. Pippi ignored them, straightening her cap in the Lexus' side mirror.

A kid hopped out of the truck, jumped up to the hilt in full National Guard mufti, looking pleased with himself and excited to be here.

"Oh, this is *just* what I need," thought Gomez. He couldn't be more than twenty-three years old…big and gangly, thick glasses. He looked like he knew his way around a modem. He introduced himself as Captain Fein.

"Tell me," Fein ordered.

"This is straight come-as-you-are. This place is like a Nagasaki waiting to happen. They could already be inside the wire, for all I know." A fifteen-foot electrified fence encircled the refinery. Good enough to keep the winos away, certainly not anyone intent on destruction.

"I have no idea what to tell you." Gomez scratched his head.

"Gotcha." Fein ran off. More trucks rolled in, followed by a single Humvee with a pintle-mounted machine gun. Very impressive, but perhaps not enough.

Still, Gomez felt a little better. A defense was forming. The sun was well past nautical dawn. The recesses of buildings and storage tanks began to take shape. Where the hell were they? What if he was wrong? Davidson was too smart. They were, right this moment, at P.O.B., blowing it to hell. In his mind's eye he saw Kessler leading the charge, man-boobs jiggling…

He couldn't stifle the laugh.

"What?" Pippi asked.

"Never mind." Gomez hoisted the black gym bag, the one he'd been dragging around for a week, out of the trunk.

It settled heavily into the dust. He busied himself in the assembly of a dreadful contraption. It was at minimum three feet long, with a great many switches and levers. The only thing that revealed that it was a weapon was the long, matte muzzle with some bulbous device attached to one end.

It was a Steyr AUG, the Austrian assault rifle, complete with handy dandy grenade launcher. The F88 variant, the really scary looking one. Gomez had modified it somewhat.

Fein the Kid jogged up to them. Soldiers could be seen melting into the shadows, looking dangerously competent. Gomez slapped in a clip.

"I've got FAST teams digging in near the roads. They've got to come by road. Right?"

Gomez nodded, wondering why Fein was telling him this stuff. Maybe he just needed someone to report to. He thought of asking what a FAST team was. Decided it would be unmanly.

"The rest of 'em are at cardinal points of the compass. They can divert to any point within the facility in say…a minute and a half."

Most of the trucks pulled away, leaving one of the two-tons and the Humvee.

"Proud of you, son." Gomez felt he should say something. "Good job." He ran out of platitudes. Fein watched them for a moment without comment, gave Gomez's space-gun a glance, then jogged off. They heard him say, *"Finally,"* as he left. Pippi raised her eyebrows to Gomez. He shrugged. Something to think about.

They adjusted their clothing, fiddling with various weapons and back-up weapons, then they ran out of things to adjust. They stood two feet apart, appraising one another fully for the first time. Something passed between them.

It was gone. To be resumed later.

Pippi blushed. "It should have happened by now," she remarked.

Gomez said nothing.

"Don't they pray to the East at dawn or something?"

"That's not it. They're waiting for good daylight. For television."

"Mmm hmm," Pippi was unfazed. Young enough to know that television really did control earth-shaking events.

Gomez drew a misshapen rectangle in the dust with the toe of his shoe. Intersecting lines filled the interior of his dust drawing. It was starting to take on a rough approximation to Viisky's diagram. He was coming around concentric when they heard it.

The sound of rotor blades, whipping in the distance.

A siren chimed in, producing a chorused wail. They looked up. Help was coming.

The beat of the blades grew louder. Another siren broke the dawn, and through it a queer whistle—like the launch of a large firework. Gomez froze, as did Pippi. The source of their attention was a ripping sound, lasting perhaps a second-and-a-half. A geyser of smoke appeared in the distance, very near a gaggle of storage tanks. A high-pitched scream sounded somewhere out along the perimeter.

Gomez hitched up his pants. Tossed his smoke in the dirt.

"That's us."

Chapter 40

AKIL WATCHED the son dispatch the single guard, wincing as the father worked the bolt cutters on the elementary fortification of the cyclone fence. The idiot was wearing sandals. Akil chided himself for not noticing that.

The lone guard did not sway him. They would be coming now.

He wished the father had used his knife. It would have given them that much more time, not to mention the additional pain the blade would provide, over the seamless death of a gunshot. Allah doesn't always bless to the fullest.

He checked once more with the rangefinder. Start it off, and then direct Hamid, the son, to fire at the tanker, which he could already see making its way up the river.

Akil wanted to be long gone before they killed the tanker. He shoved Hamid out of the way and, kneeling at the baseplate of the mortar, he set the elevation and the drift. He nodded to Hamid, who was holding a round in gleeful anticipation. Akil plugged his ears. Hamid dropped the shell into the tube.

They were surprised it made so little noise.

Akil looked up in time to see the first round hit the macadam, twenty yards from the robin's egg blue holding tank. A mini-geyser plumed from the earth. Dirt and other debris flew in a fifty-foot yellow and ochre plume.

Fragments could be heard dinging off the metal of the tank. Hamid made a slight adjustment for drift, and stood.

"Fire for effect," Akil said, in English. Hamid dropped a round into the tube.

CHAPTER 41

A SECOND GEYSER APPEARED twenty meters to the left of the first, coming from what could only be a mortar of some kind. Sporadic rifle fire resounded, but it was weak and random. They could not determine the target and, therefore, could not defend it. They were turned almost completely around.

Fein and the bulk of his men had deployed near the roads at the north end of the facility, leaving Gomez and his back-up singers in the rear, as observers. Thus, when the red glare began, Gomez and Pippi the security guard, along with Viisky the Chechen terrorist—who was handcuffed to a stolen Lexus two-seater—were the main line of defense against the latest Mujahadi assault on the United States of America.

Gomez caught sight of an Econoline streaking between the blocky pumphouses on the outside of the fence. He raised the Steyr AUG, sighting down the front reticule and…nothing happened. Crap. Before he had it completely off his shoulder he heard Pippi say the magic words, "charging handle." She reached over, yanking the big lever and hauling it back. Gomez quickly resighted as the van passed perpendicular to their position.

His first rounds kicked into the dirt abaft and short, so he led them a little more, burning up the van in a-second-and-a-half with a burst of screaming lead. Pippi grinned.

They encountered a soldier in the prone position, aiming toward the source of the commotion.

"Gimme the rifle," Pippi demanded.

"Eat shit," the man replied, ripping off half a clip in the general direction of the threat.

I hope to hell he doesn't shoot us in the back, Gomez thought, breaking into a run. He wheezed his way past the soldier and, with Pippi in tow, he hauled out past the trailer and a series of squat brick maintenance sheds, thinking as he passed that they would provide good cover.

He stopped at the last one, the one closest to the sound of the gunfire, kneeling down and peeking around the corner. Couldn't see anything from here. They sprinted fifty yards to the side of a pump house where they hunkered in the dust. Facing the southern approaches of the Delaware, a monolithic shape could be seen chugging upriver.

An oil tanker. It was the size of the Hoover building. Poorly aimed mortar rounds were splashing on the port side of the vessel.

"Oh boy."

"That's the big dog," Pippi agreed, and they crouched, perhaps two hundred yards from the southern fence line where murky activity was visible atop a small rise between the buildings. Not enough to shoot at.

Pippi, however, thought there *was* enough of a target. She jacked a full clip into the base of the rise, where from this distance little puffs of smoke kicked up like explosive popcorn. "*Let's see how they fucking like it when somebody is fucking shooting back instead of blowing up babies with fucking truck bombs.*"

Gomez stared at her.

"Suppressive fire," she said sheepishly. Her cheeks turned a rosy color as she reloaded. Gomez wondered what sort of table manners their children might have. As if to affirm her tactics, she unloaded again—on the hill. Gomez watched her arms jerk, and the brutality in her; he decided that the woman had a certain style.

"You couldn't hit Larry Kessler's ass from this distance."

"Watch me."

A shade under a minute had passed since the first action. Better than his word, Captain Fein and his men began to filter past them through the open spaces. They advanced at a duck-walk, like camouflaged spiders, as they leapfrogged Gomez' position—moving in for the kill.

The vacuum sound from the mortar could be heard like a backbeat, pumping out a round every ten seconds or so. From his vantage, Gomez could see that the crew of the tanker had become aware of their peril.

The enormous vessel was engaged in a wide, sweeping turn to the right, clockwise, away from the danger. There was now almost no small arms fire, save the occasional pop and crackle from one of the soldiers. Gomez thought, again, that something was very weird about the whole affair. They were uncoordinated. Haphazard. Like a bunch of high school kids were the enemy.

He heard Fein yelling; a lone Jihadist had struggled through the fence to Gomez' extreme left and was cut down like the cur he was.

"What a bunch of amateurs," Pippi opined.

Gomez sat up a little straighter. Something was beginning to form in his mind, in the corners. Like he had left some machinery running that he shouldn't have. A little bell made its first tiny sound, deep in the honeycomb.

He understood now. The refinery was just too damn big for them to do any real damage. Unless they had a nuclear weapon.

"I wonder?" Gomez had been about to opine that maybe Rafkin really had thinned their ranks, when the beat of the rotors—that he had not noticed for some time and were now back—grew very loud. The machine hovered briefly over the main gate. The pilot, apparently having selected a spot, plunked her down into the yard. No other helicopters were visible, nor was any additional support seen tearing into the facility. The sirens—must be local cops—had ceased. Gomez saw no police officers inside the gates.

"Speak of the dipshit."

Larry Kessler indeed jiggled, lumbering toward Gomez from beneath the still-turning rotor blades. His face was clammy with fear. Gomez thought Kessler might be in the act of shitting his pants. Running and shitting—at the same time.

Ten feet away, Kessler stumbled, falling down into the dirt next to Pippi, green as an avocado.

"Yates said I should listen to you," Kessler said

"Where is everybody?"

"They're coming. We pulled a Uey over Dover. Got here fast as we could. The guys, though…figure like, five minutes."

Kessler tugged on Gomez' sleeve.

"Senator Smeal wanted to know if it was okay to bring along an Indian-American agent. Those guys don't get *any* play."

Pippi pointed to the tanker. It was a movement in ballet, with the rounds splashing, and Fein and his soldiers encroaching on the mortar position from the north as the tanker heaved around in its dreadfully slow turn.

Gomez judged the far banks of the Delaware and said, "He might run that pig aground." Just at that exact instant, Gomez saw an old Civic running down the western fence line, doing God knows what. He had already ripped up the Econoline so he let Pippi waste this one. They could hear the rounds tinking off the engine block, then the car careened wildly and flipped into a ditch.

It rocked slowly for a second or two, then it settled.

"What is that? What is that? What the fuck is that?" Kessler shrieked, motioning at the Steyr AUG—hair on end like a crazy man, his eyes huge and red from lack of sleep—as Gomez caught motion at the edge of the ditch next to the burning car.

Gomez and Pippi opened up together. There was no further movement from the ditch.

"Got it on E-bay," Gomez replied laconically, smoke curling on the barrel.

"You did not." Kessler's eyes were like garbage can lids.

"Did too," Gomez yawned. "You can order the parts individually, each from a different site. File down the firing pin… this puppy goes rock and roll."

Kessler's mouth hung like a sea bass. "*And…*" Gomez hoisted a finger, "no sales tax."

Antoinette—or Pippi, take your pick—was tired of all this idle chatter. She stood with a grim determination, making a movement to run toward the mortar at the berm. Gomez reached up and hooked her belt, causing her to tumble to the dirt.

"Let the Army handle it."

Pippi was displeased. She glared at him. Gomez almost said that she was only a security guard. He caught himself, in the nick of time.

"They don't have enough guys. *C'mon.* We can take 'em right fucking now."

"Because this isn't it. There's something more." He was going to tell them of the diagrams, but discarded the notion. He felt the exhaustion and adrenaline mixing together in slurry, like a giant crouched on his head, boxing his ears.

"There's something more. Viisky told me two targets. She's always maintained that. Why would they do that? They could have fed us the bullshit about a single target. It's a mistake."

"You gotta be kidding me," Kessler wailed. "This isn't enough? Look at that! It's a fucking oil tanker getting shot at. What do you want?"

Gomez poked his head around the corner of the blockhouse. He saw the Shell Explorer had achieved two hundred degrees of her circle and appeared to be picking up steam. The pumping of the mortar had stopped.

Captain Fein had made progress. Gomez watched the tanker round her head and begin to make way down the river.

"We have other ports. This looks kind of half-assed."

The attackers were running headlong—alone, or in bands of two—right out in the open, not even firing. Fein and his men mowed them down while they shouted that awful blood-curdling gibberish. To what purpose?

"I mean, with all this organization it must be something more. Something that will really hurt us. Viisky said the attack on the refinery was for Russia. But Russia had nothing to do with this. They know they can't hope to put a dent in our oil. We'll just take theirs. So how are they going to hurt us?"

"They already had a damned diversion!"

"This is not a diversion. It is a disaster." Gomez was thinking of something that was *more* of a disaster. "These people don't do just one target anymore. They've graduated from the single truck bomb. Nine-eleven showed us that. So it's not really a diversion. It's just a part of a larger, coordinated attack."

Gomez thought of the drawings again. Twin circles the size of pennies at each end of the large room. He realized that the one thing missing from the drawings was elevation.

The big room with all the fans and plumbing was an industrial kitchen. And that big outbuilding with the little circles? What if that room, unlike all the little ones, had a very high ceiling? The graduated lines along the sidewalls were…bleachers. The circles were hoops.

It was a gymnasium.

"They're going after kids," Gomez slumped, deflated, and the horror on their faces validated Felik's wisdom in assigning a school as a target. Something with no military or strategic value, but then, that was not what they were all about.

"C'mon."

The only one of the three who was still ducking was Kessler, as they moved steadily toward the Lexus. Pippi followed, casting toward Gomez for information. He averted his eyes. They got to the coupe, where Viisky was crouched behind the fender with her arm still hanging up around the wheel.

She needn't have bothered. The sounds of gunfire were dying out, down to a few raggedy bursts, with the occasional pumped shout of command. Gomez got in Viisky's face, kneeling in the dust.

"Which school?"

"Is school of president," Viisky said immediately. She'd been waiting for the question. It did little in the eyes of Gomez to redeem her misdeeds. She could have told him earlier. The war inside her was not yet over.

Kessler recognized the voice. He took a hesitant step toward the car, to look inside…like maybe Gomez had a pet python in there.

"Better stay back. She's a biter."

Pippi smiled.

Gomez thought of the marks on his sternum, from the shower.

"You could have called the guys in Newark. Saved them a long night." Kessler shook his head, trying so hard to be a leader—of someone, anyone. Kessler had finally taken notice of Pippi. He was staring at her, head cocked to the side.

"Hi. I'm Pippi," she said brightly, extending her hand. Kessler shook. Eyebrows were raised toward Gomez.

"Who's this?"

"Girlfriend."

Pippi beamed.

"Which president?" Gomez thought of them all, the living ones anyway. He doubted Al Qaeda had a beef with Alexander Hamilton.

"He's taking night courses, you think?" Kessler inquired.

"I do not know," Viisky lied. "Is told to me in, eh, faraway terms."

Gomez didn't want to have to belt her again. It should not be necessary.

A large explosion rocked them back on their heels. Gomez looked up, thinking he would see the tanker sinking, but the explosion was not that big. His eyes found a smoke cloud at the crest of the rise where the mortar had stood. Past the tongues of flame he could see Guard personnel in a somewhat more relaxed posture.

"Fein is enjoying himself." He turned back to Viisky, "Carter?"

Viisky looked like she'd eaten a lemon.

Gomez skipped right over Gerry Ford. As far as he knew, Al-Qaeda had not declared Fatwah on the game of golf. "Reagan? Clinton? Bush?"

Her eyes flashed at the last one.

Gomez glanced over at Pippi. She was confused, like they were naming the cast of some sitcom she'd missed.

"Which Bush?"

"Is more than one?" Viisky was crestfallen.

Pippi the security guard, with what was most likely a middle-school education, felt the need to exercise her socio-political acumen.

"Does it have…like a fucking cowboy hat on the roof or some shit?"

Gomez and Kessler looked at one another.

"Horn," said Gomez.

"I'm on it."

Kessler did what he did best—facilitation. While he was on the phone, Gomez trotted over to the two remaining Guard vehicles. He disdained the sluggish truck. His roving eye settling on the Humvee.

The Lexus was too small. Kessler had come in a helicopter, which Gomez did not know how to operate. Therefore…

Behind him, a retinue of law enforcement—cops, the tardy Bureau personnel, and State Police, as well as the hook and ladders that Gomez had whistled up earlier—began to filter past them toward the burning Jihadi position. Pippi pointed one arm toward the obvious while windmilling the other in a unique traffic-control arrangement.

Gomez discovered, to his relief, that the Hummer employed a standard five-speed transmission. It did not require a key. Kessler rolled over to him, sweating profusely.

"They got two Clintons and a Carter—in the city of Philadelphia. No Reagan." Kessler also had not bothered with Ford.

"And?"

"Abington. Little burb about fifteen miles from here. The George H.W. Bush Elementary School."

Chapter 42

ANTOINETTE WATCHED GOMEZ as he scribbled directions on his notepad.

Both he and Kessler were on their cell phones, talking over each other. She was on the center bench seat feeling very dangerous, flipping her braids out of the way as she saw to her reloads.

She had opined that leaving Ms. Viktorina Viisky all alone, handcuffed to that little car, was a mistake. She'd been met with a sensible shrug and the words, "Where's she going to go?"

Pippi had, hours ago, taken mental ownership of Gomez. When she heard him call his listener *Karen,* she felt the hot flush of jealousy snake its way into her giving heart.

She was not an attractive woman, not in the classic sense. She was aware of this, yet prided herself on…other assets. Gomez, seemingly, was a man who looked past the surface. Some of it, anyway. Ten-to-one said this Karen bitch couldn't hit a beer keg at ten yards with a hot target load.

Gomez mentioned the George H.W. Bush Elementary School. He was instructing this *Karen* to notify all of the other networks, both local and cable. She gathered that he was ringing the alarm bells.

They would speak of this Karen later.

The pudgy guy, Larry, was saying, "…any school with a gymnasium bigger than my hot tub…" and so forth. Antionette began to feel as if events were slipping through her fingers.

The cops would come now…drop their doughnuts and take over. Every cop, from every cop house in the Valley would get in on this. They would stand around after and treat her like some low-rent Jezebel. Like they always did.

She had gotten one, at least. The one who had crawled out of the flipped japmobile in the ditch. She had drilled him clean through the forehead from seventy yards with a 9mm+P, while Gomez's giant machine gun had done nothing more than blow ditch-dirt all over the place.

She would explain this to him one day. In case he hadn't noticed.

Her eyes moved to the ceiling of the vehicle, not for the first time since leaving the refinery. A scant two feet over her head was the cupola for the fifty-caliber machine gun. At least that's what she thought it was. She had never actually seen one, but she had watched a great many war movies with her dad. In the movies, the hero always got a hold of one of these babies and tore the enemy to shreds. She looked at it longingly… Gomez ended his call with the Karen twit. He turned to see the direction of her gaze. He smiled that smile, the one that he had at the Red Ball, and he told her, "Go right ahead."

As she clambered up into the cupola, she thought of the one she had gotten, and the way Gomez looked in her eyes—not at her chest, and she knew she could be satisfied with that.

*

They careened into the circular drive of the George H.W. Bush Elementary school in Abington to find yet another stinking minivan parked in the turnaround behind the American flag.

Three or four Middle-Eastern-looking gentlemen were scrambling out of the sliding doors. Gomez made an executive decision, yelling for Pippi to *"Go for it,"* ducking the smoking empties as she hammered the minivan to pieces, while hollering some crazy war whoop she made up on the spot.

Larry Kessler was screaming not to do that—she could hurt somebody with that fucking thing—and Gomez was yelling back at him that it was *a fucking war!*

Pippi's hunter's eyes lased in on one of them lurking around the rear hatch of the van. She cut him in half with a two-second burst. Gomez could see from his vantage as a ten-foot beam of flame reached out, and he had seen...*chunks*, when Pippi let loose with her last rounds. In a sideways glance it was clear that Kessler had seen it too. He was green again. Kessler had always had a tricky gag reflex. He was making simmering intestinal sounds, like perhaps he was about to toss his tacos.

Gomez told him not to do it in the Hummer or they'd get a bill from the Army. They arrived at a jolting stop behind an Abington township patrol car.

Gomez jumped out, leaving the door open.

The cop, hiding behind the patrol car, was struck dumb to see this massive green army jeep—some pig-tailed girl working the fifty, like a pop-up mole from hell—thundering up in front of an elementary school. He might not have understood the radio instructions in full, but thankfully he understood that the people in the jeep were the good guys.

Pippi quickly joined Gomez in talking to the cop. Gomez saw that she was amped out of her mind, pigtails quivering, eyes like softballs. She couldn't stand still, bouncing on the balls of her feet.

"*Wha...?*" the cop said meekly. His gun was snug in its holster. He looked down at his shoes and Gomez dismissed him as viable force of arms.

"Go down there," he pointed down the hill to where the entrance met the road. "Block the drive with your car. Let no one in. Except cops. Do you understand?"

The cop made affirmative motions. He walked numbly to his car, got in and left.

"You didn't get them all," Gomez said to Pippi, observing her functional incoherence. "Go back and sit with Kessler."

She, unlike the cop, made negative motions but was as yet, unable to verbalize.

"Just until you can get control of yourself."

Gomez took her by the shoulders, turned her around and started marching her toward the humvee. She continued on her own after a few paces.

Gomez lit a cigarette, examining the windows of the school… faces, pasty with fear, peeking through the windows. The Bush school was a two-story job, mid-sixties maybe, in that max-security style. It formed an elongated L, the upstroke extending a third again, of proper proportion. Lots of brick.

Two? Three? Or more, he didn't know. The only confirmed kill was that of the cut-in-half guy at the rear of the van. Really nasty. He thought maybe the rest of them got inside before Pippi lit them up.

She might have clipped one. It might help if they were wounded…or make them more dangerous.

Gonna be a bastard. Too many classroom doors. He flicked his butt onto the pavement, looking up to the sky. He muttered a short novena, thinking of Father Rivera, and headed for the door.

Chapter 43

THE DÉCOR WAS reminiscent of the Howard school, where he and Cummings had plied the wares of diversity one short week ago. There was a poster, a big glossy thing entitled, "*Harmony among Peoples!*" in which every race, creed, and level of personal hygiene was represented in a smiling line-up of world citizenry. Gomez guessed they'd all strangled each other ten minutes after the photo shoot.

He slipped past the door to the principal's office, recognizing no sound from that space. In fact, the whole place was a tomb. He had a technique, breathed again, sucked the fear up, and forced it out through his scalp. He could do that with pain, too.

It came to him then what the terrorists wanted. Why there was the first silly diversion, the amateurish attack on Marcus Hook. The oil tanker would have made an impressive bang, had they been able to shoot straight with the mortar. America would have been pissed. Missiles and fighter planes would thunder across Mid-Eastern skies.

But we were already pissed.

No, the thing here, this slaughter of children, would ignite a level of sorrow and rage never before seen in a nation with the ability to exact commensurate revenge.

Which was precisely what they wanted. The so-called clerics—the head and the heart of the movement that merely used people like Viisky, and these restless young men he was going to kill here today—knew exactly what they were doing.

They wanted Jihad. No end, or resolution, of any thousand-year-old slight. No realignment of ancient dusty territories. No caliphate of nations under the rule of some deranged mullah.

Just Jihad. The bigger the bloodbath, the better.

Only Jihad.

A woman, Latino at first glance, came strolling down the hallway, sensible shoes clocking an echo that pinged the length of the empty corridor. Clinging to her like leeches, Gomez counted four little monsters. One of them school aged, one newborn resting in the crook of her arm. Gomez considered asking her if she was deaf or just stupid, but felt it would not be entirely consistent with the mission. She smiled at him, oblivious of the machine-gun hanging from his arm.

"Joo tell me where is Miss, eh, Rrrrroberson?" Still trilling, but working at it. Gomez pointed to the door through which he'd entered, a red exit sign dangling above it.

"You gotta go to the other building. Way the hell over there." He waved his arms. "Leave this building. Go to the other one and ask for Miss Rrrroberson. Okay?"

"Thank joo!" she said airily, and left, a trail of baby snot in her wake.

Gomez found that he had spoken very loudly and trilled his r's in turn. *Jesus.*

No bloodthirsty psychopaths had arrived during their tete-a-tete. Good fortune indeed. Gomez advanced down the hallway, past classroom doors mostly closed, a few open, until he reached a T-junction. He assumed some sound could be heard if the classrooms were occupied. The wing was as quiet as the entrance hall. Karyn Macklin had done well.

Gomez's phone went off. He'd turned the volume to maximum on the way to Marcus Hook, the better to hear over the snarling women. He fumbled it, nearly dropping the accursed thing, and answered after two rings.

It was Porsche Cummings. He was supposed to do a harassment thing with her this morning at a VFW.

"Hey. I wanted to apologize for..."

"Can't chat. Gotta go." His abruptness got Cummings to hollering again. It was a teeth-rattling tirade. Gomez managed to shake her loose by promising to meet her at eight-thirty. He would bring doughnuts.

"Be a little late," he added, unclipping the battery. He threw the phone against the block wall, where it shattered.

To the right was another series of classrooms. To the left stood the boys and girls bathrooms, and farther on, what looked to be the gateway into a cavernous open space. Cafeteria or gymnasium, unless they were one and the same.

He paused, checked the Steyr AUG, safety off, trying to decide which way to go…wishing now he had a copy of Viisky's diagram, when his reverie was disrupted by a scream. Not exactly a scream, it was more of a bark, or interrupted shout. Close by, to the left.

He picked up the pace, still padding. The hallways were orange checked plastic, buffed to a gloss. They made a hell of a racket when trod firmly upon.

Halfway to the lunchroom, or gymnasium—whichever—a woman's eyes appeared, an apparition, staring at him from a distance of four feet, through the wired glass of a classroom door. The door was partially opened. The woman was badly frightened—with good reason. A terrorist, his back toward Gomez, had her by the forearm. He was yelling at her and shoving her rudely through the doorway.

It was as if *Conejito de Pascuta*, the Latino version of the Easter Bunny, had come early this year.

The woman was smart. She did not give Gomez away. For this, he was thankful. The man held an automatic weapon by the stock with his right hand, the woman by the scruff with his left. The tip of his weapon became visible beyond the door. Leading with his gun, moving slowly, like maybe he'd heard Gomez phone ring.

Halfway out, standing full in the hall, the man sensed something. Some breath or heartbeat of Gomez. Equally slowly, he began to turn.

Gomez took one step forward. The man's right side cleared the protection of the door and Gomez placed the front sight firmly against his lumbar where the spinal cord should be. Working very quickly, he fired three times.

The man jerked, an *oomph* sound escaping. He crumpled and was not fully on the floor before Gomez stepped past him, moving up the hallway.

Voices…carrying from the gym in some foreign tongue that had to be Arabic. It echoed down the hallway.

The woman's nametag said Mrs. Bee. She had screamed, loudly this time, and after Gomez made sure his target was down, he went for the gym. He heard two gunshots, picked up the pace, chiding himself for not clearing the room, but there weren't that many of them left, thanks to Pippi.

He reached the open double doors to the gymnasium. There was a small group of citizens huddling in the far left corner at the bleachers. He could see one man down—gunshot victim—as the second of the fire doors on the back wall, creaked closed.

The fire alarms went off. Their clanging multiplied the confusion, so Gomez tried to stick close to the wall as he hurried through the gym. He gave it up, running full tilt through the doors after them.

The sun was very bright, partially blinding him.

Pippi was in the Weaver stance, rocked back slightly on her heels like she was going to tip over backwards. She must have decided to cover the rear.

Good idea he thought, as she shot one of the two running men, who tripped and fell. The other ignored them, firing blindly as he ran.

Pippi advanced on the one she had already hit, plugging him repeatedly.

She kept closing on him as he lay on the grass. Little puffs of smoke came off his clothing until Gomez reached her, and slapped her on the back. They turned to follow the one going for the treeline.

Pippi had not learned ammunition management. She was out.

She followed Gomez anyway and he wondered if she was going to try to kill the next one with a head-butt or a judo chop.

The next-to-last one—that was how Gomez thought of him—only one more after this one, and then he could rest.

The fugitive struggled up a low earthen rise, clambering for the tree line and relative safety.

Pippi got out ahead of him. He yelled at her to slow down. Gomez got down on one knee, steadied the Steyr AUG with palm under forearm and fired fifteen rounds at the fleeing son-of-a-bitch. The man stumbled. Gomez waved the cloud of smoke from his face. It was unclear whether he'd hit him at this terrific distance, or if he had simply fallen down. Gomez slapped a fresh mag into the rifle and gave chase.

They were gaining on him. Gomez estimated the distance at fifty meters. Another fifty to the trees. He could hear the sirens and the helicopters now. There wasn't much time, so he fired on the run, ignoring Pippi's plea to give her the weapon.

*

Akil stumbled, crying out. There was no van…no hostages in the school…no way to escape. He wasn't even supposed to be here—he felt the hornets plucking at his clothing. He turned to see how far they were behind him, and in the smallest of moments he felt the pieces of his skull come apart as…

*

The runner was invisible. He had made it…at least over the rise, perhaps ten seconds from the tree line. Gomez slowed as he struggled upward, feeling like his chest cavity was going to burst. He was not the least bit embarrassed when Pippi gave him a helpful shove on his backside. He made it up and over, breathing unhealthily—and then saw the fallen form in the grass.

They stood there, hands on knees or hops, breathing heavily, trying to absorb it all.

Pippi turned to go. She took three steps, turned back, wound up like a European place-kicker, and proceeded to kick hell out of the corpse of one Akil Abd al Tabari, late of Damascus, Syria.

Gomez took his notepad from his jacket pocket. He glanced up to see that she was still at it. The body shifted a little. The shattered head lolled to one side. Pippi had some of the stuff on her shoe and the lower leg of her slacks.

Gomez looked away. He turned his face to the sky, and asked forgiveness as he placed a check mark next to three names on the list.

Chapter 44

A LIGHT DRIZZLE began to fall. God weeping, Gomez thought, as he parked the prowl car a block away from Davidson's house in the tony suburb of Bryn Mawr.

He was alone. Pippi had drifted awkwardly into the mix of media at the front of the school.

The last Gomez saw of her, she was smiling for the cameras.

He'd run down at full speed—using both sirens and lights the whole way—after locating the switches for both, with some difficulty. Now the siren was ringing in his head, like when you go fishing in a small boat and can feel the ocean for hours. He had now been awake and under extreme stress for too many hours.

Feeling it. Feeling his age.

There was a late-model Cadillac, a dusky blue, in the take-off position at the front of a carport. He was not the least surprised to see a white Honda Odyssey tucked in behind it. The phrase, "shallow grave" entered his mind. Cringing, as he thought how they must have died.

Now, how to go about this? It wouldn't do to get killed at this juncture. Very bad form.

He creaked out of the car, having a weird moment of déjà-vu. Couldn't quite place it. Dismissed it. He looped around Davidson's next-door neighbor's house, across the front lawn, and along a privacy fence that could stand a fungicidal treatment. The Steyr

AUG, with four rounds remaining, in one hand, the bag of commie pineapples from Paul's apartment in the other.

He arrived at an L in the fence. The corner farthest from Davidson's house abutted his yard by a whisker. Gomez dropped the bag and stuck his face against the planks.

Only one thing for it. He heaved the bag and the Steyr AUG over the fence into enemy territory, feeling the indentations where the gun had been. He must have been gripping it too hard. Over he went, sticking hell out of his ribs on the beveled wood, falling flat on his back on the grass, blowing like a beached tarpon.

Up and into the yard. He was sweating now, along with the beat of the cold rain. He dropped the machine-gun on the ground, pulled his .45 and crept up to the nearest window. The blinds were drawn, surrounded by white scalloped shutters. Three concrete steps terminated at a rear door, complete with storm windows and a wooden door behind it.

Well, he wasn't going to knock.

An idea came over him; it had blossomed in the cop car and was now in its glory. It was brilliant because he had no interest in watching a lengthy trial on Court TV. Gomez was not big on indecision and obfuscation. He was more of a scorched-earth type of guy.

A well-struck elbow made short work of what must be a bedroom window, a foot over eye level. An easy hook shot sent the first grenade in through the broken glass. He did not count off the time, had no idea how long a delay the stupid thing had anyway.

He was at the second window to the left, around the concrete steps, when it went off with a muffled bang—a messy shower of cloth, wood chunks, and various crap flying through the window hole.

Rather more quiet than he'd anticipated. The framework of the house must have dampened the sound.

Out went the pin, another lemon in the hole. He made the corner, found a smudged window of marginally higher elevation. This one put him on tippy-toe, but he broke the window. In it went. He guessed that had been the kitchen. As the second grenade went off he felt as if he was improving on his time, when he placed his foot around the corner to the front of the house. There she was.

Viktorina Viisky.

The third grenade exploded. The house shook. Viisky, at last, flinched.

His ex-intended. His potato—the woman he'd so recently thought of sailing around the world with—had her palm on his chest, like she was propping him up. He forgot to think of how stupid he had been to leave her. He had known who she was. Even though now, at this moment, her face was wet from the rain and melancholy, like she had just lost a pet. She held the Beretta in her hand. It was pointed at his stomach. Really dumb. Gomez decided that he deserved whatever he got.

He looked past her shoulder to see Lewis Davidson, natty in a tan trench coat, the shoulders repelling drops of rain. He was wearing a felt snap-brim in boardroom gray.

Feliks. The Russian killer.

Gomez realized that Davidson was ready to run. He did not seem the least perturbed that Gomez was blowing up his home. Gomez looked at the grenade in his hand. Thought about pulling the pin. They were going to kill him anyway. But his survival instinct was too great, and he remembered what he thought in the Lexus, on the ride to Marcus Hook—about how Viisky had gotten involved in the whole thing.

He looked at Feliks and said, "She's your daughter."

Feliks smiled, prodding Viisky gently in the back. Gomez understood that he would never get his gun out in time, as she looked at him with those big eyes and said, "I think I am loving you."

Gomez closed his eyes, as she raised the Beretta to his chest and pulled the trigger.

Chapter 45

THE AWARDS CEREMONY was magnificent. It was held in the old gym in the basement of the Hoover building and was everything Kessler had hoped it would be. Glittery television news chickies smeared his face with orange pancake, then he was on the podium accepting the Edgar, the Bureau's highest accolade for bravery—for his efforts at Marcus Hook. It was a crying shame Gomez wasn't here to see this.

They'd found him at four o'clock in the afternoon, six days ago, flat on Davdison's lawn. Val Sacco had finally gotten the attention of Henry Yates. Sacco explained that the cell phone Gomez had given him from Rafkin's apartment had come back with an interesting phone number culled from its memory. Davidson's number.

They'd wasted little time gathering for an assault. Hostage Rescue was sore about missing out on the Hook and the Bush school. They were ready for the chance at redemption.

Instead of finding Davidson watching the news or packing for a long vacation, they'd come upon Gomez, boneless in the grass.

The first man to reach him hightailed it back. Gomez was lying in a puddle of hand grenades.

They hemmed and they hawed, staring at the splintered two-by-fours hanging from the soot-blackened frames, where windows used to be. Someone asked how it was that none of the neighbors had noticed a bunch of hand grenades going off? They'd all shrugged.

Another ten minutes were frittered away until some HRT kid from Texas said, "Oh for Chrissake," and calmly walked up to where Gomez was lying. He gathered the hand grenades, stuffing them into a cloth pouch like he was gathering apples. The HRT kid walked past them, frowning as he chucked the bag into a trunk. The rest of them ran up to see about a pulse.

Kessler had envisioned a slightly different ending to this. One in which Gomez was seriously wounded and on the sidelines, as the heroic Larry Kessler saved the nation and thus got to chew on, or otherwise climb all over, Ms. Viktorina Viisky.

Now that was one world-class tomato—unlike that security linebacker Gomez had dragged in from somewhere. Looked like she'd had her makeup applied with a pickaxe.

But Viisky was gone, as was Davidson. A hasty bulletin to the airports had come up blank.

*

Kessler stepped down from the podium. Yates was waiting for him. The media jackals would descend upon Kessler next. They were anticipating, huddled behind a yellow rope line. They looked…itchy, like they all had hives.

"Remember, you don't know anything about any Russians," Yates instructed.

"But…"

"There were *never* any Russians," Yates emphasized, gritting his teeth.

"Okay," Kessler said simply.

And it *was* simple. Never mind the two frozen-popsicle Russian guys they'd found…or Stuart Rafkin, or any of the other Vyydraat.

They were not a threat. Yates said so. Rakfin had been duped into thinking that Feliks and the Viisky woman were Russian, when they were really Chechen.

"I still don't get it," Kessler admitted.

"You don't have to."

The media took its fill.

Yates took Kessler by the arm, "You did fine. Now you have to go to the hospital. Senator Smeal is going to be there."

Yates made a sourpuss and left.

Kessler wandered off to the parking garage, thinking of something more prestigious than the piece of shit he was driving. A GS16 salary would allow him to purchase something nicer, say… something like that little Lexus coupe Gomez had stolen. Sharp-assed car. He could get one in black, maybe, or red. Women liked red.

Kessler parked in C lot, tucking his ticket into the visor. Made his way past the fog-eyed families and their chittering brats, over to a bank of elevators, where he got off on the fourteenth floor…a smile for the hot little number at the nurse's station. She was a little on the chunky side, but she knew him, so even though visiting hours had not yet begun, he waltzed past the counter and into the trauma unit.

The room held a *constellation* of assholes. If the assholes had a club, this would be the asshole jamboree. Reporters, chiefs of police, city officials from multiple jurisdictions and, of course, upper-tier Bureau officials, all crowded the tiny space. Kessler could barely make out the lump on the bed. Tubes, wires, and beeping plastic junk climbed from a multitude of freshly drilled orifices.

The Director himself was just leaving. He fled past Kessler with a posse of three, allowing Kessler just enough room to squeeze inside.

Senator Roger Smeal was holding forth, something about the diversity of the forces that had cast the mighty power of our Great Nation against the scurrilous dogs of Al-Qaeda.

Gomez spoke. A quiet settled over the room as they strained to hear his words. They came out in a croak, befuddled from the medications.

"But Senator," he said, a twinkle in his eye, "the terrorists were all Muslims."

Smeal's conditioning kicked in hard.

"I didn't mean to say that *all* Al Qaeda were dogs. Of course not." Todd Smint tugged his sleeve, to no avail. Smeal was going for it.

"I *love* Muslims. Most of my best friends are Muslim. In fact, I had lunch yesterday at the Willard. My waitress was Muslim."

A newspaper guy, with a silver ponytail and wrinkles of wisdom, burst into a ragged laugh. It was contagious. No one could help it. Soon Kessler, too, was doubled over, trying to contain himself.

The Great Man heard only applause.

"She had one of those shiny things in her head. You know… those little jewely things?"

Gomez lost it. He was shaking with laughter. Kessler saw the ghastly security guard sitting in a chair at his head. She seemed to be cautioning Gomez not to overdo it. He could split open. Things might fall out.

"We are so very proud of your accomplishments," Smeal said to Gomez, flashes popping. "I will be sure to include *millions* of Latinos in my Administration."

Smint dragged Smeal from the room, just as Smeal was promising to name a Latino *woman* to his ticket. The newspaper guy asked Gomez to explain The "Commission."

Kessler broke in. "He's too weak." Thus, it fell to Kessler to describe the Federal Enforcement Commission for Equality of Service.

"Fekhas?" The guy asked, rolling the acronym on his tongue. Suddenly he got it, and once again the little room sounded as if a particularly good party was underway.

"That is the stupidest shit I've heard in my entire life." The reporter guy was doubled over, beet red, making a squeaking noise. After some difficulty, he found his words, "I gotta go."

In time, the rest had gone. The mayor of Philadelphia, looking lost and alone, trudged back from whence he had come. He had not gotten to say anything to the reporters.

Finally it was Gomez, Pippi, Kessler, and the doctor, who put a stethoscope to Gomez' heart. She admonished him about smoking. "This is a really good opportunity to quit. You can't smoke them in here."

A severe, older woman, she intimidated Kessler. She followed her lecture with an answer to a question about Gomez's medical condition with phrases like pericardial sac, staph infection, and other confusing medical bullshit.

Kessler took the doctor's elbow as she came through the door. He asked how Gomez was *really* doing.

"Oh, he's all fucked up."

Kessler saw that she wasn't kidding. He smiled back lamely, wondering whether she had meant physically, emotionally, mentally, spiritually, or some other new-age category—then she too, was gone.

Gomez and the girlfriend were nose-to-nose in conspiracy. A notepad lay between them…plotting something. Gomez handed it to the woman, who drew a crude circle. Kessler was reminded of crocodiles, or those primitive Scottish clans that slaughtered people with mallets.

Kessler decided not to bother them. There was something he'd meant to ask Gomez, but it could wait. He slipped quietly from the room and down the hall, out into Lot C, and drove off into the rain.

The Novembrist

Joseph Donnelly

Winter 2009

Made in the USA